FORCED ENTRY

FORCED ENTRY

Stephen Solomita

G. P. PUTNAM'S SONS
New York

G. P. Putnam's Sons
Publishers Since 1838
200 Madison Avenue
New York, NY   10016

Library of Congress Cataloging-in-Publication Data

Solomita, Stephen.
    Forced entry / Stephen Solomita.—1st American ed.
        p.   cm.
    I. Title.
PS3569.0587F68   1990   90-8298 CIP
813'.54—dc20

ISBN 0-399-13559-6

Printed in the United States of America

1 2 3 4 5 6 7 8 9 10

This book is printed on acid-free paper.
                    ∞

Special thanks to Harriet Smith and Jack Finn who taught me about the tenant–landlord wars played out in New York over the last ten years. Thanks also to Jim Silvers, who taught me something about towers and taxes. And to Eddie Sedarbaum and Howie Cruse who showed me the sights in Jackson Heights.

THIS BOOK IS FOR MY FATHER

PROLOGUE

October 11

MAREK NAJOWSKI, casually elegant in a cashmere sweater and wool-flannel trousers, ran his short, square fingers through his blond hair, then stepped out onto the balcony of his Brooklyn Heights co-op, fully expecting the view, as it always did, to calm him. To ground him and return him to his goal.

He swept his eyes across the black, choppy waters of the East River, stopping to caress the monuments, Governor's Island to the south and the Brooklyn Bridge to the north, which framed his view of southern Manhattan. It was cold for New York in October (though he felt entirely comfortable in his thin sweater), and a brisk wind had blown the smog out to sea, scrubbing the air between the skyscrapers the way his mother had scrubbed the corners of their first apartment in Flatbush.

Marek had come a long way from Flatbush, a long way from the heap. He could allow himself to gaze at the towers of lower Manhattan that defined his dream without feeling utterly insignificant. The developers had taken the land along the waterfront and transformed it, erecting black glass towers so high they dwarfed the older stone buildings, hiding many of them altogether.

But not the Woolworth Building. Unmistakable, with its pale-green facade, it looked, to Marek Najowski, like an old lady fresh from the beauty parlor. Or, better yet, from the plastic surgeon, her brazenly displayed jewelry calling attention to the face-lift, the breast-lift, the blue eyes shifted just slightly to green by tinted contacts (and, thus, perfectly matching the emeralds at her unlined throat).

"Hey, Mikey." Marek Najowski always called himself by the nickname his mother had given him, in defiance of her old-world Polish husband. "Mikey, you ready yet?"

"Not yet, sir," he promptly answered.

Like a weight lifter pumping curl after curl, he began to recite the list of waterfront towers: Wall Street Plaza; Liberty Plaza; New York Plaza; State Street

Plaza; Battery Park Plaza. Each a separate building devoted to the practical needs of the financial world; each with a personal address dedicated to the power of money.

Marek, calmer now, shook his head in wonder. The Donald Trumps and Harry Macklowes, who'd gotten in on the ground floor of the fifteen-year building boom (which had wound down abruptly in 1989), had made billions. With the help of politicians willing to cut almost any deal to keep the big Wall Street houses from moving across the Hudson, they'd literally transformed the profile of lower Manhattan, especially on the west side of the island, where the World Financial Center, flanked by a community of 17,000 people, stood on a pile of landfill so new that some of the road maps printed in the early part of the decade showed only the Hudson River.

Marek Najowski had been a young man when it'd started, a college graduate working his old man's plumbing supply business in Greenpoint, but he'd gone into real estate about the same time, buying up three- and four-family homes in Hackensack and Jersey City, then renovating and reselling, usually for a profit. In his own mind, he was every bit the intellectual equal of the Zeckendorfs and the Kalikows. Having anticipated the explosive development of the Jersey waterfront with a precision that shocked even him, he was convinced that if he'd begun with enough capital . . .

Well, he mused, no sense in dwelling on the past. He wasn't dead yet, though middle age was adding to the strain of what he had to do. Sweeping the skyline one more time, he allowed the sharp blaze of fluorescent light to pierce the fabric of his dreams before he turned back to the interior of his apartment. He always found the quantum leap from the magnificence of Manhattan's financial district to the reality of his two-bedroom apartment depressing, a reminder of how far he had to go before he managed to heave himself to the top of Manhattan Mountain. Not that he wouldn't make it. Not that his $450,000 Brooklyn Heights co-op (with, he firmly believed, the *best* view to be found below Central Park South) wouldn't be enough to impress the other side of the deal he had to make tonight.

Marek glanced at the small brass clock on the mantel. A quarter after eight. Fifteen minutes until D Day. Marek had been waiting for this moment for twenty years, for the day when he'd clinch the big deal that would jump him from a small-time New York asshole into a bona fide player (though not in the league where the Kalikows played; not in this life). Of course, in his fantasies, the big deal had always been consummated in the immaculately groomed inner sanctum of one of the investment bankers who maintained offices throughout the financial district. But none of those silver-haired, silver-tongued demons would give him the time of day. And none would have the balls to cut the kind of deal he was determined to land.

He looked up at the clock again. Eight twenty-five. Time for his game face. He walked quickly into the bedroom and stood in front of the full-length mirror, carefully checking his appearance. At six foot two, trim and athletic ("Body *and* mind," his old man had explained), his build denied his forty years. His blond, wiry hair was as thick as a boy's and lighter than his father's. Even his face, with its heavy bones and small, even features, was smooth and untroubled. Only a few lines (crow's feet? laugh lines? he couldn't remember the proper term) from the corners of narrow, Slavic eyes that glowed a fierce, brilliant green. Without benefit, he noted, of contacts.

"Play it like one of the boys, Mikey," he told his reflection. "Be the man who's coming to make the big deal of the day. The big deal of your goddamned life."

The bell rang precisely at eight thirty, followed by the sharp crack of a brass knocker against solid oak, and Marek Najowski, adding a bounce to his walk and a smile to his lips, went to greet his guest.

But, despite his earlier request, he found three men instead of the one he'd been expecting. No surprise, though, considering the caliber of the man with whom he was dealing. The short, thick, walleyed man, with the habit of shifting his unblinking stare from eye to eye, had been born Martin Ryan, but was known universally as Martin Blanks, a name derived from an incident that had taken place when he had been eight years old. In a rage after a fatherly beating, he'd waited for his dad to go to sleep, then taken the family .38 from its hiding place and pulled the trigger three times.

Unfortunately, the unloaded gun had made a series of impotent clicks just loud enough to awaken Martin's dad. Which, of course, drew another beating, this one bad enough to require surgery and the attention of the police who had passed Martin over to the Bureau of Child Welfare and, eventually, a series of foster homes and group institutions. What with being raped, raping, and dodging rape, it had been ten years before Martin had been able to go back home and put a bullet in his father's head. He had been eighteen at the time, just old enough to qualify for an adult prison, Clinton, where he was strong enough, finally, to avoid rape by confronting prospective rapists. And to stop committing rape. And even, sometimes, to prevent rape by taking young "chickens" under his wing.

Thus, the ten years he spent behind the walls of the Clinton Correctional Facility passed without major incident and he emerged from prison with enough connections to assemble a gang of ex-cons and become a major player in the blossoming cocaine trade on the old sod—Hell's Kitchen (the politicians liked to call it Clinton, an irony that did not elude Martin Blanks) which included everything west of Times Square, from 34th to 57th streets.

Marek Najowski nodded to the impassive Martin Blanks and stepped back to allow him and his cohorts to enter. "I thought you were coming alone," he admonished.

"I lied," Martin Blanks answered. Without being commanded, his men fanned out to look through the apartment. To look for anything that might endanger Martin Blanks, whose paranoia, honed in the city's juvenile system, was legendary.

"Look, Marty, I kind of expected you'd bring company. It only makes sense.

But some things in life you have to be alone for. Some things don't work with more than two people. Am I right, or what? So do me a favor, once you satisfy yourself, send them home and we could talk in private. Please."

Martin Blanks said nothing, patiently waiting for his men to finish. He took in his host's cashmere sweater, the wool-flannel trousers, the Bally loafers, even the two thin gold chains, one with a crucifix, hanging outside the sweater. Blanks had been turned on to Najowski by a neighborhood lawyer named O'Brien. O'Brien was a child of Hell's Kitchen. He'd gotten an education, but hadn't run away to Westchester or Connecticut. He'd stayed to defend and advise his boyhood chums, one of whom had been Marty Blanks.

"Nothin'." Stevey Powell, followed by his baby brother, Mikey, both ex-heavyweights, emerged from the kitchen to await further instructions.

"Go back to the house," Martin Blanks ordered curtly. "You know which one I'm talkin' about. I'll be back when I'm back."

"Should we take the car?"

"Yeah. Mr. Najowski wouldn't mind drivin' me home. Ain't that right?"

Marek Najowski, his grin jumping into place as if Martin Blanks had flipped a switch, nodded eagerly. Every instinct told him not to confront his guest. To let Martin Blanks enjoy his cocky attitude. "No problem. I was hoping we could go for a little drive, myself. Something I wanna show you in Queens." He waited patiently until they were alone, then offered Blanks a snifter of brandy.

"Bring the bottle in the car," Martin Blanks replied shortly. "I'm runnin' close tonight. I gotta be in the city by eleven the latest. Time's money, right?"

Still grinning, Marek Najowski passed the bottle of Paul Remy over to Martin Blanks, who wasted no time in sampling the contents while Marek slid into a wool jacket, an Ungaro houndstooth check which made no more impression on Martin Blanks than the cognac or the fire.

Ten minutes later, as they drove up Montague Street in Marek's white Jaguar sedan, Marek turned to Marty Blanks and began his pitch, playing the part of the engaging rogue with complete confidence.

"Tell me somethin', Marty," he said. "When is money not money?"

"Don't call me 'Marty,' " Martin Blanks responded shortly.

"Am I offending you?" The Jaguar accelerated effortlessly. Without a sound. "Because you're the last guy I want to offend. Hey, I'm the same as you. I grew up in Flatbush. I went to school with the nuns. I made my First Communion at St. Bernadette's, for Christ's sake."

Marek began to weave the Jaguar in and out of the trucks and cars, pushing it just a little faster than the traffic allowed, talking quietly. "So what should I call you?"

"Martin," Martin Blanks replied evenly.

"Is that what your friends call you?" Marek asked innocently. He was looking for the answer he got. Expecting it.

"No."

Marek laughed, shaking his head ruefully. "Whatever you want, Martin. Ya gotta go with the flow. Am I right, or what? You could call me Marek. I used to go by my mother's nickname for me—she was Irish, by the way—Mikey. I even had my name changed legally when I was about twenty-five. Changed it to Michael Najowski. Then, last year, I changed it back to Marek. You can't run away from what you really are. In more ways than one." He paused to thump on the leather armrest between Blanks and himself.

"I don't know what you're talkin' about," Blanks answered, his eyes straight ahead as the Jaguar slowed down to creep past a stalled Buick.

Marek Najowski didn't reply for a moment, concentrating on the traffic as he maneuvered the Jaguar up the Tillary Street ramp and onto the Brooklyn–Queens Expressway. "Tell me something," he finally said. "Were you in Hell's Kitchen before the Puerto Ricans took it over?" He knew, of course, that Martin Blanks had been taken from his family (and his neighborhood) before he was old enough to go out on the street, but the question was purely rhetorical. "Me, I grew up in Flatbush. On East 28th Street off Clarendon Road. Up until I was ten, it was all white. Italians, Irish, Poles, Germans. I'm talkin' about working people, Martin. Cops, firemen, plumbers. Come Sunday morning, St. Bernadette's ran six masses and every one of them was packed. All the kids I knew went to Catholic school. Maybe it wasn't paradise, but it worked. People took care of each other. They took care of the apartments where they lived. They took care of the *neighborhood*. Am I right, or what?"

Despite his original intentions, Marek Najowski was unable to keep the anger out of his voice. But he'd caught Martin Blanks' attention. The Irishman was looking at him with curiosity, waiting for the end of the story.

"Then the scum started moving in," Najowski resumed.

"This I already figured." Martin Blanks grinned for the first time.

"They came down from Atlantic Avenue. First to Eastern Parkway, then Empire Boulevard, then Linden Boulevard. Only a few, in the beginning. I remember the nuns telling us to get along. 'They're your brothers and sisters in God.' And the politicians coming across with the same bullshit.

"Well, the nuns stayed locked up in the convent and the politicians didn't live anywheres near Flatbush. They didn't come home to find them pissing in the hallways. They didn't see the scum throw bags of garbage out the window 'cause they were too lazy to carry their crap down the stairs. My father came to America after the war. He was raised up tough and he tried to get my mother to move out. Meanwhile, she's tellin' him to show 'Christian charity.' Well, here's what Christian charity means to the scum. One day, my mom was coming home from shopping. Three o'clock in the afternoon. As she's walking up the steps to our apartment—to her *home*—two of them come up to her. One grabs her pocketbook. No trouble, right. She gives it up, but the other one still gotta hit her. Gotta punch her in the mouth so she falls backward down the stairs. Know what, Martin? My mom's still alive. She don't know me, of course. She don't know nothin', but tubes and diapers."

"And, nat'rally, you blame it on the blacks."

Najowski shook his head. "You don't understand. No matter what society you pick—I don't care if it's all white or all black or what it is—there's a heap at the bottom. It's boiling. Literally boiling. Like bees crawling over each other in the nest. You could go to Sweden where they're whiter than white or Uganda where they're so black, they're invisible. Everybody wants to get out of the heap. It's just natural to want to rise up. But how many do it? How many rise up and how many stay on the bottom? My mother struggled all her life, only to get destroyed by an insect from the very bottom of the heap. That's not gonna be my fate, Marty. I already came too far for that."

They drove in silence while Marek Najowski allowed his heart to slow down. Allowed the red curtain in front of his eyes slowly to peel away. Finally, when he was ready to resume the persona he'd set for himself earlier in the evening, he spoke again.

"So tell me," he said, "when is money not money?"

"I give up." Even Martin Blanks, who'd seen violence in all its forms, from gang rape to cold-blooded murder, didn't have the heart to stop Najowski.

"When it's in a suitcase under a bed. Then it's a pile of shit. Am I right, or what?"

"I don't get the point," Blanks replied. Suddenly, he didn't like where the conversation was going.

"You could make millions in the drug business and what does it get you? I mean how long before you get busted? Or until some rival burns you for your connections? A year? Two years? Five years? Next time you go upstate, you won't come back until you're an old man. Not only that, but they'll take all your money. These days, when you get busted, they seize every dime and when you come out of jail, you're just another asshole on welfare. See, Martin Blanks, right now all you have is a penniless future in an upstate jail." Najowski flashed Blanks his most winning smile. "Am I right, or what?"

The reality was undeniable. A week before, Ali "Supreme Boy" Reynolds, one of South Jamaica's legendary crack lords, had had all his properties seized while awaiting trial in a Rikers Island dormitory. Everything the feds could lay their hands on, including two apartment buildings in Miami, a 7-Eleven in Tennessee, a yacht anchored in the Flushing Bay Marina, and a stretch Mercedes. Since the racketeering laws, state and federal, had taken effect two years before, major drug dealers stood to lose their assets before the trial even took place. Theoretically, if they were found innocent and could prove they'd acquired their property through honest toil, they could recover. It's the second part, of course, that provided the problems. A sharp lawyer might find a way to get a dealer off the hook, but even a genius can't find a technicality that accounts for an unemployed man's possession of hundreds of thousands (sometimes millions) of dollars in assets.

"Ya know somethin', Najowski? You got a big fuckin' mouth," Blanks said finally. His short, square body was rock-hard, a hundred and ninety pounds glued to a five-foot-six-inch frame; his head was broad and the heavy bones over his small, blue, Irish eyes made him seem dull and stupid. He was neither, though he sometimes played the fool.

"Yeah," Najowski replied, "but am I right, or what?" He nudged the Jaguar into the right lane and they exited the Brooklyn–Queens Expressway at Roosevelt Avenue and turned east, crisscrossing the streets between Roosevelt Avenue and 37th Avenue, the main commercial blocks in the neighborhood known as Jackson Heights. Dozens of small shops declared the prosperity, the middle-class character of the area: food, clothing, hardware, pharmacies, stationery. The neighborhood might have been set in any large city, except that half the signs were written in two languages and there were as many Orientals on the streets as whites.

"Pakistanis and Koreans," Najowski said, anticipating Blanks' question. "With a few Indians and Hong Kong Chinese. The neighborhood used to be Jewish, Italian, and Irish. This is where they came when they got enough money to leave the slums and it held up until the late 60s. Then the spics—Puerto Ricans, Dominicans, Colombians, Mexicans, Cubans—started to arrive and a lot of the whites got out. The Koreans came around 1980 with the wogs right behind. Now you find young professionals trying to beat Manhattan rents."

"Why'd they run?" Blanks asked. "This neighborhood is clean. There's nothin' happenin' on the streets. I don't see no sign of drugs. They look like they come outta church."

"It gets worse further east and along Roosevelt Avenue. There's drugs in the bars. There's even a dirty movie and a topless bar a couple of blocks from here. Hookers work the bar and sometimes the streets. That's gonna be a big thing for us. That movie and that bar."

Najowski pulled the car to the curb in front of 337-11 37th Avenue, an eighty-unit building with the name Jackson Arms carved over the entryway. Leaning back in the bucket seat, he watched his guest survey the neighborhood. Najowski had asked his connections to tell Blanks that Najowski wanted to propose a real estate deal. Nothing else. Now Blanks was looking over the property, impressed with the obvious quality of the housing, as Marek had hoped.

"Still looks like a good neighborhood," Blanks observed neutrally. "These people take care of their shit. Not like in Flatbush, where you used to live." He turned to his host and grinned innocently.

Najowski, ignoring the cut, changed the subject. "The way I figure, the mob is your best bet. They can take your money, for a percentage, and make it legitimate. But you'd have to trust them. You'd have to make them partners and, most likely, wops being wops, they'd have no reason to give an Irishman a piece of the action. Not once they got up a relationship with your suppliers and your customers. After that, they'd probably drop you in a field with a little hole behind one ear. Am I right, or what?"

"And you got a better way. Nat'rally. You want me to become a landlord. Well, I went to a lawyer, an old friend of mine, and he told me I can't make no money buyin' buildings more than fifteen years old. All them old buildings are rent-controlled. He says I'd be better off puttin' the money in the bank. I'd get more return. Plus, the landlords are in a computer now. Up in Albany. All that's gotta happen is one of the big pigs types ya name into that computer and you don't have no more property."

Najowski turned away from Blanks, staring out the side window long enough to make both of them uncomfortable. When he finally turned back, he was visibly upset. "You think I don't know this? I'm a landlord, for Christ's sake."

"You know about rent control, all right," Blanks said evenly. "But maybe you think that *I* don't know about it. Maybe you think I'm another Irishman with potatoes and whiskey, instead of brains, between his ears."

"What would you do if I ripped you off, Martin?"

"I'd kill ya. I wouldn't have no choice."

Najowski grinned enthusiastically; it was going exactly as planned. Let the asshole have his macho victories. It was the last card that mattered. He leaned in close to Blanks as he prepared to flash the bait. "Now listen carefully, Martin. This is where it gets good. Two years ago, Morris Katz, the Jew who owns this building and the two buildings running down 74th and 75th streets, sent his tenants notice that he wanted to convert his real estate from rental to co-op. Without gettin' into it too deep, you should know the laws about conversion are written in such a way that the *owner* of the property has to beg the *tenants* to buy or move on. You can't throw anybody out. Not even if their leases have expired. So long as they pay the rent, tenants have the right to renew their leases until they're carried out in a box. That's why Morris offered to sell the occupying tenants their apartments at a price thirty percent below the market price. That's called the 'insider' price and it means the tenants could buy a hundred-thousand-dollar unit for seventy thousand. That's a thirty-thousand-dollar profit. You'd think nobody in their right mind could refuse thirty thousand dollars. Am I right, or what?"

Najowski held up three fingers for Blanks' inspection. "Three people took it, Martin. Three." He paused to let the information sink in. "There's two hundred forty units in these buildings and I can get them for just over fifteen million dollars. Two million up front and the rest in a ten-percent mortgage which Morris will hold. I can swing the two million. Two million ain't a problem for me. Morris Katz is the problem. He bought the buildings in 1960 for two and a half million and the profit is gonna be taxed like ordinary income. Morris wants something under the table by way of compensation. Also, Morris don't trust banks. Or anything else run by Christians. He wants a million dollars in gold coins—one-ounce Mexican pesos—at the exchange rate on the day before the closing.

"I don't have cash, Martin. Or any way to get cash without attracting a lot of attention, but I know Morris Katz could get eighteen million if he wasn't in such a hurry to get out."

"What the fuck is an eighty-three-year-old man gonna do with a million dollars in gold?" Blanks interrupted, frowning. The whole deal had something wrong with it.

"Check this out, Martin. The Jew wants to sail his yacht to Jamaica, where he'll pass out the coins to any little native gal who can get him off. He lost his wife and kids in the concentration camps in World War Two and he spent all his efforts makin' money after the war. Didn't have time to start another family and now he's gotta have compensations."

"I still don't see what it's got to do with me," Blanks insisted. "What do I want with a rent-controlled building that even a Jew couldn't make no money on?"

"Well, you understand that when Morris tried to convert, he had to send his tenants a written proposal, right? That's called a red herring. In that proposal, he had to establish the value of each unit. The average price of a unit in one of Morris Katz's buildings, to an outsider, is just over one hundred thousand dollars. Multiply the number of units times one hundred thousand and what do you get?"

"Twenty-four million," Blanks replied without hesitation. "You're talkin' about a nine-million-dollar profit."

"No." Najowski grinned like a little boy. The bait was taken. All that remained was the formal setting of the hook. "Not nine million. The co-op assumes the mortgage, so the profit, minus legal fees and cosmetic repairs, is closer to twenty-one million dollars. But that's for *empty* units. That's if the Koreans and the Jews and Pakis already living here are encouraged to find other housing. I admit I can't do it. I got no way to get those assholes off my property. But *you* got a way. I'll bet you got a lot of ways."

Marek paused again, his grin widening. "Listen, Martin. This neighborhood might look like paradise, but Morris' buildings are only three blocks from an alley that runs off Broadway. There's a fuck-flick moviehouse there and a topless bar and, late at night, drugs and whores. If that scum took a notion to move the few blocks to our real estate, who could blame us? If it moved into our vacant apartments, how could we, as helpless landlords, blocked from *real* ownership of our property by ass-kissing politicians, be held accountable? And if these scum were to concentrate in a single building and conditions became so bad that we were able to *empty* that building, you, Martin Blanks, could be out of the dope business in two years. Am I right, or what?"

"And all I gotta do is trust you with a million bucks?" There was a challenge in Martin Blanks' words, but not in his voice. The figures were too astounding.

"Trust is not part of our arrangement," Najowski announced. "The units'll be operated by a management company for five percent of the gross rents. The properties will be owned by a corporation registered in New York. That corporation will be wholly owned by a corporation registered in the state of Delaware, where the disclosure laws are very weak. The Delaware corporation will be owned by a third corporation registered in the Bahama Islands, where the bankers make the Swiss look like gossip columnists. Each of us will own half the stock in that final corporation. Now, maybe the CIA could find us. Or the FBI.

But there ain't much chance the FBI or the CIA is gonna give two shits about some asshole tenants from Jackson Heights.

"Plus, Martin, you should consider that I can empty fifteen percent of the building just by checkin' leases. The Pakistanis and the Indians never do anything straight. One tenant moves out, a cousin moves in. Like they never heard of paperwork. And a lot of them are illegals. They'll fly the minute they see an eviction notice.

"The Koreans are better about the paperwork, but they won't fight. They'll be off as soon as there's a threat of drugs or violence. That's 'cause they're afraid their kids'll turn out to be Americans.

"Now, if we don't rerent the empty apartments, they'll attract squatters. Junkies. Whores. Alkies. The Jews and the Christians'll fight; they think the rent laws can protect 'em. When they find out the truth, they'll leave. Or we'll buy out the few we can't convince. The only real question is whether *you* can overcome their addiction to low rent."

Martin Blanks grinned from ear to ear. "That's the least of the problems, pal. I can make the cocksuckers wish they'd moved to fuckin' hell instead of Jackson Heights." He paused, then ran his fingers lightly over the Jaguar's leather seats. "I meant what I said before, though. If you rip me off, I kill you, if it means I gotta die myself."

Najowski echoed Blanks' smile. Despite his guest's reputation, Najowski felt no fear at all. "Martin, listen with both ears. If you want to stop being a criminal, you should learn to protect yourself with lawyers instead of threats. Look around, then buy yourself an attorney who accepts cash payments. Maybe the one who recommended you in the first place. Now, where could I drop you?"

Marek took his time driving back into Manhattan. Instead of running the BQE south and coming in through the Midtown Tunnel, he drove northeast, to the Grand Central Parkway and the Triboro Bridge. At 116th Street, he exited the Parkway and cut across Spanish Harlem, to Fifth Avenue, then turned south. Once past Mt. Sinai Hospital, with Central Park on the west side of the Avenue, the squalid tenements miraculously gave way to the most expensive real estate in Manhattan.

Martin Blanks was suitably impressed with the opulence surrounding them— the doormen and the long canopies extending to the curb, the glittering chandeliers in ballroom-sized lobbies, the beautifully dressed couples hurrying into their homes. For a short time, right after his parole, Martin Blanks had held, at the insistence of his parole officer, the exalted position of assistant janitor in a similar building on York Avenue. He had no more love for these people (or desire to live among them) than he'd had for his father on the day he pulled the trigger, but the years upstate had made him cautious. They could bite, these people, despite the fragile bodies and the bullshit facade. If he crossed them, his parole officer would certainly send him back to prison, so he tiptoed when in their exalted presence and, now that his parole was complete, ignored them altogether.

Still, watching the canopies pass, the doormen bowing and scraping, he had to concede the rich several truths: there were no cops coming to put them in jail. No rivals longing to put a bullet between their eyes. Or employees tempted to head south with a year's profits. They didn't hold their economic lives together with guns and shanks and tiny vials of rock cocaine; they were safe in a way he had never known.

When the white Jaguar pulled to the curb on 47th, between Ninth and Tenth, the whores and dealers were out in force. Despite the cool weather, knots of people dotted the tenement stoops, buying and selling. Hell's Kitchen had been Irish first, then Italian, then Puerto Rican. Now adventurous New York professionals, drawn by its proximity to midtown, were renovating individual tenements, but welfare hotels and decrepit slum buildings still dominated the neighborhood, furnishing the dealers with a ready clientele. Later, after midnight, the wolf packs, black and Latino kids from the outer boroughs, would roam the same streets, looking for prey, but, for now, the transactions were peaceful, if noisy.

This was Martin Blanks' territory and, though he hadn't been involved in the retail end of the business for several years, he was a role model for the street people, and a dozen voices greeted him as he stepped from the white Jaguar. The whores, the dealers, the neighborhood thugs . . .

Martin listened for a moment, then turned to Marek Najowski and said, "First thing is I'm gonna talk to that lawyer you mentioned. Then I'll be in touch."

ONE

January 4

CONNIE APPASTELLO, seventeen years old, waited impatiently in the first-floor hallway of the Jackson Arms for Yolande Montgomery to finish. Occasionally pressing her head to the door of apartment 1F, she could hear Yolande's caressing voice and the trick's steady grunts. It *sounded* like he was nearly done, so it probably wouldn't take that long. Still, Connie cursed Solly Rags, her pimp, for setting up two whores in a studio apartment. Unless one or the other turned a car trick, the situation was impossible. It could take a half hour to get these old shitheads hot enough to part with fifty bucks. How could you tell 'em they had to wait in a hallway 'cause the bed was full? And even if she was smart enough (which she definitely was) to maneuver the trick and make enough money to satisfy the rapacious Solly Rags (by freezing her ass off, mostly) she still had to stand around and be stared at, like some mutilated freak, by these asshole tenants (who probably never laid eyes on a working girl before) while Yolande did her thing in the apartment.

Finally (it seemed like forever), the door opened and a short, heavy man, buttoning his coat, hurried past her down the hallway. Connie pushed inside without waiting for the door to close. Yolande was lying in the bed, nude, her ample black body at ease. "What's happenin', baby?" she asked. "You still hurtin'?"

Connie ignored the question. She went right to the bureau against the far wall, to the glistening mirror with its heap of white powder. Quickly, expertly, she pushed a small pile to the center, chopped it with a razor blade then snorted it up, one line into each nostril. As the drug came on, she silently wished for a vial of crack, for that quick, overwhelming rush of ecstasy, but crack was forbidden, at least for the time being. They were opening up new territory, Solly explained, and they needed to keep their heads reasonably straight.

"Fuck that prick," Connie said. She admired her cheerleader reflection in the mirror for a few minutes, trying to gauge the coke's quality by the quality of her blue eyes, her full mouth. Then she found a pimple on her cheekbone, a tiny, red area that looked like it might develop into something really nasty. She consoled herself by cutting another line, chopping briefly, and snorting it up.

"You better take it easy with that blow, baby," Yolande called. "Ain't no more comin'. Solly say he won't be back."

Instead of answering, Connie stripped off her clothing: pink feathery jacket, electric blue micro-mini, five-inch spike heels, bright red push-up bra and matching panties, black, acrylic leg warmers. Nude, she climbed into the bed and cuddled up against Yolande, casually throwing a slender leg across the older woman's body. Tricks find such moments incredibly erotic, but Connie (for the moment) just wanted to cuddle.

"What a night," Connie said. "You wouldn't believe the fucking night I had." She laid her arm against Yolande's, noting the contrast between Yolande's dark, oily skin and her own baby-powder complexion. Six months into the life, Connie admired Yolande tremendously. Yolande had been on the street for years. Had actually been in jail, on Rikers Island, six different times and done a two-year bit in Bedford Hills for nearly killing a pimp. Yolande made sure Solly Rags didn't beat Connie more than absolutely necessary and that he put a gram on that mirror every night. It was one thing when the two girls worked the Lower East Side. There was every kind of dope on the street and they could always hold a few dollars back from their tips. Now Solly had them somewhere out in Queens and they had to rely on him to keep them high.

"Ya know, Yolande," Connie said, "that Solly can be a real prick."

"Did he beat you bad, baby?" Yolande, who'd begged two Seconals from a trick, was floating somewhere between the bed and the ceiling.

"Uh-uh. He just slapped me around a little. It didn't hurt much, but I wish he wouldn't do it right in the fuckin' car with Tony watchin'. It was really embarrassin'. Then he put me out on the street." She paused, giving Yolande an opportunity to join her in her indignation. "Ya believe that? I begged him, 'Solly, at least lemme work the bar,' but he goes, 'Yolande got the apartment, so you gotta find a car trick worth fifty bucks.' He said he don't care if I stay on the street all night. I gotta come back with another fifty bucks or I know what's gonna happen to me."

Connie pushed herself even closer to Yolande. The cocaine was more potent than she'd originally thought. Thank God. Maybe they'd do each other, she and Yolande, after all. She pressed her nipples against Yolande's back, running the tips of her fingers across the tightly curled hair at the top of Yolande's thighs, then took a deep breath and continued her narration of the night's events.

"So I'm walkin' up and down by the movie, but it's so cold no one's even goin' to the skin flicks. The streets are goddamn *empty. Finally* this little Jap car pulls up. Guy about forty, looks like a trick's sposed ta look—a little fat, a little bald, a wedding ring, a cheap suit and tie. He asks me how much and I say, 'Fifty,' cause that's what I gotta get fa Solly and I don't care what the trick wants me to do.

Well, he don't hassle about the money, so I get in the car and it's so warm I don't never wanna get back out, but the trick says he don't wanna do it in the car. A Toyota ain't big enough.

"I swear I tried everything. I stripped down outta my jacket. I put my legs on the dashboard and let my skirt ride up. He saw everything I got but he stuck to his guns. No car trick. We gotta do it on a bed or he's goin' down ta Queens Plaza and pick up one of them faggots work by the bridge. I mean *why* did Solly pick this asshole neighborhood without even a fuckin' motel that lets whores in?"

Suddenly, without any transition, Connie stopped talking and both women got out of bed and walked over to the mirror, cutting up four thin lines and sorting them out. Connie went first, pressing her buttocks back against Yolande's thighs (the way she knew Yolande liked) as she leaned forward to do her lines. Yolande, who preferred women to men (for companionship or for sex), responded with a casual swipe at Connie's butt.

A few seconds later, huddled together in the warm bed, Connie, without prompting, continued her story. "Well, fuck it, I *couldn't* let the trick get away. I mean it's like a Tuesday night and there's no traffic out there whatsoever, so I told him, 'Okay,' and we drove back here, but just like I figured, you got the pink cover on the doorknob and there ain't no way I can get to the bed. Meanwhile, the trick is hard and ready, hands up under my skirt, kissin' me all up by my neck and down my chest.

" 'Let's do it here, baby,' I said.

"I could see that fifty flyin' off ta Queens Plaza like it had goddamn wings, but the idea of doin' it in a hallway turned the freak on. He said, 'You really wanna do it right here? You don't care if people see us?'

" 'No, honey, I ain't worried about it.' I squeezed him through his pants and his dick jumped so fast I thought he was gonna come on the spot. He went in his pockets and turned over the cash and I got on my knees. I figured I could maybe work him fast enough so's he'd get off without no one seein' us, but just when he's about ta come, I feel him stiffen up and I see this old lady outta the corner of my eye. She standin' there watchin' us and she looks like she's about to croak or somethin'.

"Shit, I thought the trick'd lose his hard-on and I'd have ta fight ta hold on to that fifty, but he starts laughin' and callin' out ta the old broad.

" 'Hey, bitch, you wanna bite on this, too? I got enough for both of ya. C'mon down here.'

"Then he started pumpin' like crazy, alla time callin' out to the old lady did she wanna do this and wanna do that. The old lady was shakin like she was in an earthquake, but she didn't say nothin'. As soon as the trick came, she ran by us (except old ladies can't run no more, they kinda stumble). You shoulda seen the look she gave me—like I came outta one of those horror movies. Like I was a demon. I guess I can't blame her, though. I mean it's *her* goddamn house and everything. I'm just lucky the old bitch didn't have a gun 'cause she woulda shot me fa sure."

Yolande took her time answering. "This ol' lady didn't say nothin'?" she finally asked.

"Not one word. She was too fuckin' scared, or maybe she was in shock. Alls I can remember is she was standin' there shakin' like she had some kinda disease."

Connie giggled and slid in closer. She was definitely in the mood, now that she was sure Yolande wasn't mad at her. She let the backs of her long, polished nails slide down the smooth skin of Yolande's belly.

"Cops probly gonna be here," Yolande said flatly, pushing Connie away. "What're we gonna do then?"

Connie, who was very stoned, sat up in bed and pouted. "Well, what was I supposed ta do, Yolande? You think I wanted to do that trick in the hallway? I was *freezin'*. It's twenty degrees and the wind was blowin' up my skirt so hard I thought I was gonna die."

"Okay, okay." Yolande, still cradled in the warm indifference of the Seconals, reached out a hand and drew Connie back in close to her. "I ain't gonna say nothin' ta Solly Rags 'bout this. You keep your mouth shut, too. Hear me, girl?" She leaned across and kissed Connie's lips. "We just gettin' started. Solly say we'll be runnin' the whole buildin' a few months from now. Be jus' like the Lower East Side. Dope everywheres. We gonna have about three apartments workin' tricks. Long as we don't fuck it up. I got plans for both of us."

Connie laid her head on Yolande's shoulder. Yolande was so butch. Maybe she really could take them out of Solly's control. If that happened, she promised herself, she'd never hold out on Yolande. Gently, she kissed Yolande's throat. Right underneath the Adam's apple where she knew Yolande liked it.

"I'm gonna have a little conversation with Solly Rags," Yolande announced. "Hell, you beautiful. No reason we can't get us some telephone work 'till it warms up. Maybe do shows. Let you play the little girl. Solly told me he want us out where the people can see us, but it ain't gonna help if we freeze ta death. I'll talk to him tomorrow. Lay down the law."

Again, without transition, both women got up and walked across the room, to the bureau, the mirror, the cocaine.

TWO

January 5

SERGEANT PAUL "PORKY" DUNLAP hated everything about his job as Community Affairs Officer of the 115th Precinct on Northern Boulevard and 92nd Street in Queens. The position had been created more than fifteen years before, after the scandals exposed by the Knapp Commission, on the theory that an individual police officer whose only duty was to present a positive front to the communities served by the various precincts, would act as some kind of counter to the negative image created by the special prosecutor's relentless attack on corrupt policemen.

At the time, an ambitious Sergeant Paul Dunlap (who had not yet eaten his way to his nickname) had seen the position of Community Affairs Officer as a pathway to rapid advancement in the department. Twelve years later, having failed the lieutenant's exam twice (the last time in 1984, after which he'd given up) he knew the position for what it actually was—an endless parade of bullshit lunches and jerk-off dinners, a hairbag nonstop flight to retirement. The Elks Club, the Knights of Columbus, the East Elmhurst Improvement Group, the Jackson Heights Merchants' Association, every goddamn church in the precinct . . . the list was endless.

Two years after stepping into the role of Community Affairs Officer, Sergeant Dunlap, though he still hoped to escape his fate by passing the lieutenant's exam, had realized several things. First and foremost, no Community Affairs Officer would ever make an arrest unless he happened to step into the middle of a robbery while off-duty. Second, and nearly as important, without good collars and without passing the lieutenant's exam, there was no place for him to go in the job. Third, he couldn't give the position of Community Affairs Officer away.

Four years into the job, after failing the lieutenant's exam for the first time, he had made several futile attempts to get free, at one point feigning illness for so long, the precinct Integrity Officer began an investigation into possible misuse of sick time. As a result, he was ordered back to work and found himself in the office of Captain Serrano, Precinct Commander, where he was told that his options were Community Affairs or early retirement. He could expect no transfers, either to another precinct or to another position.

"Hey, *shmuck*," Serrano had explained, "wake up and die right. You got a perfect job you could do until you're sixty-five when you gotta take retirement. You get to wear a suit every day and you never gotta sit on a toilet waitin' for some junkies to do a deal. What's the matter with Community Affairs? It's pig fuckin' heaven."

"Then how come nobody wants it?" Dunlap had countered. What bothered him most was the feeling that he wasn't a real cop. While the others bragged about street encounters, vicious fights, important arrests, Porky Dunlap kept his mouth shut in the squad room and stayed away from cop bars.

"Because most cops're stupid kids who still wanna play cowboys and Indians," Serrano patiently explained.

"They laugh at me, Captain," Dunlap moaned. "It's like I should be on Madison Avenue instead of the One One Five. I don't get respect from anybody."

"Tough shit. Do ya fuckin' job or hand in ya papers. Every house gotta have a Community Affairs Officer and you're mine."

Porky Dunlap put on seventy-five pounds in the next two years, ballooning up from one eighty-five to more than two sixty. Nobody cared. He was the invisible man in the precinct and only the odd businessman bothered to dig a sly elbow into the flab surrounding his ribs.

During that same period, the sergeant developed four basic speeches. One each on drugs, robbery, street crime, and burglary. He gave one of these four, depending on the place, the circumstances, and the hot crime of the day, to any group requesting his services, even to the smirking high school students jammed into the auditorium for his annual talk on the dangers of drugs. Inevitably, some of the seniors remembered the speech from prior assemblies and laughed out loud when Paul Dunlap described the agonies of a heroin junkie trying to kick the habit.

And so the years went by: eight, ten, twelve, fifteen. Porky learned to do his job well; he was recognized by the more influential citizens in the community (if not by the cops in the One One Five) and called upon whenever the good folks needed reassurance. His life became routine and monotonous and even though his paycheck bloomed, what with all the appearances at night time meetings of this or that organization, he never quite lost the sense of being a civilian employee instead of a third generation New York City cop. His best buddy in the house was a computer operator who ran the network connecting the precinct with the mass of information stored in the state files.

This explained Porky Dunlap's utter consternation when Sylvia Kaufman knocked firmly on his door, then entered without waiting for permission. He'd been casually daydreaming about the speech he planned to give to the American Legion that evening and the endless rounds of drinks the Legionnaires would buy once he was finished. It was a pleasant dream. Far more pleasant than the old lady who, still without permission, pulled a chair over to his desk and sat down.

"Are you the Community Affairs Officer?" she asked.

"Yes. I'm Sergeant Dunlap." Porky's manners and speech had been honed by frequent contact with influential civilians. He smiled automatically while his mind raced over the possibilities. The kind of people he ordinarily dealt with never entered the precinct unless they were actually filing a complaint in a criminal action. In which case they went to one of the real detectives. Not him. "What can I do for you?"

"The officer downstairs, the one behind the desk where you come in, suggested I speak to you about a crime I witnessed. My name is Sylvia Kaufman."

Porky Dunlap shifted uncomfortably, well aware of the joke being played on the two of them. The woman had to be a nut and the Desk Sergeant simply wanted to get rid of her without being second-guessed by some lieutenant if the old lady's grandson happened to work for CBS.

"When did this crime happen?" Dunlap asked. He was wondering what a complaint form looked like these days; he hadn't filled one out in years.

"Last night. I was inside Annie Bonnastello's apartment until nearly midnight. She had a stroke two years ago and she needs help with the heavy cleaning. Her apartment is on the first floor, the same as mine, but we're on opposite sides of the building . . ."

"Could you give me the address of the place? Let me get a fix on it? The One One Five serves a pretty large area."

"337-11 37th Avenue. Two blocks from where Broadway crosses Roosevelt Avenue."

"That's Jackson Heights, right?"

"Correct." Sylvia paused, waiting for another question, her thin body rigidly straight. She was sixty-five years old, but still strong and confident. Illness, though she tended it in others, seemed quite foreign to her. True, she sometimes thought about death, but she fully expected to function right up to the end. No wasting diseases for Sylvia Kaufman, who'd spent thirty-five years in the public school system without taking a sick day. When Porky Dunlap kept silent, she went on with her recitation. "As I walked through the lobby to the western wing, which is where I live, I witnessed an act of public prostitution. I would like to file a complaint."

At the sound of the words "public prostitution," Porky Dunlap did a mental double take, though he maintained a concerned expression, the one he used when listening to the laments of recently burglarized businessmen after speeches at the Elks Club. "Prostitution? In public? In Jackson Heights? That's pretty rare." The question came automatically, because, at heart, Porky Dunlap was still a cop and when confronted with an unusual situation, cops instinctively probe.

"That's what has me so worried," Sylvia Kaufman said evenly. "We're only a block from the el on Roosevelt Avenue, but our building has always been good. No drugs. No loud parties. Even when the Spanish started moving in twenty years ago and everyone said the neighborhood was going, we managed to keep it together. It's just that lately . . ."

"Tell me exactly what you saw?" Dunlap asked.

Sylvia Kaufman took a deep breath. She'd grown up in a different era and remembered the old Catholic Legion of Decency with its list of condemned movies. Her friend, Annie Bonnastello, always consulted it before going to see a film. Nowadays, according to the media, girls threw away their virginity before puberty. But in her day, women didn't talk about sex. "I saw a very young woman, a girl, really, performing an act of oral sex on a much older man."

"Right in the hallway?"

"Yes. The man made obscene remarks to me. He invited me to join in."

Though he kept the scepticism out of his voice, Porky Dunlap jumped to the same conclusion as the Desk Sergeant. Nut case. Now all he had to do was figure out how to get rid of her. "Did anyone actually touch you?"

Sylvia searched for a way to explain what she'd seen and how she'd felt. She'd been very tired when she left Annie's apartment. Her eyesight wasn't so good when she was tired and the hall was dimly lit. (It seemed to get dimmer and dimmer as the years went by.) She'd heard sounds, first. Someone was grunting and there was a wet sound that might have been a kiss. Sylvia's first thought was that Fay Gelardi, who lived on the fifth floor, was at it with her boyfriend again. The one her parents hated; the one she was forbidden to see. Fay's parents were old country and were deathly afraid of the kinds of corruption available to New York teenagers.

Sylvia, who thought of herself as tolerant, had cleared her throat by way of a warning, but the reaction she'd gotten was totally unexpected.

"Check out the old bitch. Hey, old bitch, what's doin'?"

The images had suddenly jumped into focus. Two strangers, a man and a woman. The woman (just a girl, really) was on her knees and the man's trousers were down around his ankles. She was holding his erection with one hand while she looked back and forth from Sylvia to her lover.

Sylvia took a deep breath. There had to be a way to express her sense of violation, of impending doom. She felt like the first human to spot the aliens in a science fiction movie.

"No," she finally said, "the man had an orgasm, and I passed by them and went into my apartment."

"Did you see any money actually change hands? How do you know it wasn't a couple of kids who got carried away?"

"The man was in his forties, wearing a suit and tie. The girl was no more than eighteen. She wore some kind of bright pink jacket that looked like it was made of feathers and a very short skirt that barely covered her buttocks. The jacket was open and I could see her bra. It was red and designed to leave her nipples completely exposed."

The sergeant squirmed in his seat. He was taken with the old woman's concise recitation of the events. Putting her in the "nut" category had relaxed him, but her manner was anything but typical of the confused elderly who occasionally wandered into the precinct. This woman was steady as a rock.

"The girl lives in apartment 1F with another woman," Sylvia Kaufman continued. "Apartment 1F is a studio. They sleep all day and work at night." She hesitated a moment, unsure of herself, then rushed on. "The building changed hands about two months ago. There's a new management company. They fired the super and they haven't hired anybody to replace him. We have to carry the garbage out ourselves. And there are empty apartments all through the building where people have been evicted. Precision Management says these apartments were not occupied by the individuals who signed the leases, but the former owner never cared. He just wanted his rent."

"Hold up a second." The story, though familiar enough in poor neighborhoods like Corona, a black slum which lay east of the precinct house, simply didn't fit the pattern for Jackson Heights. Even in the 60s, when the Latinos had arrived, the majority of the entering Puerto Ricans, Dominicans, and Colombians had been hardworking and determined to exercise their right to a slice of the American dream. Street crime had never become a major problem.

Porky Dunlap, processing this information, was again caught up in the anomaly. The situation stunk of outside manipulation. Then he pushed the contradictions back and returned to reality. "If you have problems with the building, you have to go to HPD. Housing Preservation and Development. Get them to send out an inspector and write up the violations. As for the prostitution—unless you saw the money change hands and you can prove the money was given in return for sex, we can't make an arrest. Now it's true, public indecency is a misdemeanor, but it's still your word against this girl's. Even if we took your complaint and brought her in, we'd have to write a Desk Appearance Ticket and release her on her own recognizance. And *you'd* have to testify in court. The worst she'd get, assuming she was found guilty and had a history of prior arrests, is a fine or a few days in jail. And she'll know who made the complaint and her pimp'll know, too. You might find yourself subject to personal harassment without really accomplishing a damn thing. It's not worth it." Satisfied with his impromptu lecture, he sat back and waited for her to respond.

"Well, what am I to do? Simply ignore it? My husband and I lived in that building for thirty years. I pay three hundred dollars a month rent. If I had to leave, there's no place in the city I could afford. Even with all the new people, I still have a lot of friends in the building. It's like a community."

"You should have brought your husband with you. The more people who sign a complaint, the more likely someone'll take action. Always keep that in mind. Numbers impress."

"My husband passed away in 1982," Sylvia replied evenly.

"I'm sorry." Suddenly Porky Dunlap found himself wishing he could really help, that he could be a cop for once, but the situation, assuming she was describing it accurately, was not a problem for the NYPD. "Look, your move is to organize the tenants. A strong tenants' association can get action from any landlord. That's what you really need. Put enough heat on the landlord and he'll take action against this whore and her roommate." He noted the look of dismay on her face; she'd expected the police to solve all her problems and now she was being asked to organize a mass movement. "Look," he said, "as Community Affairs Officer, I've visited tenants' associations during rent strikes. I know a little about how they work. You don't organize all at once. First, make a list of the tenants you've known for the longest time. The ones you can count on. Get them together and explain the situation. See if they agree that something has to be done. How many units in the building?"

"Eighty."

"How many vacant?"

"I'm not sure. Maybe fifteen."

"That leaves about sixty-five occupied. If you can organize ten people and have them knock on five doors each, you can get in touch with nearly every tenant in the building. Get up a petition and take it to the landlord asking that the prostitutes be moved out. See, I don't think you *really* have anything to worry about. Those buildings are pretty solid, not like the tenements, and I just can't see a landlord allowing the property to fall apart. Sometimes when a building changes hands, it takes a little while for the new management to get organized. Still, the sooner *you* get organized, the better."

Sylvia Kaufman knew she was being dismissed and she didn't like it, despite the sergeant's obvious sincerity. "Isn't there a vice squad to go after the prostitutes?"

"There is," Dunlap admitted, "but the penalty for prostitution is so light, enforcement is a waste of time. And arresting the girls doesn't help, because the pimp's certain to dump new girls in the same apartment. If you really want to put heat on prostitutes, get somebody to stay in the lobby and harass the customers. If the johns can't be anonymous, they'll stop coming." Porky Dunlap stood up, clearly indicating that the interview was over. "There used to be a time when a vice cop'd go up, have a few words with the whores or the pimp and they'd be on their way. Nowadays, unless we got the warrant in our hands, the scum just laugh in our faces."

THREE

THOUGH he'd only known Stanley Moodrow (formerly Detective Sergeant Stanley Moodrow, NYPD; now retired) for a year, Detective James Tilley, NYPD, considered Moodrow to be his best friend and, in his opinion, best friends weren't supposed to surprise each other. They were *supposed* to know each other too well for surprises. They were *supposed* to be open to each other.

He, Tilley, had kept his part of the bargain, becoming more and more predictable as he settled down to life with his new bride, Rose Carillo, and her two children, Lee, now eight, and Jeanette, six. Moodrow, on the other hand, continued to surprise, without putting space between himself and the much younger Jim Tilley.

For instance, Tilley had predicted to Rose, who'd known Moodrow longer than he, that retirement would be the end of Stanley Moodrow. "Moodrow's the ultimate loner," he'd explained. "Know how many friends he's got in the Department? One and a half. Captain Epstein is the one and I'm the half. And maybe Epstein only because he kept himself between Moodrow and the sharks at Internal Affairs. And maybe me only because I sat next to him for a few months before he passed in his papers."

Moodrow's first surprise had been a new career which had begun within weeks of his retirement. It had happened so suddenly that Tilley (though Moodrow continued to deny it) suspected Moodrow had begun to set it up even before he walked away from the job. And it wasn't simply the transformation from cop to private investigator that amazed Jim Tilley. Too many ex-cops take up careers in private security of some kind for *that* part of it to come as a surprise. It was the exalted level on which Moodrow had made his appearance that had had Tilley explaining the wild inaccuracy of his prediction to an unsympathetic Rose, who'd always thought of Stanley Moodrow as the ultimate role model in the survivor sweepstakes.

For Stanley Moodrow had not become one of those sleazy half-criminals who maintained closet-sized offices near Times Square. Moodrow didn't follow errant husbands, looking for a photograph explicit enough to cancel potential alimony awards; he worked exclusively for New York's finest criminal lawyers— investigating alibis, searching out witnesses, probing for skeletons in the prosecution's closet. As an ex-cop, he had the right to carry a gun and to have his application for a private investigator's license processed by the NYPD in less than

a week. After thirty-five years in the job (and to the great delight of his employers), he also had access to working cops and, sometimes, to the confidential
reports the prosecution keeps away from the defense by declaring them irrelevant
and, therefore, not subject to the legal process of discovery.

Thus Stanley Moodrow, much to his *own* surprise, was an instant success; the
demand for his services rising day by day. And, as if that wasn't enough, two
weeks after beginning his new occupation, Moodrow realized that his assignments would almost always involve the same shoe-leather methods he'd used as a
cop, a similarity for which he was infinitely grateful. Like most cops, Moodrow
equated retirement with oblivion and his new career, as he'd explained to Jim
Tilley on more than one occasion, was unexpected enough to be rated as
miraculous. Which is why he had again surprised his former partner . . . by
rejecting it.

"All right," Moodrow had explained, "I admit humans are supposed to be
happy when they get a miracle. I'm not a complete fucking idiot. I'm *supposed* to
be happy."

And he would have been. Except for one tiny, yet inescapable, detail: virtually
all of his work involved efforts to free guilty men. As his whole life had been
devoted to putting the guilty behind bars, this small fact had worked its way into
his heart, attaching itself, like a tapeworm, to his conscience.

"Yeah, I understand the system," he'd protested to Tilley and Rose over a fiery
dinner at one of the Indian restaurants that lined 6th Street between First and
Second avenues. "It's a war between the defense and the prosecution, and
the defense lawyer's *obliged* to get the client off the hook. I heard all that shit
about the founding fathers not trusting the government and maybe they were
right, but I'm not a lawyer and I'm not obliged to keep some shyster's scummy
client—pardon me: scummy *rich* client—out of jail. I admit they pay me
good, but I retired on a three-quarters pension. With the overtime on the
last year, it's enough so I don't have to worry I'm gonna finish up sleeping
in doorways. Which means if I keep doing this, it's because I want to. It
bothers me."

The end had come when he'd been asked to dredge up a few individuals
willing to provide an alibi for a Wall Street executive named Evan Rhenquist,
a brutal rapist who openly bragged of his crimes during meetings with his
lawyer, George Feingold. Feingold, who specialized in pulling "not guilty"
verdicts from juries like magicians pull rabbits from hats, had found Rhenquist's braggadocio quite amusing, but Moodrow's first instinct had been
to bury his massive fists in the defendant's smug face. The thought of Evan
Rhenquist going back out on the streets through his efforts left Moodrow
utterly disgusted.

"I didn't actually hit him," Moodrow explained on the night he began what
was to become a monumental drinking binge, "because I was working for
Feingold. I couldn't take the man's money and then fuck up the man's client, but

I told Rhenquist that I wouldn't piss in his mouth if his heart was on fire (which didn't bother him worth a shit) and walked out. Now I don't know what to do. The only thing I have going for me is an offer to head up the security in a pharmaceutical warehouse. I got the contact from a friend of Captain Epstein."

"So what's wrong with that?" Tilley asked.

"It's in the middle of New Jersey. I'd have to move. To fuckin' New Jersey. It's a fate worse than life."

Moodrow shrugged his massive shoulders, then rose from the chair. It was the first time Tilley had ever seen him worried, ever seen him pace the floor. Even in the middle of the most intense investigation, Moodrow had inevitably been calm when he'd discussed a case. Now Tilley, watching his former partner closely, had the sinking feeling that his prophecy regarding Moodrow's retirement was about to come true. Moodrow's broad, almost featureless (almost ageless) face was beginning to show signs of real wear. Like the ex-cop could see his future and he didn't like it worth a damn.

The weeks that followed had done nothing to diminish Tilley's fears, even though Rose assured him that Moodrow would eventually pull out of it. Moodrow drank hard and long, drank until he fell into bed at night. Tilley knew his partner wasn't afraid of death, that Moodrow was a fatalist who thought that life was only a series of postponements. Sex was a postponement; money, too; they could sometimes push away the depression that often lies at the core of the cop's attempt to square his sense of justice with the reality of the inner city. But the most effective postponement was the job itself. Many cops marry it, including Moodrow, only to find themselves widowers in middle age. Then, with no family and few friends, they have to face the consequences of their deal. Moodrow faced them by launching himself into a bar-by-bar tour of the 7th Precinct (just as he used to when looking for a suspect) and Tilley became afraid that Moodrow would substitute a bullet for the bottle, choosing the most final of all cop consolations.

Then, one Thursday night, Tilley received a phone call from an obviously sober Moodrow asking that he and a new girlfriend, a lawyer named Betty Haluka, be invited to dinner on Saturday. After a brief consultation with Rose, Tilley eagerly agreed, but Tilley's questions, inspired by intense cop curiosity, went unanswered. Moodrow was on the run; he was feeling great; he'd speak to them on Saturday night.

Tilley decided not to wait. With Rose, the kids and Moodrow's date around, there was no way he was going to get any straight answers. He wouldn't even be able to ask the questions. Thus his presence in Moodrow's apartment on Saturday afternoon while Moodrow prepared for his date.

"Whatta ya think of this suit?" Moodrow asked, taking it out of the plastic garment bag and holding it up to the light. "It's only a couple of months old. Cost me two hundred at one of the showrooms on 7th Avenue. I know the owner pretty well. Did him a favor once."

Tilley eyed the plain, brown wool suit Moodrow offered for his inspection, concluding that it had so little to distinguish it, it might have been any age younger than shiny and any price lower than expensive. "I think it's the real you, Stanley."

"Do the 'real me' a favor and don't be a smartass," Moodrow replied evenly. "I wanna make a good impression. She's a fucking *lawyer*."

"Does that mean she specializes in litigation involving intercourse?" Tilley, who expected no answer and got none from the imperturbable Stanley Moodrow, still paused for effect. "Don't be a prick. Tell me how you met her." Tilley sipped at his Budweiser speculatively. "You know everything about Rose and me, probably including our love life. I gotta know how you met this broad."

"You know what Rose would do, if she heard you say 'broad'?" Moodrow asked innocently. "She'd serve Lower East Side prairie oysters tonight." He paused long enough to giggle at his own humor. "Betty wouldn't take shit from anyone, either. That's what I like about her."

"You want me to beg, or what, ya fuck?" Tilley asked, tossing a pillow at his ex-partner. "Tell me how you met the woman. The last time I saw you, you were puking on your shoes in the Killarney Harp. Now you're glowing like a goddamn Hare Krishna health freak."

"Actually, Betty called *me*. She's a Legal Aid lawyer."

"A what?" Just the sound of the words "Legal Aid" made Tilley's hackles rise. Legal Aid lawyers were the ones who pored over the police reports and the warrants, looking for an undotted "i" or an uncrossed "t." They were the ones who worked you over on the witness stand, implying that your shield, the gold shield of the detective coveted by generations of cops, was no more than proof of your incompetence and corruption.

"I was sitting here one afternoon," Moodrow continued, "trying to wake up (this is about a week ago) when the phone rings. A lot of the time when I'm hung over, I don't answer the phone, but this time the fucking bell was going off between my ears. My whole brain was vibrating and I couldn't think of any way to stop it without picking it up.

"It turns out to be this Legal Aid lawyer, Betty Haluka. She says she got my number from the mother of one of her clients, Estelle Lopez, who I happen to know. Then Haluka says she thinks her client's innocent, but she can't prove it by herself. She's got an incredible caseload and there's an attack on a cop involved, so the Assistant DA won't help her investigate and, naturally, the cops don't wanna hear about it, either.

"Now here's the kicker. The client, Henry Lopez, is charged with assault, atrocious assault, drug possession, weapons possession, loitering with intent to sell narcotics and resisting arrest. He's got a string of priors and even though his priors are all misdemeanors, if he goes to trial and he's found guilty, he's gonna get twenty years. On the other hand, if Lopez wants to plead guilty, they'll drop everything but the assault and let him off with a year at Rikers Island.

"At first, I was gonna hang up the phone and forget about it. That's how bad I was hung over, but I was curious, too. I wanted to hear about the case and why she thought the guy was innocent. And why it mattered if he was guilty or not. There were plenty of times I let a scumbag hang for a crime he didn't commit if I thought the neighborhood was better off without him. Maybe I'm not supposed to play God, but that's still how I did it.

"Anyway, I asked her to run it down for me and here's what she says. The cop, Lekowski, and Lopez have completely different stories and there are no other witnesses. The cop, who was assigned to a buy-and-bust operation, says he observed Henry place several glassine envelopes, which the cop had reason to believe contained heroin, into the right-front pocket of his trousers; naturally, Lekowski, being a good cop tried to arrest Lopez, whereupon Lopez punched him in the face, forcing Lekowski to draw his gun in order to complete the arrest. A subsequent pat-down turns up four bags of dope and a used syringe. Case closed.

"Lopez says he was standing in front of a tenement in Bushwick, enjoying the heroin he injected about an hour before the incident. He admits having the dope on him, but he says when he copped there was just him and the dealer present, so there's no way Lekowski could have seen him handle it. He also admits that he busted Lekowski's nose, but he says he was provoked and Lekowski didn't identify himself until after it was over which, if he's telling the truth, would make it entrapment.

"All of a sudden I'm interested in spite of the fucking hangover. Don't forget, this is a middle-aged woman I'm talking to. Usually they're so goddamned stuffy, they make me feel like I got asthma. Especially civil servants, which is what Legal Aid really is. Anyway, she tells me Lopez swears that Officer Lekowski, who looked like an ordinary junkie, walked up to him and said something in English which Lopez didn't understand. Lopez doesn't speak English very well, especially when he's stoned, and he responded to the cop by saying, 'No habla.'

"Then Lekowski, in perfect Spanish, told Mr. Lopez that his mother (who is dead, by the way) was a whore with a cunt as big as the entrance to the Holland Tunnel. Furthermore, Henry himself was a queer, a *pato*, and his asshole had been enlarged while receiving multiple infusions of the AIDS virus from his father.

"Henry used to be a fighter before he took up heroin, so he naturally belted the cop out. In fact, Lopez knocked the cop down the stairs in front of the building, but he was too stoned to even *want* to do anything else. Lopez says he was shocked out of his underwear when Lekowski got up with a pistol in one hand and a badge in the other.

"Then Haluka stops and, me, I'm so into the story, I don't make a sound. Imagine a middle-aged lady lawyer saying shit like 'a cunt as big as the Holland Tunnel'? Without laughing behind her hand or something? How many women you know would say that?"

Tilley, still intensely curious, answered the question seriously. "I know some lady cops who wouldn't blink. I think Rose could say it."

"To a stranger?"

"She might," Tilley insisted.

"All right, but Rose is a lot younger and she knows about the street. I can tell from Betty's voice that I ain't talking to a member of the younger generation. This woman comes from a time when ladies didn't talk like that."

"Fine," Tilley agreed with a wave of his hand. "Go on with the story."

"So, for a minute, neither of us speak. Then Betty says, " 'I think I know what's bothering you.' "

" 'What's that?' " I ask her.

"She says, 'You're thinking Henry Lopez is probably a scumbag and he deserves to go to jail.'

"And you're saying that he isn't?

" 'Look, Mr. Moodrow,' she says, 'I *know* Henry's a junkie. He's got six arrests for misdemeanor possession of heroin with four convictions, plus one arrest and conviction for burglary. But Henry Lopez is not a violent man and he doesn't deserve to face twenty years in jail for the crime of pleading not guilty. Because that's really blackmail. If he forces the State to undergo the expense of a trial and gets convicted, they'll fry his ass for the next two decades. The man's only twenty-five. He's got a family and most of the time he works. I can show you letters from former employers. Who gains from putting him in jail, especially for a crime he didn't commit?'

"Normally I wouldn't even listen to bullshit like this, because, personally, I think most of the people who get busted are guilty. It's very rare that someone gets popped who ain't a criminal of some kind. But if I *gotta* work with criminals and the law, if it's *really* in my fucking blood, then it's better to work with people who're at least innocent of the crime they got charged with. The difference between Betty Haluka and the other lawyers is Betty didn't ask me to get Lopez off the hook. She just wanted me to find out if he was really innocent.

"Of course, at the time, I didn't know exactly *what* she wanted, so I asked her what she expected me to do and I told her if I found out Lopez was a real asshole, I wouldn't have anything to do with his defense, even if he was innocent.

"She said she didn't have a problem with that and what she wanted was simple. At a preliminary hearing, the cop claimed that he didn't know a single word of Spanish. If she could impeach Lekowski by proving that he could speak the language, it would blow the case wide open. Lekowski was the only witness against Lopez. Of course, I mentioned that Legal Aid has its own investigators, but she said the investigators' unit is so small they can only work on major cases. If I don't check out Lekowski, nobody else will."

Moodrow, now seated on edge of the bed, stared into his former partner's eyes just as if the story was finished. Tilley, who knew his friend too well to show his annoyance, simply asked, "What happened?"

"Shit, Jim, I wanted to ask her out right then and there, but I didn't have the guts. I figured she'd think I was muscling her for the date . . ."

"I'm talking about with Lekowski and Lopez," Tilley said mildly. In the course of their friendship, he'd grown to relish the long conversations with Moodrow. Most of the time, when they were partners, they'd begun their working day in Moodrow's apartment. The intimacy was addicting, especially as Tilley's most recent partner was a burnout with the unfortunate habit of withholding information in order to take sole credit for the collars they made together.

"There wasn't that much to it once I got going," Moodrow said. "I gave a twenty-dollar bill to the Records Clerk in Lekowski's precinct and got a look at his package. There was a notation that he went to Queens College for three years before he came into the job, so I went out to Queens College and spent another twenty for a look at his transcript. Five semesters of conversational Spanish with nothing lower than a B+. Betty took it to the Assistant DA handling the case and they dropped all the charges. Now I'm getting calls from every Legal Aid lawyer in Manhattan. Like I was a miracle man."

Tilley settled back in the ancient overstuffed chair Moodrow ordinarily used as a hanger, shaking his head. Moodrow never ceased to amaze him. "Now tell me about Betty Haluka," he commanded.

"She's about forty-five, dark-haired, pretty good-looking, but with very strong features. Full mouth and nose. She was dressed for court the times I seen her and it's hard to tell how she's built. If I had to guess, I'd say she's a little chunky, but I think there's muscle under there. She's been twenty years with Legal Aid and she's not burned out. She claims she's made enough peace with herself to be satisfied that she's doing the best she can with a fucked-up system." Pausing, he walked to the closet and took out his other suit, a plain navy blue that Tilley knew was too small for Moodrow's massive frame.

"What kind of name is Haluka?" Tilley asked.

"Haluka's a Turkish name. Betty's grandfather was a Turk, but Betty thinks of herself as a Jew. She says her family hasn't stopped traveling since the Romans threw them out of Israel. Turkey, Armenia, Spain, England, Hungary. Wherever they went, it got bad for them sooner or later, so the family adopted the ability to make quick exits as a survival tool. They came here from Berlin in 1934, early enough to get out *with* the bankroll."

Moodrow stopped right in the middle of his narrative, holding both suits, the blue and the brown one, at arm's length. He shook his head. "So whatta ya think, Jim? Which one?"

Tilley, who, at 28, was too young to appreciate the idea of "one last chance," nevertheless understood that Betty Haluka was very important to Stanley Moodrow. He didn't spend any time dwelling on the reason why, though he had a flash of one of Moodrow's most recent girlfriends, a twenty-five-year-old waitress that he, Tilley, would have dated himself, had he been single. But the waitress's youth had, obviously, meant little to his friend, while the chunky Betty Haluka had pulled Moodrow out of a long-term drunk. "You know something, Stanley," Tilley said. "You'd do a lot better if you shopped at one of the specialty men's stores. You're too big to buy clothes off the rack. Even if you know the guy who makes the suits."

Moodrow looked at Tilley sadly. Tilley was slim and muscular, actually elegant, in the jeans, flannel shirt, and Harris Tweed jacket he was wearing at the moment. Moodrow knew that even if he, Moodrow, coughed up a grand for a custom-made suit, he'd still look like a refrigerator in drag.

"Do you know how much those specialty shops charge? Besides, I'm on a culture trip." He held up the suits again, inspecting them carefully.

"Put on the brown one and let's see how it fits," Tilley advised. "I hope you got a clean white shirt. And your overcoat is pressed."

"Shit," Moodrow said, heading for the closet, "I forgot all about the fucking coat." He picked a lump of wrinkled wool off the floor and shook his head. "I'll go without a coat."

"Gimme the goddamn coat," Tilley responded at once. "I'll go out to Muhammad's on First Avenue and get it pressed. Meanwhile, take a shower and look for a tie. The woman's a lawyer, for Christ's sake. You look like a slob and she's gonna dump you."

Moodrow thought about it for a second, then relaxed. "No way," he said. "She's seen me. She knows what she's getting into."

FOUR

January 17

SYLVIA KAUFMAN, working on a third cup of tea, looked over the beginnings of the Jackson Arms Tenants' Association from the safety and comfort of an overstuffed chair in her living room. Not exactly the powder-puff brigade, she decided, but not Superman's League of Justice, either. She smiled inwardly, recalling the hours sandwiched between grandson and grandaughter before the family moved out to Los Angeles. What with Wonder Woman, Superman, Batman, and the blond who swam like a speedboat, Aquaman, no problem ever defied the animated efforts of the Justice League.

Her oldest friend, Annie Bonnastello, had come, of course, arriving before the others for a cold supper. Though Annie refused to let her stroke "slow me down," she'd crossed the lobby with the aid of a walker. The nights were always hard for Annie; her joints (or her spirits) seemed to tighten with the setting sun. Sylvia couldn't imagine her friend, a widow for more than fifteen years, riding to the rescue, even in Wonder Woman's invisible airplane. But Annie could still vote, could still sign a petition.

Yong Park, on the other hand, short and muscular, his features composed and suitably inscrutable, looked perfectly capable of dispatching an army of evil prostitutes. But Yong Park worked a sixteen-hour day—from five in the morning, when he drove out to the Hunts Point produce market to personally choose the fruits and vegetables for his small grocery, until nine in the evening, when he, his wife and three of their four children closed shop. Park hadn't wanted to come to the meeting; it meant leaving his business two hours early, but when Sylvia told him that Al Rosenkrantz, Precision Management's Project Supervisor, would be on hand to hear their complaints and accept their petition, he agreed to attend.

Unfortunately, it was almost eight thirty, a half hour past the time for starting, Rosenkrantz hadn't shown and, though Yong Park's face was still expressionless, Pat Sheehan looked very uncomfortable. Sylvia had long ago recognized Pat's roommate, Louis, as a gay man and she supposed that made Pat a homosexual, too, though he didn't look particularly feminine. Sylvia's friends in the building often made jokes about the strange couple sharing three and a half rooms on the fourth floor.

But Sylvia never found the jokes funny, though she kept her opinions to herself. Louis was very ill; he looked as thin and frail as Sylvia's own husband toward the end of his illness. Of course, it was cancer that took Bennie Kaufman, and Pat's lover probably had AIDS, but they looked almost the same. Pat Sheehan wasn't really one of those close friends Sergeant Dunlap had told her to invite, but Pat was always friendly in the supermarket or the laundry room. Sylvia had asked him on impulse and been surprised when he accepted.

"This Rosenkrantz guy gonna come, Sylvia? Cause if he ain't even gonna come . . ." Inez Almeyda folded her arms across her chest. Twenty-eight years old, she was inevitably angry about something. Sylvia had come upon Inez a few weeks after the Almeyda family moved into their fourth floor apartment and been assaulted with the inadequacies of the world surrounding them. All of it, except for her husband and whomever she happened to be talking to.

"In my country, we get rid of these women without signing no petitions," Inez continued. That was her second theme. *In my country.* As if, Sylvia thought, Cuba was paradise. Inez's husband, whenever *he* mentioned Cuba, made it sound like the bowels of hell.

Andre Almeyda interrupted his wife, asserting his authority along with his opinion. "We're jus' gonna wait," he said firmly, shutting Inez down as no one else could. "No matter if this guy from the management come or no, we gotta do something. We cannot have our kids seein' them *putas* in the hallway." He made

a motion, as if to spit on the rug and Sylvia's eyes widened until she realized that
the gesture was only a gesture. The Cuban Almeyda family were born-again
Christians, *Evangelistas*, and attended prayer meetings twice a week. Their
oldest, an eight year old, went to the church school instead of P.S. 78, right
around the corner.

"Did anyone see what happened to the front door? Did anyone happen to
notice the lock don't work? The key don't go in the door? The tong thing don't
snap back in the goddamn hole? We got no security whatsoever. Did anyone
happen to notice?" Mike Birnbaum glared at them before answering his own
question. "Hoodlums. Drug addicts. Whores. When Morris Katz owned these
buildings, he ran them like palaces. Now we got new management we don't even
know who it is. How can a company be an owner? We should have bought our
apartments when we had the chance. Then *we* decide who lives here."

Mike Birnbaum, reversing form by outliving his wife, was eighty-one years
old and even angrier than Inez Almeyda. Angrier than in his youth when he'd
won prize after prize fighting Christians in YMCA boxing rings and liked to
refer to himself as a "belligerent Jew." Long retired, he subsisted on a pension
from the Department of Health and was chronically broke.

The conversation, as the group gave up on the arrival of Al Rosenkrantz,
Project Supervisor for Precision Management, began to pick up. Sylvia, who
busied herself with coffee and wedges of spice cake (her best, with the lemon
icing), noted that only one of her co-conspirators was minimizing the danger to
their way of life. Predictably, it was Myron Gold. Like Mike, Annie, and herself,
Myron was one of the old-timers.

"So what's the big deal?" he asked, spreading his hands to show his amazement. He'd been raised in the building, then gotten married and divorced,
before returning to 2B after his father's death. His mother, Shirley Gold,
recovering from surgery to remove a tumor from her jaw, only left the apartment
for biweekly chemotherapy treatments at Physician's Hospital, a few blocks away.
"You remember two years ago we had those people in 3F?" Myron waited
patiently for them to recall the unofficial chapter of the Iron Horsemen, a
motorcycle gang dedicated to speed, alcohol, and heavy metal. They'd moved
in, en masse, with a mousy blond secretary who'd lived in 3F for a year before
developing a taste for group sex and Harley Hogs. "All right, so it took a little
time. Who can expect speed when you're dealing with city hall? But, can
anyone deny the fact Morris got 'em out of there? These creatures in 1F may not
be pleasant to look at, but they're only a nuisance. Not a cause to make a whole
association. I mean some of us are talking about lawyers and housing inspectors.
Gimme a break, already."

"Then what about the superintendent?" Mike Birnbaum stared at Myron
Gold with barely disguised contempt. Myron was a "get-along" Jew, an assimila-
tionist. The kind Mike and his old man had always hated. The kind that moved
back in with mommy when things got tough. "No super anymore and last night I
froze my ass off. Pardon my French." He nodded to the women. "I'm eighty-one

and I gotta carry down my own garbage. Since Morris left, the whole joint is a piece of . . ." Noting the look of dismay on Andre Almeyda's face, he pulled himself up just in time.

"What of the other buildings?" Muhammad Assiz, a Pakistani and a Moslem, had only been a resident of the Jackson Arms for ten months. Sylvia didn't know him very well and she hadn't invited him. She did want some of the Asians to attend and she'd spoken to an older gentleman in front of the mailboxes. His name was Aftab and, while he couldn't come himself, he wanted to send a younger man. "As an observer. So we can be seeing what it is before we are signing anything. The management is already after us. You see many empty apartments where formerly we were living and things are very dangerous for us right now. But we will send one young man to observe. Muhammad Assiz, who is very intelligent, a doctor in our country, a technician in yours."

Sylvia, tuned to the immaculate politeness and the wide smile, didn't register Aftab's anger until later, but, angry or not, there were twelve Pakistani families in the Jackson Arms and she'd need all of them if things got worse.

"Why in the other buildings is there nothing happening like this?" Muhammad Assiz, a polite smile gracing his smooth, brown skin, allowed his musical voice to express the very essence of reason. "There are many Pakistanis living in these other buildings and there is no problem there."

That was the big question, Sylvia thought. And nobody has an answer. Morris owned three buildings. Two of them were running along with no changes. With the same supers, the same tenants, the same basic services. As if Morris Katz was still in charge.

"Exactly right." Myron Gold seized Muhammad's idea without registering the suspicions troubling the Pakistani. "There's no reason to believe that just because a drunken super gets tossed on his butt like he deserves, the Nazis have invaded Jackson Heights." He let his voice rise on the final phrase, ending his statement with a question mark, then tossed Mike Birnbaum his most significant look. Myron Gold wasn't about to be bullied by an eighty-one-year-old man.

"But you don't *know*, right?" Mike Birnbaum couldn't let Myron have the last word. They would carry him out in a sheet before he let a *putz* like Myron make him look bad. "Two days ago, I phone up these *gonifs* who call themselves Precision Management. I tell 'em, 'Look, from you I don't wanna hear word one. I want you should refer me to the landlord. I wanna talk to the landlord direct.' You know what the *shiksa* done to me? She hung up. Don't even tell me to mind my own business. Bang. She hangs up."

"What's the point?" Myron asked, looking at the others for support. "What *is* the damn point?" He hated coming down to the old man's level, but the bastard was so infuriating, so blindly stubborn.

"The point," Mike Birnbaum continued, a long bony finger cocked nearly in Myron's face, "is it could be *Hitler* owning our homes and you don't got no way to prove me wrong. Also tell me this—if the *gontser machers* ain't up to no good, why they gotta hide?"

Mike's question, like that of Muhammad Assiz, hung in the air, and Sylvia Kaufman, with no notion of how to run a meeting, how to keep the focus of conversation on a particular goal, was allowing the evening to degenerate into a personal debate that excluded the very people, the Almeydas, the Parks, the Assizes, who formed the majority of tenants. She had an instinctive understanding of where the evening was headed, but no idea how to bring it back to its original purpose.

What followed, unfortunately for the Jackson Arms Tenants' Association, did provide a focus for the meeting, a vehicle which carried them off in an utterly wrong direction. Mike Birnbaum, energized by Myron's failure to provide an answer to his question, was gearing up for another assault, when the outside bell rang. Sylvia jumped up to buzz her visitor in, then remembered that the outer lock was broken and there was no reason Mr. Rosenkrantz (if that's who it was) couldn't walk right up to her door. Nevertheless, she activated the buzzer designed to release the lock on the lobby door, then opened her own door to await their visitor.

"Al Rosenkrantz," the fat man said, shaking Sylvia's outstretched hand as he rushed past her. "Sorry to be late, folks." He pulled off a tan London Fog trench coat and handed it to his hostess. "We had an emergency in the Bronx. Heatless building. I had to light a fire under the repair crew." His small eyes, overshadowed by heavy brows and pinched by sallow, puffy cheeks, darted from person to person and he nodded whenever he made eye contact, absently running a finger along his thin, dark mustache.

"What about an emergency right here? I froze my butt off last night." Mike Birnbaum was the first to find his voice.

"Please, call me Al," Rosenkrantz began.

"I don't call you nothin' until I see results," Birnbaum returned.

Sighing, Rosenkrantz positioned his fat body over a kitchen chair and sat heavily. "Please, everyone, call me Al," he repeated, then spoke directly to Mike Birnbaum. "I don't know who I'm speaking to . . ."

"A tenant," Birnbaum answered, folding his arms tightly across his thin chest.

Rosenkrantz, looking sharply at the old man, couldn't have asked for a better beginning. The senile bastard would make a perfect dupe. "Mrs. Kaufman," he said, turning to Sylvia, "I agreed to come here tonight so that I could hear your complaints firsthand. As you know, Precision Management has been in charge of your building for less than three months. In that time, we've made some changes, but we feel that, in the long run, these changes will reflect the true needs of the owners *and* the tenants."

"Is this why you are throwing us into the street?" Muhammad Assiz, his voice sweet as sherbert, interrupted Al Rosenkrantz's set speech. "Since you have taken the buildings, only the Pakistani people have been evicted. Tell me why this is."

Rosenkrantz smiled indulgently. "Please," he said. "Your name. What should I call you."

"Muhammad Assiz."

"Muhammad, I've been in this business for fifteen years and I have never been involved in a deal this big where the new landlord didn't check leases. The first thing any landlord wants to know is who is living in which unit and are they living there legally."

"So he could get a rent increase," Birnbaum snorted.

Al Rosenkrantz accepted a cup of coffee and sipped at it gently, before answering. "A lease," he began in his most reverential tones, "is a profound legal document. A lease is a contract that defines the conditions of a binding, long-term relationship. The lease is so important to urban life, that New York City has created a special court, the Tenant–Landlord Court, to enforce the provisions of leases. I tell you a landlord has as much right to require that his tenants live within the lease, as the tenants have to demand the landlord honor the obligations specified in the lease." He paused, deliberately seeking out Myron Gold who was staring at Mike Birnbaum as if at a cockroach on his kitchen table. When he got a nod from Gold, an acknowledgment of his irrefutable logic, he began again. "But these are all problems associated with a new relationship. Believe me, six months from now every one of the empty apartments will have been rerented. A new super—one who can stay sober long enough to fix those locks when the savages break them—will be in place. Everything will be returned to normal and you'll be laughing at your suspicions. Look at the other buildings on the sidestreets. We've brought them through the transition without a hitch. Just give it a little time."

Andre Almeyda, restraining his wife, spoke up first. "Mr. Rosenkrantz."

"Please, call me Al."

"No, Mr. Rosenkrantz. I am Cuban. Born in Cuba and I learn in Cuba that not everyone who shakes your hand is a friend. I want to know why you allow these whores to move into our building? I raise my little girls to believe in our Lord Jesus Christ and I don't want them to see such things."

"Good. I'm glad you brought that up." Accepting a slice of cake from Sylvia Kaufman, he flashed her a quick smile. He could feel the sweat forming in the roots of his thick, black hair; it was the one thing he couldn't control. He took a quick bite of the cake, savoring the tang of the lemon icing, before answering. "When I first heard of these alleged prostitutes, I went into the files and personally checked the lease on 1F. The unit is currently rented to a man named Sal Ragozzo. One of our field men paid a visit to 1F just last week and found Mr. Ragozzo in residence. According to the lease, we cannot evict just because the tenant has roommates. Now, if the police make an arrest and get a conviction, we can have them removed without a problem. That would be a clear violation of the morals clause in the lease. But without some proof, I believe we'd lose in Tenant–Landlord Court." Quickly, with a little sigh of disgust, he wiped his forehead with a white handkerchief. "Still, as a demonstration of Precision Management's good faith, if you can bring us a petition with . . . let's say twenty names on it, we'll serve Mr. Ragozzo with an eviction notice and see if he decides to fight. Meanwhile, I do feel that you should demand police help. Put some heat on these scum right away. One thing I personally guarantee, Precision Management will double-check the references of all new tenants. There will be no repeat of this unfortunate situation, which, I should add, was *inherited* by Precision Management. Apartment 1F was rented to Mr. Ragozzo by Morris Katz three weeks before the closing."

Pat Sheehan watched Al Rosenkrantz's performance with private amazement. Sylvia Kaufman's assessment of Pat as gay was only partially accurate. Certainly, his roommate, Louis Persio, was a feminine homosexual, but if that's all "gay" meant, Pat Sheehan would have rejected the label without a second thought. The couple had met while doing felony time in Dannemora State Prison. The homosexual unit happened to be full on the day Louis Persio arrived and the administration, with typical sensitivity, assigned him to the first available cell, which happened to belong to Pat Sheehan. What followed was a contract, every bit as sacrosanct as Precision Management's leases, in which Louis Persio agreed to satisfy Pat Sheehan's pent-up sexual fantasies while Pat Sheehan guaranteed Persio's physical and sexual survival in the institution. What followed that, after a year's cohabitation, was only love, but it surprised the shit out of both of them. Especially Pat Sheehan, who found that even after their release, even after he'd spent a weekend in bed with an enthusiastic seventeen-year-old whore from the stable of an old jail buddy, he still wanted Louis Persio.

When a second and a third and a fourth visit did nothing to diminish the intensity of this need, Pat Sheehan, ever the realist, hopped the 7 Train out to Persio's Jackson Heights apartment, a single suitcase dangling from his hand. That had been four years ago, two years before Louis had woken up one morning with badly swollen lymph glands and a fever that defied aspirin and ice packs.

Fortunately, nobody had ever caught wind of the roommates' jail backgrounds. Being gay was enough trouble. Pat was short, only five foot seven, but weighed a solid hundred seventy-five pounds and was prison-hard. Louis Persio, by Dannemora standards, was a fox and foxes are not protected with bullshit. Pat, however, tried to avoid any display of his street sense; he passed his days driving a UPS delivery van, which was a very good job for an ex-con, and he didn't want any complaints getting back to his Parole Officer, Juan Profantes. Profantes was overlooking Pat's relationship with Louis Persio. For the time being.

But even if Pat Sheehan's smarts had been repressed for a hundred years, he could still spot a bullshitter like Al Rosenkrantz. The guy *smelled* like bullshit and Pat sniffed the odor like an old con probing for fear in a new prisoner. Pat had read the move when the pimp first showed up with the two women. Nobody could sign a lease with Rags Ragozzo without washing their hands immediately afterward. The guy sweated olive oil. Like fat Al Rosenkrantz with the drops starting to slide along his temples. Rosenkrantz was so obvious that Pat Sheehan was tempted to call him on it. To slap him with his bullshit. He could feel every warden he'd ever known speaking through Al Rosenkrantz's lips. "If you give the institution a chance, the institution will work with you." The lies made him want to vomit.

But Pat Sheehan held his peace. He didn't tell his fellow tenants what (or who) was coming in behind the whores, though he'd made the new tenants in 4B, right across the hall from his own apartment, as heroin junkies the minute he'd found them struggling with their few pieces of cardboard furniture. Shit, he ought to know about dope. That's why he went away. Because of an unfortunate accident in the middle of an armed robbery while trying to get the money to sustain his habit.

"A *gonif* you can't recognize?" Mike Birnbaum shouted at Myron Gold. "You got to wait until he cracks your skull before you wake up?"

FIVE

February 20

JONATHAN "BORN" MILLER was, among other things (crack addict, mugger, prostitute, pimp), a vegetarian. At twenty-four years of age, and fresh from Rikers Island, he felt himself to be at peace with a world he finally understood. True, he was using crack again, but at nowhere near the suicidal pace that had preceded his incarceration. He had been crazy back then, crazy enough to smash the side window of a car waiting for a light at 39th and Ninth, just off the Lincoln Tunnel. He remembered reaching through the broken glass to grab the old broad sitting behind the wheel; he could still hear himself screaming at her for money like she was deaf. A poor helpless old vic in a pearl gray Mercedes–Benz, with cars in front of her and behind her. Where could she go?

Into her purse. Into her mother-fuckin' purse for a can of mace. When she splashed that shit in his eyes, he stumbled back into the side of a moving delivery van and the mirror knocked him just flat enough for the police to arrive before he could crawl away. Who would believe such bad luck? Who could believe the mace after staying awake for three days and nothing to hold his head up? On top of which, the old cunt, instead of hauling ass like they always do, waits calmly for the pigs, then files a complaint.

The arresting officers (after they put a *major* beating on his ass) charged him with assault, assault with intent to kill, assault with a deadly weapon (the window glass), reckless endangerment (to the other drivers on Ninth Avenue), possession of a controlled substance, felony possession of a controlled substance, possession with intent to sell a controlled substance and paraphernalia. It was enough, considering the string of plea-bargained misdemeanors that had dominated his street life, to effectively put him away until his sixtieth birthday.

But the DA was sure to cut a deal in return for a guilty plea. All those charges were only there to frighten him into taking the *wrong* deal. That's what the jailhouse lawyers, who listened to his case in return for the chicken cutlet sandwiches he smuggled out of the captains' dining room, predicted. But he didn't buy it. Fact is, he only turned to those bullshit artists because he never had a lawyer of his own. Never went to court, either. Or saw a cop or heard from anyone in law enforcement except for correction officers, who had less than no interest in his legal situation.

Six months later, his body strong from hundreds of hours in the gym, he had his act together, courtesy of an older inmate, Brian "DeadDog" Patterson, who had taught him (in exchange for certain reciprocal sexual favors) how to discipline his mind while he nourished his body by cleansing his system with fruits and vegetables. Only then, when he was pure in mind and body, when his act was tight and he was ready for the world, did he seek out a correction counselor and ask why his case hadn't gone to trial. Three days later, after a chagrined Assistant DA named Myra Baines admitted to a phenomenally sarcastic Judge Calvin Smith that inmate Miller's case had somehow been closed before his trial, Born Miller was out on the street.

Strong and confident, he wandered back to St. Nicholas Avenue, in Harlem, and begged twenty dollars from his mother. "I got to get me a place to stay, mama, else the man gon' dump me back in the jail. I'm on probation."

His mother, Marla, nodded maternally, then handed over the twenty because she was afraid of her son. She knew about his prior record, of course, both as a juvenile and as an adult, and she didn't understand why they had let him out. She *did*, however, fully understand that twenty dollars would get rid of him, at least temporarily. At least long enough to make preparations for his return.

After six months of abstinence, the first hit on the pipe stem exploded simultaneously in his brain and his crotch. He was in a crack den/shooting gallery on 143rd Street and one of the women, a Dominican crack whore, offered to get him off for a hit on the pipe.

"Suck first, bitch," he growled, careful not to betray how desperately horny he was. The girl, called Choch, turned the trick so fast and so efficiently, that Born Miller alternately fucked and smoked until the vials were empty. Then he went out to look for money.

At first he considered returning to his mother's apartment, but now that she knew he was on the street, she'd either have her brother there or refuse to open the door. Born Miller wasn't afraid of the brother, but he wanted crack and he wouldn't get it there, no matter how many times he kicked ass. Better to take his chances in the street.

Ten minutes later, he was in a room on the second floor of an abandoned tenement near Convent Avenue, watching for prey, when three kids, teenagers, strolled by. The boys were fresh in their Task Force jackets, Guess jeans, and white Reeboks. One, the smallest, had a dope rope, a gold chain thicker than Miller's thumb, hanging all the way down his chest. Man, did Born Miller want that fucker. That chain would keep him stoned for two weeks. Keep him stoned until he connected with DeadDog who was up in the Bronx somewhere.

The kids stopped to bullshit. Miller could see their lips moving, though he couldn't hear what they were saying. Then a miracle happened. Two of the boys left, walking west toward Riverside Park, while the third, the one with the chain, already unzipping his fly, turned into a narrow alleyway alongside the tenement.

Born Miller's spirits jumped almost as high as they would when he fired up the pipe again. The broken piece of cinderblock someone had chipped out of the window seemed to leap into his hand. The boy with the chain was right below him, as if waiting for the hand of God to descend, and Born, leaning out over the empty windowframe, let the cinderblock go like a World War Two bombardier over Berlin.

The stone seemed to drift downward, as gently as a parachutist dropping onto a spring meadow, but when it found the boy's head, it made a very audible sound, a solid chunk, and the boy, still pissing away, dropped to the concrete and lay motionless as the blood ran down along the side of his face and pooled up under his head.

Born Miller took the chain to a pawnshop in Chinatown and sold it for a straight one hundred dollars per ounce. The pawn broker, a squinty-eyed ancient who peered at him from behind two-inch plexiglass, would get three times as much when he offered it at retail, but Miller didn't mind. The fucking thing weighed more than twelve ounces and the cash made a satisfying pocket print when he slipped it into his worn Levis. Talk about fresh—he had enough to tighten his threads and still beam up for a week.

"Say what, my man," he called to the Chinaman before walking back onto Bayard Street. "Could y'all direct me to a public phone. I have to make an important call." The Oriental responded with a shower of high-pitched Chinese, but Miller wasn't insulted. It's hard, he speculated, to disrespect a man who's about to get as high as he was. "Bye-bye, li'l Chinaman," he called. "Don' eat too many wontons."

He found a phone on the corner which not only worked, but, even more miraculously, was not in use, and dialed DeadDog's phone number.

"Speakin'," the voice on the other end announced without preamble.

"That y'all, DeadDog?" Miller asked.

"Born Miller?"

"That's my name. Dope is my game." He tried to be cute. The man always liked him when he was cute.

"Homeboy," DeadDog shouted. "Just the man I been waitin' on. I got plans for you, baby. We openin' up new territory and you gonna be the main man. You gon' be mah banker."

Born Miller, under DeadDog's spell as if they were both still at Rikers, nodded as he took in the information. Most drug operations revolve around a banker who collects the money and a mule who hands out the dope, a structure which makes it hard to rip off both ends at the same time. DeadDog was in the midst of setting up a crack and smack distributorship in a quiet Queens neighborhood. "Virgin territory, y'unnerstan' what I'm sayin'? No competition. We gon' start workin' out this apartment, but we be on the street in a month. Turn these white boys and these yellow boys on to some good crack and we have more customers than we can handle. Y'unnerstand what I'm sayin'? Y'all hold yo head together, you gon' be one rich nigger."

Born Miller dutifully memorized the address DeadDog gave him, but the minute he was off the phone, he headed straight up the Bowery to the Lower East Side, where every kind of drug was readily available. The first dealer he saw, part of a crew that worked Allen Street, sold him twenty vials of crack and a battered .44 caliber Charter Arms Bulldog for three hundred dollars, throwing in a dozen extra rounds as a sign of good faith.

The tool felt good tucked into his waistband. It made him feel bigger, an insurance policy to prevent some punk from lifting his roll the way he'd yanked the gold off that brother's neck. He did have every intention of heading out to Queens, but he made the mistake of ducking into a doorway for a quick hit on the pipe and didn't stop sucking on it for two days, when a sudden burst of paranoia warned him that if he didn't move soon, DeadDog's offer would, indeed, be dead.

Two hours later, he was standing across the street from 337-11 37th Avenue and wondering just what kind of bullshit DeadDog was tossing these days. Except for a trio of moving men filling their truck with furniture, there wasn't another black face anywhere on the street. Born was wearing his working clothes: nondescript Levis, cheap sneakers, a down jacket that reversed from black to blue and a throwaway Yankee baseball cap. His hair was close-cropped, without any of the fashionable designs black barbers shave into the scalps of their customers.

"You got to be cool on the streets, my man," DeadDog had explained. "These boys with the fancy cars and the dope ropes all gon' do long bits. Y'all shove yo shit in the man's face, he get you if it take twenty years. Shit, the pig got all the money, he can afford to wait. Y'unnerstan' what ah'm sayin'? We talkin' *survival* here."

But *this* scene didn't have any cool to it. If coming into a white neighborhood (as far as Born Miller was concerned, the Orientals were even whiter than the maggots) and opening a crack den wasn't throwing it in the pig's face, he wasn't a stoned-out coke freak. Born Miller was accustomed to tenements and projects, had never been outside Harlem until mama took him to the circus on his fifth birthday. He could deal with situations that would paralyze ordinary citizens; could, for instance, creep through an abandoned tenement on a pitch-black moonless night in search of a dealer. Or of prey.

Unfortunately, there were no abandoned tenements in Jackson Heights. The apartments and the two family homes, Born Miller noted in amazement, were nearly spotless. Even the shrubbery and the lawns had the look of a neighborhood holding its own against the tide of urban decay. How could DeadDog be such a fool? Anyone trying to work these streets would be busted in a minute. This was a place you came to do a quick rip-off, then subway up to Corona where the brothers lived. But even as he started to turn away, a black woman, Yolande Montgomery, came through the door of 337-11 and walked left, toward Broadway.

"Man," Born Miller said out loud, "the sister's a damn bulldyke. This shit is *wrong*." Born Miller didn't like it when things didn't make sense; he didn't like being confused. In fact, that was the only good thing about jail—you were never confused. It always came straight at you. Not like this shit. He *knew* he wasn't ready for it, not after two days of crack, but he couldn't seem to walk away, either. Then his eye found a stairwell leading to a long unused basement door and he walked down the steps without hesitation, pulling out the pipe stem as he went.

Five minutes later, his head was on straight, but he still couldn't bring himself to enter the building. "Ain't no up to this scene," he whispered to the neurons popping off inside his head. "DeadDog know how bad I hate these white mother-fuckers. Can't do mah shit when the maggots be on my case." Finally, too stoned to stand still, he walked back along 37th Avenue, trying to mix with the pedestrians, but the shoppers, whites and Asians for the most part, made him even more uncomfortable. No matter how good the crack felt, he was aware of its darker side, of its potential for terror and panic. He felt like a declawed, toothless lion wandering among a herd of elephants. If they stampeded, he'd be trampled in a second.

Impulsively, he turned into the Happy Sea Produce Market. He hadn't eaten in a couple of days, maybe an apple or some grapes would help take the edge off. He was rummaging through the apples when he noticed Mee-Suk Park looking at him. Her glance was casual, actually benevolent, but Born Miller felt it burn him as furiously as the perfunctory commands of the Correction Officers on Rikers Island. Why was that damn gook watching *him*? Was he some kind of freak that she should stare at him like that? He hated the Koreans worse than the Jews. At least the Jews hired blacks to front for them. The slopes didn't trust nobody.

He strutted to the cash register, staring straight into her eyes. If the bitch was a Jew, he thought, she'd have turned away by now. The gooks were mother-fucking *hard* to read. He couldn't see anything in her eyes as she took his apples, dumped them on the scale, then punched the buttons on the register with practiced skill. When he paid her, she slapped the change down on the counter, ignoring his outstretched palm, and proceeded to the next customer. In an instant, the panic changed to anger. He had two pockets stuffed with crack vials and a .44 pressing against his gut. Why should he fear a slanty-eyed cunt?

Born Miller was what police like to call an opportunistic thief. He had no special *modus operandi*, but was content to accept whatever the day happened to offer. Thus, when he saw the New York Telephone envelope lying on the counter, he automatically noted the address: Yong Park, 337-11 37th Avenue, Apartment 3H. He looked around the store again, counting the Oriental faces busy with the fruits and vegetables. Koreans, Born Miller knew, worked very hard. Most of the time, the whole family was involved, especially when it was busy. Maybe he'd make a quick stop in 3H before he checked out DeadDog's scene. Everybody know the gooks ain't trustin' no banks. Might be any kind of money hidden behind the mattress.

On the way back to the Jackson Arms, he stopped in the stairway to *really* do his head up, knowing full well that he wouldn't be coming down for a couple of days. Not until he connected for enough smack to grease the runway. When he walked across the street to 337-11, he was buzzing from his crotch to his eyeballs, but he noted the broken front door with surprise. Definitely wrong for honkey heaven. And someone had torn out the mailboxes, jimmied them with a steel bar so they hung out like broken teeth. And the elevator smelled of piss, the door closing in little jerks, the cage shaking so wildly that Born thought he was back in the projects.

Apartment 3H, as Born expected, had two double-bolt locks in addition to the landlord-supplied burglar's special under the doorknob. DeadDog had introduced him to the fundamentals of lock-picking in Rikers, but he didn't have the patience to spend weeks setting up a score. He knew there was a much simpler way and once he had 3H properly placed within the geography of the Jackson Arms, he went back outside the building, to the rear, and began to climb the appropriate fire escape.

It was after three o'clock and most of the housewives had gathered up their broods and retired to the kitchen. The sun had begun to drop behind the skyline of Manhattan; it peered dimly through gathering clouds. None of this, though it undeniably aided him, ever pierced the glow suffusing Born Miller's brain. In his mind, the deed was already accomplished and he stopped on the first landing to listen to the voices in apartment 1H while he fired up the pipe.

Five minutes later, he was outside Yong Park's window, staring, undismayed, at the window gate. "Pussy shit," he said, then climbed to the railing and casually executed a graceful leap to an adjoining window ledge. He was prepared to crack the glass with the butt of his newly acquired .44, but the window slid upward at his touch and he was inside without making a sound.

He listened carefully for a moment, crouched by the side of a bed, but there was no one in the apartment. Only the soothing hiss of crack dancing up and down his spine. Still cautious, he went from room to room, carefully opening doors, his "tool," his .44, in his hand.

The trick when doing burglaries, he knew, was to get in and out as fast as he could. It was like banks, in a way. Every second counted. Unless you were so fuckin' stoned, your mind was on Pluto. Unless you were so fuckin' stoned, you were *hopin'* the assholes'd show up.

Born Miller giggled, as he thrust the barrel of the Bulldog .44 into his waistband and pulled out the pipe. This time the crack lit up what he called "the safety zone." He had the revolver, a dozen vials filled with tiny white pellets, a pocketful of twenty-dollar bills and every hope of a big score in the great here and now. That was the safety zone. The Cave of the Untouchable. Fresh and tight.

He started in the back, in the adult bedroom, with the mattress and the boxspring, slicing the covers neatly, working his hand around the yellowing foam. Nothing. He went to the bureaus, pulling out the drawers, overturning them on the bed, examining the contents. He ripped open a jewelry box, snarling at the cheap costume pieces, then smashed it to pieces on the top of the bureau.

"Sweet baby, show me *gold*." He stuffed the two chains and the earrings that tumbled out of the secret drawer into his pockets, *knowing* this was only the beginning, then yanked both bureaus away from the wall, examining the backs for taped packages, tipping them against the bed so he could check the bottoms. The wall mirror followed, crashing to pieces.

He was on top of his game, now, working up a real sweat. After all those months in Rikers, his act was *tight*. Bad Born Miller come up to breathe. Check him out.

He took down the large cross hanging on the wall by the headboard with every intention of pissing all over it. Show the slopes where his head was at. But when he tossed it on the bed, the back slid out in his hand and a roll of bills tumbled onto the mountain of clothing already placed on the torn mattress.

The bills, a thick stack of twenties and fifties, were in his hand almost before they hit the bed. He cradled them in his palm as if holding a lover's breast. A little voice whispered, "Get out quick. Get in. Get out." It was DeadDog's voice, but this was too good to be believed. He sat on the edge of his bed, pulled out the pipe, inflated his brain to its proper level and was preparing to count the loot, when he heard the front door slam shut, the sharp clack of multiple locks being thrown, the sing-song voice of an older woman lecturing a child.

Born Miller looked around the room calmly, noting both the chaos and the open window. "Check this shit," he whispered softly. The pipe was still in his hand and he was tempted to light it instead of either fleeing or preparing for battle, but he put it back into his pocket and strolled, his shoulder dipping with each step as he picked his way through the debris, to the open window. The old lady (he could almost see her wrinkled face screwed up so far her eyes were black lines against pale yellow skin) was still jabbering away. Why should he fear something so ugly? He flashed back to his first years in school, to a handful of Oriental children who always knew the answer. To the sullen grandmas waiting to see them safely home.

He looked at the window ledge and imagined himself stepping out and making the leap to the fire escape. There was a time he would have done it just to impress the homeboys on St. Nicholas Avenue, but DeadDog had cut that macho shit dead.

"You come in the window; you go out the door," DeadDog had told him as they lay together on the cot in DeadDog's cell. "You ain't never take nothin' you can't hide in yo pocket. No televisions. No VCRs. No stereos. Y'unnerstan' what ah'm sayin'? You don't give the man no reason to search yo ass, so once you out the door, you home free."

Out the mother-fuckin' door, he thought. Ain't no gook gon' push Born Miller through no window. Fuck, no. Not when the boy got himself a .44 near touchin' his dick.

He crept to the door and listened closely. The old lady and the kid were still going at it, the sharp meaningless sounds chipping away at his head. The need for the goddamned pipe was beginning to fill him and he knew he wasn't about to get to it until after he offed the bitch. He wanted to crash through the door and just do it, but he remembered DeadDog's instructions on cool, on how that urge to get the shit over with had put him in Rikers in the first place. Quickly, his ears still glued to the voices outside, he found a pair of panty hose in the pile on the bed, ripped one leg off them and pulled it over his face. "Okay, maggot," he whispered, "here I come."

He dropped to the floor and looked through the keyhole just as the old woman began marching the child along the hallway toward the bathroom. The kid was tiny, no more than three or four, and she was crying silently. The granny was as ageless as her body was shapeless, a sausage stuffed into a pink housedress. Her eyes, as she came right toward him, were tiny and lost in her wrinkled, ivory face.

He waited until he had just enough room to open the door before he rushed out into the hallway, the pistol raised above his head. The old lady, suddenly mute, stared up at him and her eyes widened until they were nearly as round as his.

"That's a favor, bitch," he said, bringing the butt of the gun down across the top of her head. "Makin' them eyes round. People gon' think you white." He raised the gun again, but she was already dropping to the brown carpet. Blood was dripping from the tips of her stiff, black hair and the housedress had ridden up, bunching around her hips. Born Miller stared down at her heavy thighs, at the white strip of cotton running between her open legs.

"Ain't this some shit," he whispered. His crotch was already aflame as his fingers busied themselves with the pipe and a small vial of tiny white pellets. "Party time," he announced to the pipe, to the warm buzz pulsing in his body, to the little girl with the red ribbon in her hair.

SIX

February 27

THE subway platform was nearly empty when Stanley Moodrow boarded the F Train at the Houston Street Station, despite the hour. It was six o'clock in the evening and the rush was in full swing, but there were few commuters (and less work) that far south on the F Train's run through Manhattan. Later, as the F passed through midtown before turning out to central Queens, the subway cars would fill until commuters, exiting or entering, would have to force their way through the doors. It was the worst part of the day for a majority of New Yorkers, this extraction of a second payment for their daily bread. They understood the phrase "by the sweat of your brow"; the eight-hour day is a forgotten idea to most of them. But this other labor—to be stuffed into featureless subway cars on a rainy Tuesday evening, to ride for an hour (if everything was running on time) with the stink of wet wool, or, worse yet, the stench of a homeless beggar, pitiful or not, sharp enough to bring tears to your eyes . . . It was too much. It was unfair.

Moodrow, on the other hand, was oblivious to his surroundings. Already comfortable on a bench near the doors separating his car from the next (two adolescents, smelling cop all over him, had fled the seats the moment he entered), he could allow himself the luxury of daydreaming. The only benefit of rush-hour subway rides is the lower potential for the kind of violence that keeps the tabloids humming. At the height of the morning and evening crush, the muggers rest, while the pickpockets and the perverts wait for the car to give a sudden, covering lurch.

Being neither pervert nor pickpocket (and with zero potential to be a victim of either), Moodrow could ignore the commuters and concentrate on his memory of the previous Saturday evening, especially Betty Haluka's determination in the face of Jim Tilley's complaints. Because Tilley, as Moodrow expected, hadn't been able to hold his cop resentment inside, despite Rose Carillo's attempts to soothe him. Not after the first few drinks.

"Well, I'm Irish," he'd said, his voice carefully neutral in deference to Stanley Moodrow, "and we don't have very good imaginations, so I'd just like to understand how it feels to work with those people. You know what I'm talking about? To take some pig who stabbed his best friend fifteen times and get him off because the arresting officer didn't do the paperwork right. How does it feel to put that man back out on the street?"

Betty looked over at Moodrow, as if expecting help, but Moodrow had no help to give. Jim Tilley was articulating the anguish of every New York cop. The department was making more and more good arrests (despite the restraints imposed by *Miranda*) and it was extremely disheartening to see a man originally charged with attempted murder out on the streets after doing six months for simple assault.

"Do *you* understand why?" Betty asked Moodrow.

"Maybe," he shrugged, "but I'm retired now and I always thought the system was bullshit, anyway. Besides, I never argue with my mouth full." So saying, he shoved a handful of Doritos into his mouth and chewed judiciously.

With no help from her date, Betty raised her glass for a refill and eyed Jim Tilley carefully. She might, she knew, have appealed to Rose. Rose would certainly try to head off any potential ugliness. But Elizabeth Shirley Haluka didn't appeal for help in situations she thought she could handle. Not after a third glass of burgundy and two plates of Irish lamb stew. Not after a second iced Stoli (without the twist). And especially not after making an irrevocable decision to take the giant ex-flatfoot, Stanley Moodrow, into her bed that night. She knew why Moodrow was leaving her to face Jim Tilley. It was because he wanted her, too. Wanted her enough to take a chance.

"I don't like it," Betty finally answered, sipping at her iced vodka. "But it's not my fault. Most of those 'technicalities' come about because some gung-ho cop decides he can see a bag of dope lying on a dresser from his position on a rooftop sixty feet away. Or because, in his zeal for aggressive law enforcement, the same moron conducts an illegal search and the murder weapon can't be used in court. And, even with that, I don't get those kinds of dismissals in more than two percent of my cases. It's not really a factor."

"Look," Tilley said, catching a meaningful look from Rose Carillo that prompted him to ask his question without anger. "Two months ago, I pulled a speed freak named Ronald Starise off another speed freak named Vera Blisso. Starise cut her face in a barroom argument; there were fifteen witnesses. Me and my partner hauled Vera to Bellevue and they spent four hours stitching her up. Pumped three units of blood into her while they were sewing. Yesterday I heard Starise got sentenced to a year for assault. I don't think that's right."

"Well, don't blame me," Betty said. "I don't even know the guy. Besides, you're talking about plea bargaining. The big lie. That's not anything the defense controls. Unless the case is very weak, the DA makes the offer."

Moodrow, a glass of bourbon in his hand, was intrigued, despite his intention to keep out of it. "What's the 'big lie'?" he asked.

Betty grinned at Moodrow, unconsciously leaning toward him and away from Jim Tilley. "Once upon a time there was a politician named John Whore. This politician, in his endless quest for re-election, went out and took a poll. He asked the voters what they wanted to do about crime and the voters said, 'Please kill all the criminals. But if you can't kill them, throw them in jail and keep them in jail until the flesh rots off their bones.'

"John Whore (as a responsible servant of the people should) passed this message down to the police who began to make more and more arrests. At first, everybody was pleased as punch. The population of upstate prisons went from twelve thousand in the early seventies to more than forty-five thousand today. But then John Whore took a second poll and this time the voters said, " 'Hey, you guys are doin' a great job. Really great. Just don't make us *pay* for it.'

"Now here's the truth, Jim: a little over ten thousand criminals were sentenced for felonies in the Bronx last year. Nine thousand five hundred involved defendants who pleaded guilty. That's plea bargaining, right? Only five hundred involved trials. And those five hundred equaled the largest number of cases that, given the number of judges, Assistant DAs and courtrooms, *can* be tried. Understand what I'm saying? If the nine thousand five hundred criminals who plea bargained their way into lighter sentences all decided to ask for a trial, the system would come to a complete stop. Likewise, if the judges decided to send every one of those criminals to jail, the jails would be so overcrowded that some other judge would force the state to let most of them go. All this because a politician took a couple of polls."

"So everybody pays," Rose Carillo said. "If they don't pay with money, they pay with bullshit courtrooms and junkies crawling through their windows." Now that the kids were in their rooms, she was playing catch-up with rum and cokes. Her first instinct was to like Betty Haluka, recognizing Betty as a fellow survivor. But Rose had once been the victim of a brutal husband and had felt, firsthand, the effects of a criminal justice system that seemed to be failing everyone and she couldn't shake off the simple solution to crime which had all the criminals safely in jail. "Because if those people go back out on the street, they're gonna hurt other people. You know that."

Betty said nothing for a moment, looking inward for the right words. When she did begin to speak, her voice was very gentle, as if she sensed the experience that lay behind Rose's question. "There's three kinds of defendants. First, there's the druggies. Crack or dope, it's all the same. They go out and commit minor crimes to keep themselves high. Or they become small-time dealers for the same reason. That accounts for ninety percent of my clients. Second, there are people like Henry Lopez, who Stanley told you about, who're actually innocent. They get it worst, because the system is set up to *force* defendants to plea bargain. Third, there are psychopathic criminals capable of such mindless violence, no argument on Earth could justify their continued freedom. I can't get used to them. Not even after twenty years in Legal Aid. Not after a thousand years in Legal Aid."

"But you defend them, too," Rose said. "You have to. And sometimes they go back out because of your defense."

Betty thought about it for a moment, weighing her answer carefully. "Actually, they go back out because of plea bargaining. The cops made more than a hundred thousand arrests last year. I'm counting misdemeanors, too. The courts can't deal with that and sometimes really bad people slip through the cracks. But remember, it's almost always the District Attorney's office that sets the deal. I try to haggle, but the deal is usually presented as a take-it-or-leave-it proposition. It's only when the prosecution's case is weak and they're afraid to go into a courtroom that anything like 'bargaining' takes place."

"And how do you handle that?" Moodrow asked, sitting on the edge of his seat. "When you know someone should be put away forever and you hear the judge give him two years?"

"Or her," Betty smiled. "We get women crazies, too."

"Her or him," Tilley said. "How does it feel?"

"Do you like everything about being a cop?" Betty asked. "You don't have to do shit work sometimes?" She didn't wait for an answer. "When I have no choice, I do it and try to forget about it. Like everyone else involved in the justice industry. Like the Assistant DAs and judges and even the cops."

"Do you ever have a choice?" Rose asked, sensing something behind Betty's answer.

"Once in a while, you have to even up," Betty said, her voice darkening. "You have to step outside the boundaries of professional ethics. If you don't, you go crazy." Even as she went ahead with her story, she had a sense that she shouldn't be saying this, but somewhere between the alcohol and Stanley Moodrow, she'd lost her sense of self-preservation. It drowned in sudden trust. "About six months ago, I went to one of the court pens, where they keep the prisoners, to confer with a burglar/rapist named Morton Heller. He told me he had to speak to me in private; there's something I had to know. Usually, that means a client wants to inform on someone in exchange for less time.

"So I arranged for a conference room which took about three hours, because there aren't enough of them, either, and I went in to talk with Mr. Heller. Fortunately, I had enough sense to let the Court Officer cuff him to the table. That's standard procedure, but most of the time I don't bother. I want my clients to trust me."

Suddenly, the three of them, Moodrow, Tilley, and Rose, were sitting on the edge of their seats. All slightly drunk and waiting, like kids, for their bedtime story.

"The minute I came into the room, he started telling me about the women he raped and how he couldn't wait to get out of jail so he could crawl into *my* room next. He told me exactly how he'd hurt me and what he'd do sexually and how he'd make me pretend to like it. And while he explained all this, he masturbated with his free hand.

"Nice, right? Of course, I'd seen all the complaints (he was up for four counts of rape along with assorted assaults, atrocious assaults, and robberies) and the depositions the victims gave were really bad. The rape was the least of it; he beat them, cut them, terrified them. And he dragged it out. He came into their apartments just after they went to bed and he stayed all night.

"Well, Morton Heller was stupid as well as disturbed and he had this sense of his own power, of his invulnerability, that set him up nicely for what I decided to do to him. I said, 'Look, Heller, you can sit around jerkin' off if that's what you want, but I think there's a good chance you could beat this.'

"The truth is I had just come from a meeting with the Assistant DA and I knew the case against Heller was rock solid. The DA was offering twelve years to life for a plea bargain, which means Heller would have to do at least ten, even if he took a plea. Heller, by the way, was only twenty-five, so if he did ten, he'd still be young when he came out. Young enough to ruin some more lives.

"Anyway, Heller stopped playing with himself and asked me how I could get him off. I said I didn't think all the victims would show. I ran down a line of bullshit about two of the victims failing to pick him out of a lineup. I told him I'd contact any witnesses who could give him an alibi. I told him that since he never turned on the lights in his victims' apartments, the identifications wouldn't hold up.

"Maybe I should have been an actress, because the asshole bought the whole bit. I went back to the Assistant DA and informed him that my client was determined to go to trial and there was nothing I could do to dissuade him. You realize that once I speak to the client, the prosecution can't get near him without tainting the case, so there was no way the Assistant DA could get a hint of what I was doing. He just shrugged his shoulders and we went before the judge and got a trial date.

"About halfway through the trial, Heller figures it out and goes crazy. Fortunately, I was questioning a witness at the time, so there was enough space between us for the court officers to get to Heller before Heller got to me. He tried to tell the judge what I'd done to him, but every defendant blames the lawyer when a case goes bad, so the judge didn't want to hear about it. He asked Heller if he'd like to change his plea to guilty and Heller was so crazy by this time he agreed.

"Boom! Down comes the gavel and two weeks later, the judge sentences Heller to the max on every charge: four counts of rape; four counts of sodomy; two counts of felonious assault; two counts of aggravated assault; four counts of kidnapping; four counts of robbery. It adds up to life plus a hundred and forty-five years. Case closed."

There is a unique moment in the lives of lovers. A mostly unremembered eyeblink that inevitably drowns in a wave of lust. It is the moment when man and woman are naked for the first time; when eyes slide across vulnerable flesh. Betty Haluka looked over at the giant who walked toward her. His body ran in a straight line, from his armpits across his ribs, his waist, his hips, his thighs. The difference—the ultimate injustice—in size between men and women passed quickly through her consciousness. He was monstrously big; she could exert no physical force against him. To voluntarily accept that surrender; to knowingly be that vulnerable—she could not complete the act without trust. The emotion was implied in the touch of his lips on hers and when her nostrils were full of the fragrance of the hairs on his chest, she took hold of him and leaned forward to whisper in his ear.

"You can forget about getting on top."

When Moodrow came back to himself, the F was pulling into the Continental Avenue station, one express and five local stops further than he'd planned to go. He glanced at his watch as he left the train to wait for an express going in the opposite direction and noted that he'd be a little late for the meeting with Betty's Aunt Sylvia, which was no big deal. He didn't expect much to come from his trip. Maybe, if the place wasn't too far gone, he'd have a private talk with the pimp or one of the dealers. See if he couldn't scare them away.

SEVEN

THE second meeting of the Jackson Arms Tenants' Association, Sylvia Kaufman noted from her position at the front of a hastily rented bingo room at St. Ann's Roman Catholic Church, was going to be far better attended than the first. Unfortunately, the tenants, instead of uniting around their anger at the abomination that had taken place in the Parks' apartment, were standing in little ethnic knots, talking among themselves as if protecting state secrets: five families of Koreans, with wives and children near the folded bingo tables; a dozen Asians, Hindu and Moslem, united in their distrust of the whites who, they believed, controlled their destinies; a large group of the old-timers, led by Mike Birnbaum, who liked to blame all problems on the 'new people'; and, finally, the Hispanics (including a group of Mexicans she hadn't known existed before this evening) surrounding the Cuban Almeydas and two Colombian families who'd been in the building for almost ten years.

Curiously, none of the groups appeared to be intimidated and Sylvia wondered if they were showing off for each other or if they were too angry to be afraid. Certainly, some of the tenants *were* intimidated. Yong Park and his family had secluded themselves behind closed doors. Their fruit and vegetable business was shuttered while they prepared to move into a two-family building in Flushing, a building owned by Mrs. Park's brother. And Myron Gold was going, too. Just like that. Announcing to Sylvia that his mother, Shirley, couldn't take the winters anymore—not after the surgery. They were Florida-bound as soon as the paperwork could be completed on their Ft. Lauderdale condo.

Shirley Gold had kept her head lowered all through that conversation, wanting to show neither her tears nor the unhealed scars from the cancer surgery on her jaw. She and Sylvia had been neighbors, if not friends, for decades; there should have been a better way to part. But Shirley Gold *was* tired. Haggard, really; and the tragedy that had fallen on the Park family only added to it.

"So that's it, Sylvia. We're going down south where it's warm all the time. Mom can't take the winters and, to tell the truth, I can't either."

As Sylvia expected, Myron had not even bothered to show up for the meeting. But he'd found the time to go from door to door, trying to sell the furniture they couldn't take with them into the fully furnished condo.

"Excuse me."

Sylvia, startled, looked up at the giant standing next to the desk at the front of the room. Somehow, she hadn't noticed him coming. Which seemed, in light of his size, clearly impossible. The word "Alzheimer" clicked on in her consciousness, as it always did when she was forgetful. Even while he introduced himself, she wondered if everyone over fifty had the same association after a moment of inattention. Each time it happened, she consoled herself by recalling the day and date, a sure sign, she believed, of continuing intellectual continence.

"Yes?" Looking into the small, dark eyes of the man who stared down at her, she felt that something was wrong with him. Or different, at least. Something strange, but not, in itself, threatening. Then she realized that he hadn't smiled and he wasn't blinking.

"My name is Stanley Moodrow. I'm a private investigator. I used to be a cop. Betty Haluka told me a little bit about your situation. She asked me to come down here tonight."

"Betty called me this afternoon," Sylvia said, taking his hand. Her fingers, she noted, lay flat in his palm, like a baby's head on a pillow. "I'm afraid I don't have much time to talk tonight."

"Have you gone to the police?" he asked. "I know a lot of cops and I could probably help you out there."

"I phoned the precinct and Sergeant Dunlap assured me that he would be here tonight," she replied politely. "Sergeant Dunlap is the Community Affairs Officer."

"I'll talk to him when he comes in."

Out of the corner of her eye, Sylvia, though she was too busy to consider it for more than a moment, saw Pat Sheehan start to enter the room, only to freeze in his tracks when he saw Moodrow. Then Al Rosenkrantz squeezed by Pat, trying to say "hello" to everyone at once, while Pat retreated through the doorway.

"Mrs. Kaufman." Rosenkrantz wasted no time in coming up to her, ignoring the Yiddish epithet (which he didn't understand, but which he was sure meant him no good) tossed at him, like spit, by Mike Birnbaum. "I'm so sorry. I can't tell you how badly I feel."

"Well, I think you should say that to Mrs. Park." Sylvia stepped away from him. She wasn't the injured party. Nor was she about to go into mourning. She wanted to save her home and she was determined to do it in the only way she could comprehend: by organizing and by raising money.

"Is Park here?" Al Rosenkrantz asked. "He called us yesterday and begged to be let out of his lease. Of course, considering the awful thing that happened, we agreed immediately."

"No, Mr. Park isn't here," Sylvia said quietly. "He's in his apartment."

"Is the granny going to be all right?"

"Yong Park's mother is still in the hospital. She's all right physically, but she's in shock. She won't talk to anyone. Not even to her son."

"Such a waste . . ."

"Mr. Rosenkrantz, I'd like to get started. I promised you a chance to speak to us, but I can't give you the whole meeting." Her resolve hardening, she watched Al Rosenkrantz, probably looking for Myron Gold, retreat to a chair off by itself.

"Please, may I address the meeting? I got a message for these *faygelah* guests you invited."

That was Mike Birnbaum. As expected. Controlling Mike Birnbaum, though it was absolutely necessary, could easily turn out to be the most difficult part of her job.

"May I address the meeting?" he repeated loudly.

"I wish you wouldn't, Mike," Sylvia said, resurrecting a small piece of the union delegate who'd represented the teachers in her school for almost ten years. "Not until after we begin. I've done a few things today that I'd like to tell everyone about."

"Sylvia," Birnbaum raised his hand to wave her off, "whatever you say is okay by me. I'm an old man. I can't even be in charge of myself. But I got to say I think it's *meshugge* you should invite people to this meeting who ain't tenants." He indicated Rosenkrantz, Moodrow, and Porky Dunlap, who'd come in as he was speaking. "Two I don't trust and I don't know. One I don't trust and I *do* know."

Before Sylvia could frame a reply, Paul Dunlap approached her and began, without permission, to address the Jackson Arms Tenants' Association. For a moment, she considered pushing him out of the way, but he was enormous and he wasn't bullying her. He was enthusiastic. And she might need him later on . . .

"My name is Paul Dunlap. Sergeant Paul Dunlap from the Hundred and Fifteenth Precinct on Northern Boulevard. I just want everyone to know that the man who broke into the Park apartment and attacked Mrs. Park, was cornered in Manhattan and killed after shooting at officers trying to arrest him. The man had jewelry in his pocket that Mr. Park identified as belonging to his mother, and there were other, chemical, identifications on his clothing. We're completely convinced that we got the right man. The case has been closed."

Of course, Porky Dunlap had had nothing to do with the demise of Born Miller. Born Miller had been about to be arrested for trying to break into his mother's apartment when he'd suffered a fit of temporary insanity (substance-induced) which had compelled him to pull his .44 on Patrolwomen Rita Mintz and Patty Ruthven. They'd pumped nine rounds into his chest before the pistol cleared his waistband.

Even worse, though Sergeant Dunlap wasn't about to announce it, the connection between Born Miller and the Park family had been made through a credit card in Park's name which Miller had been carrying in his wallet. The jewelry had come as an afterthought, while the "chemical identifications" were entirely his invention.

But Porky Dunlap, noting the smiles of relief on the faces in the room, was more than content to bathe in the gratitude due an overworked cop who had just made a timely arrest. It never occurred to Dunlap that his announcement would undercut the gravity of Sylvia Kaufman's meeting, but Sylvia felt it. She felt the hope of organizing the tenants (which she defined as getting them to pay dues, to part with their money) slipping away from her, as it had on her first attempt to establish the Jackson Arms Tenants' Association.

"Please, please." It was Al Rosenkrantz, who also recognized the import of Born Miller's death and was anxious to add his considerable weight to the evening's momentum. "May I please address the group? I'm due in the Bronx in an hour and I have several announcements to make."

"I guess we're all glad to hear that Mrs. Park is going to be okay," he began, ignoring the hostility focused on him, while noting that it came from sources besides Mike Birnbaum. "Nobody could feel worse about what happened in the building than Precision Management," he continued, his eyes moving from face to face. "And nobody could be happier about what happened to the animal who did that to Mrs. Park than I am. Of course, you already know that the scum got into the Park apartment through a window by the fire escape and you might want to consider security gates for your own windows if you don't already have them. Please don't think we're putting the entire burden on you, however. That's what my announcements are about.

"First, you'll be glad to hear that by tomorrow afternoon, the Jackson Arms will have a full-time, resident superintendent. Richard James Walsh." Now he was getting some smiles and he returned them, careful to make eye contact. As expected, the Irish name was reassuring. He'd originally planned to drag Richard Walsh with him, to display Richard's whiter-than-white face to the whole bunch, but Walsh had begged off, claiming a family problem. "And the *first* thing Dick Walsh will take care of—you have my word on this—is that disgrace in the lobby, including the mailboxes and the locks. Also, starting day after tomorrow, you can use the compactor shoots to get rid of your garbage.

"Second, we've decided to put security in the building. A twenty-four-hour doorman to watch the lobby and make sure that anyone entering the premises has a good reason to be here. There'll be two shifts during the week, with relief on the weekends. These men will be dressed in blue uniforms and will carry mace and a nightstick; they're being provided by Aback Security and they'll remain in place until you people are satisfied that your homes are safe. We expect their presence to eliminate much, if not all, of the vandalism that's been going on in the lobby.

"Third, you'll be pleased to know that we've served Salvadore Ragozzo, the leaseholder on the apartment where the alleged prostitutes live, with an eviction notice and we'll see him in Tenant–Landlord's Court by the middle of March. We'd *like* to have some of you tenants down to testify about what you've seen. I've already taken up a lot of time, so I won't ask for volunteers tonight, but anyone who would like to testify should call me at my office. I'm leaving some business cards on the table here, so you won't have any trouble finding me if you need me." He tossed the cards on the table, fanning them out and thanking the Lord that he hadn't been interrupted. In spite of the chilly room, he was beginning to sweat. Maybe if they didn't ask too many questions, he'd get out of here before he fucked up another shirt.

When Stanley Moodrow heard Sylvia Kaufman pronounce the title "Community Affairs Officer," he nearly grinned. It was his own appointment to the position of Community Affairs Officer of the 7th Precinct that led to his retirement. Sending the CAO was equivalent, in his mind, to sending a form letter extending "deepest regrets." Porky Dunlap's speech, thrilling as it may have been to the tenants, had only added to his contempt, especially the claim about chemical tests, which, in his opinion, was just so much cop bullshit. In most cases, you had to beg the forensic unit to process that kind of evidence; sometimes it took months. It *never* took less than a week. Not unless the media was looking over the commissioner's shoulder.

Al Rosenkrantz was a more difficult problem. Sure, he oozed insincerity, but he worked for a landlord. He was *supposed* to look like he loved throwing old ladies into the street. What he actually offered, on the other hand, was a fundamentally sound way to protect a building and would probably be enough to keep the Jackson Arms secure. Walking from the subway, Moodrow had taken a good look around. In the course of a long career with the NYPD, he'd been everywhere in New York at one time or another and his memories of Jackson Heights involved a stable, middle-class neighborhood, with clean streets and well-tended shrubbery around the houses and apartment buildings. His stroll had convinced him that little, if anything, had changed and that the landlord, whoever he was, had good reason to protect the property. In any event, the tenants were apparently buying Al's solution. Their only questions revolved around "when" and "for how long."

Moodrow left early, resolving to come back to visit Sylvia Kaufman at some later date. There was nothing he could do to help her with the organizing, but that didn't mean he couldn't go to work. He walked back to the Jackson Arms and checked the names in the tenants' directory near the buzzers, running his finger down the line until he found the one he was looking for: Sheehan, 4A.

"Fuck," Pat Sheehan said, opening the door. "Whatta you got, eyes in the back of your head?"

"Only for you, dear," Moodrow returned. Stepping into the apartment, he made a quick, professional sweep of the living room, noting both the clean, inexpensive furniture and the shrunken man who lay quietly on the couch.

"Don't get comfortable, Moodrow, 'cause you ain't stayin' around. I'm only lettin' you in here, so I can get rid of you. For permanent. I'm clean and I been clean since the day I got out. I'm a UPS driver and I don't get involved in nothin' worse than a few beers. If I wasn't on parole, I'd spit in your face."

"Does that mean you don't like me anymore? The amount of time we spent together before you went upstate, I thought we was real buddies." Standing in the center of the living room, his hands in the pockets of his overcoat, Moodrow seemed very permanent. "But, hey, Pat, a lotta things have changed since you roamed the Lower East Side. Like, I'm not even a cop no more. I retired. Now I'm a private eye."

Pat Sheehan had no idea whether or not Moodrow was telling the truth, but he was certain that Moodrow's primary aim in coming out to Jackson Heights had nothing to do with him or with Louis Persio. Not that Moodrow wasn't dangerous. When you're on parole, everyone connected with law enforcement is dangerous, because you can be remanded to custody on the mere *word* of a cop (or a parole officer after a cop whispers into his ear)—incarcerated and held without bail pending a parole hearing which might or might not come up before some con shanked you while you were asleep.

"So whatta you supposed to be? The Equalizer? I mean, you used ta be a fat Dirty Harry, but you ain't a cop no more, so you must be somethin' new."

"*Fat?* Get offa my face. And the fucking Equalizer's at least ten years older than me. I'm more like the Thin Man. You know: elegant, suave, cosmopolitan. My whole life I wanted a Waspy girlfriend called Nora, but all my old ladies came from little countries between Germany and Russia." Moodrow, uninvited, sat in an armchair near the kitchen and stretched his legs out. "Why don't you introduce me to your friend?"

Sheehan thought about it for a moment, trying to detect any trace of sarcasm in Moodrow's request. He found none and went on to make the introduction. "This is my lover. Louis Persio. Louis, this is Stanley Moodrow from the 7th Precinct. Formerly from the 7th Precinct. Now retired."

Pat Sheehan didn't bother to add the facts about Persio's condition and

Moodrow had seen far too many cases of AIDS to have to ask. Persio nodded slightly at Moodrow. The right side of his face was covered with a flaking eczema and, though his eyes were bright with fever, they also burned with intelligence and with the knowledge of impending death. It wouldn't be long, Moodrow speculated, until Pat Sheehan was free of whatever had made him take up this burden.

"You been living here awhile, Patrick?" Moodrow asked.

"I been here more than two years, *Stanley*," Sheehan replied. "And I'm willing to talk, if you came here to help out Sylvia Kaufman. But not if you came here to break my balls. Bustin' me was one thing. Hasslin' me is another. I'm fuckin' clean and I plan to stay that way."

As soon as Moodrow understood that Pat Sheehan and Louis Persio had been in residence for more than two years, he dismissed them as part of Sylvia Kaufman's problem. Moodrow had known Pat Sheehan when Sheehan was just another junkie rampaging through the Lower East Side, had arrested him and testified at his trial. Sheehan was not a junkie anymore. He was much too healthy for that. But he would know who was operating in the building. He would see his fellow tenants with eyes as discerning as Moodrow's.

"I'm here because Sylvia Kaufman is my girlfriend's aunt," Moodrow explained. "Like I said, I'm retired, but I do private jobs. The other night, I'm laying in the bed with Betty and she starts telling me about her aunt who lives in Queens. Would I go and help her out. Hey, when you're retired, you don't have nothing but time, right? Anyway, to make a long story short, all I really know is there was a sexual assault here a few days ago and there's whores and drugs in the building. Where I come from, that ain't much to complain about, but like I said, it's a favor."

Pat Sheehan, the only one still standing, strolled across to the refrigerator and opened two cans of Coors, handing one to Moodrow, before he took his seat. "So whatta ya want from me?" he asked. There was no resentment in his voice.

"I wanna know what the fuck is going on," Moodrow answered. "And I'm not gonna find out by asking the asshole cop who showed up tonight. That fat fuck only knows from bullshit. That's his job. Bullshit."

"You think the other one is better? The one from the landlord?" Sheehan, who'd passed Porky Dunlap on his way out of the church, was openly skeptical.

Moodrow shrugged. "At least what he said makes sense for the building."

Pat Sheehan leaned forward, his eyes narrowing. "Maybe you lost your cop brains since you retired, Moodrow, but that scumbag is layin' down a carpet of shit deeper than the one in Donald Trump's living room."

"So he's bullshittin', so what could you expect from a landlord? I don't wanna waste my time with him. I need to know what's going on inside the building."

"Whatever you want, Moodrow." Pat Sheehan pulled on his beer and looked across at Louis Persio who was following the conversation closely. He waited for Persio to give a slight nod before he proceeded. "At first there was just the mailboxes and the locks on the front door. They went out about a month ago.

Then this pimp sets up two pigs in an apartment on the first floor. The pimp, by the way, is an oily fuck that's so oily no one could rent to him without knowing what he was. Next thing, the whores are givin' blow-jobs in the hallway and comin' on to the tenants. Now you got two dopers set up in the apartment right across the hall from me. They must've made me for a junkie, because they did everything but jab the fuckin' spike into my arm. Right now they're dealing dope and crack to a few steady customers, but they told me they were gonna open up the whole neighborhood to the glories of cocaine."

"And there's only two of them?" Moodrow asked.

"Two that I know of, but there's a lot of vacant apartments. That sweet landlord you like so fuckin' much's been dumpin' out the Asians and the illegals as fast as he can check the leases. With that many empties, there's gonna be squatters. Might be already, but I ain't seen 'em."

"What about the rape? What's that all about?"

"A burglary," Sheehan explained. "Dude's takin' off the apartment when the old lady comes home. Maybe she surprised him or maybe he was too stoned to run. Either way, he belted her out and then took advantage."

"With the kid watching," Moodrow added.

"Yeah," Sheehan agreed, "with the kid lookin'. But it don't figure to connect with the whores and the dope. Jackson Heights ain't got much street crime, but it does have burglaries. People here got money and that makes them prey for the people who don't. So what's new?"

Suddenly, Moodrow, his course of action firmly established in his own mind, stood up and prepared to leave. "Okay, Pat. I'm gonna go see if I can head this off before it turns into an epidemic."

"Is that a joke?" Louis Persio spoke for the first time.

"What?" Moodrow asked, confused.

"About the epidemic?"

"You're too sensitive," Moodrow replied. "If you think I got a problem with you or your condition, you're mistaken. The only problem I got is with my girlfriend and this building." He hesitated momentarily, measuring his thoughts. "See, I have this deep conviction that if I don't save these poor, helpless tenants, who just happen to be going through what half the people in this city live with every fucking day, my old lady is gonna walk away from me and I like her too much to take a chance."

"I want you to do us a favor," Persio continued, ignoring Moodrow's reply. "Do us a big favor and we'll be your eyes and ears. We'll be rats." He began to cough, his emaciated body seeming to ripple beneath the green plaid blanket covering him. Sheehan rushed over to help, but Persio shook him off. "I waited a long time in my life to become a rat," he said.

"Why don't you just tell me what you want," Moodrow said neutrally. The idea of a trade-off appealed to his cop sensibility.

"If Pat's parole officer thinks we're part of what's going down here, he'll break us up. At the least. Convicts on parole aren't supposed to room with convicted felons. Even if the convicted felon is dying. Even if they're in love." He stopped abruptly, trying to read something in Moodrow's blank face, then settled for the neutrality. "Talk to the parole officer. Tell him we're childhood sweethearts. Tell him we're Christian fundamentalists who got saved in the joint. Because we can't move. There's nobody who'd take me, even if we could afford another apartment, and I'm not too keen on doing the hospice bit while I can still make it at home."

EIGHT

"I'M SORRY we didn't get a chance to talk before the meeting," Sylvia said. Though she didn't particularly like Betty Haluka's new boyfriend (he was too deliberately inscrutable), Betty had—for one brief summer while her mother was ill—become a second child, and so, for Betty's sake, Sylvia was polite.

"No big deal," Moodrow said, his eyes glued to the corner connecting the hallway to the lobby. "You had your hands full."

"You used to be a police officer?"

"Yeah. Thirty-five years. Made it up to the detectives. Say, do me a favor, Sylvia. Move a little bit to the right so's I could watch the lobby. I'm waiting for someone."

Sylvia looked at him closely. It was almost eleven o'clock and the rest of the tenants—the ones who'd attended the meeting, anyway—were safely inside their apartments. So who was he waiting for?

When it became apparent that Moodrow wasn't about to volunteer the information, Sylvia changed her tactics. "What did you think of Sergeant Dunlap?" she asked. "Do you think he can help us?"

"Forget about him," Moodrow said evenly. "He's a *shmuck*. That's why they made him Community Affairs Officer."

"I don't understand?"

"Community Affairs is a public relations post. It don't have anything to do with the job. The only help Dunlap could give is persuading the captain to assign a few anticrime guys to work the building. And that's not too likely, because the problem isn't bad enough. Not when you look at what's going on in South Jamaica or the Bronx. Maybe if you put together a strong tenants' association, you could persuade one of the real cops to help you. The tenants' patrol is a very good idea. Just be careful who you pick, because mostly they come around for a few shifts and then get bored. Stay at home and watch the football game." Moodrow, though he noticed the crestfallen look on Sylvia Kaufman's face when he told her about Dunlap, recited his speech matter-of-factly. Better she should know the truth. He was a great believer in truth. "And try to get that pastor at that church you were in tonight to call the precinct; he probably knows the captain by his first name. The precinct commander at the One One Five, by the way, is George Serrano. He's Catholic and he'll most likely be influenced by the priest."

"And Rosenkrantz?" Sylvia persisted. "Is he worthless, too?"

"Nobody's worthless," Moodrow explained. "But you gotta know who's gonna help if it gets bad and you could *never* count on the Community Affairs Officer. You can't count on the landlord, either, but what Rosenkrantz says will most likely get the building back together. If only because Rosenkrantz has an interest in keeping the place up. I had a talk with Pat Sheehan before I came down here . . ."

"You don't think Pat is part of this?"

"Actually, I don't. But he knows what's going on. He told me about the whores and he says there's a couple of guys dealing dope in the apartment across the hall from him. Which is what I figure the problem is all about. Crack is so addicting, the dealers feel they can make any neighborhood into a supermarket if they can find a few locals to sample the goods. There's always been drugs in the bars on Roosevelt Avenue. Coke and speed, mostly. A little dope. Now it's moved over a couple of blocks."

"Does that mean you think it can be taken care of?"

Moodrow shifted his glance just enough to look at Sylvia. The lady was very tired, that was obvious, and he was tempted to reassure her the way parents reassure their children after nightmares. "Look, Sylvia, I don't have no psychic powers and I left my crystal ball at home, so you shouldn't take what I say like it comes from the Pope. But I got every reason to think this situation could be taken care of. That's what I'm doing here. I'm waiting to have a little talk with a Chinese kid named Joey Yang who lives in 4B. I think I might be able to persuade him to move out."

"How are you going to do that?" Sylvia smiled. "If you left your crystal ball at home, that probably means you forgot your magic wand, as well."

"Betty said you were a schoolteacher before you retired. When I was in fourth grade, Mrs. Benedict always used to say, 'Stanley, you'd forget your ears if they weren't attached to your head.' "

Relief began to seep into Sylvia Kaufman, like the warmth of a hot bath after an afternoon shoveling snow. Moodrow was a physical monster; if he didn't reek of cop, he'd be terrifying. But there was confidence to go with the bulk; if he believed . . .

"I think there might be a problem when Yang shows up," Moodrow said. "It'd be better if you went inside. Just in case."

"Maybe I could be of some help . . ."

Moodrow laughed. "How about sending me the little guy who asked that I should be thrown out of the meeting? To give me a hand if Yang decides to get tough."

"Mike Birnbaum?"

"Wait a second." Moodrow stiffened as soon as he heard the sharp clank of the lobby door closing. "Go into your apartment," he ordered. "Right now."

He actually pushed her, though he was gentle, and Sylvia began to move down the hallway, fumbling for her keys. She had every intention of following his instructions, but her curiosity overcame her fear before she found the key chain and she looked back to see a small Oriental in a blue pea coat walk from the lobby into the corridor. The look of near panic that came over his face when he saw Moodrow standing in his path was so comical, she forgot Moodrow's order altogether.

"Hello, Joey," Moodrow said. It was too late to worry about Sylvia; the first rule of survival in a gun-mad city is to keep the suspect in plain view at all times. Pat Sheehan had described Joey Yang and while there might be more than one short, slim Oriental living in the building, Yang's expression upon sighting Moodrow made it unlikely that he was the victim of mistaken identity. Still, Moodrow called him by his first name and when Yang made no protest, Moodrow took the identification as confirmed.

"Don't put your hands in your pockets, Joey. In fact, don't move your fucking hands at all." Moodrow, speaking very softly (but with his own jacket unbuttoned to make the presence of his .38 more than obvious), walked quickly toward the much smaller Joey Yang, who stood frozen for a second, his narrow eyes widening with unexpected terror, before spinning and running for the door. Moodrow, anticipating the flight (and much too slow to catch the hundred and thirty pound Joey Yang) tossed his overcoat into the backs of Yang's legs, a move designed merely to slow Yang down, but which tripped him, instead. By the time Yang got to his knees, Moodrow was standing over him, smiling.

"Lemme help you up, Joey." Moodrow picked the kneeling Yang off the ground by the back of his coat and shoved him against the wall. Curiously, Moodrow was nearly as convinced of his own "cophood" as Joey Yang, who didn't doubt that he was about to be arrested for a second. "You don't have a gun in there, Joey. You ain't carrying no gun, I hope. How come your hands ain't against the wall? What the fuck's the matter with you? That's better. For a second I thought you was gonna tell me you never been busted before and I wouldn't like it if you told me lies."

Moodrow's right hand was darting in and out of Joey Yang's pockets like the head of an exploring python. Dipping, searching, pulling back. He found the gun Pat had warned him about in the waistband of Yang's trousers, but that was the least of it. In a plastic sandwich bag taped to the small man's thigh, Moodrow discovered thirty bundles of heroin. Three thousand dollars, retail, the following day's supply for Yang's slowly expanding operation.

"This is really bad for you, Joey," Moodrow continued. " 'Cause you got a gun on you which is an automatic year, even if you don't have no priors, which I think you got. Also, they changed the dope laws now, so this much smack is a B felony unless you rat your people out. Which, even if you do rat, you still gotta do *some* time. This kinda weight and the judge don't have discretion."

Moodrow stuffed the heroin into the pocket of his jacket and the gun (a piece-of-shit .22 that was sixty percent likely to misfire) in his overcoat pocket where it wouldn't be a temptation for Joey Yang, who was in the process of collecting himself.

"Don't I have rights?" Yang's voice had no accent and less conviction. As a third generation American, he not only spoke English perfectly, he knew that "rights" were abstractions most cops reserved for the witness stand. Especially if the cops wanted something besides a bust, as this cop obviously did. That hope of "something besides a bust" was his excuse for not insisting on his "rights." That's why he was allowing himself to be pushed into the elevator. "I hope you got a search warrant," he said by way of opening negotiations. "If you don't have a warrant, you can't use the dope against me. It's tainted."

"What do I give a shit what color it is?" Moodrow asked, tossing Sylvia Kaufman a casual wink as the elevator door closed.

"Huh?"

"Didn't you just say the evidence was 'tinted'?"

Joey Yang looked up at his captor. Was the cop joking; could he really be that stupid? "You can't take anything you find in an illegal search and use it in court," he insisted. "It's inadmissible."

"Wrong, Joey." Moodrow's voice was suddenly much harder. "Cause I'm gonna say you opened your coat when you came through the door and I saw the gun in your belt. That gives me the right to do anything, but kill you. For instance, just because you have that fucking gun, I could justify any kind of a beating. A broken nose, cracked ribs, a closed eye . . . All I gotta say is, 'I observed the perpetrator put his hand on the gun.' Now, if you had remembered to tape the gun, you could say it was a plant, but I'll bet my left testicle that .22's got your prints all over it. Let's face facts, you could do a lotta time, Joey, and, if you don't mind my saying so, little dudes, like you, don't fare too well in the joint. They tend to get victimized by the other prisoners."

Suddenly Moodrow put his arm around the much smaller man and hugged him close. "Joey, you look like you're smart enough to know that I know what I'm talking about. Smart is not always a good thing for the dope business, but in this case, it could help you out, because when I explain that my intention is not to make a bust, you could believe it without me sayin' it over and over. Of course, that don't mean you couldn't still find yourself in the joint. It only means that if you do the right thing here, you could walk away. Tonight. You could really walk away."

Neither of them spoke until the door to the elevator opened onto an empty fourth floor corridor. Having advanced the bait, Moodrow was waiting for Yang to bite. The deal he was offering—freedom—was too good to resist, especially when compared to New York's penal system, and Moodrow was convinced that Yang would come around.

In fact, Yang, as Moodrow had predicted, *was* contemplating life at Rikers Island, where he would be subject to one sexual assault after another. Small and slender, with ivory skin and thick, jet-black hair, the wolves would be unable to resist his charms. In an instant, despair overwhelmed him as completely as a rush of injected heroin or smoked cocaine, translating itself as the intention to do "whatever it takes" to get out of the situation.

"Tell me what you want," he finally asked.

"I wanna go in the apartment and talk to your partner for a little while, but I'm concerned he might have a gun in there and use it to shoot me. I really hate it when they do that, so I was thinking that you could start earning your freedom by helping me get inside. By telling me the code you gotta give before you unlock the door. So your partner could know it's you coming in."

They were in the corridor now, walking toward 4B. Moodrow was right about Joey Yang's intelligence. Joey had grown up middle-class ambitious and been admitted to Columbia before discovering cocaine. He knew the consequences of killing a cop in New York; his own people would drop the dime.

"Knock twice before you turn the key," he said.

"Not me," Moodrow whispered, gathering the back of Yang's pea coat in one huge hand. "You, Joey. You go in first." He pulled his own .38 and held it out where Yang could see it. "And no mistakes. Not one. Like forgetting to tell me if you know there's someone in there besides your partner."

"There's one other person. I forgot."

"Who's that?"

"The whore from downstairs. Connie Appastello. We keep her stoned and she fucks for us when she's not working."

Moodrow, without putting the gun down (and without letting go of Joey Yang), knocked twice on the door to 4B, then quickly turned the key in the lock, before pushing the door open to find Georgie Vallone sitting next to Connie Appastello on the couch. Vallone, in powder-blue jockey shorts (replete with full erection) looked even more surprised than Connie who, though naked to the waist, made no move to cover her breasts, reaching instead for the crack pipe. Until Moodrow's voice froze her in her tracks.

"Not a fucking twitch," he warned, his eyes darting from corner to corner. Apartment 4B was a studio with a tiny, obviously empty, kitchen, but the door to the bathroom was closed. "You, Vallone, come off the couch and lie flat on the floor. And you, the whore, you lie on top of him." He leveled the gun. "Do it fast." As soon as they were down, he pushed Joey Yang onto the pile and went to the bathroom door, careful to keep his bulk out of the line of fire as he pushed it open. It was empty and, as he walked back to the pile of squirming bodies, the pleasure he always took in his work coursed through his body like a blush.

"Okay, so here's the story," he began. "I only got two sets of cuffs and there's three people. So even though I'm gonna cuff you around the steam pipe in the corner (where you could all start moving to, by the way), you're gonna have one hand free. You shouldn't let that influence you into doing anything stupid, okay?" He nodded to Connie, who was off the floor. "You wanna get dressed?" he asked, then noticed that her eyes were glued, not to her clothing, but to a crack pipe fashioned from a one-ounce bottle of Jack Daniels. "Guess not. How about you, George? You cold?"

"Fuck you."

"Pardon me? Did I hear you employ bad language in front of a woman?" Moodrow's voice was even, despite Vallone's mounting rage. The Italian was very muscular, but his eyes had the look of a man who'd been stoned for a long time and the little speech he finally gave was so stupid, it proved that fact to Moodrow. Beyond a shadow of a doubt.

"You can't shoot me," Vallone said, turning to face what he, too, had no doubt was an ambitious cop making an arrest. "I don't have a gun, so you can't shoot me. You gotta take me with ya hands."

"No problem, asshole."

Moodrow, always quick to seize an opportunity to get his message across, threw a short, economical right lead that landed against the side of Vallone's head with stunning force. It disoriented Vallone to the point where, even if he was thinking of retaliation, Moodrow's several heads were spinning too fast to be hit. In fact, it seemed like several shoes rushing up to crack into his legs, kicking them out from under him, and several hands that hauled him back to his feet. Which was just as well, because if Georgie Vallone wasn't so confused, he might have noted how rapidly the left side of his face was swelling.

"Connie," Moodrow said confidently, "here's two sets of handcuffs. I want you to start by putting one ring on . . ."

He went about it methodically, as a good cop should, letting Connie wrap the cuffs around the pipe until the three were securely fastened. Then he tossed the apartment, inch by inch, recovering Vallone's and Yang's personal effects, as well as more than four hundred vials of crack and an expensive 9mm Smith & Wesson.

"Do you like stories?" Moodrow asked, going over to the sink.

"Please, can I go?" Connie begged, the panic finally cutting through the cocaine. "I don't belong here. I live downstairs. I'm not a dealer."

"That's very rude, Connie. I was talking to Georgie."

"Listen," the prostitute continued, taking a deep breath before pushing her breasts at Moodrow. "If you like what you see, we could work something out. Men love my techniques; I get all kinds of repeat business and I'll do you whatever you want."

"Cut the crap, already." Moodrow was afraid she'd panic, maybe scream. If the neighbors called the cops (perhaps *because* it was a dealer's apartment), the sergeant might let him off the hook because he was once a cop, but he would have to chance a patrol sergeant's mood and Moodrow was committed to not taking chances in his work. "I have about as much interest in your ass as I do in getting a blow-job from a snapping turtle. But I'm not interested in busting you, either. What I got is a personal interest in this fucking building. Understand? I got a personal interest in the people who live here and they don't like you. They don't like your dope or your tits. They don't like freaks coming in here and raping old ladies. They don't like junkies or crackheads or pigs that give blow-jobs in hallways."

Now he had their attention. The "maybe you won't have to go to jail" gambit never failed to get the attention of the truly guilty. "What you two scumbags are gonna do is move out. Tonight." With all the nonchalance he could muster, Moodrow turned on the water in the sink and began, vial by vial, to empty the jumbo pellets into the swirl of hot water running down the drain. The steam rising up around his hand as he disposed of nearly ten thousand dollars' worth of crack and smack, was part of the intended effect. "Which shouldn't upset you, because you ain't been here long enough to make real friends."

He went on and on, chatting almost to himself while he completed his work. It took nearly half an hour to open every crack vial and heroin envelope, to gather up the clothing, the small pieces of jewelry and stuff them into garbage bags, to rip apart each piece of furniture in a brazen display of personal strength. To unload the two pistols, letting the cartridges drop to the carpet, then tear the handles from the stocks before dumping what was left onto the garbage heap in the center of the room.

"What's happening now," he finally announced, touching Georgie Vallone's swollen eye gingerly, "is that I'm keeping the keys to this apartment and I'm gonna lock the door after you leave. Of course, you could always come back and break the door down, but you notice that I threw the vials and the envelopes on the floor, so if you try to get back inside, one of those neighbors who don't like you worth a shit is liable to call the cops. These cops, because they're investigating a possible felony, will have probable cause to enter the premises without a warrant. In which case all traces of dope remaining in this paraphernalia are admissible. They ain't even tinted a little bit."

NINE

March 1

THERE were two premature victory celebrations following Moodrow's summary eviction of the undesirables in 4B. Sylvia Kaufman's, in deference perhaps to her years, got under way first and combined two goals. There was the celebration, of course, but Sylvia Kaufman was too savvy to believe that all her problems would disappear just because Stanley Moodrow had strong-armed a couple of junkies. It was a relief to see the trash moving out for a change; the traffic had been going the other way for a long time, but the new super, an overweight, red-nosed Irishman who reeked of alcohol, hadn't fixed the front door locks, citing the expense and the necessity of getting an estimate approved by Precision Management before the repairs could go forward. She'd complained, of course, only to have Al Rosenkrantz respond to her phone call by insisting on his own helplessness in the face of company policy. He urged her to be patient for a little while longer and "everything would straighten out."

Sylvia, whose strategy for life had developed in the classrooms of New York, believed that patience was a luxury reserved for the properly prepared, and preparation was, therefore, the second aim of her celebration. Preparation for a tenants' patrol that would, itself, accomplish two aims. The patrol, if not exactly girded for battle, would at least make sure the doors were locked and the junkies weren't injecting themselves in the lobby, while the close, working relationships the tenants formed in the course of protecting their own homes would weld the small group into the nucleus of a much larger association.

Over the past few weeks, Sylvia Kaufman had come to realize that someone had forgotten to light a flame under the melting pot called Jackson Heights. Though the tenants (in deference, perhaps, to the neighborhood's middle-class character) were publicly polite to each other, most of the ones Sylvia knew were privately scornful. It wasn't just the old-timers, who were all white, against the immigrants, who were any number of shades. Sylvia could vividly recall standing near the broken mailboxes, open-mouthed, while one of the Korean women complained about the odor of the Pakistanis. "They no clean," she had insisted in the face of Sylvia's call for tolerance. "They no wash."

"You notice who ain't here, Sylvia?" Mike Birnbaum's voice yanked her away from her speculations. "You notice who had such a big mouth, but ain't here when it counts?"

75

Once again busy serving tea and her best peanut butter/chocolate swirl cookies (so fresh they could be molded like soft clay, which nobody seemed to notice), Sylvia responded with a sigh. "You know how sick Shirley is, Mike. Myron *had* to go."

"All I know is when it was time to stand up and be counted, that cutey little *faygelah* went south with his mommy. *This* you can't deny." Having gotten the last, last word on Myron Gold, Mike Birnbaum settled back to enjoy his cookies. In some respects, the events of the past few weeks had been a tonic for Mike. Born Miller's violence confirmed Mike's belief in the imminence of personal danger while Moodrow's muscle validated Mike's own belligerent response to that danger. As a bonus, his growing responsibility to the tenants' association kept him away from the "Lucy" reruns that had long dominated his old age and, best of all, Myron Gold had run away to Florida, the land of the dead.

"I think we should work out a schedule for the times of patrol," Sylvia suggested. "We need to know who can volunteer on which days."

"And we need a fire patrol, too," Paul Reilly, the retired fireman from 3L, was determined to be heard and respected. "We have to go to each apartment and make sure everyone has working smoke alarms. By Jesus, the last ten years I was stationed in the Bronx, it seemed like every fire was started by a dope addict or an alkie squatter. They get stoned and forget about the candles they light. Or they break down the walls and splice into electric lines with hi-fi cable."

The ice broken, they all began to come in with suggestions and Sylvia went back to the kitchen. Disagreements were part of the bonding process; let each fight for his own idea of how the patrol should be run. In the last analysis, they would come out of the meeting with at least one firm resolve: to save their homes. Already, Inez and Andre Almeyda were joining voices with Mike Birnbaum to suggest that patrolees carry baseball bats and look for an opportunity to "drive" their point home. The Almeydas had always been "new ones" (or "new scum," when he was among friends) to Mike Birnbaum.

"I don't go along with that kinda talk." Paul Reilly, who, like many ex-firemen, had difficulty breathing, spoke with just the touch of a brogue. "By all that's holy, I'm too old to go to jail," he wheezed. "Besides, I confess to Father Patrick at St. Ann's and he has the biggest mouth in the Diocese."

"We don't even know if there's anything left to confront," Jimmy Yo said. He was a student at Columbia University and lived quietly with his parents in 4G; so quietly that prior to Jimmy's unexpected arrival at the meeting, the Yo family was no more than a trio of Oriental faces Sylvia occasionally passed in the hallway. "I want to hear a little bit more about the cop. What's his name? Moodrow? I think we need to understand exactly how he got those people out of 4B; I live down the hall from 4B and I know, for a fact, that one of the dealers usually carried a gun. I don't think they went easily."

"Moodrow is an *ex*-cop," Sylvia explained for the fourth time. "I witnessed his confrontation with one of the dealers. He was very forceful, but we agreed, when we spoke on the following day, that it would be better if I didn't give out exact details."

"Because what he done ain't kosher with the *real* cops." Mike Birnbaum winked at Paul Reilly. Maybe Paul wasn't too anxious to bludgeon the perps, but he and Mike were old friends. Mike greatly admired the courage of anyone crazy enough to run *into* a burning building.

"I didn't see anything of what went on upstairs," Sylvia continued, smiling at Mike Birnbaum. "But the one downstairs had a gun. Moodrow took it away from him."

"That's the point," Jimmy Yo broke in. "If this cop . . ."

"Ex-cop," Sylvia reminded.

"If this ex-cop is going to stick around, it changes our strategy. For instance, Moodrow should set up the patrol routine; he must know much more about it than we do. He should advise us on the use of force, too. We're just speculating, but he undoubtedly *knows* whether we can forcibly eject those who don't belong in the building."

"I think he has already told us this," Muhammad Assiz, his voice as carefully composed as his delicate features, spoke for the first time. Unlike most of the Hindu and Moslem Asians, Muhammad was breaking through his instinctive dislike of Westerners. He'd twice come down to Sylvia's apartment, unannounced, to discuss developments within the building, and Sylvia had been impressed with the core of resolution that lay beneath the brilliant smile and the musical voice. "I think by Mr. Moodrow's action we have before us an example to be followed. We are the only ones with something to protect and that something is our lives in this place. Three families in my community have been served with eviction notices for failing to care for their apartments. This is the new way they attack us—after there are none left to evict for improper leases. The landlord thinks we will run without a fight, but we will not run. We have decided to stay and, by the Will of Allah, to prevail."

Sylvia, her duties as hostess completed, took a chair next to Assiz. "Maybe we need an education committee," she said, changing the subject. As a Jew, the "Will of Allah," even when applied to the destruction of a common enemy, made her nervous. "I've done a little research over the past week and I found a group called the Metropolitan Housing Council that helps people with our problems. Especially with the education part. They'll send someone down to advise us. Also, my niece, Betty, is a lawyer, though she specializes in criminal law."

"Maybe I can help with this." Jorge Rivera, fifteen years out of Lima, Peru, was short and incredibly thick, a barrelchested man who'd spent his teenage years as a porter in the Andes Mountains, working up high where the air is thin. Sylvia could remember the day he moved in. As the first of the Latins, he had not been welcomed. "I volunteer once a week for a Latino outreach program. Mostly our work has been with the illegals, but we also run a conversational

English course. If you would like me to do this, I will meet with the Metropolitan Council and learn how to be in the Landlord–Tenant Court. Then I will set up an education committee to prevent illegal evictions."

The meeting ended at nine o'clock, but it took fifteen minutes for all but Mike Birnbaum and Annie Bonnastello to leave. Even as she saw her guests off, Sylvia began to weigh the good and the bad. Only nine people, representing eight apartments, had come to her tenants' patrol meeting. Not exactly an army, but Assiz, Almeyda, Birnbaum, Rivera, and the others represented every major ethnic group in the building (except for the Koreans), and were solidly behind the Association. If . . .

"Sylvia, wake up." Once again, Mike broke into Sylvia's speculations. "Where were you, huh? You had your head up in the clouds, maybe?"

Sylvia, silently reciting the day and date, turned back to Mike with her own question: "Tell me what went wrong tonight, Mike. You'll know, if anyone does."

"Too much waiting for the cop, Sylvia. Too much waiting for someone else to come and save us."

"He's an ex-cop, Mike," Annie said. "He doesn't actually have a badge."

"My point exactly. To come and help us like this . . . I gotta say he's a *mensch*, naturally. But that don't give him no more right to say what goes in this building, than we do. I seen it all happen before. I seen the big *machers* kiss Hitler's ass. 'Oh, please, Mr. Hitler, don't attack my country. I'll be a good boy.' I seen how, when the garment workers went over to the unions, some of the workers said, 'Trust the boss, kiss his ass and he'll let us keep our jobs.' Okay, I'm an old man, but I'm not yet such a Chelmite I could swallow that baloney. What I say is break a few heads now, before it's too late. We got nearly thirty apartments empty. How many more gotta be empty before the dope addicts start using the Jackson Arms for a hotel? Break heads and throw the scum out."

Even as Mike Birnbaum defended his position, Rose Carillo and Betty Haluka, twenty-five miles away on the Lower East Side of Manhattan, were toasting Stanley Moodrow's success. All three waited for Jim Tilley, who was delayed (as usual, according to Rose) by paperwork at Central Booking. Betty and Rose were drinking mimosas, a blend of orange juice and champagne that Moodrow, committed to a cloudy brown slop marketed as Oldfield's Wild Turkey Bourbon, refused even to look at.

"What you're drinking ain't alcohol," he explained, sipping at his own drink. "It's not even a color alcohol could be. That's a color rich people paint on their bedroom walls."

"We're toasting you anyway, Stanley," Rose said.

"Right," Betty echoed. "To your victory in Jackson Heights. May it be the first of many."

"It was no big deal," Moodrow protested. "If it wasn't for Betty's personal interest, I wouldn't even mention it." They were seated together, he and Betty, on a couch in Rose's living room and Moodrow turned to look at her. "I shouldn't really say this, but what's going on in your aunt's building is everyday life for a lot of the people who live in this city. Not that I'm putting your aunt down. Your aunt is a nice lady and I gotta admit she's got heart. Like you and Rose. But that don't make me a hero." His eyes wandered across Betty's features—the strong nose, full lips, prominent jaw. There wasn't an inch of surrender in her face. Not an inch.

"But how about what you did for Betty's client? And for me before that? And for a hundred people before that?" Rose cut a thin slice of Gruyère and placed it on a cracker before handing it to Moodrow. In spite of her longterm (and Betty's recent) attempts to civilize him, Moodrow insisted on stuffing three or four different kinds of cheese, smothered with Pulaski's Dark Mustard, between the largest crackers on the platter. Inevitably, when he bit down on the mess, crumbs drifted over his suit while little jets of mustard dribbled onto the tips of his fingers. "Face it, Stanley, you're a hero. You've always been a hero."

"Your husband calls me 'Don Moodrow,' " Moodrow snorted. He was working on his fourth drink. "He thinks I got a complex."

"What's a 'complex'?" Rose asked.

"That's what they called obsessions in 1950," Betty returned, squeezing Moodrow's hand. She was pleased with him, both as a lover and an ally, and very grateful for the help he'd given to her aunt. Betty had been inside the bureaucracy for so long, people who could actually accomplish things were as exotic to her as creatures from Mars.

"What about the prostitutes?" Rose asked.

"I told the one, Connie, to let her pimp know I'll be paying them a visit in the very near future," Moodrow replied. "What I'm hoping to do is inform prospective perps that the Jackson Arms has an angel looking out for it. It's like putting an extra lock on your door. Maybe it won't keep out a master thief, but if you don't have anything a master wants, the rest of the bums'll go look for easier prey. Likewise, if I make it tough for the drug dealers, they'll find a market that's easier to crack. Get it? Crack?"

TEN

STEVEN HOROWITZ, like Born Miller, had always been an opportunistic thief; he stole whenever the possibility of theft existed. But, unlike Born Miller, Steven had matured of late, refining his operation to the point where he was in danger of developing an m.o. His specialty now was credit card fraud; he bought counterfeit cards (bearing real numbers), along with supplementary identification, from a small printer on 49th Street, in Hell's Kitchen, and used them in suburban malls throughout Long Island, Westchester, and New Jersey. Which is how he became Steven Horowitz; it was the name on the VISA he was currently using and matched his identification. His real name was Saul Merstein, but his legal name (the name which underlay his various incarcerations) was Scott Forrest; he'd changed it when he was 19.

Despite an occasional indulgence (for recreational purposes only) in the kind of quick hit that had characterized the beginnings of his career, Steven was satisfied with his present trade. It paid well and involved little risk. The cards cost seven hundred dollars (five hundred, if he brought in his own numbers) and were guaranteed to have three thousand in credit. Most had a good deal more, but no card, not even that ten-thousand-dollar American Express back in November, had resisted Steve's attempts to find its credit limit for more than three days.

Usually, the hit was limited to a single item with a four- to five-hundred-dollar pricetag—videocassette players, gold chains, good watches. Steven, smiling his golden smile, would flirt with the salesgirls while they processed his charge. He could afford to flaunt it, because he wouldn't be the one coming back to return the merchandise. His partner, Louella Walters, two hundred pounds of indignant black fury, made the returns. Louella could make a sales clerk break out in hives.

"Mah momma gimme this watch on my birthday and I do not want the mother-fucker. Now please make out yo fuckin' slip and hand me my money. You makin' a mistake if you think you gon' mess with *my* money."

It didn't always work. Many of the stores *never* made cash returns on charged merchandise. Others only returned cash for low-ticket items. Louella handled these situations either by direct sales to dozens of neighbors for about three quarters of the ticket price or, if they needed money quickly, by dumping the goods on a forty-cents-to-a-dollar fence.

They'd been working the scam successfully since the day Steven was released from the Men's House of Detention, in Brooklyn, where Steven had the good fortune to share a cell with Louella Walters' boyfriend, Darryl Porter. It was Darryl who'd turned him on to the credit card scam. Darryl Porter who'd explained the value of the black–white partnership. Darryl Porter who'd taught Steven about crime and the life.

Steven Horowitz was no fool. The scam was a gift and when he, like Born Miller, beat the rap (the good judge had taken one look at Steven's golden smile, his small, straight nose, his respectably cheap gray suit and dealt him five years probation), he went directly to Louella Walters' modest home in St. Albans, Queens, and applied for work.

And that was, of course, another difference between Steven Horowitz and Born Miller. Because Steven was a freshly scrubbed, clean-cut, whiter-than-white honkey whose good looks had (so far) survived the ravages of an advanced heroin/cocaine/alcohol cross-addiction, he was able to rise above the avalanche of harsh sentences typifying the new severity in law enforcement. Steven, like Born Miller, had spent his whole life with his middle finger in society's rectum, but society was more than willing to give Steven Horowitz another chance. That's why he was out on the street clearing nearly a grand a day. More than enough to afford what he wanted from life: dope to make his eyes sparkle; coke to make his smile widen; alcohol to make him fearless. And vicious.

He was certainly flush when he came into the Jackson Arms, pushing past the broken door locks. Flush and looking to party on the good dope and crack he'd been copping in 4B. Like Born Miller, he was surprised by the neighborhood, but he wasn't threatened by the middle-class couple who pushed past him as he went toward the elevator. Whereas Born Miller had frozen in near panic, Steven turned up the golden smile and got a smile in return. Not surprising, considering his disguise: navy down parka, ski cap with small, white tassel, pressed khaki trousers, scuffed cordovan penny loafers. He felt good and looked good and that's exactly how the public saw him.

Unfortunately, Steven's good feelings took a major downturn when nobody answered his repeated knocks on the door of 4B. He put his ear to the door, hoping for the sound of a running shower, but everything was quiet.

"C'mon, ya little gook, answer the fucking door," he said, slapping it with the palm of his hand. "C'mon, Vallone, take the spike outta ya fuckin' arm and lemme in."

Steven's impatience had nothing to do with any impending symptoms of drug withdrawal. Unlike Born Miller, his addictions, though well-developed, were under control; he even kept a bottle of prescription Dilaudids in his medicine chest as a kind of health insurance. Besides, he could go to any of a dozen places in Corona or South Jamaica to get what he needed. What bothered Steven was the certainty that, wherever he went, he wouldn't get anything like the quality available in 4B, especially the coke which was unreal in its intensity.

"Anyone helping you?"

Steven spun on his heel, automatically flashing a confused smile. "I'm looking for my auntie's apartment. Her name's Weinstein."

"Yeah?" Pat Sheehan had been chasing junkies away from 4B ever since Moodrow had evicted the tenants. At first, it was a labor of love, but he was getting tired of it. He drove ten-hour shifts for United Parcel and took care of his partner when he was home. Louis had been running high fevers in the evening, fevers that responded to the prompt administration of ice packs and alcohol rubs. "Well, there's no dope in your auntie's apartment, pal. The cops closed down the store."

"Pardon?" Steven Horowitz knew, of course, that he was dealing with a fellow graduate of New York's penal system. But the guy had some kind of hard-on and Steven figured him for an asshole trying to go straight.

"The store is closed," Pat repeated. "Permanently closed by order of the police. So it'd be best if you stopped bangin' on the door and took off."

Steven Horowitz wasn't afraid, though he found Pat Sheehan formidable; he'd functioned in far worse situations. On the other hand, though he held on to his smile, Steven *was* absolutely enraged. His first instinct was to smash the smaller man, to crush him, but as an experienced opportunistic thief, he knew there was no opportunity in an even contest. It wasn't like jail where you had no place to retreat to. "Hey, man," he said, "I'm just lookin' to get high. You know how it is, right?" He continued to smile as he turned, not toward the elevator, but toward the stairwell.

Steven was almost down to the next level before he stopped to compose himself. The flip, from soon-to-be-stoned criminal to humiliated, retreating junkie, had been much too sudden; it only added to his need for drugs. But there was no sense in going out on the street with a bad attitude, either. The first thing he had to consider was how to get high. He was tempted to settle for a crackhouse on 105th Street, in Corona. It was only ten minutes away, but the crack in Corona was all comeback and he would probably have to go inside to buy it. If he drove to the Liberty Park Houses, in South Jamaica, on the other hand, his regular people would come up to the car. And the crack was clean, pure cocaine; the dope reasonably potent; the home he was sharing with Louella less than twenty minutes away. Fuck the faggot upstairs. Nothing would prevent him from enjoying the fruits of his labor.

When a thoroughly calmed Steven Horowitz stepped into the third floor corridor, the first thing he noticed was the open door to apartment 3H. As this (and not a fistfight with a rock-hard Pat Sheehan) was what he defined as opportunity, he walked over to take a closer look. He was in the mood to indulge his nostalgia for the old days, when his criminal career consisted entirely of taking things directly from their owners. But the apartment was stripped and empty, the floors strewn with the odds and ends of moving: torn boxes, pieces of tape, chunks of packing.

With a barely perceptible shrug, Steven started to turn away, then heard the elevator clank to a stop and the door wheeze open. The old man who stepped out did such a double take upon sighting him, that Steven nearly laughed, but Steven, even while his mind worked furiously to analyze the potential for opportunity, managed to control himself. Instead of laughing, he flashed his brightest golden smile.

"Hi," he said, drifting back to a conversation with Darryl Porter in which Darryl had explained the philosophy and the technique of the push-in, a form of robbery that could be done without weapons if the victim was old enough to guarantee control. Control. Steven could hear Darryl's high, sharp voice even as he measured Mike Birnbaum.

Can you control the vic? That's the first rule. You gon' be with the vic a long time, so you best be able to control him.

"And what could I do for you?" Mike Birnbaum asked. Mike had never liked golden smiles.

"Looks like we're gonna be neighbors," Steven said. "My name's Steven Horowitz."

Can you get the vic in his apartment 'thout bein' seen? Don' forget, if some nigger see you go inside, he prolly gon' do his nine one one bit and you still be fuckin' with the vic when the man come to bust yo ass.

"What kind of name is that for a Jew? Steven?" Despite the sarcastic tone of his reply, Mike Birnbaum was more than happy to discover that his new neighbor would be a clean-cut Jewish boy instead of the black drug dealer he expected.

"My parents wanted me to be a good American," he countered with a shrug. "You should pardon the expression." Steven Horowitz, born Saul Merstein and legally Scott Forrest, was amazed; he'd thought the old Jews had died out long ago. The little mousey ones who gave their kid names like Izzy and the sharp-tongued whiners who soaked up that slimy fish like it was caviar? They were supposed to be long gone.

Suddenly, he was pissed-off again. The night had been shitting all over him, but now he had an opportunity to get even. And to make a few dollars.

Who know how much the poppy love got in his mattress? One time ah catch this ol' nigger come pushin' her shoppin' cart with the house keys in her hand. Man, she look like she sleep in the subway. Smell like piss. Ah figure ah'm lucky if she got ten bucks. Turns out she got her "sick money" in a stocking in the back of her closet. Twelve hundred fifty-five dollars. Ah was jus' comin' out the institution and that "sick money" set me up in bidness.

"So when do you move in?" Mike turned the key in the lock and pushed his door open. He was a thrifty man and had remembered to put out the lights before he left. The rooms within, Steven Horowitz noted, were dark.

Is there anybody in there waitin'? Sometime you be pushin' grandma through the door and grandson be there with a damn baseball bat. Put "Louisville Slugger" all over yo ass.

"I think I'll move in now," Steven said quietly.

"Without no furniture?"

"You got furniture. You got enough for both of us."

Mike Birnbaum, despite his bravado, was an old man; when Steven Horowitz, by way of fulfilling the name given to this crime, pushed Mike into his apartment, he seemed to fly down the darkened corridor, thus covering requirements number one, two, and three. The prey was under control. Nobody had seen. The apartment was unguarded.

Do the vic know y'all mean bidness? Don't let there be no doubt. You fiend that vic till he understand the onliest way you gittin' outta there is if he come across wit' the goods.

Steven read the fear in Mike Birnbaum's face even before he turned the old man over and pulled him to his feet. Steven had seen it many times in the Brooklyn House of Detention, seen a kid so shitass panicked he'd open his mouth before the wolf had his cock out. Steven could smell that fear in the old Jew, but he drove his fist into the Jew's face anyway. Three times. And the frail hand that floated up protectively was no more than a fly to be brushed away.

Do you know what you lookin' for? Can't be spendin' all day hangin' on to the vic. Make yo move and get out. Make the poppy love tell you where he got the shit hid, cause he know if he don't, you gon' kill him.

"How do you want this, old man? Because we could do this the easy way or the hard way. You know what I'm sayin'? Like I don't give a shit how we do it. Like I hope you make me hurt you. Like you're just an old fuckin' kike who shoulda dropped dead ten years ago. Like they shoulda burned your ass in the motherfuckin' ovens."

ELEVEN

IT was just after five o'clock on a weekday afternoon and it was snowing hard in New York. Not a blizzard, by any means; just a brief, intense, snow shower as the temperature began a sudden drop from the mid-thirties to the mid-teens. The warm streets and sidewalks were turning the snowflakes to water as soon as they touched down and, far from a winter wonderland, the black pavement seemed even blacker as the moisture lifted road oils from the tarry surface as deftly as a Crime Scene detective lifts fingerprints from glass.

For most of New York, committed to subway and feet, the snow was a pleasant diversion that would disappear by morning. A minor incident to enliven the coffee break, but not enough to slow the city's nightlife for a second. On the other hand, for the drivers of the eighty thousand cars, trucks, and buses that invade Manhattan every day, the first swirl of snowflakes was sufficient cause for out-and-out panic. The commuters from New Jersey, Westchester, Connecticut, and Long Island resolved their business as early as possible and rushed for their cars (or their limos) at almost exactly the same time. Similarly, the truckers who feed the monster skyscrapers rushed through their deliveries, then dashed toward the bridges and tunnels just as the suburbanites wheeled their BMWs out of four-hundred-dollar-a-month parking spaces.

The result, as usual, was chaos and Marty Blanks, along with Steven and Mikey Powell, his two bodyguards, was trapped in the worst of it. Blanks was headed south on what was left of the old West Side Highway; he was on his way to Brooklyn Heights and a business meeting with his partner, Marek Najowski, but he was getting absolutely nowhere. Mikey Powell was driving, his brother alongside, while Blanks, lost in thought, had the backseat to himself. The brothers were furious, the long line of gray cars stretching out through the snowstorm forcing them to deal with frustration when they'd lived their lives by smashing anything that annoyed them. Marty Blanks, on the other hand, having spent nearly twenty of his thirty-one years in institutions, felt no anxiety whatsoever. He'd long ago adopted the prison cliche that "what doesn't kill me makes me stronger" as a driving force in his life. While the Powell brothers fumed silently (they knew better than to vocalize their annoyance in front of their boss), Marty Blanks leaned against the leather seat and relaxed.

"Hey, Marty," Mikey Powell thrust himself into his boss's thoughts, "Whatta ya say we take 23rd Street over to the East Side? Try ta get on the bridge from the Drive. We ain't goin' nowhere this way."

"It ain't gonna be no different on the East Side," Blanks protested. "It's snowin'."

"That what I say," Steve Powell, who'd been fighting with his older brother since he could walk, chimed in. "When it snows, everything gets fucked up in New York. We just gotta live with it."

"Yeah, but we don't *know* what's on the East Side," Mikey insisted, his logic irrefutable. "It might be the same or it might be better. It *can't* be no worse." He gestured toward the wall of metal surrounding them. "We ain't moved a hundred yards in the last ten minutes. I don't want ya ta be late, Boss."

"Forget about 'late,' " Blanks replied evenly. "This meeting's gonna be two hours of bullshit and ten minutes of business. I don't even know why I put up with this guy." He settled back against the seat.

"So whatta ya want I should do? Yiz want me ta stay on the West Side or what?"

"Take 23rd across to Ninth Avenue, then cut down to 14th Street. 23rd gets fucked up past Fifth Avenue. Take 14th over to the Drive, but don't hurry. I couldn't give a shit what time I get there."

While Mikey Powell turned the Buick into the 23rd Street Marina, swinging in a circle to face east on 23rd, Blanks settled back to consider the nonsense that awaited him in Brooklyn Heights. Najowski, who couldn't seem to decide whether he was a country squire or one of the boys in a neighborhood bar, would be dressed in some kind of asshole tweed jacket. His shirt would be Irish linen and his flannel trousers slightly wrinkled. He'd be wearing ancient, immaculately shined loafers and checkered argyle socks.

And there'd be a lecture about the "heap," too. About the ones who escape and the ones doomed to remain. About the ones "born to rise" and the ones who give up, who settle for drugs and welfare handouts and baby after baby after baby. Then they'd sit down to a steak and fries dinner served on Wedgwood china. It amused Blanks no end to take a sterling silver fork and use it like a dagger to spear peas. Najowski always pretended not to notice, making allowances for Marty's crude behavior, his foul gutter language. Too arrogant to consider the possibility that his partner hated his guts.

Blanks had long ago resolved someday to alter the contours of Najowski's face. But not until the deal was over; not until their business was concluded. The money and the lure of legitimacy was too big for Blanks to jeopardize the deal. That was the most amazing part—that the money was there to be made with so little personal risk. The attorney he'd finally chosen, Paul O'Brien, a child of Hell's Kitchen with tie-ins to most of the Irish street gangs that ran the West Side docks, had confirmed each facet of Najowski's proposal.

"Lemme put it this way," O'Brien had explained. "Those buildings you're thinking of buying are in pretty good shape, right?"

"Damn good shape," Blanks had replied. "Better than anything in Hell's Kitchen."

"Well, kiddo, think about this: if you could snap your fingers and make those buildings disappear, the vacant lots would be worth more than the lots with the buildings on them. With empty lots you could build and get top dollar whether you go rental or co-op. No rent control. No bullshit. That's why the South Bronx is gonna be the next big area for development. You got hundreds of vacant lots from where the city demolished burned-out buildings. You know what I'm talking about?"

"Do me a favor and spell it out," Blanks had replied. "I need an education, before I get in too deep. Also I hate this scumbag Najowski, and I don't wanna go within fifty feet of him unless the money's right."

O'Brien, who loved to lecture, especially after a few belts, pulled a bottle of Bushmiller's from a desk drawer, poured a double into Marty Blanks' glass, then filled his own to the top. "Okay, let's do it. In the early 70s, for reasons unknown, the city began closing firehouses in poor neighborhoods. They called it 'consolidating,' but the result was slower response time and, of course, greater structural damage to tenements that had been substandard from the beginning. Then the fiscal crisis hit and forty-five hundred firemen were laid off. Marty, it was 'burn, baby, burn' for the next ten years. The South Bronx lost more than a hundred and ten thousand apartments in that period. That means tenements so destroyed the city had to knock 'em down and cart the rubble off. You go to places in Brownsville or the Bronx, and the skyline looks like an old man's mouth. All empty spaces, and that's the kicker. For the last six or seven years, the speculators have been flipping real estate like crazy in the Bronx. Sometimes two or three times in a year. Units worth sixty and seventy thousand a few years ago are trading for three hundred and up. And empty lots are worth more than lots with buildings on them. I tell ya, Marty, the city owns most of those lots and that translates as lost tax revenue. It's only a matter of time until they start auctioning the parcels off. Then the big boys will come north and the South Bronx will enjoy a 'Renaissance.' "

"I don't see what this has to do with me," Blanks had interrupted. "There's no burned-out buildings in Jackson Heights. No vacant lots. We're talkin' about two hundred and forty occupied apartments."

Paul O'Brien had lifted his glass, saluting Marty Blanks, draining the few inches of Irish whiskey left in the glass. His ears and throat had burned red for a moment as the alcohol rushed into his bloodstream, but his hands were steady as he refilled both glasses. "The only point I'm making, is the difference between full and empty. An empty lot is worth more than a lot with occupied apartments. That's the usual condition. But the best imaginable situation, if you stop to think about it, Marty, has got to be a lot with a solid, *empty* building on it, which is what you're shooting for."

Blanks had sipped at his drink, letting the information run through his mind.

He was convinced that the money was right, but there were questions remaining. "What will the cops do if we start harassing the tenants? If we have to make some examples? Are the cops gonna stand by and let it happen?"

Paul O'Brien had shrugged his shoulders. "They didn't do anything about it here. I've been representing landlords in Hell's Kitchen for the last fifteen years and I've seen a lot of players clean up by dumping tenants illegally. For instance, everybody laughed at the landlords who owned the welfare hotels. The ones for male adults. How much money could you make off people on welfare? Well, the tenants in those hotels didn't have any rights under rent control; they were transients and when the building boom got started twenty years ago, the landlords hired every kind of scum to get them out. I'm talking about smashing down doors at five o'clock in the morning and beating some half-delirious alkie into the hospital. I'm talking about fires and robberies and rapes. I'm talking about old men who never left their rooms after dark. Who pushed the bureau up against the door to keep the wolves out.

"The city lost thirty-five thousand rooms before the reporters figured it out and began to put heat on the politicians. That's when the City Council declared a moratorium on demolition of welfare hotels. You know the new hotel on 44th Street? The Macklowe? You know how it got to be built?"

"No idea," Blanks replied shortly.

"Four days before the moratorium went into effect, at midnight, a contractor working for Harry Macklowe knocked down four buildings: two tenements and two hotels. He didn't have any permits; he didn't even have the gas and electricity turned off. The media screamed, but there was no way to put the buildings back up and no criminal charges were ever filed against Harry Macklowe. The city fined him two million bucks and the mayor made him wait two years before he could start construction, but the Hotel Macklowe, all forty-three stories, is standing on 44th Street right now and I guarantee it's worth upwards of a hundred million. Understand what I'm saying? The two hotels and two tenements were worth, at best, a million and a half."

Blanks had been impressed, but he kept his voice neutral. O'Brien was from the neighborhood; he had no reason to lie. The favor of free counsel was a marker that could always be called in and Blanks had been well aware of it.

"I gotta ask you one more question," Blanks said. "There's somethin' that's botherin' me. You seem to be advising me to do this deal, but I keep readin' in the papers that you can't sell real estate in New York. What I gotta ask myself is why I should put large money into a scene that ain't happenin'?"

O'Brien, much to Blanks' surprise, laughed out loud. "What's going on out there has nothing to do with your project," he'd said. "New York City has a two percent vacancy on rentals. The only way to get a decent apartment in a neighborhood you're not scared to live in is to *buy* it. So what if it takes you a year to sell the apartments instead of six months? We're talking about twenty million dollars. Also, you have to figure it'll be two years minimum before the assholes are out of there and the paperwork with the state is completed. Recessions don't last long in this country. They make voters crazy."

Blanks finally broke into a smile. "I guess the only question left is if the middle-class tenants in Jackson Heights are gonna run like a bunch of alkies on welfare."

The dinner went almost entirely as expected, the only special touch being the black woman, Marie, who cooked and served the meal. Najowski smiled each time she appeared in the kitchen doorway, then flashed Blanks a conspiratorial glance. Blanks returned the look evenly, but noted the tracks on Marie's arms and the fact that, instead of an ordinary maid's uniform, she was dressed in a torn black housecoat and never raised her eyes from the floor. After some consideration, he made her for an expensive hooker specializing in what the trade calls "freak shows." He wasn't surprised to discover that his partner was a freak, but he didn't shy away from his own conviction that doing business with freaks was a dangerous way to make a living.

"Has my servant caught your interest?" Marek asked as the coffee was served. "Stay here a moment, Marie."

"What you do is your business," Blanks replied. He could sense what was coming and he didn't want to watch. He'd always believed the only way to rape a prostitute was to hold back payment. Now he was learning otherwise.

"This," Marek said dramatically, gesturing to Marie, "is the absolute bottom: the drug-addicted Negro whore. All dignity gone and no thought beyond her next fix. When I fuck her, I use two condoms and rubber gloves. Am I right, or what, Marie?"

"Yessir," Marie responded softly. "Yessir. You're right."

Blanks finally glanced at the prostitute. She was standing quietly, eyes on the floor and her face showed nothing of what she was feeling. Blanks looked at her arms again—the needle scars were old and healed. How much was Najowski paying her? Four hundred? Five hundred? Suddenly, Blanks got a glimpse of the self-indulgence at the bottom of Marek's use of the woman. It sickened him.

"Now I don't want you to think I'm prejudiced against Negroes," Marek grinned. "It is true, of course, that the Negro sits at the absolute bottom of the American heap. But when French Aristocrats and Roman Senators spoke of 'the mob,' they were talking about white people. In fact, I'd go so far as to say you could define 'the mob' by watching the crowd at a British soccer match. It's just an accident that the Negroes collect all the welfare and commit all the crimes in America. Isn't that right, Marie?"

"Yessir. You right, sir."

"You're a good woman, Marie. You're a credit to your heap. Now, go into the bedroom and wait for me. I shouldn't be too long. At least," he winked at Marty Blanks, "not as long as the ones *you're* used to."

Marek waited until the prostitute was gone before he began his report. "There's good news and bad news," he said quietly. "We've got thirty-five empty apartments. Nearly halfway there. On the other hand, the dealers you set up in 4B took off a few days ago. They were chased out."

"This I know already," Blanks replied. "I saw one of the guys in the neighborhood the next day. He says it was a cop that put the heat on, but he didn't actually see a badge. Anyway it don't mean shit. In fact it's better for us."

"Tell me how." Najowski, settled down to business, showed no trace of the friendly worker. His investment was much larger than Martin Blanks', especially considering how long it would take him to replace it should the deal go bad. Their goal was empty apartments, but empty apartments don't pay rent. They'd be operating in the red within weeks.

"I made a mistake when I spoke to them personally. Lucky for us the cop was too stupid to ask how they got there in the first place. He washed the dope down the sink, busted up the furniture and slapped them around, but he never asked who set them up. From here on in, I'm gonna go through other people. And not even the same people all the time. Meanwhile, I need seven apartment numbers. I got people set to go in. Squatters, alkies, dopers, crazies—you name it, it's gonna be livin' in Jackson Heights."

Najowski smiled for the first time. "How'd you do this so fast?"

"Don't worry about how I do my end of the deal. You asked for pressure and that's what I'm gonna deliver."

"I'm not trying to pry," Najowski said sharply, then immediately softened his tone. "You think these people will stay? What if the cop tries to drive them off?"

"That's the best part. The guy who's leading them in, Kricic, is political. He's been involved with squatters all through Hell's Kitchen and the Lower East Side and nearly came in his pants when he heard about empty apartments in a middle-class neighborhood. Anybody tries to evict is gonna have to do it in front of a TV camera."

"And this man, Kricic, is bringing dealers with him?"

"No. He's only bringing two families. But when he gets there, he'll defend everyone. At least until he figures out what's goin' on. It don't matter, anyway, 'cause you're gonna serve 'em all with eviction notices in a couple of weeks. It's gonna be like a revolving door, with more comin' in than goin' out. Now, how 'bout you tell me your end."

"I had the lawyer, Bill Holtz, go through the leases with Rosenkrantz. They picked out twenty tenants they think might run and served them with eviction notices. Little things—late payments, failure to keep the property up, failure to allow the landlord access. Nothing that'll hold up in court, but we'll get postponements, refuse to accept rent, claim we weren't paid. A lot of these people don't speak English very well. They come from countries where cops make people disappear forever. Some of them will run."

"We losin' money yet?" Blanks changed the subject.

"Not yet. But next month's receipts won't cover the bills."

"You got credit lined up?"

"Holtz has an Arkansas S&L willing to keep us going. As long as we stay on schedule."

"We're ahead of schedule right now and I haven't even started putting on the pressure. What about the tenants' association?"

Najowski shrugged. He didn't like being questioned, but Blanks' commitment to the project was more than welcome. "They got some kind of patrol going, but they weren't able to organize the building. Mostly due to Rosenkrantz. That guy could sell tanning oil to a Negro."

"Enough with the jokes. My boys're waitin' for me in the car and they're probly gettin' restless. I wouldn't wanna miss my ride."

"The attack on the old Jew, Birnbaum, will bring some of them into Sylvia Kaufman's circle. She's the one who organized the tenants. But that doesn't mean they won't run. The Pakis are almost completely cleared out. A bunch of Koreans went with Park and the rest are getting ready to fly. The spics are too macho to be intimidated. They'll probably go over to Kaufman."

"Only until I get some blown-out rapo to fuck one of their daughters up the ass. I'm workin' hard on that right now. And I got a little surprise for the tenants' association, too." Blanks stood up and went to the closet for his coat. "But enough is enough," he announced. "Everything's goin' smooth. I don't think them faggots'll hold out for more than a couple of months." He shrugged into his coat, then turned back to his partner. "And, by the way, next meetin', how 'bout you come to me? The traffic gettin' out here is murder."

TWELVE

MARIE PORTER hated doing the Freak. That's the way she thought of him, even though *all* her clients were freaks; even though everyone in the life called them freaks. Even though what she did was shows for the freaks, performances, and the only limits professionals like herself were supposed to put on the freaks involved pain, both giving and receiving. The saddest part was that Marie usually thought of her customers by their first names. She *liked* her clients, but the Freak was the Freak and always would be.

Not that she'd outright refuse him. That would disappoint her pimp, George

Wang. George Wang was her savior. He'd spotted her when she was working Madison Avenue, too dark to play the ingenue despite being sixteen years old.

Marie had begun her street life as a throw-away: her mother had locked her out of the family apartment when she was fifteen. For a year, she'd lived with relatives, attended school, struggled to stay alive. Then an uncle had introduced her, first to the serenity of heroin and then to what all prostitutes call "the life."

Within a month she was the property of a pimp named Hector Cortez. Hector, called Poppy, specialized in teenage flesh, male and female, and kept his workers diligent with the lit ends of Marlboro cigarettes. In his estimation, teenagers were prone to run off unless properly terrorized.

Marie, who was more than properly terrorized, had seen no way out, and thus George Wang's coming had been nothing short of miraculous, though many in the life would have thought it a routine piece of business.

"I see you on street and I think you very beautiful." He had been very elegant in an off-white, double-breasted, linen suit with matching tie and Marie had been properly impressed. With his narrow eyes and thin drooping mustache, George Wang looked as if he'd just walked off the set of a 40s gangster movie. "Got wonderful body—no fat, but not too hard. Very smooth skin. Very pretty. Then I think this girl in wrong end of business. This girl very dark skin. Customer think she just another black whore. They mostly want blond virgin from Iowa. You know this true?"

Marie had laughed, sipping at a cup of coffee. They were in a diner near the Triboro Bridge, in Astoria. Far from Poppy Cortez. "Man, I'm tellin' ya . . . Them johns all look for that baby-white pussy. Balder the better. White bitches shave the pussy, then flash the trick. Can't say as I blame 'em. If the trick think you near to bein' cherry, he comin' up with fifty like puttin' a quarter in the phone. Me, I gotta fight for a twenty-dollar blow-job. And I'm still young. What's gonna happen when I'm thirty?"

"Good." George Wang had taken Marie's hand and pulled it toward him, stroking the jet-black skin. It didn't seem possible for flesh that black to be so reflective, yet her teenage body glowed with vitality. "Exactly so. You understanding make my job very easy. I have customer alla time ask for black-skin girl. They think dark girl exotic. Pay plenty. You never get this from street pimp. My customers all scared of street pimp. They think old Chinaman very safe."

Marie had withdrawn her hand, placing it firmly in her lap. "You nice, pops, but don't handle the merchandise, 'less you buyin.' Now tell me what I gotta do before these rich 'customers' part with the big bucks."

"How many way you can fuck?" George Wang had asked. "Once you do sex in three holes, you finished. No more place to put it. Street whore sell all three holes, so why street whore get forty dollars and my whore get two hundred? Secret is not in fucking at all. All extra money earned before fucking start. You understand this?"

"Shit, pops, my man say, 'Get 'em in and out as fast as you can.' He believes in volume."

"Pimp is correct. If you only getting thirty dollar, you must do many tricks. But what if you get three hundred dollar? Then you no have to rush. Then you take your time. My girls all performer. Fucking is shortest part of way they turn trick. If you want, I give you apartment uptown. Ninety and York. Doorman building. First three months you only go out with other girl maybe one time each week. I train you to become actress. Customers all want fantasy. You must learn to give them fantasy the way you give pussy on street. As long as customer pay, you never hold back. You think you can learn this?"

Marie had nodded solemnly. "I can learn, pops. But what's in it for me?"

"My name ain't 'Pops,' you little asshole. My name is George Wang and that's what you'll call me."

Marie looked into the pimp's black eyes, catching a glimpse of the iron will sitting patiently behind the frail exterior. "What happened to your accent?" she asked lamely.

"What'd I tell you before? About the customers and their fantasies? The accent is for the assholes. There's nothing these stockbrokers like more than having a chinky sell them pussy. They think it's cute, something to brag about at Harry's Bar after work." He paused to let the point sink in. "We split everything fifty-fifty, but I guarantee you'll make a grand a week after three months. If you don't get it off the customers, I make up the difference. You on dope?"

"Yeah," Marie had admitted. "But it's just a chippy. I ain't strung out or nothin'."

"I get you dope and needles. Good quality. Reliable. I don't give a shit about your personal life, but if you get too fucked up to work, you're out on your ass. In fact, that's the penalty if you break any rule." He sipped at his drink, waiting for a question or a protest, but Marie, utterly amazed by his transformation, kept her mouth shut. "The rules are very simple. You take a job, you make the customer happy. That means you show up on time and make the customer believe his fantasy has come to life. All your assignments come from me. You do private business and I throw you out. You even take a phone number and I throw you out. That's the rules: make the customer happy and don't fuck me over. You accept, I'm gonna make you rich."

As it turned out, many of her customers were women. Rich white women. They virtually always went the same way. She played a maid (a maid wearing blazing red bra and panties under a translucent black uniform) who seduces her mistress. And seduce them she did; she took them in the bedroom, the kitchen, the laundry room, the attic, the bathtub (they went nuts when she soaped their backs, her hand slowly dropping, dropping . . .). She did them with vacuum cleaners, broom handles, scrubbing brushes, towels, washcloths— anything that came to hand. And she did them until they couldn't take any more.

They were marvelously easy, so into the fantasy they shivered when she brushed against them and cried when they came. Then, of course, they'd pull her back onto the bed, pushing her legs up into her chest, devouring her.

Curiously, none, no matter how inept, ever failed to bring forth Marie's deepest, loudest, most professional orgasm.

The men, on the other hand, usually wanted humiliation. Wanted her in leather and stainless steel, cursing them, forcing them into one demeaning act after another. They'd get *so* hot. Begging her to get them off. And she would, finally. After they'd proven themselves worthy, she'd run her fingers down the length of their bellies, take them in her hand. It was all they needed.

These days, George Wang always referred to Marie as "my best." Even when she was working with another girl. And Marie was perfectly willing to allow the pimp to think of her as property. What counted was that he never touched her, that she could walk out whenever she wished, that her money was in a bank in her own name. A pro, as George Wang had explained on many occasions, helps the tricks retain their fantasies and George Wang, though she was infinitely grateful to him, was Marie's ultimate trick.

The only dark shadow in Marie's career (besides the Freak) had been her drug habit. Initially, her habit had kept pace with her economic success. But after a year of expansion, she had realized that dope, if left unchecked, would drive her back onto the streets (and into the hands of another Poppy Cortez). She was too tough for that. Too accustomed to being her own woman. With George Wang's encouragement, she enrolled in a residential treatment program at Barclay Hospital in a rural corner of Albany County. The doctors at Barclay put her on a thirty-day methadone withdrawal program. The first day, they gave her enough methadone to satisfy her craving for heroin. The second day, they gave her a little less. She was ready to climb the walls on more than one occasion, but it never became impossible to bear and by the time the program was completed, her habit was gone.

And that's the way it stayed. In control. Just like her life was in control. Marie was able to see her prostitution as a kind of scam, a hustle she was putting on the trick. In a way, sex was her ultimate triumph. Except for the Freak. The Freak got the better of her. Whenever Marie left his apartment, she felt cheated, even though George Wang assured her that the four-fifty they were getting was proper compensation for the services she provided.

"You forgot about the customers who scream 'Nigger' while you whip them? You forgot about the customers who say the same thing while *they* whip you?"

"They don't hurt you. All they want is to get off."

"How does Marek hurt you? You serve dinner, you fuck him, you go home. Where's the hurt?"

"It's not that easy. I go there in rags. I play the part of his slave. He ridicules me in front of his friends."

"They don't touch you, do they? We'd have to get more money for that."

"The laughing is worse than being touched. I'm not even allowed to look up. I have to keep my eyes on the damned carpet. Have to say 'Yes, sir' and 'No, sir.' Serve his shitty dinner. He gives me long lectures about 'Negroes' and the crimes they commit and the drugs they use. He tells me the whole country is standing on my back and he keeps me around to remind him of the bottom. He keeps me around for inspiration."

"Make sense, Marie. I send you to a house where you scrub the toilet on your knees, then give head to a sixty-year-old white woman. That doesn't bother you at all . . ."

"Mrs. Blum loves me. After we finish, she serves me pastries and coffee. Tells me about her wicked grandchildren. You're a smart man, George Wang, but you don't know shit about tricks."

"Don't say 'trick.'" He waved a long bony finger. "Trick is a street word. You're not on the street. You call them customers. Then maybe you'll understand. Look, if you were selling lettuce, you wouldn't give a shit about the character of your customers as long as they didn't threaten you with violence. It should be exactly the same when you sell pussy."

"Well, the Freak could hurt me," Marie insisted. "I have no doubt the Freak could hurt me. The Freak wears five-hundred-dollar sport jackets, but he has the eyes of a mugger. Redneck eyes that hate everything they see."

George Wang threw up his hands. "You've been with him more than thirty times and he's never laid a hand on you. He doesn't even go with other whores. In fact," George Wang grinned, "I think Marek's in love with you. You should be flattered."

Marie sighed impatiently. "I never minded when other tricks called me a nigger or a black whore, because they were in a fantasy and the fantasy was no truer than their ordinary polite lives. But . . ."

"Too much college," George Wang interrupted. He considered himself an expert at appraising a customer's potential violence and he found the Freak perfectly acceptable.

"Just let me talk for a while. All right? You listen, for a change. The Freak isn't in a fantasy. He's not pretending, either."

"But did he ever hurt you?" George Wang was getting sick of the conversation.

"No. He pinches me, shows me his strength, but never quite hurts me."

"Look, if you're determined to give him up, I'll back you on it. You know that, Marie. I'm only asking you to give it a little while longer. After all, the smart response to a repulsive trick is to up the ante. We're getting four-fifty out of him. Let's increase it a hundred bucks and see what happens. I mean if you look at him the right way, you'll see that he's just a poor slob who has to buy his pussy. Like every other john in the trade."

THIRTEEN

"I DON'T believe this," Moodrow said, waving his hands at the empty road in front of him and his girlfriend, Betty Haluka. "It's six o'clock in the afternoon and the road's empty."

"Mike Birnbaum wasn't your fault," Betty replied. She was sitting close to him, one hand laid casually on his knee.

"I wasn't talking about Mike Birnbaum," Moodrow snapped. "I was talking about the damned road; I figured an hour and a half for the ride and we'll be there in fifteen minutes. On the Brooklyn–Queens Expressway. It's unbelievable."

"It's not unbelievable," Betty insisted. "It snowed this morning."

"What's that got to do with it?"

"If it snows in the early morning, the commuters take the subway. Then the snow melts and the evening rush is easy. I thought everybody knew that."

They were riding in Betty's 1982 Honda Civic. At Betty's request, Moodrow was driving, somehow manipulating the tiny pedals despite being twisted into his seat like a sponge in the mouth of a bottle. His head was pressed against the roof of the car, with only a narrow brimmed fedora to cushion the potholes (placed with all the wonderful randomness of a minefield) carpeting the roadway.

"I guess you're right," Moodrow finally answered. "That's the only thing it could be. It was snowing pretty heavy around seven this morning. The commuters must've got scared off by the traffic and left their cars home. Then the snow turned to rain and now there's nothing left. All the driving I done, I shoulda known about that."

Betty smiled, squeezing closer. "People from Manhattan never understand about traffic in the boroughs. In fact, they don't usually admit that there *are* boroughs. Even cops who come out here all the time. Besides, Mike Birnbaum wasn't your fault."

"Jesus, Betty." Moodrow sighed, shaking his head. "We oughta let that go."

"I think you're blaming yourself," Betty insisted. "There was nothing you could have done short of moving a cot into the lobby."

Moodrow took his time answering. The Honda didn't have much acceleration and Moodrow, who wanted to pass a creeping garbage truck, was trying to press the Honda's gas pedal to the floor without catching the edge of his shoe on the brake, a task that was momentarily commanding all his attention. "The thing is," he finally said, "that I don't really *know* that I'm not responsible. It's possible that I screwed it up. Maybe I should have been stronger with the junkies I threw out of the building. Maybe there was some other apartment I should have checked out. One thing I learned as a cop is that some of the time it *is* your fault. Especially with crimes like child abuse where the cop who goes to the scene has a lot of discretion. Sometimes they don't make arrests when they should. Sometimes they don't see the signs right in front of their eyes. You tell the captain that the kid looked okay when you saw him three days ago and the captain puts your bullshit in the report, even if the kid is lying in the morgue. But in your heart you know you made a mistake and that someone else paid for it."

They were on their way to the Jackson Arms and an emergency meeting of the tenants' association, but they were nearly an hour early. Betty suggested a coffee shop, but Moodrow asked if she'd mind driving around for a while.

"I don't mind," she responded. "I just thought you might like to get out of the car."

"Driving helps me think," Moodrow shrugged.

"Think about what?"

"Like where this nightmare came from." They were driving on Roosevelt Avenue, under the elevated 7 Train, a "subway" line connecting much of northern Queens to Manhattan. Both sides of the street were lined with businesses. Businesses that sported clean windows and freshly painted signs, that boasted of prosperity in their very facades. Usually, in neighborhoods that were sliding downhill, the cancer grows first in the shadows under the el. The dark spaces conceal the activities of the dealers, the whores, and the hunters. But there were no kids skulking in the alleyways. No adults, either, except for shoppers running in and out of the stores or diners patronizing the many restaurants—Chinese, Korean, Indian, South American—that dotted every block.

"I'll tell you something," Moodrow finally said. "The existence of all these restaurants proves the neighborhood has money. Poor people eat at home."

"What's the point?" Betty asked. "Jackson Heights was always middle-class."

"Then where did they come from? The whores? The two dealers? If they didn't come from the neighborhood, how did they find the empty apartments? Coincidence? Cops hate coincidence, Betty. The idea that it 'just happened' makes cops want to puke."

They were still a half hour early when Moodrow pulled the Honda to the curb across from the Jackson Arms. Several people turned from the sidewalk to enter the building. Working people, obviously making their way home after a late day.

"Betty, you mind going in to your Aunt Sylvia's by yourself? There's someone I need to talk to in an upstairs apartment. I'll probably be finished before the meeting starts."

"I don't mind," Betty said. "You know I can almost *see* your mind going away from me. When you go into your cop mode, you don't have room for anything else."

They parted at the elevator, Moodrow waiting until she was out of sight before pressing the floor button. As the elevator slowly creaked toward the fourth floor, banging repeatedly against the side of the shaft, Moodrow, who'd been sincere when he spoke of being "on duty," was, nevertheless, thinking about Betty Haluka. He'd dated women, unlike Betty, who were outside his caste. Above it, actually. Usually, they were condescending, but occasionally they tiptoed around his feelings like junkies trying to conceal a dime bag of dope. There was never a hint of permanence with any of them. Betty, on the other hand, spoke to him like they were colleagues. Almost like they were both cops.

The elevator door, after a hearty yank by Moodrow, slid open on the fourth floor, and Moodrow walked down the hallway to Pat Sheehan's apartment, noting, out of pure habit, the stairwell between the elevator and the apartment door. He knocked softly on Pat Sheehan's door and, again out of habit, held his breath as he listened for footsteps.

They came promptly—a quick march across the apartment, followed by a chorus of snapping locks. Moodrow knew it wasn't Pat Sheehan; Pat walked much more quietly. Though not alarmed, he eased off to one side of the door, opening his coat to give his hand a path to the worn .38 hanging under his left arm.

"Yessir?" The black woman who opened the door inspected him carefully.

"I'm looking for Pat Sheehan," Moodrow replied. He tried to bluff her with eye contact, but she didn't seem to be impressed.

"Pat ain't home yet," she announced. "He's workin' late."

"What time is he expected?"

"Soon, I hope."

"You're the health aide taking care of Persio, right?"

"That's right." She stood in the doorway, her thick torso firmly planted between him and the interior of the apartment.

"Ask Persio if he'd mind talking to Sergeant Moodrow." He used his former rank deliberately, expecting her, as she did, to step back and make eye contact with Louis Persio. As soon as the door opened far enough to allow him to pass through without pushing against it, Moodrow stepped into the apartment. "How ya feeling, Persio? You look a lot better tonight."

Louis Persio was sitting in an armchair watching the nightly news on a battered Sony. He was, in fact, feeling much better than he had on Moodrow's first visit. Massive doses of antibiotics had broken his fever, destroying the microbes in his throat and lungs. He felt in control of his thoughts for the first time in months.

"It's a temporary condition," he responded, smiling broadly. "This is Marla

Parker, angel of mercy. Marla, this is Moodrow. He's not a sergeant anymore. He retired from the police. Now he just pretends, like the rest of us."

"Pleased to meet you," Moodrow said immediately, extending his hand.

Marla Parker, furious over being fooled, kept her own hand by her side. "I'll be in the bedroom," she said to Persio. "If you need me."

"I have a big problem," Persio announced as soon as the bedroom door closed behind the aide. "For some reason I can't possibly imagine, the landlord, whoever he is, feels that I'm less than a desirable tenant. The bitch sent me a dispossess notice. Can you imagine me appearing in a courtroom? I'd need a makeup man."

"They gotta put down a reason on the notice," Moodrow responded quietly.

"What difference does it make?"

"You want my help?"

"Yes. Not for me. For Pat."

"Well, if you want my help, don't bullshit me. Just tell me what it says on the notice."

Persio pushed himself further up in the chair, the effort bringing sweat to his forehead. He was very serious when he turned back to Moodrow, despite a smile tugging at the corners of his lips. "It says a lot of things. It says I don't keep the place up. That I miss rent payments. That I live an immoral life with an illegal roommate. That my illness poses a health hazard to the other tenants. That I'm a slimy faggot who shouldn't (and needn't) be tolerated by decent human beings."

"That's not a notice," Moodrow observed. "That's a fucking book. Is any of it true?"

Persio's smile finally got the better of him. "Only the last part."

Moodrow, more comfortable here than he would ever be in Sylvia Kaufman's apartment, peeled off his coat and sat on the couch across from Persio. "So whatta ya want from me?" he asked genially.

"First things first," Persio replied. "For some obscure reason, it's been ages since I've been able to assume my Superman identity, so I definitely need your help. But I also understand about the police and *quid pro quo* and, well . . . Pat saw the guy who hit the old man downstairs. We're almost a hundred percent sure, but Pat won't go near the real cops. I swear it's almost a superstition with him. Like not opening umbrellas in the house. But we decided to talk to you. That was Pat's decision. He trusts you."

"You know the details?" Moodrow asked.

"Well, I didn't actually see the man, but Pat spoke to him. Pat'll be home any moment, so what I want to do is talk to you about the eviction before he gets here. I think he'd be angry at what I have to say."

"No problem. Why don't you get it off your chest. I'm probably gonna wait for Pat, anyway, so it won't hurt to pass the time with pleasant conversation."

"There's no way I can appear in court five or ten times to fight this notice. I don't have the strength and Pat knows it. He didn't say what he was going to do, but I'm terrified that he'll go to Rosenkrantz and try to muscle the fat bastard into dropping the eviction. I don't want to see Pat in jail before I die. It's selfish, really, but I don't give a shit—the best I have is a few months and I want Pat with me. I thought maybe you could talk to Rosenkrantz for us."

"I don't mind talking to him for you," Moodrow answered. "But I'm not a cop anymore. Even if I was, there wouldn't be any way I could influence a straight guy like this."

"Please. Do the best you can. I don't have the energy to fight this."

Moodrow held up his hand. "Okay. I get the point. I'll make a definite effort to get the landlord to pull his bullshit eviction notice. Now you wanna tell me about the mugging or do we have to wait for Pat?"

"We already decided to help you," Persio explained. "Pat and me know what's going on in the building and the people here don't deserve it. I mean we'll never really be part of the building. Not two gay ex-cons in Jackson Heights. But this is a community. A very, very *straight* community, true, but a community nonetheless. What's going on here is a crime . . ."

"Look, Louis, I'm in a little bit of a hurry. There's a meeting about to start downstairs and I wanna listen to what the tenants have to say. Why don't you fill me in on what you know. I can always talk to Pat later."

"Fine with me," Persio shrugged. "Pat saw the guy right before Birnbaum was attacked. The guy was banging on the door where you threw out the dealers. In fact, there was a whole procession of customers and mostly we ignored them, but this asshole kept banging away and Pat finally went out in the hall. He made the guy for a junkie with money, maybe even a part-time user. Pat told him, in a fairly nice way, that the dealers were gone and he should be gone, too. Now tell me if this isn't the icing on the cake? The asshole gets so turned around, he goes down the stairs instead of the elevator. Those stairs open onto the third floor within twenty feet of the old man's apartment. I mean it *has* to be the same guy."

"You said the man was there to buy drugs? How do you know?"

"When Pat told him there was no dope to be bought, the guy didn't even bother to make an excuse. He got pissed that Pat was throwing him out of the building, but he didn't try to make himself an innocent. Besides, Pat was a junkie for ten years. You don't think he can tell?"

"Exactly when did this happen? How close to the assault?"

"Jesus, you're hard to please. A half hour after Pat confronted the man in the hallway, we heard the sirens. The cops knocked on every door in the building that night."

"Okay. Enough." Moodrow stood up, throwing his overcoat across his left arm. "I appreciate the help and I'll be back after I speak to Rosenkrantz."

"That's it?" Persio asked in amazement. "You don't want a description? You're not going after this scumbag?"

"Fuck that. Let the cops go after the mugger. I'm sure they have a description from Birnbaum. Ya know, it's a funny thing, but at first I thought maybe the attack on Birnbaum was deliberate. I didn't have any good reason to believe this, but I couldn't get it out of my head. I'm still gonna check it out with the cop who caught the squeal, but right now I'm satisfied that it was violence left over from when the dealers were here. A week from now, everything'll quiet down."

"It already has."

Moodrow grinned. "See what I mean? The problem's taking care of itself. Anyway, I'll either see Rosenkrantz tonight, if he shows up for the meeting, or I'll run him down in his office tomorrow. Then I'll be in touch with you. Have a nice night."

As it turned out, Al Rosenkrantz did attend the emergency meeting of the Jackson Arms Tenants' Association. He was holding forth when Moodrow made his appearance in Sylvia Kaufman's apartment, only this time the questions were much more unfriendly and he was sweating profusely. The tenants wanted to know why the lobby wasn't fixed, where the security was, why the eviction notices kept going out. Rosenkrantz responded by attacking the cops. Crime in New York, he insisted, was out of control. It was up to the police to prevent crime, not real estate management companies. But Precision Management *had* sent an eviction notice to the drug dealers in 4B shortly before they left. Sal Ragozzo had also been served. True, management might have made a mistake in its choice of a superintendent for the building, but the lobby would be repaired and a security desk set up within the week.

Moodrow, sweeping the room professionally, noted the presence of Community Affairs Officer Paul Dunlap, as well as the association's regulars. Apparently, the attack on Birnbaum had failed to fire up the rest of the tenants. Betty, off by herself, finally caught his eye. She smiled and waved him over.

"I miss anything?" he whispered, sitting beside her.

"Birnbaum was badly beaten. He's not going to die, but he's an old man. His daughter was here and she said she was taking him to her home in New Jersey. The cop over there spoke for about two minutes. He said it was a robbery, the kind that happens a hundred times a day in New York, but he didn't have any suspects. Then Rosenkrantz waddled up. He's been the target for most of the anger in the room, but he's holding his own. He keeps insisting that things are going to get better."

"You think he means it?" Moodrow asked.

"It's hard to believe that he actually *sent* dealers into the building. This is not the South Bronx. On the other hand, Al Rosenkrantz is definitely a slime ball. No doubt about it."

"Well, I got a way to sound him out a little without making him too suspicious." Quickly, Moodrow filled her in on his conversation with Louis

Persio. "I'm gonna brace Rosenkrantz as soon as he leaves the apartment. Try to corner him in the lobby. I want you to come with me. So I can hear what your impressions are."

Betty smiled broadly. She had a wide mouth and when she grinned, her face seemed to explode with pleasure. "Great," she responded. "Do we get to slap him around?"

"You been watching too many cop movies. Remember, I'm trying to help Persio out and I'm not gonna get a favor by attacking Rosenkrantz. We'll just talk to the guy and see what he has to say."

Before Betty could reply, there was a solid knock on Sylvia's door, the sound of wood on wood. Dunlap, who was nearest the door, opened it to find Mike Birnbaum, his cane raised to give the door another shot. The left side of his face was badly swollen and his skull was heavily bandaged behind the ear, but he was erect and furious. When Porky Dunlap tried to take the old man's arm, he was pushed away with a contemptuous glance.

"What'd I tell you?" Birnbaum asked triumphantly. "Hoodlums, *gonifs*. The *dreck* of the universe comes in here since Morris sold the building. We didn't buy when we had the chance and now you see what happens. My own daughter tells me I gotta move to someplace in New Jersey. I'd rather move to Siberia." He began to hobble toward the front of the room. "I know you told me I shouldn't talk too much at the meetings, Sylvia, but now I gotta say what's on my mind. So tell this *putz* to go back to his cave and let me speak."

Rosenkrantz gave way at once. He tried to do it gracefully, but Birnbaum's parting comment hit the Project Supervisor right between the shoulder blades, driving Rosenkrantz into a sudden, stifled rage.

"Remember this," Birnbaum shouted to his retreating back. "The *pisher* of a *gonif* is also a *gonif*. A man who works for a hoodlum is also a hoodlum. It don't matter if he carries a fancy briefcase. I want all you people to listen to me. I made my life here in this building. When I first moved here, it was mostly Irish and they tried to run me off. The women called me 'dirty Jew.' The men said 'sheenie' and 'kike.' I'm not gonna be such a *schnorrer* I gotta brag about the fights I had. The point is I came here to stay and that's what I intend to do. I ain't gonna die in New Jersey. New Jersey is already dead as far as I'm concerned. Queens is where I lived since I came back from the war and Queens is where I'm gonna die."

Rosenkrantz paused, the apartment door held open, until Mike finished, then stepped through. None of the tenants were paying any attention to him, but Moodrow and Betty Haluka quietly followed him into the hallway.

"Mr. Rosenkrantz," Moodrow called out. "Can we talk to you for a minute?"

Rosenkrantz swept his questioners quickly, knowing they weren't tenants. Wondering what they wanted. His anger had not begun to abate and would not until he placated it with ten milligrams of Valium and several shots of Scotch. "Sure," he said, extending his hand. "Always glad to talk. I'm Al Rosenkrantz."

"Stanley Moodrow," Moodrow replied, taking Rosenkrantz's hand. "I'm a private investigator." He flashed his license quickly. "This is Betty Haluka. She's an attorney. We just wanna speak to you for a moment about a tenant who got a dispossess notice. This tenant is very sick and can't really cope with appearing in court."

"Who is it?" Rosenkrantz asked.

"Louis Persio. On the fourth floor."

"The fag?" Rosenkrantz said in amazement. "You want to talk to me about a diseased criminal faggot?"

"Look, Mr. Rosenkrantz," Moodrow persisted. "I saw the eviction notice and the only real grounds for eviction you put on there is the failure to make payment. All that other stuff, the roommate, the illness, the homosexuality— you can't evict for that in New York." He hesitated briefly, hoping for a nod of agreement from Rosenkrantz, but Rosenkrantz's face was frozen in disbelief. "Look, Persio claims that he made the rent payments on time. He says he's got the cancelled checks, so maybe you could settle this face-to-face in the guy's apartment. Instead of going to court. Persio's very sick; he's dying. You're gonna get the apartment in a few months, anyway. What's the rush? Why push it?"

Rosenkrantz shook his head, his anger at last finding an outlet. "I don't believe this. I don't believe it. For the last half hour I've had a roomful of assholes shitting all over me. Now I'm getting muscled by a shyster and some amateur policeman. Well, listen, Private Detective Moodrow, you don't mean shit to me. You're not a tenant and you have no standing in these talks. As for Ms. Attorney over here, if she thinks Precision Management has acted improperly, she can take us into court. She'll find we have considerable resources when it comes to protecting our own interests and the interests of our clients. And one more thing before we part company. Louis Persio is a criminal fag. It's not my fault he took it up the ass until he got AIDS. It's not my fault at all, but I'll tell you this. I hope the sissy goes directly from here to the emergency room at Elmhurst General. I hope they line him up on a cot with all the other diseased bastards waiting for treatment. I hope they keep him there fifteen or twenty hours, the way they usually do, while his lungs fill up with pneumonia. I hope they keep him there until cancer eats his face away. I hope . . ."

At no time did Moodrow, who was stunned by Rosenkrantz's sudden fury, consciously command his body to move, but somehow Precision Management's Project Supervisor was lying on the sidewalk, one hand pressed to his nose.

"You mother-fucker," Rosenkrantz cried. "You'll go to jail for this."

"I don't think so." The voice, hearty and firm, came from the hallway behind Moodrow and Betty. It was that of Paul "Porky" Dunlap. Ever curious, as a cop should be, he'd followed the trio into the lobby. "I don't think there's a cop in the One One Five who'll arrest a man for defending himself. And, by the way, I don't think it's very nice of you to attack a man who Sylvia tells me has been helping out the tenants so much. And this 'shyster' you mentioned is Sylvia's niece. Sylvia told me they were like mother and daughter, so what you did wasn't right, Al. In fact, if you don't take a quick hike, I might have to put the cuffs on you myself."

FOURTEEN

April 2

IT was raining hard when Maurice Babbit left his Inwood apartment at the northern end of Manhattan Island for the long subway ride to Queens. The kind of cold spring rain that had fat weathermen giggling about April showers and May flowers. If there was anything in this world that annoyed Maurice Babbit, it was April showers. Not that he gave a shit about May flowers, either, but water was a more potent enemy than beauty. Water put out fire. Or most fires. Nothing could put out his favorite fire. Nothing could put out napalm. It stuck to people like the slimy goo kids play with. Like wet burning plastic snot. In Nam, they'd assigned him to the "native ward" at the big hospital near Bien Hoa where he'd learned about napalm from tending injuries to the fried friendlies.

That was his own name: fried friendlies. If he'd had army buddies, they'd've loved that one. He didn't. Didn't have any buddies or anybody to talk about the fires with. Not until he got sent to jail. Not until he got himself put in a place where he couldn't walk away. Poor Maurice. Life in Middleburg hadn't prepared him for the army and the army hadn't prepared him for the Clinton Correctional Facility.

The main thing about the army was they wouldn't let him fight. He still didn't understand it. They sent divisions of shit-scared babies into battle, while he carried slop in a hospital. If they had the slightest sense of what they were doing, they would have put a flamethrower on his back, a handful of incendiary grenades in his pocket and shipped him off to a platoon of tunnel rats. Shit, he would've paid *them*.

But they didn't. (Was there anything behind their decisions? Any reasoning? Were they really as arbitrary as lightning bolts?) And it wouldn't have made a difference, anyway. Not unless he'd been killed. Maurice could have torched a million hooches and he'd still be hungry for a good blaze. He set plenty while he was in Nam; set them in the slums of Saigon where the houses were made of wood and cardboard so dry it burned like paper.

Afterward, after watching until the embers were black coal, he retained the images like individual photographs. Like stopping a movie to study the details of a particular frame. A woman running. A man slapping at his burning trousers (that one comical). Children crying or moaning or silent in the street. Maurice would take these pictures to the nearest whorehouse (never far away in wartime Saigon) and pass the night. Funny, he could remember every detail of every fire, but the whores, when he bothered to think about them, were a fuzzy parade of chirping dinks.

"You want fucky me now? You want me sucky you?"

Nowadays he carried his own napalm in one of those plastic lemons they sold in supermarkets. Carried it whenever he went out onto the dangerous streets of New York City. His own personal mixture of gasoline and soap. He had it with him now, in his pocket, and he caressed it as the subway tore south. If he popped the cap and sprayed his napalm on the old nigger sitting across the car, it would stick like glue. If she rubbed it, it'd spread all over her. If he lit it up, it would burn down into her flesh.

If Maurice could have had it his way, he'd've burned them all. It was bad enough to live in the slums of Inwood (he couldn't go back to Middleburg; not after the fire that put him in Clinton) where every other Puerto Rican had a pocketful of dope. That the niggers coming onto the 1 Train as it passed through Harlem should make him feel like a faggot begging for mercy seemed like one of the injustices God reserved for assholes like Job. When they weren't actually robbing people, they smoked weed and blasted that mindless music until it made his brain rattle. Then they stuck their feet up on the only empty seats and dared him to do something about it. Grinning that fuck-you badass grin.

Maurice didn't like to be put down. He didn't like that at all. When they fucked with him in the joint (and they did; they fucked with everybody), he'd burned one right in his cell. Charcoaled the black mother-fucker even blacker than he was born, with napalm he'd made out of turpentine from the woodworking shop. The turpentine had cost him five cartons of Salems and come by way of a hustler who didn't give a shit if Maurice burned up his granny.

Maurice had gotten away with the fire, even though all the cons (including the snitches) knew he'd done it. Maybe the pigs didn't have proof or maybe they didn't give a shit. You couldn't always tell with them. But the fire got the attention of Paul Ziff, an aging professional arsonist. In return for cigarettes and an occasional pint of jailhouse hooch, Paul had taught Maurice the art of fire. And the relationship of art to economics.

The train rumbled into the 145th Street Station and Maurice automatically scanned the incoming passengers. It was ten o'clock at night, prime time for the wolves to be heading downtown in search of prey. But except for a homeless bitch who'd make the whole car stink of piss, the other passengers were ordinary workers, and Maurice, his knapsack cradled against his chest, began to day-dream about the day he'd flicked his BIC.

The job, he recalled, had been special from the beginning. He made fires that cleared buildings and fires that scared people; he made fires to destroy inventories and fires to destroy competitors. All that was old stuff and he could make his fires so that the insurance companies would have to pay. In spite of the suspicions of the fire marshals who thought *every* fire was arson.

But this time Maurice's employer didn't give a damn about the fire marshals and what they suspected. No insurance company was about to write a policy on a piece-of-shit tenement in one of the ravines near Yankee Stadium in the South Bronx. Not on the only one still standing on the whole block. Maurice's employer (though nobody told Maurice) owned the block. He wanted the building *gone*.

Maurice was the subcontractor for the job. He never met the man who ordered it. But he was proud that the broker had chosen him. Of course, any building could be leveled if you brought enough gasoline or explosive to the task. But that would take hundreds of pounds of dynamite or thousands of dollars' worth of C4. Fortunately, there were three families living in the building (as well as the usual assortment of squatters in the apartments that had already been emptied by smaller fires) and natural gas was still coming into the tenement. That would make the job easy and the reward Maurice got from watching the blossoming of his work especially great.

He was hoping for an explosion, but he knew he wouldn't get that as soon as he walked down into the basement. The small windows were all broken and the gas would never build up enough pressure for an explosion. Too bad. But it wouldn't interfere with the job. He went directly to the gas meter and shut off the gas between the meter and the street with a notched tool that had cost him a thousand dollars. Then he cut a two-foot length out of the pipe that led from the meter to the various apartments. When he turned the gas back on, it would pour from the pipe at full pressure and it would keep on pouring at several hundred cubic feet per minute until the gas company shut it off from the street.

The final steps were easy. The broker had made good on his promise that all dopers would be out of the basement. The junkies were the only ones who could fuck up the deal, because, sure as shit, there weren't any straight people coming down to look for the fuse box. Not at night. Not in dope heaven. Maurice piled newspapers under the missing section of pipe. Soaked them with gasoline. Set a battery-operated alarm clock, its wires deliberately shorted, one hour ahead. It was crude, but it wouldn't take more than a spark to get this one going. In fact, it was only a guess whether the alarm would go off before the gas reached a spark in one of the apartments above.

When he turned the gas back on, the stink of it was overwhelming. He tried to think of the smell as the flowering of his efforts. Not that he was stupid enough to hang around. He left immediately, then climbed the hill overlooking the single tenement (standing like the last tooth in an old lady's mouth) and settled down to wait.

When it went off, it was just like firing up the stove a few seconds after the gas'd been turned on. That same sound. WHOMP! And then the flames instantly there, covering the first three floors and screaming upward.

Only a few people got to the roof and there was no place for them to go once they got there. No other roofs to run across and the fire was too hot to get a ladder anywhere near it. In fact, there was nothing the firemen could do except turn off the gas and it took them almost forty minutes to do it. By that time there wasn't any more building and the little figures had already jumped. Maurice called it, "the job where I flicked my BIC."

Despite his reveries, Maurice had made the transfer to the 7 Train and was cruising along the elevated tracks in western Queens. He wished that this fire, tonight, was meant to be as big as that one had been. But the broker didn't want any damage. He wanted smoke and a fire that wouldn't come back on the landlord. A scary fire for some shithead tenants. A lesson fire.

Maurice got off the train at 74th Street in Jackson Heights. It was eleven o'clock and the streets were pretty much empty, as they would be in a working-class neighborhood during the week. Usually, he got the creeps when he was out late at night. What with the neighborhoods where he mostly worked, it was a miracle if he even got to the project without some doped-out spook trying for his wallet.

But he wouldn't have any problems here. The rain had everybody running for home. Maurice turned down a ramp leading to the basement door of the Jackson Arms, a six-story apartment building on 37th Avenue. The door was open, the lock already busted out. He peered into the dimly lit interior, listening carefully. As expected, it was quiet. He could feel the quiet closing in on him. Maurice was a professional and he didn't let himself think about fires while he worked. Each job was a series of problems. Like a crossword puzzle. It was the first thing Paul Ziff had told him about setting fires for money. You had to separate the pleasure from the work.

This building, for instance, had been built after LaGuardia had become mayor and it had a fire retardant ceiling in the basement. Ordinarily, it would take an hour for the hottest fire he could set (but not as hot as "flicking my BIC" not *that* hot) to burn through. So the first problem was how to get the smoke up into the first floor apartment where the employer wanted it. Fortunately, the landlord had redone the heat and hot water pipes sometime in the fifty years since the Jackson Arms had been built and his contractor had been sloppy, as they all were. Maurice could see light filtering down from the apartment above. The pipes would be a tunnel for smoke. They'd be the only way for the smoke to get out of the basement.

None of this was a surprise, of course. Maurice had come a week before to check it out. If the pipes hadn't been cut through, he wouldn't have taken the job. But there were several bonuses that he hadn't expected. There was a bed made of two old newspaper-stuffed mattresses on the floor directly beneath the target. Most likely, the janitor used it for afternoon naps and some squatter had taken it over. There was a pile of human feces behind the burners and a faint smell of urine in the dank basement air.

Mattress fires, Maurice knew, make incredible amounts of smoke, but very little fire. Which was exactly what the employer wanted. Just a smoky fire to wake up the tenant in the apartment above. A message fire.

Maurice opened his pack and placed four small candles on the floor, lighting them and making sure they were stuck firmly to the concrete. Then he dropped the cover: a dozen crack vials (empty, of course) and as many tiny envelopes around the mattress; a pile of burnt matches; three bent teaspoons, their bottoms blackened with soot; a dozen bottlecaps; a peanut butter jar of filthy water tinted pink with his own blood. As an afterthought, he placed two syringes (well-used spikes he'd gotten from one of the shooting galleries that infested Inwood), on the mattress as a little joke. Most of the plastic would burn away, but the needles would sit in the charred mattress. Waiting for a fire marshal's investigating fingers.

Finally, he set a candle directly on the mattress and lit it, then repacked his bag. He checked every inch of the area he'd been through, walked it back and forth to the outside door, making certain he hadn't dropped anything. Not a lost button or a busted shoelace or *anything*. When the candle flame reached the edge of the first newspaper, he was ready to leave, but he waited a few moments, until the black smoke rose in thick clouds toward the ceiling. Just to make sure.

He did have one regret as he walked to the subway. In a quiet neighborhood like Jackson Heights, he couldn't hang around to wait for the firemen to show up. He consoled himself by remembering that there wouldn't be much to see, anyway. No "fried friendlies." No "flick my BIC." Just a lot of smoke.

FIFTEEN

THE dark, oily smoke curling up into Sylvia Kaufman's bedroom was heavy with moisture. It stunk of grease, at first, grease and human sweat, the sum total of all the bodies that had ever sunk into the ancient mattress burning on the floor of the basement, but as the smoke began to accumulate, it quickly became caustic, irritating the sleeping woman's nose and throat. It continued to rise, of course, propelled by the heat of the naked steampipe, and might have found a way out through the poorly cut hole that allowed the steampipe to pass from the first to the second floor, but a tenant, Mathew Healy, long gone from the Jackson Arms, finding the light and noise filtering through the hole objectionable, had stuffed it with pink insulation.

The smoke, with no place to go, began to press downward again, drifting toward the old lady sleeping in her bed. Sylvia's bed (her wedding bed) was close to the radiator, a concession to age-weakened circulation, and the first thin wisp of smoke fell directly across her throat. Then, propelled by a cooler draft pushing under the bedroom door, it moved toward the closed windows at the eastern end of the room. The windows, cold to the touch despite the presence of storm windows, chilled the warm smoke until it gave up its moisture, dropping beads of oily water onto the glass.

The smoke, lighter now, broke into four waves, running along the wall to the corners of the room, to the floor, to the ceiling. Gradually thickening, it piled up against the eastern wall, then slowly pushed back across Sylvia's bed until, at last, it found a way out. A small gap between the top of the door and the frame sucked the warm, smoky air into the hall where it quickly rose up into the sensors of the smoke alarm.

Sylvia was dreaming of Betty Haluka and her own daughter, Marilyn, when the alarm went off. The cousins were still girls in the dream, maybe ten years old; she, herself, though she never looked in a mirror, was obviously a young woman. It must have been raining, because the children were in the house; Sylvia insisted the girls play in the fresh air when the weather was nice. In any event, Marilyn was seated at the piano, pounding out a popular tune, a Walt Disney tune, "Happy Talk," and all three were singing.

At first, Sylvia, trying to keep the sound inside her pleasant dream, mistook the buzzing fire alarm for the doorbell. She looked to the door, willing the intruder to be her husband, but the buzzing continued long after an ordinary visitor would have released the button. Suddenly, the dream evaporating as an idea took hold of her waking mind, she knew the buzzing could only be her alarm clock, inadvertently set. Instinctively, her eyes still closed, she reached out to shut it off, pressing the correct button (she'd done it thousands of times in the course of her working life) on top of the clock, but the buzzing only grew more insistent. It demanded that she attend to it immediately, that she close it down, no matter how badly she wanted to dream.

The first thing Sylvia became aware of, upon opening her eyes, was the darkness. True, her nose and throat were sore, but the inflammation seemed no worse than the precursor of a spring cold. The pitch black was more puzzling. Exploring it, she glanced toward the windows at the eastern end of the room; they overlooked a well-lit courtyard (too well-lit for her taste) and, normally, a ribbon of light framed the shades. This morning, however, they were invisible.

Puzzled now, she began to drag herself toward full waking; she reached out blindly and snapped on the lamp by the side of her bed. The hundred-watt bulb, normally blinding if turned on before dawn, cast only a dim glow, like the sun rising into a dense fog. She stared at it for a moment, obviously confused, then, without transition, she was wide awake and her mind was screaming, "Fire." Just the one word, endlessly drawn out. A howl of terror.

Sylvia didn't stop to consider why there were no flames. Why there was no heat. She didn't try to find the source of the smoke or even to assess the danger. Instead, she sat up straight, her frail body, propelled by a burst of adrenaline, rising into even thicker smoke. That same adrenaline, pounding in her chest, quickly exhausted the oxygen in her blood, forcing a deep, involuntary breath. The choking that followed drove her into panic; though fully awake, she could form no thought more coherent than the absolute compulsion to get out as quickly as possible.

To Sylvia, "out" meant through the bedroom door, down the hallway and out of the apartment. The window might have been a better bet (the fire could very well have originated in some other part of the apartment); she might, in fact, be running directly into the flames. But, choking, retching, her lungs filled with smoke, she could only formulate that single imperative—GET OUT!

Jerking herself into action (moving faster than she had in years), she tried to swing her feet over the edge of the bed, tangled her trailing foot in the blankets and fell heavily to the polished oak floor. She landed on her right hip and the sharp crack told her the bone was broken even before the pain roared up to overwhelm her fear of the smoke and fire. For a moment, she thought she was going to lose consciousness; she almost hoped for it. But the smoke was much thinner close to the floor and as she lay motionless, waiting for the pain to subside, her mind cleared and she found herself suddenly calm.

All the realizations she might have had before lifting her head from the pillow suddenly flooded Sylvia's mind. There was no heat and no visible flames and she became almost certain that the fire had originated in some other part of the building, probably somewhere else in the apartment, which made the windows the only sure way out. She was lying on the floor with the bed between herself and the windows and she couldn't see them; she would have to crawl to the foot of the bed and use the wall to guide herself to the eastern end of the apartment.

Then she realized that the windows were closed, the outer storm windows firmly in place (there hadn't been a lot of heat lately and all the tenants were protecting themselves against drafts); she would have to stand in order to open the windows and the dull ache pulsating in her hip (and threatening to explode at the least movement) would never allow her to remain erect long enough to get through the glass. For an instant, she had a picture of herself breaking the glass with the straight-backed chair in the corner and diving through, then she rolled a few inches to the right, exerting a slight pressure on her hip, and the eruption of pain dispelled her fantasy as surely as an open window would have dispersed the smoke in her bedroom.

As Sylvia understood it, she was left with two possibilities, both clearly formed in her mind—she could chance the bedroom door or wait for rescue where she was. The telephone (how many times had she resolved to put an extension in the bedroom?) was in the hallway, on a small table about fifteen feet from the bedroom door. If she got through the door, she could pull down the telephone and call for help. In any event, she could test the door by touching it. If it was hot, there was fire behind it; if it was cool, she could open it and get out.

Not that it was going to be easy. Besides the pain (which she didn't want to think about, not yet), there was the simple fact that she couldn't see the door; if she took off across the carpet, searching for the shortest line, and missed, she might lose her way altogether. How, after all, would she know which side of the door she was on? No, she concluded, the only realistic way to get out was to crawl to the head of the bed, then use the wall for a guide.

That was her final decision; afterward there was only the pain to deal with. Tentatively, an inch at a time, she thrust her arms to their fullest extension, dug her fingernails into the carpet and pulled herself forward, moving a few inches before the pain, hot and thick, overwhelmed her. Instantly, she resolved to stay put, to wait for rescue and just as quickly, the pain causing her to take a sudden, deep breath, knew the smoke was thickening, that her lungs were old and fragile, that if she were to be rescued, it would have to be soon.

For a moment, as the pain subsided, she listened for the sound of fire engines, for the pounding of the sirens (which no longer screamed, as they had for most of her life, but now sounded like a ship's foghorn). She heard nothing, not even the crackling of the fire, but her coughing diminished until she was able to maintain herself by pressing her mouth close to the carpet and sipping at the air. That was enough, for the time being.

After several moments, a new idea, a very foreign thought from her point of view, began to filter into Sylvia's mind. She began to think that she might die. That night, in her own bedroom. The idea frightened her more than the fire. She had spent much of her working life in neighborhoods that terrified other New Yorkers; many times, over the years, she'd faced down adolescent students who were quite capable of attack, who wouldn't hesitate to pick up a weapon if one were handy. She'd refused to allow herself to be intimidated. Never. Not once had she let fear control her actions; if she did, she knew, she would never have found the courage to go back.

But fear of pain was different; one stood up before a blow was struck in order to prevent the blow. The only preventable aspect of this situation was pain. Or, just possibly, she had to admit, death. Death might be preventable if there was no fire on the other side of her bedroom door. Or if she could bear the pain. She tried to sense the smoke without breathing it, to determine if it was getting worse, but all she could decide was that her eyes were burning and she could breathe if she was careful not to raise her head.

She lay still for several, seemingly infinite moments, drifting back and forth between the two courses of action, until a third possibility, a possibility so simple she couldn't believe she hadn't thought of it (as usual, the word Alzheimer crossed her mind, as it always did when she was careless or forgetful); she'd simply pull herself as far as she could. If she didn't make the door, she'd be no worse off, even if she lost consciousness. The smoke, she was now convinced, *was* growing thicker. If she waited much longer she'd be too weak to try. She summoned up every bit of her resolve, all the intention that had so characterized her life, and began to move. Careful to keep her weight over her left hip, she again dug her nails into the carpet, pulling herself toward the head of the bed, toward a hole surrounding a steampipe, toward a cloud of black, oily smoke.

She managed to move the length of her body before the rising heat brought her to a halt. The smoke was much worse here, but it could be getting worse throughout the room. The heat, on the other hand, was definitely a new phenomenon. Somehow, though she couldn't see any flames, she was drawing closer to the source of the smoke. The puzzle intrigued her momentarily, enabling her to ignore the pain in her nose and throat, then she realized the only possible explanation. The fire was in the basement; the smoke was coming up from the basement. There was no flame because of steel plates in the basement ceiling (there wasn't supposed to be any smoke, either), but the smoke must be coming up through a hole in the floor.

If the smoke was coming from below, the bedroom door was, indeed, a legitimate way out; the air had to be cleaner out there. That was the way to go; the way to go right now, before the smoke got any worse. She tried to move backward, but was unable to make any progress with only one leg. If she turned left, in the general direction of the bedroom door, she would have no landmarks once she left the side of the bed.

I'm going to die if I stay here, she told herself. The statement seemed curious; it seemed like the kind of statement she might hear in a college philosophy class, an absurd consideration designed to undermine her resolution. She smiled contemptuously, then began to turn her body away from the bed, toward the door and escape.

She lost her sense of direction almost immediately, veering to the right, toward the head of the bed. The smoke was very heavy now; she held each breath as long as she could, trying to avoid the oily taste that scorched her throat each time she tried to breathe. Funny, her leg wasn't bothering her much. It seemed far away, as dull and empty as the bedside lamp when she'd turned it on a few minutes before. The leg was the easy part; it had always been the easy part. Will, on the other hand . . . well, that was another problem altogether.

She made no conscious decision to stop, no conscious decision to lay her head on the carpet. She felt light-headed, almost girlish, as she inevitably did on those few occasions when she took a glass or two of wine. What, she thought, was I worried about all this time? There was certainly no problem here; she could breathe as easily as she could on those country vacations she took with her husband forty years ago. And she could also, for the first time, see the smoke, see its separate tendrils finding their way through the air currents. The tendrils looked like currents, like charts of ocean currents in the geography textbooks (although the charts were always multicolored and the smoke, of course, was gray or black).

But, monochrome or not, the smoke was beautiful nonetheless, undeniably beautiful and not the least bit frightening. She listened for sirens, for the sounds of rescue. Thinking it wouldn't make any difference, now. Even if they came, it would take them a long time to find her, because they'd probably go to the basement first; they'd go to the basement, put out the fire and, only then, come looking for old ladies trapped in their apartments.

She fell asleep a few minutes later, knowing it was sleep because she returned to her original dream. Marilyn was a terrible pianist, barely able to pound out the chords while the fingers of her right hand doggedly poked their way through the melody, but her clumsy attack went unnoticed as all three bawled the words to the song, laughing as they went along. Sylvia, watching the girls (they were seated alongside each other on the piano bench) wondered why it couldn't always be like this. Betty was so close to the family that she and Marilyn often fought like sisters. Well, better to be thankful for the peaceful times than perpetually angry over life's problems; Sylvia was a firm believer in a positive attitude, despite the leading exponent of that philosophy, Norman Vincent Peale, being not only a *goy*, but some kind of Protestant priest.

Marilyn was enthusiastically missing the last few chords of the song when the bell rang. Not the persistent insect buzz of the smoke alarm, but a deep gong that continued to echo through the house after the button was released.

"I'll get it," Sylvia said. "It's for me." In her dream, she didn't ask herself how she knew the visitor was looking for her. Marilyn had lots of friends in the neighborhood and they often came calling. But she did know.

"What do you want to do next?" Marilyn asked Betty.

" 'The Wayward Wind,' " Betty responded without hesitation, fishing through the sheet music spread across the top of the piano. "Here it is."

"Okay, you do the train whistle," Marilyn commanded, already searching for the opening chords.

Still smiling, Sylvia suddenly found herself by the open door. She was surprised to see her husband standing there; he rarely got home before six o'clock. "Bennie," she cried happily, "what are you doing at home? It's only four-thirty."

"I came to get you," he answered.

"I don't want to go anywhere," Sylvia said, doubtfully. "I'm having such a good time with the girls. We haven't had this much fun together in months."

"Don't worry about them." He reached out and took her hand, an old familiarity that Sylvia, awake, would never have remembered. "The kids are doing fine. You come with me, Sylvia. There's something I've got to show you."

SIXTEEN

April 3

"THE thing is, I can't go to funerals anymore." Moodrow was standing by the window, trying to explain himself to Jim Tilley. He was looking out at the street, his back to the kitchen table where Tilley was playing with a cup of coffee. "When Rita died four years ago, I sat through the wake for two days. It was the worst thing that ever happened to me. Not the death, Jim. Sitting through those hours with her body right there in the room was a fucking nightmare. My blood was on fire. I felt like if I stayed there another minute, I'd ignite, but I sat by the coffin anyway. It was very bad. In those two days, I did all the funerals and wakes I had left in me. I can't do no more."

Tilley, who'd never seen his friend in this mood before, tried to frame a response, but after a moment's reflection, decided that no response was necessary, that Moodrow was only pausing for breath, that he needed a sounding board, not a counselor.

"What's making me crazy is that I know I fucked it up," Moodrow said, turning back to the table. He was looking for the solid ground of police procedure. "I should have . . ."

"Wait a second," Tilley reminded him patiently. "I don't know what happened out there except there was a fire and a fatality."

"It was arson," Moodrow said flatly. "And the lady that got killed was named Sylvia Kaufman. She's having her funeral right now. While we're talking."

"You know for sure it was arson? You found a gas can and a blowtorch?" Tilley, like all cops, preferred to deal with the details of investigation. It's always easier, when viewing the body of a raped and battered woman, to think in terms of semen traces and genetic matching. Of entry wounds and exit wounds instead of breathing, bleeding tissue. Instead of holy life slipping out of the body.

"It'll be arson, Jimmy. Take my word for it. The fire was all smoke and no heat. It was a warning that got out of hand and it was a professional job. No gasoline can. In fact, no accelerant at all. Gasoline, kerosene . . . they cause damage, Jimmy, and whoever set this fire didn't want damage."

"What does the fire marshal think?"

"I haven't spoken to him yet." Moodrow poured himself a cup of coffee, his fifth of the day, and sat down across from Tilley. "I have a problem with that. I'm not a cop anymore and I don't know if he'll even talk to me. For sure, he ain't gonna let me argue if he thinks it's accidental."

"No problem," Tilley said. "I'll go out there with you."

Moodrow looked up, appraising his friend. "I appreciate the offer, Jimmy, but I'm trying to line someone up from the One One Five. Make it an official police investigation."

Tilley was, to his surprise, relieved at not having to partner with Stanley Moodrow and he made a note to think about why he was relieved as soon as he had the chance. In the meantime, he kept to his role, absorbing his friend's mood and method. "I hope you're not thinking of that Community Affairs Officer. What's his name?"

"Dunlap. Paul Dunlap, but I hear the cops in the house call him Porky."

"Maybe you should find a real cop."

"From where?" Moodrow waved Tilley's objection away. "Dunlap'll be okay as long as he lets me run the show. Plus he's got a big advantage in that his job consists mostly of giving speeches and not too much of that. He doesn't usually work during the day, which is another plus. I spoke to him over the phone this morning and he seemed eager."

"Is he coming here this afternoon?"

"They'll all be here later. They're at the funeral right now. You knew Sylvia was Jewish, right? According to her religion, she has to be buried within forty-eight hours. Then her family sits around her apartment for a week. It's called sitting *shiva*. I think it's better to do the mourning without the body around. It's easier. Anyway, Sylvia's daughter, Marilyn, flew in from Los Angeles yesterday and she's going to sit *shiva*, so I guess I'll go over there tomorrow. That won't be a problem. It's being near the body I can't stand."

Once again, Jim Tilley chose silence. He pushed back his chair, went to the refrigerator, and cut himself a piece of cheesecake.

"The thing that bothers me," Moodrow continued, "is that I should have known what was going on, but I was an asshole. I thought it was funny. Not the assaults, but the idea of a bunch of middle-class citizens running around in panic over something we see everyday on the Lower East Side. I checked the building and found two drug dealers and two prostitutes." He stopped suddenly and raised his right hand in front of him, curling his fingers into a fist. "I got big hands. All my life, I've been using them to solve problems, especially in the job. I figured I could be a hero. Toss the dealers out on their asses and save the Jackson Arms. I shoulda known better."

"How?" Tilley finally asked. "You don't even know right now what's happening out there."

Moodrow ignored him. "Where'd they come from? Why'd two street dealers pick a neighborhood where there's hardly any customers? They couldn't have come from the streets because the action around there is almost nonexistent and what does take place, takes place behind closed doors, in the bars or the apartments. With this crew, the whores and the dealers, it was like they were out for publicity. It didn't make sense and I should of seen it." He paused for breath, looking over at Tilley, who was staring into his coffee. "Jim, I had the fuckers in that apartment. The dealers. I had them right there and I didn't ask 'em where they came from. I didn't ask who sent them. That Chinese kid was so scared he woulda given up his mother to stay out of the joint. And I didn't even ask."

Tilley, looking up, tried to find a safe comment and then opted for the truth. "You should have asked," he admitted. "You definitely should have asked."

Moodrow got up and went to the window again. He was looking for Betty, though he couldn't help being impressed by the spring day unfolding outside his window. It was the first really warm day of the year and residents of the Lower East Side had abandoned their tenement apartments in favor of the streets. Radios blared. Children shouted. The dealers, who worked their corners in all weather conditions, shrugged off heavy jackets. "Looks like the homeless won't have to worry about freezing anymore this year," Moodrow observed. He forced the window open for the first time in weeks.

"What?" Tilley asked.

"It's getting warm," Moodrow said. "No more frozen bodies in the park."

Tilley refused to respond, bringing the conversation back to the point. "Ya know, you weren't running the show out there. What makes you think Sylvia would have installed an alarm in the bedroom, based on your suspicions?"

Moodrow didn't hear the question. He turned away from the window, crossing the room to take his chair again. "When they lowered Rita's body down, I wanted to get in with her. It wasn't that I couldn't face the pain. I was having trouble with the anger. As long as I kept the anger, I didn't have to face the pain, but I knew there was a chance the anger might get out of control. That I could use it on the wrong people. So I pretended that I needed the anger to make sure Rita's killers were punished. I pretended Rita needed revenge, but I knew, when they put her down in that hole, she was gone forever."

"And what about Sylvia? Does *she* need revenge?"

"With Rita, I was the one who needed revenge. I had to do it personally, because I was in love with her, but I only knew Sylvia well enough to be sure she didn't deserve to die that way. As for what I want to do—right now the best thing I could do for Sylvia is to save the building. And to get whoever did this to her. The one who set the fire and the one who ordered it." Moodrow suddenly straightened in his chair, taking up a working posture. "Tell me what you think's going on out there?" he demanded.

"The first thing that sticks out," Tilley responded eagerly, "is the coincidence that drugs and whores came in right after the building changed hands. But let's pretend that it was just a coincidence. No connection whatsoever. Then I'd say that some major dealer is trying to expand by setting up small-time dealers in a neighborhood where he won't have to fight to keep his turf. The big dealers have a very hard time expanding in neighborhoods where drugs are sold on every corner. In those neighborhoods, you gotta kill to grow. Also there's a lot of dealers who think that anyone who tries crack, from derelict to chief executive, is gonna get hooked. I don't agree a hundred percent, but, from that point of view, it makes sense to jump into a clean territory. The second possibility is that the new landlord and the problems are connected. There's plenty of instances of landlords hiring goons to empty out buildings, so it wouldn't be a rare phenomenon, even if it doesn't usually happen in neighborhoods as clean as Jackson Heights. It's also possible that the landlord is personally into drugs. Crack dealers have lots of money to invest and just maybe a middle-level pusher figured a way to make his investment pay off double. When you think about it, the neighborhoods that go bad in New York go bad one block at a time. If this building and a few others turned into real horror shows, some of the small homeowners might try to get out while property values are still high. I don't think it would work, but that doesn't mean someone couldn't be giving it a try."

"You forgot about the arson," Moodrow interrupted. "What kinda drug dealer uses a professional torch?"

"If it *was* arson," Tilley returned quietly.

"It was definitely arson."

"I admire your hunches, Stanley. You got more street sense than anyone I know and you're probably right. But I'm a cop and I took an oath not to believe anything until I had evidence. If there was no smoking gas can, then I gotta hold off on making any conclusions."

Moodrow got up and walked back to the window, pulling the curtain aside to look up the block. "I wish they'd get here," he said.

"Who?"

"The people I invited to help me with the investigation."

"What's the rush?" Tilley asked, repressing the urge to ask who they were. He'd find out soon enough. "You're not just sitting around. We're working here."

"When they come I'll know the funeral's over," Moodrow explained without turning around.

Tilley, surprised by the answer, found himself wishing for a cigarette, despite having given them up when he was eighteen. He didn't want the cigarette to smoke; he wanted to play with it. To light it, to move it through his fingers. Again, he searched for a reply, but could find none. Moodrow's revelations, though intensely personal, were delivered so matter-of-factly that ordinary sympathy was out of the question. What could he say: "Gee, Stanley, I'm real sorry you have trouble handling funerals"? Finally, he settled for a change of subject.

"You say you don't need to get revenge for Sylvia, right?"

"Yeah."

"You fucked up in Jackson Heights. No doubt about it. You walked around that building with your head up your ass and maybe you think the only way you can pull your head out is to get the mutts responsible. Maybe you want revenge to make your fuck-up right."

Moodrow turned away from the window, crossing the room to stand over Tilley. He was enormous, a huge block of a man whose square, flat body mirrored his habitual lack of expression. "The thing that's bothering me right now," he said, "is that I'm happy to be in a real investigation again. Since I retired, I've been doing little pieces of work. One or two day jobs that turn out to be all legwork. For a long time I've wanted to be in deep, and now I am."

SEVENTEEN

LEONORA HIGGINS was the first to arrive. An old friend of both Moodrow and Tilley, she hugged each in turn, then held Moodrow at arm's length. "Damn, Stanley," she said, "you're even more rumpled than when you were a cop."

Moodrow smiled for the first time that day. "And what about you?" He pointed to her outfit. "You got no business draggin' that *Vogue* bullshit down to this neighborhood."

Leonora, an Assistant District Attorney who ordinarily dressed in tailored navy business suits, performed an obliging twirl. "It's the new me," she declared. "What do ya think?"

She was wearing a white cotton tank top over cotton pants that rose almost to her breasts and a white duster that hung to her ankles. The effect was made even more startling by her dark brown skin and a coarsely woven tribal scarf in the brightest shades of red, orange, and blue.

"You look uptown," Moodrow said flatly. "You always dressed a little uptown, but now you're doing the penthouse."

Leonora, frowning, poured herself a cup of coffee and took a seat at the kitchen table. "Screw you, Stanley. I knew you when you were nuts." She added milk and sugar to the coffee and stirred it slowly. "They're talking District Attorney for me, Stanley. Serious people. I'm on my way to a dinner party after we get finished here. With the kind of people who make District Attorneys."

"Congratulations. With a little luck, you may get to prosecute me someday." Moodrow turned away. His contempt for administrators came as no surprise to either Higgins or Tilley. "The only thing you could do with a fucked-up system," he continued, "is once in a while stuff something decent through the cracks. Most everything you do as a cop just feeds the bullshit politicians. It doesn't do shit about crime and it doesn't make the people any safer. But when you get to be a Commissioner or a District Attorney *all* the cracks disappear. Then you're just a slave to the same vultures who've been eating this city for two hundred years."

Higgins smiled. Moodrow's reaction was expected, but it stung, nevertheless. Curious . . . the names of the people pushing her to make a run could be found on the pages of New York's newspapers almost everyday. Why should she look to this old dinosaur for approval?

"Do you know about the fire and what's going on in Jackson Heights?" Tilley asked diplomatically.

Leonora shook her head and Moodrow went through the history of the Jackson Arms, from the change of ownership to the smoky fire that had killed Sylvia Kaufman. When he'd finished, she took his hand and apologized for her flippant mood.

"Forget about it," Moodrow said. "Tell me what you make of the murder."

"Are you talking about the woman who died in the fire?" she asked.

"Of course."

"What makes you think it was murder?"

"It was murder." Moodrow, obviously annoyed at this second challenge to his instincts, was sharp, but not sharp enough to intimidate his old friend.

"Don't bullshit me, Stanley," she replied evenly. "If any cop had the nerve to bring this to my office looking for warrants, I'd laugh him all the way back to the precinct."

"Look, Leonora," Moodrow insisted, "don't worry about the proof. I didn't call you here because I want some kind of a warrant. I wanna find out who owns three buildings on a quiet block in Jackson Heights. Now I plan to speak personally to the management company and the lawyer who's representing the landlord, but I have grave doubts the prick from the management is gonna tell me anything and talking to lawyers is like howling at the moon. In other words, I'm gonna make the effort, but most likely I'm just wasting time. On the other hand, I also know that landlords have to register with HPD. That's the city, right? Housing Preservation and Development? And I also think there's some new state agency that registers base rents for apartments. I was hoping you might be able to tap into these departments. See what's in the files."

Higgins grinned (as did Tilley) with admiration. "You always were a practical son of a bitch," she observed. "Even after Rita, you did all the logical things. Sure, it wouldn't be any trouble at all for me to pull the files. I could do HPD tomorrow and probably get to DHCR within a couple of days. The Department of Housing and Community Renewal. That's the state agency that watches the city agency that watches the landlords get rich." She burst out laughing. "This isn't really funny, but it shows how hard it is to stop the decay. There was a building I was involved with on Pitt Street, right here on the Lower East Side. A landlord named Furman bought it for $300,000, and two weeks later the back wall started to collapse. The landlord wouldn't make repairs, so the tenants took it to Housing Court, whereupon the judge ordered an inspection. The inspector told the court the wall could go at any minute, so the judge issued a vacate order that made every tenant homeless. Still, the tenants didn't give up. They went back into Housing Court to force the landlord to repair the building. The Housing Judge ruled for the tenants (despite the landlord's claim that it would cost more than he paid for the building to put it back in shape), but the landlord appealed to the Appellate Court, a process that ate up about nine months, during which the empty building continued to fall apart. Finally, two weeks before the Appellate Court affirmed the lower court ruling, there were six separate fires and the roof collapsed. Now it's an empty lot waiting for gentrification."

Betty Haluka arrived next, along with Sergeant Paul Dunlap. She'd lost both her parents years before; Sylvia Kaufman was all that remained of her childhood. Instinctively, she allowed herself to be wrapped in Stanley Moodrow's arms for a moment, then pulled away. His arms were enormous; they enclosed her completely and she was afraid that if she stayed in them for more than a moment, she would never have the courage to come out. When she pulled away, though, she was dry-eyed.

"Are you sure you want to go ahead with this?" Moodrow asked.

"More than anything," she replied. "There's really nothing else for me to do."

Moodrow, his face neutral, introduced Dunlap to Tilley and Higgins. Leonora smiled briefly on learning that Betty worked for Legal Aid. As an Assistant DA, most of the lawyers she faced in court worked for Legal Aid. To some extent, no matter how civilized the contest, the participants in an adversary proceeding are bound to look at each other as competitors. "Where do you work?" she asked.

"I've been working with the Prisoners' Rights Project for the last six months. We're trying to do something about Rikers Island."

Rikers Island, which lies right next to LaGuardia Airport in Queens, contains seven separate jails, and houses more than 18,000 prisoners. A federal judge named Morris Lasker had called it one of the most violent jails in America and various reform groups had been trying to change it for years.

"That's probably why I haven't run into you," Leonora returned. "I've been doing a lot of work in Manhattan recently."

Moodrow, who recognized the natural antagonism, but knew it wouldn't interfere with his plans (there was no chance he'd *let* it interfere), turned his attention to Paul Dunlap. Dunlap was an NYPD sergeant, while he, Moodrow, was a retired cop with a private investigator's license. There was no reason to suppose that Dunlap would submit to Moodrow's authority, but Moodrow had already decided to dump him in favor of Jim Tilley if he refused.

"Did you go to the captain?" Moodrow asked. Shaking Dunlap's hand, he was surprised to find it nearly as big as his own.

"Yeah," Dunlap returned, careful to keep his voice matter-of-fact even though he was bursting with excitement. It was like being let out of prison. "The captain wants to treat it like a homicide. At least until the fire marshal says otherwise. It seems the pastor over at St. Ann's has been calling him three times a day about the troubles in the Jackson Arms."

It had been Moodrow's idea, but Dunlap had carried it through. Though he had little experience with crime, Dunlap knew every priest, reverend, and rabbi in the One One Five. St. Ann's pastor, Father John Casserino, though by no means a drunk or anything close to it, had a certain fondness for Scotch whiskey and the company of Community Affairs Officer Paul Dunlap, who regaled him with fabricated stories of rapes and robberies and murders. So it was no trouble for Father John, who'd been listening to complaints about the Jackson Arms from a number of parishioners, to put a bug in Precinct Commander George Serrano's ear about the same time Porky Dunlap wandered into Serrano's office, humbly requesting that he be allowed to follow up on the suspicious fire on 37th Avenue. Since "follow up," in Serrano's estimation, meant no more than waiting for the fire marshal's report, the Precinct Commander had readily agreed.

"You wanna play cops and robbers, Dunlap?" Serrano had burst out laughing.

"It's not that, Captain. It's just that I know some of the people there . . ."

"Say no more, Dunlap. It's your case. I spoke to the fire marshal about an hour ago and he'll be at the scene tomorrow morning. *Adios*, and don't miss no speeches."

The final member of Moodrow's task force arrived ten minutes later. Short, immensely barrel-chested, his dark hair glistening, Jorge Rivera nodded shyly to the others. As a tenant of the Jackson Arms, he had as much right to be there as any of the others, but, as usual in the presence of native-born Americans, he found himself tongue-tied.

"George," Moodrow said, automatically Anglicizing Rivera's first name, "lemme introduce you to my friends." After the handshakes and the smiles, he continued, addressing the whole group. "I spoke to George Rivera yesterday and he's agreed to act as our contact with the other tenants. I picked him because he does volunteer work, which is to say that he's an active man. As opposed to most people who only exercise their mouths. Now I know it's too soon after the fire and I'm supposed to wait until people recover, but I don't think we have the time. Not that I'm saying I know what's going on, because I don't, but I'm *sure* that there's no random happenings here. Somebody's got a long-term plan and that somebody has a big headstart on us. If we wait even a few days, the fire marshal is gonna bury his report, along with every bit of evidence from the fire scene. This is also true for the evictions that went out last week. They'll be moving into court while we cry into our hankies. I don't like to put it so hard, but that's what I think is happening."

It was Betty's place to affirm or deny Moodrow's speech, and she affirmed it without a second thought. "My role here, as I see it," she began, her voice strong, her eyes fixed on Moodrow, "is to try to slow down the deterioration within the building. As soon as we can get together a tenants' petition, I'll start an HP action in Tenant–Landlord Court. The judge will order an inspection and, when the report comes back, follow up with whatever repairs are needed. That'll get us started. Hopefully, with Mr. Rivera . . ."

"Jorge," Rivera broke in, pronouncing it Hor-hay, with the accent on the first syllable. "Please."

"If Jorge can give me some help, I'll interview any tenant who's received an eviction notice. I've been temporarily transferred to Legal Aid's Tenant–Landlord division, small as it is, and I'll be able to stay there indefinitely. Plus, I'll have the use of a paralegal who's familiar with the field. I spoke to him yesterday, right after Stanley called me. His name is Innocencio Kavecchi. He told me that we can start an action in Supreme Court instead of Housing Court. It's possible, though unlikely, the judge will issue an injunction ordering the landlord to stop harassing the tenants if the eviction notices—they're called dispossess notices, actually; eviction notices come after the judge makes a decision—are completely without foundation. Either way, it'll serve to let all interested parties know that we intend to fight."

"I already have this with the evictions," Jorge Rivera announced. "I have been collectin' a list of tenants with eviction notices and makin' copies. I was gonna take them down to the Council on Housing, where they said they might be able to help us with a lawyer, but if you're gonna do this, it's even better. I know all these tenants personally now, and I ask respectfully to please don' make no mistakes. These are my friends." He handed a manila envelope to Betty Haluka. "Most of the evictions say the tenants haven't been payin' no rents. The tenants say they mail the checks, but the checks don' get cashed. Anyway, it's only one or two months. Nobody gets thrown out in New York for not payin' one or two months' rent, but some people are scared, anyway."

"Let me read these over tonight," Betty said, accepting the envelope. "We'll do interviews over the next few days."

Leonora Higgins followed with a quick rundown of the two agencies involved in regulating New York real estate. "I should be able to get you a profile of the landlord within a few days. It's all on computer now. And there's one other possibility I hadn't thought of before. The building is almost certainly owned by a corporation. I can't say I'm up on corporate law, but every corporation doing business in New York has to file tax returns and I think the original charter, which would be on file with the Department of State in Albany, lists the president and the treasurer. They might not be stockholders, but they'd be a good place to start if you wanted to find the stockholders."

"Perfect," Moodrow declared when Leonora had finished. "I'm glad everybody took the time to come down here. I thought we needed to get started right away, but it's too soon to meet out in Queens. Better to let the people get over the . . . Better let them get over what happened." He surprised himself by not being able to say the word "death," but refused to spend any time thinking about it. Dunlap was next and Moodrow had to find some way to let the sergeant know that he was working *under* Stanley Moodrow without driving him away. Of course, if Moodrow had known that Porky Dunlap was so eager to be a cop he'd willingly serve under the deadest hairbag juicer, in or out of the job, he might have been a little more confident. Nevertheless, finesse not being one of Moodrow's greater accomplishments, he launched into his own plan.

"Sergeant Dunlap and me are gonna investigate the arson. It's too much coincidence that it happened to start right under the apartment of the leader of the tenants' association and that the way it went off there was no damage, except smoke, to any part of the building. We're gonna make sure nobody buries this fire, because it's too hard to prove arson one way or the other. That's tomorrow, right, Paul?"

Dunlap, caught off guard, could do no better than affirm Moodrow. "Yeah, the marshal's gonna be on the scene tomorrow morning."

"Whatta ya say we join him? Look over his shoulder."

Dunlap shrugged. "No problem," he said.

"Once we finish up with the fire marshal," Moodrow continued smoothly, "we'll talk to Precision Management and at least get the name of the lawyer representing the landlord. We can also press Rosenkrantz for an exact schedule of repairs. Not that he's gonna do anything, but the sooner we expose him for a liar, the sooner the other tenants'll come to the association." Moodrow turned his attention to Jorge Rivera. "In the end, it don't matter what we do here, if the tenants don't hold together. It's your home, Jorge. You gotta stand up and fight or you won't be able to live there six months from now."

Much to Moodrow's relief, Dunlap had made no protest at Moodrow's assertion of his own authority and Moodrow was ready to dismiss the group, when someone knocked firmly on the door. Moodrow, who was anxious to be alone with Betty, called out for his visitor to enter. The short, thin young man who pushed the door open was a stranger to everybody.

"Hi," the man called out, his active features seeming to go in all directions at the same time. "My name's Innocencio Kavecchi. Forget the 'Innocencio.' Call me, Ino. Eeeee-no. I'm third generation, right, but my father had this weird sense of humor. Is this the place where I can find Betty Haluka?"

"I'm Betty Haluka," Betty said. "You're the paralegal, right?"

"That's me," Kavecchi said. "Eight years with Legal Aid. Talk about your basic death-in-life, right? The whole time with the housing division. There's nine parts in Manhattan Tenant–Landlord Court and I know every judge in every part. I can walk over to HPD and talk personally to every clerk on the floor. You need a printout on violations for a building, but the landlord should never know, so you don't wanna write up an order? Ten bucks during business hours. Twenty at night. I tell ya, boys and girls, when it comes to housing, I'm an effing freak."

"What about evictions?" Jorge Rivera interrupted. As a man who coveted his own dignity, he was offended by the paralegal's strident voice and sharp mannerisms. "Can you do somethin' for evictions?"

"Actual evictions? That gets hard."

"He means dispossess notices," Betty broke in.

"I got it." Kavecchi turned back to Rivera. "Legit dispossess or b.s.?"

"The second," Jorge replied.

"For b.s. evictions, we go into Supreme Court and say, 'Your honor, my clients will suffer irreparable harm if not given immediate injunctive relief.' Then the judge says, 'Get yer ass outta my courtroom and back to Tenant–Landlord Court before I report you to the Ethics Committee of the New York State Bar Association for terminal stupidity.' Then you go to the Tenant–Landlord Court and, *if* you got all your tenants organized, you consolidate the cases and only have to go into court once. That's for a baseless dispossess. For a legitimate dispossess, we use time. There's eight judges hearing landlord complaints and there's thousands of complaints. Ya think ya just hop in and outta there? I mean in Tenant–Landlord Court you could stretch time as thin as the security in a welfare hotel. Ten months to a year before the landlord can get a tenant off his property."

"What about complaints against the landlord?" Dunlap asked. "How much time does the landlord get?"

"Same thing for both sides, right? Fair is fair. If you could stretch out your problems, why shouldn't the landlord be able to stretch out his? And don't forget, you got eight judges hearing landlord complaints in Manhattan every day. There's only one judge hearing tenant complaints. But it's the same in every court. If all you need is time, you could make it go on practically forever."

Betty was sitting at the foot of the bed, her back to Moodrow. She was dressed for bed in a gray T-shirt and a pair of white gym shorts with a thin red stripe running along each hip. Moodrow, who knew she was thinking about her Aunt Sylvia, watched her sturdy, muscular body carefully, noting both the wide back and the slumped shoulders.

"Are you ever afraid to die?" Betty asked without turning around. Her voice was softer than usual, but there was curiosity there, too.

"I don't think so," Moodrow answered quickly. "I know it's hard to be sure about something like that, but I think I'm more scared of other people dying."

"But you've been in situations where you might die?" she persisted. "Where you had to arrest someone who turned out to be armed, for instance."

"Actually, the fires are the worst. Where you have to go inside and try to warn the people. I'm not that good about fires. I don't know what could happen, and most of the time I didn't have any backup."

"Were you afraid in the fires?"

"Definitely. But even fires weren't the worst. No, the most I was ever scared was in a fight I had with an EDP on a roof. That's 'Emotionally Disturbed

Person' for you civilians. The guy thought I was a devil. He called me 'Moloch.' Kept screaming, 'We die together, Moloch.' "

Betty, turning for the first time, stared directly into her lover's eyes. "You thought he might push you over the edge of the building."

"Yeah. He was chargin' me and I was dodging out of the way. It was late at night and we were in the shadow of a much bigger building, so it was very dark. I was wearing my winter blues, still on patrol, and I couldn't move very well."

"Did you think . . ."

"All I could think about is how much I wanted to shoot the fucker. But the EDP didn't have a gun, so I couldn't use deadly force. Never mind about the mutt wants to cross-block me into the next universe. That's only my judgment and my judgment don't count. If I shot that bastard and claimed self-defense, I'd have to prove it in a courtroom and, guaranteed, I'd be off the force no matter how the trial came out."

"So what did you do?" Betty asked after a moment's silence. She was turned all the way round, sitting cross-legged at the end of the bed. "You must have been terrified by the thought of going over the edge of that roof."

"I didn't do nothin'," Moodrow declared innocently. "The mutt had a heart attack. Right in the middle of the fight, he grabbed his chest and went belly-up on the tarpaper. Started flopping around like a fish on the beach. Crazy, huh? Turned out he'd found three gallons of turpentine in an abandoned basement and been soaking it up for almost a week. Musta gone to his head."

"Are you making this up, Stanley?" Betty had cross-examined hundreds of cops in the course of her career. She could smell perjury like a beagle scenting a fox. "I *know* you're making this up."

"Yeah," Moodrow grinned. "It didn't really happen like that. Actually, I shot the fucker right away, then planted a knife on him."

"Now you're lying about that, too." She took a swipe at his leg, but caught the sheet instead, pulling it off his body. She stared at him for a moment, impressed with his bulk. He really didn't have any fat on his body and it seemed immoral, to Betty, that a human being that big should go through life without a weight problem. She ran a finger over his calf, curling it over the tips of his toes. "Will you make love to me?" she finally asked.

"It's not my strong point," Moodrow replied, "but if ya let me wear the tiger-stripe panties, I'll do my best."

EIGHTEEN

April 4

TALKER PURDY was having the hardest time getting used to his new digs. He hadn't felt so unnatural, so out of place, since his mother had dragged him from the teeming slums of London to deposit him, at ten years old, in the teeming slums off Fourth Avenue in South Brooklyn. *That* took a lot of getting used to, because the neighborhood was mostly Spanish and the other kids spoke and understood broken *American*–English. At best.

So, Talker, despite his belief that he'd emigrated to an English-speaking country, had quickly discovered that his East End yowl might as well have been Hungarian for all the effect it had on his ability to communicate. The local kids at P.S. 242 had instinctively begun to treat him like a freak, to pack up and to use him for a target. A few confrontations, however, had put an end to that. As it turned out, Talker Purdy was dead game and had the scars to prove it. Dead game kids were hard to find, even in Sunset Park, and Purdy had cooperated in his own acceptance by learning Puerto Rican Spanish. And thus earning his nickname: Talker. His real name was Percival. Percival Purdy.

After passing that first test of heart, very little of what he encountered in the course of a rebellious adolescence bothered Talker Purdy, and he finally developed into a taciturn (though criminal) young man. Even when the pigs took him over to the baby unit on Rikers Island for the very first time, he accepted each indignity with grace and patience. Sure, they'd try to fuck him. The other prisoners, especially the black ones who took him for some sort of half-breed Rican, would move on his ass; they'd move on his gold, too, or even his fucking sneakers. They'd move on whatever he had, regardless of its value, because that's the way it was in the baby jail on Rikers. But he knew people, too, and he knew enough to service his own pack. Take someone else's ass. Take someone else's gold. After a week, he had a place in a serious crew and steady access to the pleasures of prison.

What he really couldn't get through his head was that the Spanish people who lived in the apartments surrounding his new home went to work in suits. He knew they were Spanish, because they spoke Spanish to each other, but they were as far from his bro's in *el barrio* as the old white people who kept appearing in the lobby to stare at him through thick, cloudy glasses. Where were the kids?

How come these white people didn't have babies? How come the Spanish people who did have babies kept them locked up in their apartments? And what about the wogs? He knew all about the wogs; he'd been old enough when he'd come over to remember the wogs from London. What he remembered is that you could do almost anything to the wogs and they wouldn't fight back unless they outnumbered you ten to one. Then they'd tear you to pieces.

Talker Purdy's best friend and mentor in the criminal world was Rudy Ruiz, who was called Rudy-Bicho by his friends even though *bicho* meant "prick" in Spanish and should have been an insult. Talker and Rudy-Bicho were testing out the lobby of their new home in Jackson Heights, sitting on a small ledge that, once upon a time, had held house plants. They were listening (or, at least, Talker was listening; Rudy-Bicho was somewhere else altogether) to the Spanish jazz of Hilton Ruiz. The prominent horns slashed at the staccato beat, exciting Talker Purdy, who tapped out the stops and starts of the exotic rhythms perfectly.

"*Mira*, check out these feets, man," he told Rudy-Bicho seriously. "I shoulda been a dancer. Or I shoulda been a singer."

"You should take your fucking head out of your *culo* and start lookin' around."

"What's the matter with you, man?" Talker asked sincerely. They'd both shot the sweet *decata* only two hours before and they were waiting for an afternoon delivery from their new regular connection, who lived above them on the fifth floor. They did armed robberies to support their moderate habits (not bullshit street rip-offs, but jewelry dealers, furriers, securities messengers). The man they worked for, a wiseguy who lived in Bensonhurst, provided information and bought all the merchandise for twenty cents on a dollar. Not a lot, but since the individual hits were big and came off reasonably close together, Rudy-Bicho and Talker Purdy were living the rent-free high life in Jackson Heights. Which is why Talker Purdy was so surprised by his partner's mood.

"I don' like the way these *patas* keep watchin' me like I'm some kinda bug," Rudy-Bicho finally said.

Talker Purdy, who hadn't realized he was being insulted by his fellow tenants, blushed bright red. For all his learning Spanish and dumping his cheapside English accent, he couldn't rid himself of a schoolboy complexion that flashed a deep scarlet whenever he did something stupid. Which was often. "But we livin' here for nothin', man. And we got dope right next door. And don' forget there's no peoples here to rip us off. I don' even see no cops."

Rudy-Bicho reached over to take the much larger man's shirt in his hand, twisting it as he pulled his protégé closer. "How come you go in the joint and you don' learn nothin'? These people look at you like that, they disrespect you, *maricón*. You let them disrespect you today, tomorrow they have their *bichos* so far up your *culo*, you gonna be chokin' from it."

"*Excuse me! Excuse me!*"

Talker Purdy, jarred by the loud voice, was even more startled by the apparition limping toward him. He made the old man for a poppy love, for the kind of

victim he'd often stalked before he'd connected with Rudy-Bicho and taken up
armed robbery. In Talker's world, rabbits didn't approach lions.

"You got business here, you should make a lounge out of this lobby?" the same
figure demanded.

Then a second man came over, one of those weird spics who wore a suit to
work. "What is your business here?" the suit demanded.

"We live here," Talker Purdy explained patiently. He was playing for time
while he tried to get a handle on the situation. "We're neighbors."

"*Chinga tu madre,* mother-fucker," Rudy-Bicho said. His voice took on a
prison-sharp edge which (though it went unrecognized by Mike Birnbaum and
Andre Almeyda) alerted Talker Purdy to the fact that he was supposed to get mad.
"How come you got the balls," Rudy-Bicho continued, "to come over here and
talk to me? A bug comes and talks to me and I gotta put up with this shit? Don'
you know, Señor Whiteman, that I could crackle you up like a fuckin' *cu-
caracha?*"

When Stanley Moodrow and Paul Dunlap entered the lobby of the Jackson
Arms, they saw exactly the same phenomenon, yet they reacted quite differently.
What they saw was an Hispanic male, approximately twenty years of age, five
foot ten inches tall, 165 pounds, with one hand around the throat of an elderly
white male, approximately five foot two inches tall, 120 pounds. There were two
other males, one Hispanic, approximately thirty-five years old, and one white,
approximately twenty years old. The latter pair were standing face to face, as if
just about to enter combat.

Paul Dunlap, whose contact with violence was limited to breaking up fights
between drunken Legionnaires, was uncertain. He stopped for a moment, trying
to get a handle on the situation. Stanley Moodrow, on the other hand, unbuttoned his jacket before the door closed behind him, bellowing, "Stop! Right
now! You, mother-fucker! I'm talkin' to *you!*" He pointed to Rudy-Bicho with his
left hand. "Let that man go or I'll rip ya fucking heart out. Right the fuck now,
faggot. And you, too." This time he pointed at Talker Purdy, who was just
beginning to anger. "Sit ya fucking ass down and shut off the goddamn radio.
Here, fuck it, I'll shut it off myself." He took two steps across the lobby and drove
the toe of his brown wing tips through the radio's speaker.

The initial silence was deafening. As Moodrow had hoped, it froze the
participants in their tracks. In his estimation, he had come upon a scene that was
almost, but not quite, out of control and his best move was to keep the lid on.
Rudy-Bicho (making the two enormous men for cops) released Mike Birnbaum,
who staggered back several steps. Andre Almeyda, who'd been eagerly closing
with Talker Purdy, stopped in his tracks. Talker Purdy, confused and bro-
kenhearted, stared at his radio with evident surprise.

"Dunlap?" Moodrow's sharp voice broke the momentary silence.

"Right behind you." Dunlap elbowed his way between Moodrow and Purdy, announcing, "Assume the position, asshole," in the most bored voice he could muster.

Moodrow turned immediately and walked across to Rudy-Bicho Ruiz, who reacted by folding his arms across the chest. "The *maricón* attack me and I'm defendin' myself. I wasn't doin' nothin' when he attack me. He attack me for nothin'."

Moodrow, though he took in the words, paid no attention whatsoever. He wasn't looking for explanations; he'd just witnessed a felony and had absolutely no interest in explanations until the perpetrator was properly secured. Dominating the smaller man with his sheer bulk, he yanked Ruiz erect and spun him toward the wall, talking all the while. "Get up against it, prick. Get your fucking legs back. You make one twitch, I'm gonna crack your neck." His hands were moving over Ruiz's body, searching for a weapon, before he stopped speaking. Finding nothing, he yanked the man's arms behind his back and cuffed him tightly.

"You're under arrest," he began automatically, forgetting that he had no powers of arrest and that he wasn't a cop and that the loss of those powers was the reason why Paul Dunlap was with him. "You have the right to remain silent. If you choose to speak, anything you say can be used against you." He went through the whole speech while he searched Ruiz down to his underwear and his socks. Having found no weapon, he was hoping for drugs, but, again, he was disappointed. Still, there was no question about the assault. It would stand up and if the man had any serious priors or if he was on parole, he might do real time.

"So what's going on here?" Moodrow, much quieter now that the scene was under control, asked Mike Birnbaum.

"I come into *my* lobby and see two animals they wouldn't even let in a zoo." He wanted to say, "two spics" (if he'd been with his friend, Paul Reilly, the ex-fireman, he would have), but Andre Almeyda was an ally, so he held himself in check. "Nat'rally, I ask myself what they're doing here. My lobby don't look like the Waldorf Astoria. My lobby don't look like the jail on Rikers Island, where these animals probably came from. Maybe they think it's a day care center? Maybe they think they're in *shul*? Maybe they're looking for a *minyan*?"

"Mike," Moodrow brought the old man up short. "Do me a favor and get to the point."

Birnbaum tossed Moodrow his angriest look, but got only a blank stare in return. "I went up to this *macher* here." He pointed to Ruiz. "I asked him what he thought he was doing in my lobby and he grabbed me by the throat without so much as a word."

"That's true," Andre Almeyda chimed in. "I was coming from the mail and I see it happening. Mike didn' do nothing to this guy."

"We live here, too!" Talker Purdy suddenly cried out. "We're neighbors." The frustration was coming down on him hard. He was an easy-going man, but if they took Rudy-Bicho away, he wouldn't be able to do the jobs anymore. And he wouldn't have any good dope, either. In fact, without Rudy-Bicho's connection in Brooklyn, he'd most likely have to take up his old profession, which policemen like to refer to as "opportunistic thief."

"Tell me exactly what happened," Dunlap asked Andre Almeyda. "Especially about this one." He jerked his head toward Purdy.

As Andre launched into a detailed explanation of the assault (an explanation which, incidentally, exonerated Talker Purdy), the lobby began to fill with curious tenants. Moodrow's first instinct was to protect the crime scene, but after glancing over at Dunlap, who seemed to be enjoying the show, he allowed the witnesses to assemble. Thus, almost a dozen tenants were present when Anton Kricic, his luminous, orange-red hair flaming in all directions, emerged from his first floor apartment to confront Moodrow and Dunlap.

"This man has as much right to be here as any resident," Kricic screamed. He was extremely tall, taller than Moodrow, but stick-thin, with a narrow face framed by a halo of very curly, very long hair.

Dunlap put up a hand to stop the apparition. "What're you talking about?" he asked, innocently.

"You have no authority to put this man out. He's a human being with a right to shelter. You can't put him on the street again." Kricic, though he stopped coming forward, tried to make it clear that he was not about to be bullied by a couple of middle-aged cops. Not with this many witnesses handy.

"What's your name?" Moodrow asked quietly. He was beginning to get the feeling that he'd been out-maneuvered again, that something new was sneaking up on him, and the feeling was making him very depressed.

"Anton Kricic," Kricic announced proudly. "I live in apartment 1F. In fact, my name is already on the mailbox."

"Do you have a lease?" Moodrow asked.

"That's not your business," Kricic shouted.

"This man is under arrest for an assault," Dunlap explained angrily. He didn't care to be told that he had no authority any more than Moodrow did. "It has nothing to do with tenants and landlords. Now, I'm telling you to step back. I'm directly ordering you to remove yourself from the crime scene. If you don't, I'm going to place you under arrest for hindering a police officer, which is a D Felony. The penalty for commission of a D Felony is an indeterminate sentence of up to seven years in prison. Now move your ass outta here."

Kricic sneered, though he did, in fact, step away from Dunlap. His purpose in coming out had been to confront the other tenants with the reality of his existence. He had hoped, of course, that the arrest had something to do with the fact that Purdy and Ruiz were squatters with no legal right to their apartments, but he settled for the confused looks on the faces of his neighbors as he walked back to his apartment unmolested. Once they realized that he was living rent-free, they would protest to the landlord, who would move to kick him and the other squatters out. That would be a great day for the homeless: the day when the media chronicled the squatters' physical eviction from warehoused apartments the landlord was deliberately keeping off the market.

Back in the lobby, Dunlap stepped closer to Moodrow, raising his eyebrows in a silent question.

"Forget about him," Moodrow said calmly. "We'll look into Anton Kricic later. As for this mutt . . ." He gave Ruiz a little tug, pulling him closer. "Call the One One Five and get a sector car down here. Give the collar to whoever shows up. Let 'em get statements from Andre and Mike and use them to write up the complaint. We can act as witnesses, but let's not get trapped down at Central Booking. Let the uniforms sit around all day. We got a lotta work to do and it's shaping up to be a very bad day."

NINETEEN

As soon as the two patrolmen had arrived and been briefed, Moodrow and Dunlap walked from the lobby to Sylvia Kaufman's apartment, their original destination when they'd happened upon Birnbaum and Ruiz. It was an obligatory visit for Moodrow, in light of his relationship to Betty Haluka and the Jackson Arms, but he didn't see himself as an investigator. Nor was he going as a friend of the dead woman. He was occupying an uneasy middle ground, a position he'd occupied many times in the course of his policeman's life. His best bet was to understand himself as a simple acquaintance (as Dunlap was doing), but the dual anger he felt (with himself for playing the fool and with men who kill with no regard for the manifest innocence of their victims) was too powerful to allow him that refuge.

Somebody had put up a card table outside the apartment door, and set a carafe of coffee on it. A smallish, middle-aged man sat on a kitchen chair by the table. "Hello," he said, smiling up at them. "I'm Herb Belcher. Sylvia Kaufman was my mother-in-law. I suppose one of you must be Stanley Moodrow. Betty's boyfriend."

He stuck out a hand and Moodrow shook it briefly before introducing Dunlap. "Betty's inside. Are you going in?" Belcher asked.

"Yeah," Moodrow answered. "We're not gonna be long, though."

The first thing Moodrow saw, after ducking into the apartment, was a thick candle burning in a glass cylinder. It reminded him of the Russian Orthodox Church where he'd gone as a boy. Even the smell of smoke was like the smell of the incense pouring from the metal censer swung by the priest. Then he remembered the last time he'd been inside a church; not surprisingly, it was at the last funeral he'd attended. A thought popped up in his mind: this can't be the same, because you didn't really know Sylvia Kaufman. Followed quickly by: it *never* should have happened.

Marilyn Belcher, who had been Marilyn Kaufman prior to setting off for UCLA twenty years before, a heavyset, graying woman, was sitting on a low stool when Moodrow walked into the room. Betty was kneeling beside her on the rug and both were crying. Marilyn wore a dark gray dress decorated only by a torn black ribbon pinned below her left shoulder. She was in her stocking feet, her face free of makeup. Her hair, which had been cut and feathered so carefully in a Santa Barbara salon a week before, was barely combed now.

Later, Betty would tell Moodrow that Marilyn's grief, already compounded by the sudden, violent nature of her mother's death, had been aggravated by the years she and her mother had spent apart; Marilyn was blaming both herself and her husband for lost opportunities. At the time, however, Moodrow saw only the face of a woman made frantic by grief, a woman very near to tearing at her own flesh. The emotion was so strong, it stopped him as soon as he entered the room. It stood in his way and held him back, like the force field in a Hollywood science-fiction movie.

Sergeant Paul Dunlap (which is the way he introduced himself to Marilyn Belcher), on the other hand, had attended more than a hundred funerals in his official capacity as Community Affairs Officer. He walked directly to the women and began to offer his condolences in a strong, clear, hearty-Irish voice. "I'm so sorry," he began.

If Betty hadn't come over and taken Moodrow's hand, he might have spun on his heel and walked out of the apartment. He'd turned his head away from Marilyn an instant after reading her grief, preferring to concentrate on the fruit and cake displayed on a coffee table, the white sheets covering the mirrors, the sharp, destructive odor of the smoke. The smell of smoke dominated the apartment; it stung Moodrow's eyes and burned his nostrils, reminding him of the job ahead.

"Don't stay long," Betty, an unconscious angel of mercy, whispered. "Marilyn and I need to talk."

The smell of smoke, powerful as it was in the apartment upstairs, was far worse in the basement. It rushed over Moodrow and Dunlap as soon as the elevator door opened, causing both to jerk their heads away from the open door as if they'd just come upon a moving rat in a narrow corridor.

"Jesus Christ," Dunlap muttered. "You smell that?"

Moodrow didn't answer. Once over the initial shock, he eagerly snorted the odor up into his nostrils, using it like ammonia in the nose of a fainting virgin in a romantic novel. It pulled his attention away from the apartment above and focused it on the fire marshal in the spiffy uniform with the peaked hat. The man was standing in a large room just past a series of cheaply partitioned storage sheds. He had his hands on his hips, obviously impatient with his not-unexpected visitors.

"Sam Spinner?" Dunlap asked. "I'm Paul Dunlap, from the One One Five. This is Stanley Moodrow."

Sam Spinner suspected that the two cops (he knew that Dunlap was a cop and he assumed Moodrow was Dunlap's partner) were there to second-guess the investigation. *His* investigation. He was a short, thick man with a heavy face dominated by allergy-tormented blue eyes. Allergies had been the curse of his career and he was especially allergic to smoke.

"What's up?" he asked curtly. Cop briefings were obligatory courtesies extended by one department to another. Spinner couldn't avoid them, but he didn't have to like them. Or to make them pleasant.

"I spoke to you on the phone yesterday," Dunlap said evenly. "So you already know what it's about." Dunlap (as Sam Spinner had predicted) believed that all crime was the property of the NYPD. Including arson.

"Oh, yeah, that's right. You're the Sherlock Holmes who talks about arson *before* he even comes down to the scene. You're a psychic, right?"

Dunlap threw Moodrow a sharp look before responding. He was trying to tell Moodrow that, as far as Sam Spinner was concerned, they were in trouble. Moodrow, who never doubted that he would eventually find proof of deliberate arson, was unimpressed.

"I take it you've completed your investigation?" Dunlap asked.

"Except for the lab tests," Spinner announced.

"So whatta ya think?" Moodrow was all smiles as he suddenly entered the conversation. "Did you come to any conclusions yet?"

"Well, I sure don't think it was arson." Spinner turned to the more sympathetic Moodrow. "I think you cops are barkin' up the wrong tree."

"See," Moodrow said, turning to Dunlap, "I told you it wasn't arson. No way it *could* be arson. You're buyin' me lunch, Paulie. Don't forget our bet." He turned back to Spinner, still grinning. "I got a partner sees murder every time he farts."

Spinner laughed. He didn't like cops much. Most of them, he knew, held the Fire Department's investigatory division in contempt, especially the detectives. "He oughta buy ya two lunches fa this one. I been through every inch of this basement and I don't see nothin' but an accidental fire."

"But how do you know for sure?" Dunlap asked. "I mean, gimme a goddamn break. This guy eats like a horse."

Spinner drew himself up. If they wanted a lecture on fire investigation, he would be glad to give them one. "First thing, there ain't no sign of an accelerant anywhere. No gasoline, no kerosene, no lighter fluid, no nothin'. I took samples, nat'rally, and I'm gonna put 'em through the chromatograph, but I guarantee they're gonna come out clean. Second thing is the mattress where the fire started. It's been there for years. All ya gotta do is pick it up and look at the concrete underneath to see that. Third thing is there's been people using this area for living quarters. There's well-decayed human feces behind the boiler. There's urine stains in several places along the back wall. There's food particles . . ."

"How come there's no damage? How come nothing got burned?" Dunlap continued to probe, asking his questions curtly while staring angrily at his partner. In every respect, he appeared to be no more than a dumb flatfoot pissed at being caught on the wrong side of an argument.

"Mattress fires don't make a lotta heat. Smoke, yeah. Clouds of black smoke. Especially when they got motor oil soaked into one corner like this one did."

"I thought you said there was no accelerant?" Dunlap said.

"Motor oil, unless you got tremendous heat, puts a fire out. Ain't you seen all the ads on TV about engine heat and the oil don't break down? You practically gotta use napalm to ignite motor oil. Here, lemme learn you a little something about fires." Snorting triumphantly, he led them to the back of the room where the remains of the mattress, a jet-black rectangle almost lost against the smoke-scorched wall, still lay. The fire had evidently begun in the center of the mattress and, fueled by the newspaper padding, spread to the edges. One corner was almost untouched and it was here that Sam Spinner pointed. "See this here?" he said. "Where it ain't burnt? This corner is soaked with motor oil. I figure there musta been oil in the middle, too, but when the fire reached where the oil was thick, it went out. That oil, in case ya thinkin' about askin' me, is gonna show up in scrapings we took off the wall and ceiling. It don't mean nothin' in terms of heat, but it makes very dense smoke."

"How do ya know someone didn't pour the oil on the mattress, then set the fire?" Dunlap asked.

Spinner looked at Moodrow, gesturing over at Dunlap. "Some guys don't like ta lose," he said, sarcastically.

"You got that right," Moodrow agreed.

"The reason," Spinner announced, turning back to Paul Dunlap, "why I know how long the oil has been in the mattress is that I picked up a corner of the goddamn mattress and checked to see if there was oil on the bottom. That mattress, my friend, is soaked through and the oil in the mattress is gritty and dry. That's because it's been there for a long time. No way it coulda been put there even a week ago." He glared at Dunlap contemptuously, leaving a long, empty silence before taking up the thread of his logic. "Now the third reason why this fire was accidental is the presence of drug paraphernalia. Crack vials, glassine envelopes, syringes, candles, bent spoons, scorched bottle caps, etcetera, etcetera. Evidently, the neighborhood druggies come down here ta get their jollies and somebody didn't blow out his candle. Could be the asshole just nodded out, as junkies are known to do. He nods off and, when he wakes up, the fire is too strong to put out. Or maybe he could put it out, but he don't give a shit. Whatever the case, he takes off for parts unknown without havin' the decency ta call 911."

"It sounds right to me," Moodrow interrupted. He had less than no interest in Spinner's speculations. What he wanted was a rundown of the physical evidence, which he'd already been given. Now it was time to see if there was any profit to be squeezed from that evidence. "It's too bad about the lady upstairs."

Spinner's eyes dropped to the floor. "I feel like shit about that," he said, piously. "The bad breaks she got are almost unbelievable. First, when the landlord decides ta put in new pipes, he hires a lumberjack with a chainsaw instead of a plumber. The hole on this goddamn retrofit is nearly twice as big as the pipe. Second, the guy livin' above the old lady stuffs the hole around *his* pipes with insulation so the smoke can't go up. Third, she's got the windows closed tight, the bedroom door shut and the smoke alarm out in the hallway. See, that's another reason why this fire was an accident. What did an arsonist stand ta gain? How could he know all those things would be that way upstairs? I mean about the windows and the smoke alarm? It don't make sense anyone should do it deliberately."

"Say," Moodrow interrupted, changing the subject abruptly, "did you mention you dusted that paraphernalia you found? I don't remember."

"For fingerprints?" Spinner was incredulous.

"Yeah." Dunlap joined in, even though he didn't know what Moodrow was getting at, either. "For goddamn fingerprints."

"It's just paraphernalia," Spinner insisted. "Like ya find in every empty lot in the city. You're actin' like crack vials are weapons. Gasoline cans get dusted, right? Window glass. Lock handles. Since when do ya dust crack vials? Not that I didn't gather all the paraphernalia. I got it bagged and tagged, just like they taught me in fire school."

"Sam," Moodrow said, again changing the subject. "I wonder if you'd do me a favor. Would you let me take the paraphernalia over to the precinct and let our print guy take a look at it? I promise I'll have it back to you tomorrow."

"I don't know . . ." Sam Spinner didn't want to refuse his pal, and his conviction that the fire had been accidental made it possible to agree. After all, once his report was written, the samples he'd collected would be so much garbage. Still, doing favors for cops went against the grain.

"It's not for what you think," Moodrow said quickly. "It's for the narcs. There's been a lotta dope in this building and if we can find a brand name on the vials or the envelopes, or even a print we can match with a known dealer, maybe we'll finally be able to pinpoint the dirtbags bringing the dope in. Tomorrow—I promise—I'll personally bring the bag anywhere you say."

Ten minutes later, Moodrow and Dunlap stood outside the Jackson Arms, equally grateful for the fresh air. Moodrow held a large manila envelope in his right hand and both men were looking at it.

"What do you want with that crap?" Dunlap asked. "I've been going along with you. No problem. But how about letting me in on the secret?"

Much to Dunlap's surprise, Moodrow took the question seriously. "The fire was meant as a warning. It wasn't supposed to kill her. Sure, the mattress has been down there for years. The janitor who got fired when the new management took over was an alkie. He slept down there, hung out when he didn't wanna be found. Maybe he even resented the tenants so much, he pissed and shit down there. But the janitor *wasn't* on drugs. In fact, according to every tenant in the building, there wasn't any drug problem at all until six weeks ago, so how do you figure the crack vials got down there? And the syringes? And the candles and the fucking spoons? It stinks, Paulie. It fucking stinks and you oughta know it."

Dunlap flinched at the contempt in Moodrow's voice. "And what do you expect to find? You think all the prints are gonna be the same?"

"The first thing I wanna know," Moodrow replied evenly, "is if there's any prints at all."

The headquarters of Precision Management, the entire second floor of a small shopping plaza on Hillside Avenue in eastern Queens, was far from the suite of posh offices envisioned by Paul Dunlap. Five thousand feet of unwaxed, un-washed, black floor tiles, of desks lined one behind the other like beds in a homeless shelter, supported the various endeavors that made up the total busi-ness of Precision Management Consultants, Inc. There were two lawyers, their busy outlines just visible through dirty glass doors; an active insurance brokerage with phones ringing everywhere; a much quieter real estate division with three tired saleswomen talking shop; and, finally, almost as an afterthought, a small section specializing in residential real estate management.

As the two men crossed the big room, both were reminded of the detectives' room in a precinct. Virtually everything above the floor was dirty metal: gray desks, filing cabinets, dusty shelves. The legs of the desks were black with dirt and looked sticky and there was a smell of physical neglect that utterly belied the powerful drive for achievement that had created that neglect in the first place.

"I think the cops subcontract the maintenance for this fucking place," Mood-row whispered. "It's a sewer."

Suddenly, one of the real estate saleswomen, her square Irish face split into a smile, looked away from her conversation and asked, "Can I help you with anything?"

"Yeah," Dunlap said. "We're looking for Precision Management."

"It's *all* Precision Management," the woman observed.

"Al Rosenkrantz," Moodrow said, drawing the woman's attention. "That's who we're looking for."

"Sweet Al?" The woman broke into laughter.

"Yeah, Sweet Al. Where could we find him?"

"His office is against the far wall. In the real estate management division." She watched them go for a moment, before calling out. "Make sure he keeps his hands in his pockets."

When Moodrow pushed open the door to Al Rosenkrantz's office, Rosenkrantz jumped straight out of the chair. "If this guy can't control himself," he said to Paul Dunlap, "get him out of here. There's two lawyers at the other end of the building. Any repeat of the other night and I'm gonna send them after your pension."

"Why don't you sit over there, Moodrow?" Dunlap said, pointing to a dirty gray metal chair by the door. "And keep your face shut for a change." He glared at Moodrow briefly, then turned back to Rosenkrantz. "Look, Moodrow apologizes for the other day. He was way outta line. Of course, you shouldn't have said what you said, either, but that's past us now. All we want is a few minutes of your time."

Rosenkrantz, encouraged by Dunlap's apologetic tone, pulled himself up in the chair before answering. "So take your few minutes and be on your way. I don't mean to be abrupt, but I seem to be giving all my time to the Jackson Arms these days. It's really a nothing project for us."

"First thing I should tell you," Dunlap said, "is that the fire is an open investigation at the 115th Precinct. It's official, right? A suspicious fire."

"That's very interesting, because I spoke to the fire marshal not more than ten minutes ago and he thinks the fire was accidental. The building is insured through our brokerage, by the way, and the carrier is ready to cut a check as soon as the lab reports come back."

Dunlap, nonplussed for the moment, looked over at Moodrow, whose face, unfortunately, remained blank. "Be that as it may, it's still my duty to tell you that, as far as the New York Police Department is concerned, the origins of the fire remain suspicious."

"Okay, you told me." Rosenkrantz was beginning to enjoy himself. The cop was already uncomfortable and he was just getting started. "Now what could I do for you?"

"Of course, we're not here to question you about the fire," Dunlap admitted. "We're here on behalf of the tenants."

"If it's about the dispossess notices, I already heard from this Legal Aid guy . . ." He searched his notepad for a moment before spelling out the name. "K A V E C C H I. I wouldn't even make a guess as to the pronunciation. He informs me that all the tenants who received dispossess notices have retained a Legal Aid attorney to represent them. He says they intend to prepare a motion asking that all the cases be consolidated and dismissed at one hearing. Legal Aid is also going into Supreme Court to ask for some kind of injunction. This guy K A V E C C H I is very pushy; he expected me to make him an answer right on the spot. I told him that I just take orders . . ."

"From who?" Dunlap asked innocently.

"From the landlord."

"And who's the landlord?"

Rosenkrantz smiled and shook his head sadly. They were so stupid. "The

Jackson Arms and the two adjoining buildings are owned by Bolt Realty Corporation."

"That's where you get your instructions? From a corporation?"

"Bolt Realty is represented by an attorney named William Holtz."

"You got his address and phone number?" Dunlap asked.

"My secretary can give you that information."

"Why don't you get it for him?" Moodrow rose halfway out of his chair. "This is a police investigation, you asshole. Whatta ya think, you're the fuckin' mayor? Get the goddamn address."

Dunlap smiled apologetically, gesturing wildly for Moodrow to sit back down. "Please, Al, if you could help us out, we'd appreciate it."

Rosenkrantz, who had less desire to deal with his irascible secretary than Dunlap, flipped the pages of his Rolodex briefly, then handed a card bearing the address and phone number of William Holtz to Sergeant Paul Dunlap, who dutifully copied it into a small notepad.

"There's one other thing," Dunlap said. "You promised the tenants you were going to make some repairs. You know, the mailboxes and the front locks and the elevator? I tell you the truth, Al, I was scared myself when I used that elevator. It banged around like it was gonna fall apart any second . . ."

"While we're talking," Rosenkrantz interrupted.

"Pardon me?"

"All three of those things are being done while we're talking. The crews are on the scene right now." Rosenkrantz leaned across the desk to tap the back of Dunlap's hand. He was sweating profusely, but he smiled his brightest smile, nonetheless. "Look, I admit things haven't worked out as well as they could have, but I intend to keep the promises I've made. Now, for God's sake, sergeant, you and the rest of the cops have to take some of the blame. You say there's dealers and whores in the building? Then arrest them. Put them in jail. When I went to Bayside High School, they taught me that a body can't be in two places at the same time. If you put them in jail, they won't be in my buildings."

The Manhattan offices of Holtz, Meacham, Meacham and Brount, located in the Kalikow Building at 101 Park Avenue, were everything the offices of Precision Management weren't. The beige carpet pushed back against the soles of the feet like brand-new sixty-dollar Nikes. The brown burlap-covered walls sported a matched set of eight oil paintings depicting a fox hunt, from the huntsmen's breakfast to the bloody corpse held triumphantly aloft. The receptionist, suitably young and beautiful, wore a necklace and bracelet of woven gold worth more than Moodrow's entire wardrobe. Not quite sharp enough to make Dunlap and Moodrow for cops, she began to smile as soon as the door opened far enough to reveal the two visitors.

"May I help you?" Her low, musical voice was stunning, as carefully prepared as her tightly curled and slightly unkempt hair. Hearing it, Moodrow couldn't help but wonder how rich a law firm had to be to afford such an ornament. If, he concluded as he asked for William Holtz, the woman had put as much effort into school as she'd evidently put into her appearance, he'd be talking to a neurosurgeon. Still, her equally musical, "Mr. Holtz, there are two policemen to see you," failed to get them into the lawyer's office. Instead, William Holtz, tall, tanned, and heavily muscled in his middle age, strode into the reception area to confront them publicly.

"Gentlemen?" Holtz, whose dark pinstriped suit, handmade by a Hong Kong Chinese with a showroom on East Broadway, had cost more than his receptionist's jewelry, spoke sharply. He (a rare exception to the rule) accepted Moodrow and Dunlap's respective IDs and began to examine them closely.

Moodrow waited patiently, at first, then stepped in close and looked directly into the lawyer's eyes. He wasn't operating under the delusion that he could intimidate the man—lawyers are exempt from all forms of police bullying and they know it—but Moodrow's cop radar had begun to beep the minute Holtz had appeared. He could feel himself drawing closer to the end of the mystery and he wanted to let Holtz (and whoever he was fronting for) know that Stanley Moodrow was coming. That simple. That final.

"Which one of you is Sergeant Dunlap?" Though he maintained the eye contact, Holtz took a step back.

"Right here."

"I'm very busy at the moment, sergeant. I've a client in my office and I'm late for a partners' meeting. I've also had a long conversation with Mr. Rosenkrantz . . ."

"This'll only take a few minutes," Moodrow said.

"Mr. Moodrow," Holtz returned, stepping around the larger man, "this conversation will be completed much more quickly if you stay out of it. I permit you to remain as a courtesy to Sergeant Dunlap, but I'm sure you realize that you're a private citizen and have no standing here whatsoever." He hesitated, allowing Moodrow the opportunity to challenge his statement, but Moodrow let it pass. "As I said, sergeant, I've just had a conversation with Mr. Rosenkrantz and I'm familiar with the condition of the property belonging to Bolt Realty."

"We were wondering if you knew about that," Dunlap said quietly. He was half in a daze. The furnishings had gone to his head, the receptionist had gone to his crotch, and William Holtz's wardrobe had gone to his heart. Holtz, Meacham, Meacham and Brount was a long way from the Elks Club.

"Wonder no longer, sergeant. I have absolute confidence in Precision Management. Needless to say, Bolt Realty deplores any illegal activity occurring on its property and will, within reason, take whatever steps are necessary to repair the damage. Mr. Rosenkrantz has been so instructed, not only this afternoon, but on several occasions in the past." He smiled briefly. "Are we done?"

"There's just one more thing," Moodrow said.

Holtz, who stood between Moodrow and Dunlap, didn't bother to turn around. "Mr. Moodrow," he began, "do you think you can stay out of this? If you can't, we'll end the conversation right here." Again, he hesitated, waiting for Moodrow to respond, expecting and hoping the big ex-cop was infuriated and impotent.

"There *is* one more thing," Dunlap, who'd nearly forgotten, said quietly. "The landlord. We were hoping to appeal directly to the landlord. Would you have a problem giving us the landlord's name?"

William Holtz was genuinely amused. His salt-and-pepper crewcut seemed to leap erect as he grinned broadly. "Sergeant Dunlap, do you know anything about New York State corporate law? Or about the New York State housing code? Suffice it to say that my clients have no wish to be subject to the harassment of guerrillas like Stanley Moodrow. I have complete power of attorney with regard to the properties in question and am prepared to exercise my authority in a manner furthering the aims of my client. And that is all, gentlemen. That is the end of the interview. Please keep the following in mind: I will not receive you again unless a court compels me to do so. Have a pleasant afternoon."

TWENTY

MOODROW was lying in bed, alone, naked, and fairly drunk, when the calls began to come in. He was alone because Betty had decided to stay overnight with her cousin in Jackson Heights; he was naked because he was drunk; he was drunk because he and Dunlap had celebrated their first useless day by hoisting six (or seven or eight) glasses of bourbon in the course of an Italian dinner.

The first caller was the paralegal, Ino Kavecchi, who launched into his own lament so quickly, he failed to pick up a hint of Moodrow's condition. "Whatsa matter with these people?" he complained. "They don't wanna help themselves out? I mean I went to every tenant who got a dispossess. To sign them up to a petition so we could process all of them at one time, remember? Well, I couldn't even get all of *them* to cooperate. You believe that? Three of the families are gettin' ready to haul ass outta there. Don't make sense, right? I mean we're gonna defend the *shmucks* for nothin'. It took me all goddamn morning to find someone to explain it. Not that I shouldn't have figured it out, because it's simple

greed, like it usually is when people do shitty things. I mean the landlord ain't
been cashing their checks and they figure the judge is gonna give 'em a few
months to find another place, during which they still won't pay any rent. Since
they got somewhere else to go, why not take advantage and live without rent for
six months or so? I swear, if I read it in a book, I wouldn't believe it."

Moodrow's head was beginning to spin with the energy of Kavecchi's lament.
"Hold it a second," he ordered, shaking himself awake. "Did you check the
empty apartments like I asked you?"

"That's another ball-buster," Kavecchi groaned. "Holy God, what a problem I
had with *that* one. Unbelievable. I mean how am I supposed to know who's a
tenant and who's a squatter? The place is a goddamn zoo."

Moodrow was suddenly alert. "What are you talking about?"

"Like I admit I don't know much about Jackson Heights, but I was under the
impression this kinda shit didn't happen out here. The place is like the Lower
East Side. There's dealers and dopers everywhere. I mean some whore proposi-
tioned me in the lobby. And this bitch was out front, man—she pulled up her
skirt and flashed me. Then her boyfriend, when he saw I didn't want the pussy,
offered to sell me some crack. I mean I better get a haircut or something. People
are makin' me for a doper and I'm tryin' to count empty apartments."

"Innocencio . . ."

"Ino. Please call me Ino. Like EEEE-NO. I mean I'm third generation,
already."

Moodrow, groaning, suddenly realized that Kavecchi's voice was the male
equivalent of a Lucille Ball screech. "Ino, do me a favor and get to the point. I'm
not feelin' so hot."

"I thought I was gonna go nuts, but then I ran into this old guy named Mike
Birnbaum. What a fantastic break for me. I mean, like out of the goddamn blue,
this guy walks up and asks me am I from Legal Aid and Betty said he should look
out for me. He knows everything about the building. Everything."

"Just tell me how many empty units, all right?" Moodrow's voice began
to rise. His head was throbbing in anticipation of the figure Kavecchi would
give him.

"As of three o'clock this afternoon, there were thirty-two empty units in the
Jackson Arms, but the most amazing part is that a bunch more people are getting
ready to fly. I mean, it's pretty amazing. I can go almost anywhere in the slums
and get people organized. Not that a good tenants' association means a sure
winner, but without it you got no chance at all. Here in Jackson Heights, where
the people *have* a little money, they hide in their apartments like rabbits. Go
figure, right?"

"Right," Moodrow sighed. "Go figure. Thanks for calling."

"Whatta ya, tired?"

"Yeah, I'm tired."

"Well, one more thing you oughta know before we hang up. I ran into this

Asian named Assiz and he told me that a whole bunch of dispossess notices went out to the tenants in the other two buildings."

Leonora Higgins' call, which came ten minutes later, found Moodrow still naked in his bed, but far from asleep. He'd retrieved the bourbon from the kitchen cupboard right after hanging up on the paralegal and was sipping morosely when the phone rang.

"Yeah?" he said sharply.

"Stanley?"

"Leonora?"

"It's me."

"How did I know?" Moodrow sat erect. In his heart of hearts, he wasn't convinced that the owner of the Jackson Arms had anything to do with the violence, but the name or names would represent the day's only small victory.

"I have some bad news for you, Stanley," Leonora said calmly. She had no idea of Moodrow's day or of his mental condition. Her own day had been long and difficult and she wanted a hot bath, a glass of white wine, and her bed. "I got into the computer this evening after court and HPD doesn't have the name of the landlord and neither does DHCR. The property is owned by a corporation, and all the agencies have is the name of the company. Bolt Realty Corporation."

"How could they not have it? How can you fucking regulate without knowing who you're regulating? It could be fucking Hitler and they wouldn't give a shit." All of a sudden, Moodrow's headache, temporarily driven into retreat by a renewed infusion of Oldfield's Wild Turkey Bourbon, began to chip away at the bone above his right eye.

"You're only partially right, Stanley. New York *would* give a shit if it knew Hitler owned property. The politicians would have to give a shit in order to protect their butts. That's why they don't require the information. They don't want to know. In any event, according to the city and the state, the owner is a corporation named Bolt Realty. All other registered information concerns base rents, the size and nature of the property, and the conditions of the buildings. I can get you the date when construction was completed, the number of rooms, the median rent, the yearly rent roll, the base rent for each apartment, the last rent increase . . ."

"All right," Moodrow complained. "I get the hint." He rubbed impotently at the circle of pain spreading up into his forehead. "Wasn't there some other place you said you were gonna try?"

"I'm trying to get into the state corporate charters. To take a look at the original application for a certificate of incorporation. But I'm having trouble, Stanley. A supervisor in Albany stumbled onto what I was doing and threw a fit."

"Wait a minute, Leonora." Moodrow sat bolt upright. "Don't fuck yourself up with this. I don't want you to take any risks when we don't even know if the information is valuable."

Leonora, warmed by his concern, smiled into the phone. "You know something, Stanley, you're really sweet. You're a very sweet man."

"Like syrup," Moodrow agreed, sipping at his drink. He'd made a career out of manipulating the NYPD without confronting it. "But I mean what I say: don't put your ass on the line for this."

"Well, not to worry, Stanley. I'm not in any danger, but I won't be able to make another try for a week or two. If there's anything else I can do in the meantime . . ."

Moodrow didn't return the bourbon to the kitchen after Leonora Higgins hung up. Frustration is part and parcel of a detective's working life. The rule is fifty fruitless interviews for each eyewitness, a dozen freezing mid-winter stakeouts in a battered Dodge van for each dope deal recorded on videotape. Moodrow was infuriated by a system that could regulate virtually every aspect of the real estate industry without ever recording the names of those it regulated. To an outsider, it would seem impossible, but after thirty-five years in the NYPD, Moodrow understood the cards weren't the same for everyone. Hell, even the deck wasn't the same. It wasn't *designed* to be the same. Moodrow's working career had been spent on the Lower East Side, amid the tenements and the projects, and he was accustomed to the bottom of the deck. What made him nervous (fueling his headache) was the nagging fear that he wouldn't know what to do with the picture cards.

The ringing phone pulled him away from his speculations. This would be the last one and he could go to sleep (or at least turn out the light) when this was finished. It was Pat Sheehan, as he'd hoped. Moodrow had left a request for Pat to call when he'd been in Queens that afternoon, but had no real conviction that Sheehan would comply.

"Moodrow?" Sheehan's voice was sharp and impatient. "It's Pat Sheehan. What's up?"

"That's what I wanna know from you."

"First, I gotta say thank you for sending that guy around about the eviction. He says Louis don't have to go to court at all. The lawyer's gonna take care of it. So thanks, all right?"

Moodrow had no difficulty in reading the reluctance in Sheehan's voice. As an alumnus of the state penal system, hatred of the police was as much a part of his day-to-day life as the pulse in his wrist and Moodrow accepted that. Not that he wasn't willing to take advantage of the debt Sheehan owed him.

"I want you to do something for me," Moodrow said. "If you can. I know you got your hands full with Louis."

Sheehan was surprised, at first, then relieved to be able to wipe the slate clean, then wary, as befits someone who'd occupied the position both of hunter and hunted many times in his life. "Tell me what ya want, Moodrow. Louis ain't feelin' too good and I can't stay on the phone."

"First, tell me what the situation's like in the building now."

"It's drug heaven," Sheehan snorted. "Whatever ya want, right? Crack, crank, blow, dope, dust. It's all here now. Right in the open. I saw Birnbaum when I came in and he told me you busted someone. I figured it hada be for drugs, because I got approached twice on the way to my apartment."

"So the dealers are making you for a player?" Moodrow asked innocently.

"Once you done time," Sheehan observed casually, "it's like you got a tattoo on ya face. Anyone else who done time could read it the minute he sees ya."

"That's gotta be a fucking drag."

"Cut the crap, Moodrow, and tell me what ya want."

"All right. Whatever you say." Moodrow, lost in the details, sipped at his bourbon, his headache forgotten. "Lemme ask you a question, Pat. How do you figure all the drugs got in the building in the first place? Do these dealers got some kinda buzzard radar that they know when a neighborhood's in trouble? How the fuck did they find their way into Jackson Heights?"

Sheehan took a moment before answering. "It's a good question," he admitted, "but I don't got the faintest idea."

"Well, I was thinking maybe you could find out. I mean, people talk to you. You listen carefully, there's no telling what you might hear."

"I don't have time for that shit, even if I wanted to become a professional rat. Between my job and Louis, I walk around half-asleep."

"You don't have to do anything special." Moodrow's voice was soothing, persuasive. "But the people moving in must have something in common. Maybe they all come from the same area. Or they get supplied by the same wholesaler. I don't know what it's gonna turn out to be, but I'd appreciate it if you'd keep your eyes open. If somebody wants to talk to ya, let 'em talk for a while. Don't be so tough."

"Should I start buying dope again, too?"

"Hey, Pat, whatta ya think it's about?" Moodrow finally allowed the irritation to creep into his voice. "You think it's about me being a hot shit and making some kinda big collar? No way, man. This is about Sylvia Kaufman lying on the floor with a busted hip while the room fills up with smoke. Her fucking bedroom, man. Where she has a right to be safe from murderers. When was the last time you spoke to her? Two days ago? Three? Four? Now she's in a coffin and some torch is havin' a party to celebrate the success of his enterprise."

"That ain't right, Moodrow," Sheehan insisted angrily. "Sylvia was okay to me and Louis, but that don't mean I'm in her debt. She wasn't watchin' my back."

"Okay," Moodrow apologized. "I don't mean to say that you have an actual obligation to Sylvia Kaufman. But you have an obligation to me and I'm calling it in. Louis said he'd help me out if I helped you out, and I did what he asked. Now it's your turn."

"You talk good, Moodrow. For a man that's fulla shit. Meanwhile, I'm gonna help you, anyway. I'm gonna do it because I owe you, and because Sylvia was decent to me and Louis when a lotta people treated us like garbage. But mostly

I'm gonna do it because this is our home. Ya know, in the joint, the worst insult a con could give another con is to violate the man's turf. To piss on his cot or trash his cell with garbage. Then it's automatic you gotta do something about it, 'cause if you don't, you'll be washin' underwear for the rest of your bit."

TWENTY-ONE

April 13

THERE could have been ten thousand dealers in the Jackson Arms and it wouldn't have helped Talker Purdy. There could have been a dealer in every doorway, even the door where the old fuck lived, the one who got Rudy-Bicho busted, and it still wouldn't have helped. In fact, the Jackson Arms could have been the dope center of the fucking universe and Talker Purdy would still be shaking, still sweating, still shivering as if in the grip of a violent, unrelenting fever, because Talker Purdy was dead broke.

"*Maricón!*" Talker Purdy screamed at the bare walls. He knew that time was running out and he had to decide what to do before he couldn't do anything. The muscles in his back were tightening down, pulling his shoulderblades toward his spine—by evening, they'd be twisted into knots the size of golf balls. Already, his skin crawled like an army of ants was marching just below the surface. He kept touching himself to make sure his skin was still smooth. In the end, if he had to do it, had to kick, his crawling skin would be the worst symptom. And the last to go.

But the deal that *really* bothered him, and what made it so hard for him to concentrate long enough to make a decision about what to do, was that it just wasn't fair. It wasn't fair right from the first go-round. For instance, why did Rudy-Bicho get arrested? The old fuck came right up to Rudy; Rudy didn't go to the old fuck. And Rudy didn't even hurt the old fuck, either, just taught him a little bit about soft and hard. Weren't he and Rudy in the lobby of their own building? Weren't they minding their own business? Not hurting *nobody*? The pig shouldn't have arrested Rudy-Bicho or found out that he was on parole, so that Rudy's bullshit bust meant two weeks at Rikers waiting for a parole hearing. No way. It just wasn't fair.

Talker thought his biggest problem was that everything belonged to Rudy. (In a way, even *Talker* belonged to Rudy.) Rudy-Bicho was the one connected to the wiseguy in Bensonhurst. He was the one who set them up in their apartment and went downstairs to get the dope (*before* they needed it; Talker hadn't been sick in months). And Rudy had introduced him to a new kind of bitch—crack whores who spread their legs and left them spread as long as the pipe continued to crackle and spit. Thinking about them, Talker nearly managed a smile. They were fine young bitches just out of their mamas' kitchens. Do *anything* for that big rock candy mountain.

Unfortunately, Rudy-Bicho kept the money, too. Not that he was trying to cheat Talker Purdy. It was mostly because Rudy was reliable and wouldn't do anything stupid with it (like leaving it taped to the bottom of a table for another junkie to rip off), but also because Talker Purdy trusted his partner completely. Talker knew Rudy-Bicho was standup cold, because they'd watched each other's backs the time Talker did a hard bit upstate. Talker and Rudy had been there for each other in the most totally fucked-up situations; situations where they could *definitely* get themselves killed. After that, if your name is Talker Purdy, you trust your partner enough to let him hold the money. And you never think about what you'll do if he gets busted and you've been calling Rikers every day and the pigs claim they never heard of Rudolfo Ruiz. And likewise the fucking Men's House of Detention in Brooklyn and in the Bronx. And you *know* there's no way you can get to the main stash, either. It doesn't matter that you're so fucking sick, your whole body is crawling with ants underneath the skin.

Thinking about it (and especially about the old fuck who dissed Rudy-Bicho until he *had* to do something) finally drove Talker Purdy into a fury. Talker was very slow to anger. He was just bright enough to know that anger made him even stupider, made him liable to do stupid things which resulted in immediate punishment. (Like the time he really hurt the kid in junior high school. Like hurting the kid with broken glass and a metal table and whatever was handy and doing it right in the cafeteria where the whole school could enjoy the show.) It wasn't until he ended up in a courtroom (after which, despite a probationary sentence, his mom and her boyfriend had kicked the living shit out of him), that he finally calmed down, allowing himself to fall under the direction of quicker, smarter criminals like Rudy-Bicho Ruiz.

But getting so angry the tips of his pale ears flamed with frustration didn't help Talker Purdy decide what to do about being sick. It didn't absorb the snot running in a thin stream from both nostrils. There was only one cure for the condition of being sick and that was dope. For the five hundredth time, he wished for Rudy-Bicho to be there. For Rudy to explain a plan, so he didn't have to think one up by himself.

"I have to go do what I have to do," Talker said aloud, finally deciding. "I ain' gonna get sick." He shook his head. "No way, man. Fuck tha' shit." He walked, much more calmly, from the kitchen into the bedroom, opened the second drawer of the bureau, and dug under the pile of T-shirts for the two 9mm automatics. It was the first thing Talker Purdy did that Rudy had always done for him. He felt like a kid in church, handling the priests' robes, as he sat at the edge of the bed and laid the guns on his lap. They were identical Berettas, big expensive handguns with barrels that could make a vic shit his pants in a minute.

"If you ever get to shoot someone," Rudy-Bicho had told him again and again, "you gonna see some blood from all the way inside blow right out through his back." Rudy called the automatics "one-shot tools" because they were so powerful you didn't need to make sure the victim was helpless.

Talker lifted one of the pistols, the one with an ornate T burned into the walnut grip (Rudy had done that for Talker; he'd done his own with interlocked Rs), jacked a round into the chamber, then rose to look at himself in the mirror. His reflection frightened him—his face was drawn, his cheekbones hollow, his skin gray. It was not a face to make someone afraid, unless *you* were its owner. Then what you felt was goddamn panic.

He pushed the gun into the waistband of his trousers, sliding it down into the small of his back and covering it with his shirt, then left the apartment. After seeing his face in the mirror, he was convinced there was nothing to do, but get hold of the magic powder that would restore his health. There wasn't any question about where he had to go. He had to go downstairs where the dope was.

Johnny Calderone, knowing nothing of Talker Purdy's sudden poverty, welcomed him with a big grin, pulling the door wide. "Talker, baby," he cried, "come on in. I heard about Rudy. What a fucking bad break. I swear, man, the scumbags who live in this building think who the fuck they are. Somebody oughta teach the cocksuckers a fuckin' lesson. Check it out. So what could I do ya for?"

"I need some bags, man," Talker said hoarsely.

"This I already know," Calderone returned, his smile firmly in place. "Check it out. Ya look like death warmed over. How many?"

"I need a few bundles. Maybe thirty bags."

Johnny Calderone was not a trusting man. He had a hole cut in his front door and he usually didn't let junkies into his apartment; he accepted money through the hole before passing out the heroin. But he'd known Rudy for years and Talker had been running with Rudy for more than six months and sometimes you have to be a little bit human, even if you *are* engaged in a fiendish profession. "No problem, baby. Check out a chair and I'll be right back."

He strolled casually into the bathroom, to the medicine chest which held his stash of heroin. Though expecting nothing, he knew, as a professional, that he was in bad trouble as soon as Talker Purdy followed him inside; he knew he was in deep, deep shit even before he turned to confront the Beretta.

"Hey, man," Calderone said, trying to keep the panic out of his voice. "Check it out. Ya don't need that piece. I wouldn't let a friend of mine stay sick. Whatta ya think, I'm some kinda scumbag?" He opened his clenched fist to display the small bags of dope. "Check it out, Talker. My special brand: Smiley D. The absolute mother-fuckin' best, right? Take it, baby. Go ahead. Take it upstairs and get well. You can tighten me up whenever you're fresh. I'm in no hurry."

Talker didn't make a decision before he pulled the trigger. At least, he didn't *remember* making a decision. For sure, the piece jumped in his hand. It jumped in his hand and Johnny Calderone jumped back with a little red rose in his chest like the two of them (the gun and Johnny Calderone) were doing a dance.

"Hey, Rudy, man," Talker whispered, "you was right about tha' one-shot shit. The *maricón* bastard ain' movin'. But how come it din' make no blood in the back?"

In fact, the slug had exploded inside Johnny Calderone's chest, slashing through his heart, lungs, kidney, and spleen. There was a great deal of internal bleeding, but as there was no exit wound, the blood had filled the abdominal cavity, only belatedly oozing through the small hole in Calderone's chest. Talker dipped his finger in the blood, pushing his finger a little way into the wound. He had never shot anyone before (though, maybe, even here, he didn't actually *decide*; it was more like an accident) and he wondered what he was supposed to feel.

But all he felt was sick. Casually, as if the gun had made a whisper instead of crashing so loud in the little bathroom it still hurt his ears, he took the heroin out of Calderone's hand, then went to the cabinet to scoop up the rest. It wasn't as much as he'd hoped for—Calderone most likely had a second stash somewhere else in the building—ten bundles of ten bags each. Enough for about five days, if he stretched it thin.

Talker didn't really wake up until he found himself in the stairway leading to his apartment with the 9mm still in his hand. He couldn't remember closing Johnny Calderone's door and it was annoying the hell out of him. If Rudy was around, he might not even *talk* to Talker for doing something as stupid as leaving the door open and waving the gun in the hallway. Suppose he ran into one of the tenants. He'd have to kill the fucker. And the next one and the next one.

"But I got the cure, man," he said aloud, his voice echoing in the stairwell. "Smiley D is mines." Rudy-Bicho would definitely approve of *that*. Rudy loved dope.

Talker thought about Rudy's approval while he cooked up his fix. The envelopes were small and his hands were shaking bad; it seemed to take forever to empty the bags into a bottle cap. But he did get one break in that he managed to find a vein the first time he pushed the dull syringe into his upper arm. The relief was immediate, as always. He went from a sniveling, pitiful junkie to cool, straight, and controlled in a matter of seconds.

"That's bad shit, man," he said. "Tha's a bad *maricón*." Slipping down into a chair, he began a light nod, entering an almost dreamlike state. At first, there were no thoughts at all, just a gentle floating through warm, empty clouds. He might have stayed there for hours (he would have *loved* to stay there for hours), but, even as he'd cooked up a fix to cure the sickness, he knew he would have to make a move. How could he stay in his rooms like nothing happened when he just blew the shit out of Johnny Calderone?

His thoughts began to come together (gently at first, like morning dew on the flowers and shrubs when he'd worked in the Deputy Warden's garden upstate) about twenty minutes after he got off. Vague questions, in the beginning. How long would it take someone to find Johnny Calderone? Did he have a girlfriend who'd be coming by? Or a partner? Was Calderone connected to the kind of bad asses who'd come looking for his killer?

So many questions and no answers. He wasn't even sure that nobody had seen him when he walked through the hall with the tool in his hand. Maybe some asshole was peeking out through the peephole and had already called the cops.

"Rudy-Bicho, man," Talker asked, "you gotta help me out. This *pendejo* shit is so fucked up, I don' know wha' the fuck I gotta do."

Talker wasn't surprised to find Rudolfo Ruiz in his mind. Opium is the mother of dreams and he'd met every kind of life in his deepest nods.

"You got to get the fuck outta tha' room, Talker," Rudy-Bicho said angrily. "I always say you got *cojones* where your brains should be. Big deal, so you shoot tha' Johnny Calderone. You stay in tha' chair, you gonna find yourself pullin' twenty upstate. You got to get the fuck outta tha' room."

"But where I'm gonna go?" Talker asked. "How you gonna fin' me if I'm no' here when you get out?"

Rudy-Bicho laughed at him, a sneering laugh that Talker Purdy hated worse than a beating. "How come you don' think?" Rudy asked scornfully. "You so *estupido*, sometime I can' even believe you're alive. *Mira*, listen careful to what I'm sayin'. Go over to your sister's house and wait for me there. Don' you think when I find out what you done to Johnny Calderone, I'm gonna know you can' stay here no more? Jus' go to your sister's house and wait for me. Take the guns and throw the one you used on Johnny Calderone down the sewer. If nobody seen you, we can put the shit back together in a couple of days. If you been made, we go down to Miami. I got bro's in Miami. And don' forget to wipe the piece before you dump it."

Talker Purdy loved to listen to his partner explain the plans. Because Rudy-Bicho Ruiz was always positive and because his plans came out right. Talker had attached himself to a number of planners before Rudy-Bicho, and *their* plans had sent him into jail about ten times and twice to prison. "Rudy-Bicho, man," Talker said. "I'm gonna do jus' like you sayin'. I'm takin' the two guns and gettin' outta here. I'm gonna go to my sister's house and wait for you, man. Then we can go to Miami, if somebody seen me, or put the shit back together if it's cool."

"Wha' you do, *pendejo*? You blow farts from out your *culo* or from out your ears? Wha' do I tell you abou' the fuckin' gun?"

"Oh, shit, man." Talker Purdy slapped his head and laughed at himself. "I got to dump the fucking piece. The one I shot Johnny Calderone with."

"Wha' you do *before* you dump it?"

"Wipe it down, man. Tha's right. Clean tha' shit and kick it down the sewer. *No problema*, bro."

"Now you tight. You real tight. You gonna get by with this shit if you stay cool and remember what I learned you."

"I know, Rudy. Wipe the tool and dump it in the sewer."

"An' one more thing you got to do for me, Talker. *Por favor, señor.*" Rudy laughed, fawning like the greaseball waiter his father had been.

"Anythin', man," Talker replied. "You say it and I do it for you. Like *now*, man."

"All these problems we got are comin' from the old fuck who disrespect us in the lobby. You know where he live at?"

"I know."

"Go and kill him, bro. Tha's what I wan' you to do."

Talker felt himself drifting up out of his nod. He was refreshed and strong. Rudy would fade away, but that was nothing new. The lives always faded when you came out of the nod. "Rudy, man," Talker said, before he lost his friend completely, "wha' happen if the old fuck got the door locked?"

"Tha's easy, man. Take the chisel and the hammer we usin' for the locks on the truck doors and pop the lock off. *No problema*, right? Bang tha' cheap shit right off there and blow the ol' fuck away. He's the one who put me in this fucked-up place and he gotta pay."

Talker Purdy did it by the numbers. He scooped up the remaining bags of heroin and put them in the inside pocket of his jacket. Then came the two guns, Rudy's in the small of his back and his own (he remembered that he should use his gun on the old fuck so he wouldn't have to dump Rudy's piece) in front where his jacket covered it nicely. He hesitated for a moment over the ammunition stored in the dresser, but decided the several hundred rounds would be too heavy in his pockets. They'd make too much of a bulge. Rudy's clip held the full fourteen rounds and his still had thirteen. That would be enough unless he got into some totally fucked-up shootout with the pigs. Which he didn't think was even possible, because he had Rudy-Bicho's plan and Rudy-Bicho hadn't fucked up once.

Talker left his apartment, half-expecting about a thousand cops to be standing out in the hallway. A thousand cops wearing black vests in a shooter's stance with .38s pushed way out in front. But there was nobody. It was eleven o'clock at night and the citizens were settling down to the news and the bed. Even the lowlifes were laying low—the hallways and the stairwells were deserted.

He went directly to the third floor, to 3F, Mike Birnbaum's apartment, putting his ear to the metal surface, listening for sounds of life inside. Everything was quiet. Next (he wasn't *altogether* stupid) he tried the door, turning the handle, but it was locked tight, the bolt thrown. Then he took his chisel, inserting the blade between the lock and the doorframe, hoping to splinter just enough of the frame so the door, with the bolt still extended, could open outward. To his surprise, the metal-covered wood began to splinter with the first twist of the chisel; he wouldn't even have to use the hammer.

"Rudy-Bicho, man," he muttered as he worked the chisel back and forth. "You the bes', bro. You the baddes' bes' mother-fucker in the whole joint. You teach me everything, baby, and now I'm gonna get your revenge for you. I'm killin' this old fuck as soon as I get inside, then I'm gonna dump the *pistola* and go over to my sister's house and wait for you. And I'm gonna wipe the piece, Rudy. I ain' forgettin' to wipe the piece. I'm gonna wipe the piece and then dump it and then go over to my sister's house and wait."

Talker Purdy was sweating when the doorframe finally gave way. He was uncomfortable, but still very stoned. The door had come apart easily, much more easily than he'd anticipated. As he'd come down the stairs, he'd been afraid he was going to make so much noise he'd wake up the whole damn building. In fact, the noise was *all* he thought about; he never once considered the possibility that the old fuck inside might be able to make some kind of a defense, but the first thing Talker Purdy saw, as the door swung outward, was an old man standing at the far end of the hall holding a pistol, an automatic like his own.

"Aha," the apparition said. "I see you came back to finish the job."

"Where you get tha' gun?" It was the only thing Talker Purdy could think of to say.

Mike Birnbaum laughed out loud. "I took this from a Nazi in the mountains south of Milan. He was a bigshot *gonif,* just like you. Naturally, I had to kill him, *tacha.* Just like I'm gonna kill you."

Talker Purdy, suddenly realizing that it didn't even *matter* where Mike Birnbaum had gotten the gun, began to move his hand toward the 9mm in his waistband, but he wasn't fast enough. Not even close. The first slug caught him under the chin, choking and spinning him until he was facing away from his intended victim and the blood poured down his throat. "Oh, shit, Rudy-Bicho," he said, "you fucked it up."

The second bullet caught him in the back of the skull. Deflecting slightly downward, it plowed a thick furrow through his brain, killing him instantly, before exiting a half-inch below his right cheekbone.

"I got one more for you, Mr. Hoodlum," Mike Birnbaum said calmly, walking the length of the hallway to stand over Talker Purdy's corpse. "This little present is from Sylvia Kaufman."

TWENTY-TWO

April 14

STANLEY MOODROW and Betty Haluka were lying in bed when Paul Dunlap phoned with the news of Mike Birnbaum's impending arrest. It was nine o'clock on Saturday morning and they were huddled together, half-awake and beginning to search for enough energy to make love. Not that it was to have been a complete holiday for either of them. The morning's pleasure (a planned brunch just as important as the sex) was only an interlude before they went back to work. Betty expected to spend the better part of the afternoon preparing a motion for an injunction to end harassment of the tenants. The motion was a battle she figured to lose; it would be no more than a side action in the overall legal strategy. Nevertheless, she would work at it diligently and the quality of her efforts (she hoped) would not be lost on Supreme Court Judge Emmanuel Morris, who was scheduled to hear the case and who'd continue to hear it if she found an excuse to go back into the higher court.

Moodrow had planned a trip in Betty's car, to Queens where he and Dunlap would try to light a fire under Sergeant Boris Kirov, the precinct forensics officer. The fire marshal, Sam Spinner, was screaming for the return of his evidence— the drug paraphernalia Moodrow had taken from the scene. Spinner wanted the bag of vials and syringes so he could officially close the investigation.

"For Christ's sake," he'd lectured Moodrow on the previous afternoon, "have a little mercy. The landlord is waitin' for the insurance check. He needs the money to clean and paint the damaged apartment before it goes back on the market. I mean the bedroom's still sealed off as a possible crime scene. It's ridiculous."

Dunlap's call, of course, eliminated all concern, either for Sam Spinner's evidence or for Betty's Supreme Court motion. Moodrow listened quietly to Dunlap's concise explanation of the course of events, from Talker's attempted break-in to the results of interviews with several witnesses who'd come into the hallway after the first shots had been fired.

"Try to hold 'em off until I get there," Moodrow responded. "If the other tenants see him in cuffs, I'm afraid they'll give up."

Dunlap laughed. "You wouldn't believe it, Moodrow. There's about twenty of them out there now, blocking Birnbaum's door. The lieutenant's holding the lid on while he waits for the captain to show."

Moodrow got out of the bed and began to dress as soon as he'd hung up, explaining the situation to Betty Haluka as he went along. "We gotta get out to Queens right away. Mike Birnbaum shot someone."

Half an hour later, Moodrow, explaining the matter to Betty as they went along, had folded himself into her Honda and they were on their way to Queens, pushing the tiny car for all it was worth. Traffic was light on the Brooklyn–Queens Expressway (as it usually is early on Saturday morning), despite closed lanes on either side of the Kosciusko Bridge, and they arrived a little after ten o'clock to find Paul Dunlap waiting at the curb.

"What's the situation?" Betty asked as she got out of the car. Moodrow was still trying to pull his feet from between the pedals.

"Physically, it's the same as when I called Moodrow, except the number of tenants has grown. There's about thirty people out there, including some kids. Andre Almeyda's kids, to be exact. He's got his whole family singing hymns. Meanwhile, Annie Bonnastello's praying the rosary with Paul Reilly."

"In other words," Moodrow said, his feet finally on solid ground. "The standoff is standing off."

"Only physically," Dunlap replied grimly. "The captain showed up about ten minutes ago and he's determined to drag Mike out of here this morning. Not that he wants to go hard on the old man, but he doesn't like the idea of the NYPD being humiliated."

Dunlap hesitated and Moodrow stepped forward. "You want something, right?" Moodrow asked, a smile spreading across his face. "I can smell it, Paulie. I can smell it all over you."

"I'm in a bad position here," Dunlap answered firmly. "Keep in mind, I'm still a cop. I got other loyalties besides you and Mike Birnbaum."

"You're right," Betty said to Moodrow as her own instincts, honed by thousands of hours of cross-examination, kicked into place. "He *does* want something."

"I told the captain I might be able to get the old man out of there without a struggle," Dunlap confessed.

"So what's the problem?" Betty asked. "Why don't you just go talk to Mike about it?"

"I can't get past the neighbors. And, besides, he wants to see you and Moodrow. He says you're his lawyer and Moodrow's his bodyguard."

"Jesus," Moodrow said, shaking his head in wonder. "The old man's got more balls than a buffalo."

"The whole situation is scaring the shit out of me," Dunlap admitted. "I'm afraid he doesn't have any intention of giving up. Ever. I'm afraid he'll have a heart attack when we drag him out of there. But, most of all, I'm afraid that you and Betty are gonna talk him into making some kind of last stand."

"And what's the captain gonna do for Mike?" Betty said quietly, catching Moodrow's approving smile out of the corner of her eye. "What's the deal, Paul?"

"We have to book him," Dunlap began.

"Forget it," Betty said, beginning to turn away.

"We *have* to book him. We *have* to arraign him. You know that, Betty. You're a trial lawyer."

"If you think I'm gonna let an eighty-year-old client sit in a holding pen at Central Booking, you're very much mistaken. If that's what you have in mind, you can drag Mike Birnbaum through the hall without my help."

"Jesus," Dunlap cried, "give us an alternative."

"That's no problem," Moodrow interrupted. "No problem at all." Both heads swiveled toward him and he giggled softly to himself before continuing. "You forgot about bedside booking and arraignment, Paulie? You should read your Patrol Guide more often."

"That's for prisoners who're sick or wounded," Dunlap replied weakly.

"After a night and a day like the ones Birnbaum just went through, being eighty is a sickness all by itself. Nobody's gonna say shit if you take him, under police escort, to a hospital instead of the precinct. Once he's in the hospital, you can drag in a judge and do the arraignment on the spot."

Betty raised a hand, bringing Moodrow to a halt. "Wait a second," she said. "I hope you're not talking about sending my client to a locked prison ward."

"Not necessarily," Dunlap said. "We sometimes take wounded prisoners to the nearest hospital. Sometimes we arrest them while they're in the hospital bed. The only requirement is that a member of the force stay with the prisoner at all times. The captain might go for that."

"And I expect my client to be released on his own recognizance. Naturally."

"We'd have to get to the DA's office before we could guarantee it," Dunlap said. He was smiling now.

"So, go do it," Betty said. "Call everybody. We'll go talk with Mike and see if we can reach an understanding."

Dunlap hesitated. "You believe that what I said before was true, right? There's no way he can get out of this. We're gonna book him. Fingerprints, mug shots, the works."

"Don't threaten me, sergeant," Betty said, her eyes riveted to Dunlap's.

"Wait a second." Moodrow, ever the peacemaker, stepped between them. "Paulie's only doing his job, Betty. And I tell you the truth, we oughta be glad he was here today. Besides which, if Paul looks good in front of the captain, it's gotta help us in the long run. You go ahead, Paulie. Go talk to the captain and then come back to us. We'll be inside the apartment." Smiling benignly, he watched Dunlap walk away, then turned back to Betty. "You did great," he said. "If you ever decide to become a private eye, you definitely got a spot in my firm."

"Don't enjoy yourself too much, Stanley," Betty said as they entered the building. "If they charge him with manslaughter, he's gonna have to fight."

Moodrow's reply was interrupted by the cheers of the tenants packed into the hallway. The lobby, on the other hand, was packed with patrolmen who demonstrated their reluctance to let the pair through by closing ranks.

"Moodrow."

They turned to find Captain George Serrano walking toward them. Not surprisingly, he ignored the Legal Aid attorney in favor of the ex-cop. "I just want to talk to you for a minute before you go in," he said, as soon as he was close enough to speak confidentially. "I heard you were a cop. Thirty-five years."

"I don't see the point," Moodrow replied quickly. He'd never had any love for the brass. "I'm a private investigator now and Mike is my client."

"For Christ's sake, man," Serrano continued. "Let's find a way to get him out of there. We don't wanna bust heads. These are civilians, not criminals. Besides, I think the perp was already dead when Mike put the bullet in his back."

"So this whole thing is a fucking farce?"

"You know the job as well as I do," Serrano insisted. "We're *going* to make an arrest today. Hell, you're lucky the perp wasn't black. If he was black, I'd have to shoot my way through the door."

"I'm glad you told me that," Moodrow replied, already walking away. "I'm glad to hear you're doing me a favor."

Moodrow plucked Jorge Rivera and Andre Almeyda from the assembled tenants before entering Birnbaum's apartment, advising the others to keep their cool. "Don't say anything to make the cops mad. Nothing. Remember, they're not the enemy."

Inside, they found Mike and Paul Reilly calmly playing gin rummy, the gun on the table between them. "Did we get a little bit even?" Mike demanded of Betty. His face was still swollen, the bruises faintly visible.

"You got stupid is what you got," Betty returned evenly.

"For killing a *gonif*? Killing a *gonif* is a *mitzvah*, in case you hadn't heard."

"You wanna talk about it in front of witnesses?" Betty said firmly. "I work for Legal Aid, so I usually don't get to pick my clients, but when I do get the chance, I try to stay away from stupid ones. From this minute, you don't talk to *anyone* about the shooting, but me. I swear, Mike, if you wanna act like a *schnorrer* and go brag to all your neighbors what a big hero you are, I'll dump you and you'll have to go out and *pay* someone to represent you."

Mike flinched at Betty's assault and when he spoke, his voice was much softer. "How much time have I got before they arrest me?" he asked.

"I don't know. Hours, probably."

"Do you think you could fix it so I get busted before my daughter gets here? She's on her way from New Jersey."

Betty and Moodrow broke out laughing, while the three tenants just looked confused.

"That's great," Mike said, "but if you knew my daughter, you wouldn't think this was comedy."

Betty, still chuckling, drew Mike off into the kitchen where she could listen privately to his rendition of the events leading to the demise of Talker Purdy. Moodrow stayed in the living room with the three tenants. He began by explaining the deal they were trying to work out regarding Mike's arrest, a deal which seemed perfectly satisfactory to the trio, as long as Mike went along with it. Despite their defiant stance, they were all subscribers to the American dream, and fighting cops didn't come naturally to any of them. Not even Andre Almeyda, who'd once been arrested by Castro's police and held as a subversive for the better part of a week. As soon as Moodrow made it clear that Mike would not have to be locked up with *them*, each breathed a private sigh of relief.

"But the big thing, from your point of view," Moodrow continued, "is that there's cameras coming and you have to decide who's gonna represent the tenants. This is a big opportunity for you to put your case out where people can see it. The bureaucrats and the cops hate publicity. Publicity brings phone calls from angry politicians who demand action. But you gotta be prepared when you talk to the reporters. You have to know exactly what you want to say and you have to say it without slandering the landlord or the cops. Also, whoever you pick is gonna be the media's permanent contact, so you have to get it right the first time."

"And how should we do this?" Andre Almeyda asked.

"First, decide who's going to represent you, then we'll go over what to say."

"A moment, *por favor*," Jorge Rivera said. "But I think we should have the others here. Jimmy Yo and Muhammad Assiz and Mrs. Bonnastello." He turned to Andre Almeyda. "And perhaps your wife, Andre."

Rivera projected the perfect image. Naturally dignified, his large, round face, topped by jet-black hair, was nearly always composed. He smiled as rarely as he frowned. His accent, not so strong as to impede communication, would remind viewers that he was an immigrant, a hard-working man preyed upon by forces beyond his control while stronger forces (the cops, mainly, but also the landlord and the courts) stood by indifferently. Jorge was the perfect helpless victim and that's the way the association decided to play it. Rather than blame specific individuals, they would plead helplessness and demand police action.

Mike Birnbaum's affairs went equally well. After two hours of phone calls, George Serrano, Precinct Commander, managed to get permission to have Birnbaum—accompanied by two patrol sergeants, but *without* handcuffs—admitted to Physician's Hospital, a few blocks away. One of the sergeants would take him through the booking procedure, photograph and fingerprint him. A judge would arrive by evening to handle the arraignment, after which he would be allowed to return home. If, as Serrano believed, Talker Purdy had completed his transformation from moron to corpse as soon as Mike's second shot had penetrated the back of his skull, all the charges, with the exception of the gun possession, would be dismissed. And no judge in his right mind would endanger his career by sentencing an eighty-year-old Jew to hard time—probation on the gun charge was politically mandatory.

The actual operation went smoothly. The tenants in the hallway left as soon as the deal was explained to them and the sergeants led the diminutive Mike Birnbaum into a wall of exploding flashbulbs and screaming reporters. Birnbaum remembered his instructions from Betty ("If you say one word to the reporters, I swear I'll testify at your incompetency hearing. I'll see that you're sent to New Jersey with your daughter"). He kept a dignified silence, walking, eyes front, directly to the ambulance waiting outside the building and, with the help of the two sergeants, climbed inside.

A few minutes later, Moodrow escorted Jorge Rivera (who introduced himself to reporters as *George* Rivera) to a prearranged interview with a CBS reporter, then listened attentively while Rivera presented the tenants' case by enumerating the various attacks on their way of life: the fire, the drugs, the muggings, the prostitutes. The message intended for viewers was simple: if it can happen to us, it can happen to you.

Moodrow hadn't been at a crime scene involving reporters for a long time, and he was engrossed in the manic lunacy, when Paul Dunlap tapped him on the shoulder.

"I gotta talk to you a minute," he said. "Let's go where it's quieter." Without further comment, he led Moodrow outside and across the street. "First," he said, "I wanna say that I hope you didn't take no offense over what happened this morning."

"No offense," Moodrow replied. "I haven't been out so long I don't remember the line: 'You take the man's money, you do the man's job.'"

"Good. I'm glad to hear that, because it looks as if the captain is gonna keep the case open. We finally got the report on the vials and the needles from the print man." Dunlap noted Moodrow's double take, enjoying it thoroughly. It pleased him no end to see Moodrow caught off guard for a change. "At least we know it was arson," Dunlap said as he took the forensics report from his jacket pocket, consulting it to maintain accuracy as he went along. Like most cops, he felt most comfortable when he was dealing with quantities. "Okay, twelve syringes were recovered at the scene. Two were burnt. Four had multiple prints and smudges. Six were wiped clean. There were twenty-one crack vials recovered. Eight had multiples and thirteen were clean. Same with the dope envelopes and rest of the paraphernalia. A few multiples, but most of it wiped."

"Good," Moodrow said, his mind already wandering in search of a theory. "The arsonist made a mistake. He should have worn gloves when he gathered up the decoy paraphernalia, but he didn't and he had to wipe the material down."

"But you were wrong," Dunlap said gleefully, "about the mattress belonging to the old superintendent. There must have been junkies down there before the arsonist."

"What does it matter?" Moodrow replied evenly. "The arsonist was clever. He took advantage of existing conditions to set up his smokescreen. If he'd been a little more careful, Serrano would've closed out the case and I would've lost you—which wouldn't have stopped me, anyway. But he fucked it up. He made one mistake . . ."

"What if he made more than one mistake?" Dunlap asked, chuckling.

"C'mon, Paulie, don't bust my balls." Moodrow, who'd lost the routine right to use the enormous resources of the NYPD, wasn't crazy about Dunlap's teasing. Nevertheless, as he and Betty had been busting Dunlap's (and, by extension, the NYPD's) balls all morning, he could understand the justice in it.

"Awright," Dunlap grinned. "I told you there were thirteen clean vials. That wasn't true. There were only twelve clean vials. One of the clean ones had a single print, an itty, bitty pinky print, very sharp and clear, right below the cap."

TWENTY-THREE

April 18

THE absolutely best thing about whores, according to Marek Najowski, was the indisputable fact that they didn't desire their customers. For instance, Marie, the black whore scrubbing his kitchen, actually hated him; he could feel the hatred rolling off her, as real as the sweat that rolled between her breasts while he fucked her. Whenever he had the time, he made her work until she was drenched with sweat. Until, hoping to get it over with, she surrendered her body eagerly. She was allowed to leave after he came. That was part of their deal and Marek, knowing how much she wanted to hear the door close behind her (how much she wanted to be free of *him*) liked to begin caressing her, to kneel beside her while she worked and run his fingers over the backs of her legs for a few moments, then return to his chair without explanation. Probably, she didn't know how excited he was. Either that or she was too professional to rush him.

"Marie, stop cleaning and come over here a minute, please." Marek's voice was deliberately calm, almost caressing.

"Yessir."

He chuckled at her eagerness. She knew (all puns intended) that the endgame was coming. When she was standing quietly in front of him, he made a gesture with the palms of his hands and she casually lifted the hem of her skirt above her waist.

"You know, Marie, I was reading in the paper the other day about a woman who boiled her baby. She was an impoverished Negro. Like you. Authorities say she was trying to get the devil out of her baby's soul. What do you think about that?"

"I don't know, sir. I don't know about those things."

"Oh, you must, Marie. Didn't you grow up in that world? Didn't your mother beat you? Doesn't George Wang punish you when you're bad?"

"Yessir," Marie whispered, as if the information were being drawn against her will. "My momma did beat me."

Marek shook his head, chuckling softly. There was nothing they wouldn't do for money. "Move your legs a little further apart," he ordered, noting that she followed his instructions without changing expression. That was the one thing she had going for her—her control. She never lost control.

"Why did your momma beat you, Marie?"

"She beat me because I was bad."

"Isn't that why the Negro boiled her baby?"

"Yessir."

Casually, suppressing a yawn, he put his right hand between her legs and caressed her with his index finger, gently running it between the lips of her sex. She sighed, of course, but Marek knew her passion came from relief, not desire. She couldn't wait to get rid of him.

She was wet, though. She was always moist by the time he got around to the sex and that was pretty amazing. It was like trying to get an erection with a woman who didn't turn you on. Maybe she did what he would do in that situation. Maybe she closed her eyes and dropped off into fantasy. Maybe she dreamed of an enormous black cock laying against a black thigh . . .

"Have I ever told you how grateful I am? How much I owe you and your momma and the woman who boiled her baby?" Marek heard the breathiness in his voice. He wouldn't be able to draw it out much longer.

"No, sir."

"You've heard of 'the top of the heap'? It's a cliche, of course. Even Frank Sinatra sings about it. According to rumor, life at the top is so beautiful that people who get there refuse to consider what they're standing on. They never, for instance, think they're standing on poor, little Marie. I guess that's because their eyes have been riveted to the top for so long they can't look down anymore. What do you think?"

"I don't know about that, sir."

This time he pushed inside her and she groaned a little louder, her knees trembling slightly. He was tempted to dig his finger into her inner flesh, to break the careful pattern of the charade. Instead, he pressed his lips to her belly, licking at the top of her tightly curled pubic hair.

"But that's what you do when you're on top. You press down on whatever's below you. On all the human beings who want to take your place. I'll never know what it's like to be on the bottom, Marie. That's why I keep you around. To remind myself of the absolute depths, of all the alternatives to the life I intend to lead."

Marek allowed his thoughts to drift momentarily. The middle class, he knew, tried to avoid the boiling heap of struggling human beings by maintaining an illusion. They disavowed any claim to the top, using their money to create an artificial island of calm. All they wanted was escape and sometimes they achieved it. Sometimes they managed to live their whole lives in the eye of the storm. And sometimes the eye moved on, unpredictable as a hurricane, and they were smashed by the winds.

What had the two hundred and forty families living on his property done to deserve him? (What did *anybody* do to deserve *anything*?) Most people thought of the "top of the heap" as a place of delicate balance, but people really survived there by crushing anyone threatening to break into the light. The people in Jackson Heights looked at inner city footage every night on their TV sets. They enjoyed the violence the way peeping toms enjoy sex. They never thought the violence would come out to them. Just like they never expected sickness or addiction or child abuse or any of life's sharper realities.

"Lie down on the floor and pull your legs up," he ordered. He was angry now, thinking about the tenants' association and the problems it was causing him. "You could probably take on a rhinoceros without feeling a thing, but for what it's worth, I hope you walk bowlegged for a week."

The whore, Marek decided as he dressed, was a definite good luck charm. He'd had her before every meeting with Martin Blanks and the partners hadn't had a problem yet. The meeting he was heading for that evening was particularly important. It had been set up at the last minute, an emergency meeting called to formulate a response to the negative events surrounding Mike Birnbaum's arrest. It was their first setback and Marek was anxious to see how Blanks would take it. It would also be his first visit to Blanks' home and he supposed that had to be considered an honor. Certainly it meant they'd reached a higher level of trust, which was just what he wanted.

Marek went through his closets carefully. He needed a look that wouldn't be totally out of place at a dealer's pad, that wouldn't offend. (He absolutely *did not* want to appear to patronize Marty Blanks, who wouldn't appreciate *that* at all.) Finally, he chose a pair of stone-washed Wrangler jeans, a $70 off-white cotton dress shirt, and a pair of custom-made lizard-skin boots he'd picked up at a convention in Amarillo, Texas. A carefully rumpled lamb's wool-and-cashmere jacket (a lustrous, dark-gray beauty he'd pulled off the rack at Barney's for a miraculous $350) completed his wardrobe. He admired himself for a minute, then took his wallet and the change from his pants pocket and put them in the right-hand pocket of his jacket. The bulge they made was properly casual.

"Lookin' good, Mikey," he said, smoothing his hair. But he wasn't really looking so good. Mike Birnbaum's vigorous self-defense was creating a number of problems for Bolt Realty. The biggest involved a state law which allowed for the seizure of drug-infested buildings if the landlord wasn't making a "sincere effort" to evict known dealers. The tenants (no, not the tenants—the bitch and her giant companion) were pushing the issue with the fat cop from the 115th Precinct and *he* was offering a list of dealer's apartments to the narcotics unit. Several days ago, Marek had decided that Bolt Realty would have to postpone its goals for the time being. They would have to cooperate.

Marek's driver, sent by Martin Blanks to guide him through the hell of Hell's Kitchen, showed up exactly at seven-thirty, so punctual that Marek suspected he'd arrived early and parked in front of the house. He led Marek to a nondescript Buick sedan (Marek, in his more fanciful moments, had envisioned a stretch Mercedes for Martin Blanks) and held the door while Marek got inside.

"My name's Mike Powell," the chauffeur said as he pulled the car into the traffic heading toward the Brooklyn Bridge. "I work for Marty Blanks. I known him since we were little. We was foster kids in the same family for about two years."

"That right?" Marek responded uneasily. He didn't really know how friendly he should be under these circumstances. For instance, was Powell a servant? Or an executive? His suit, at least a size too small, had discount written all over it and his manner reeked of neighborhood bully. On the other hand, Powell's sapphire pinky ring was easily worth a thousand dollars and he seemed much too confident to be a servant. Marek finally decided on a test. "I suppose you know *my* name," he said.

"Absolutely. Do you mind if I call ya Marek? I ain't used to no formality."

"Sure, Mike. Whatever you want." He arranged his mouth into a smile, but was troubled by this dope dealer knowing of his association with Blanks. Presumably, Powell had no inkling of Marek's actual business with his boss; he almost certainly believed Marek to be another dealer. If Powell was ever arrested and had to give up a name or two . . . Najowski made a firm decision to arrange his affairs so that he could desert his Brooklyn Heights apartment on a minute's notice.

"Marty said I should tell ya that he can't meet you at his apartment. A problem came up and he's gonna meet ya at his office."

"And where would that be?" Marek asked.

"Uptown. At 133rd Street off Madison Avenue. But don't worry, 'cause I'll be with you all the way and I guarantee there won't be no problems." He turned and tried to grin reassuringly.

"We're not going to a place where drugs are sold, are we? I don't think I'd like that."

"*Sold?*" Powell shook his head decisively. "We don't sell no drugs out of Marty's office. Never. But if ya wanna postpone or somethin', I could take ya back to ya house. Marty says I should do whatever ya say. I'm at ya disposal. Only do me a favor and don't dispose of *me*. Get it?"

Marek, watching the big man intently, came to the obvious conclusion that his chauffeur was a moron. Probably an enforcer of some sort with pure muscle instead of brains between his ears. That was the trouble with taking a criminal as a partner—they solved every problem by killing it. How could he trust a fool like Mike Powell to keep him safe? 133rd Street was in the heart of Harlem. It was the absolute bottom of the heap, a place where he *never* went, with or without a bodyguard.

"What time will Martin be free?" Marek asked. "Maybe we can meet later in the evening."

"That I don't know. All he said was I should bring you up to him if you wanted to come."

"Can I call him?"

"He don't give that number out. Even *I* don't got it."

"Shit." He desperately wanted to turn around and go home, but the meeting was really urgent. He'd been procrastinating for several days, hoping their problems would disappear, but conditions had grown steadily worse. Now a city councilman was sticking his nose in, probably sniffing around for the publicity—a liberal with a longtime reputation for representing the little guy. Bolt Realty was going to have to convince him, and everybody else, that it was committed to preserving the tenants' "quality of life." Of course, he could always call the lawyer and make the necessary adjustments without conferring with Blanks. Instructing Holtz was his job, and Holtz wouldn't hesitate to put his orders into effect. But Marek felt it was important to preserve the illusion of partnership. And who knew how Blanks would react if he felt Marek was cutting him out?

"All right," he said finally. "Let's go visit the underclass."

In the course of his real estate life, Marek had looked at a number of slum buildings, marginal tenements that could be gotten for next to nothing and kept profitable by withholding basic services whenever possible, but he'd never bitten. The simple truth was that he didn't want to deal with blacks. Even when you managed to show a small profit, they filled your life with misery. Still, despite the simple fact that his financial investments had gone a different way, he'd been in all the big slums: Bed Stuy, Brownsville, Hunts Point, Mott Haven. He'd seen the devastation firsthand, but he'd never seen a series of buildings as close to collapse as the three abandoned tenements that greeted him on 133rd Street. The facades had broken away on all three and big chunks of stone had fallen to the sidewalk. The easternmost building was actually leaning away from the building in the center (Marek could almost see it swaying), while every apartment in the building on the west bore the scars of a serious fire.

"That's where we're going," Mike Powell said casually, indicating the fire-damaged tenement. "That's where Marty's office is, but we gotta go in through here." He pointed to the eastern building, the one that leaned out into space, walking casually toward the door (or where the door should have been) as if he was out for a Sunday stroll. When Najowski failed to move, Powell turned and smiled. "C'mon. It ain't that bad."

Marek followed without a word. He was beginning to feel that the whole situation was designed to test him in some way. Or perhaps it was a kind of insult. In any event, he concluded, his resolve hardening, it was imperative that he find out the reason for the show. He'd invested two million dollars in this project and if his partner was insane, he wanted to know it.

They walked through the empty doorway, pausing in the lobby to let their eyes adjust to the darkness. The building stank of dust and mold, but lacked the urine and garbage smells that usually announce the presence of squatters or junkies. The banister for the stairway to the second floor lay in the first floor hallway. It could only have been removed deliberately.

"Ya wanna be careful here," Powell announced casually, leading Marek through the lobby and up the stairs.

The second floor landing was even darker than the lobby with only a faint gray light drifting in from the streetlamp. Marek, struggling to see where he was putting his feet, was startled to hear Powell offer a greeting. "Hey, boys. How's it hangin'?"

Peering along the hallway, Marek could just make out two men, both carrying military-style rifles, seated on wooden chairs. The guards were in deep shadow and they didn't move a muscle, didn't crack a smile, or return Mike Powell's greeting. Their lack of reaction meant they knew it was Powell coming up the stairs and Marek realized there had to be a spotter (or spotters) hidden in one or more of the rooms. He had entered a paramilitary complex.

There were sentries on every floor, but Powell ignored them as he led Marek directly to the roof, then across to the center building and down two flights of stairs before entering one of the apartments. Marek, following, was caught off guard by the activity inside. From the street, the tenement had appeared to be deserted, but the interior of this apartment was brightly lit. Someone had knocked down the wall between the living room and the kitchen and hooked up another stove to the single gas line. Every burner was lit and the apartment was unbearably hot. Glass bottles, half-filled with a thick bubbling white paste, sat on the flaming burners. The crackling sound of boiling cocaine was clear even over the hiss of the gas. As Marek stared in amazement, realizing that he was in a crack factory, a worker snatched up one of the bottles and ran to a sink full of water, where he quickly immersed it. The water sizzled against the glass, sending up a cloud of steam.

"Actually," Mike Powell said, "this is pretty small-time with us. We supply some kids in the projects, but Marty wants to dump the crack business. He thinks we should stick to powder. Wholesale it and let someone else deal with the bullshit." He indicated the stoves and the workers who moved around them, checking the paste. "Marty says it takes up too much room and there's too many people involved."

"Take my word for it," Marek replied, "it's not a problem that interests me. Why don't we find Blanks and get this game over with?" He was furious, so furious he was having trouble controlling it. For Blanks to bring him here, to the site of an enormous potential bust, could only be understood as contempt or madness. Somehow, he didn't think he'd be able to play the jolly ethnic tonight.

"Whatever you say." Powell turned on his heel and walked, Najowski following behind, to the far wall of an adjoining bedroom. He pulled back a dirty gray blanket to reveal a hole cut through the wall into the adjoining building, then waited for Marek to go through, before dropping the blanket to cover the hole and walking back into the kitchen.

The first thing Marek Najowski saw as he entered Marty Blanks' office was money. Stacks of it piled on a table in the center of the room. Though Marek was used to dealing in large sums, he'd never seen this much cash except on television. He was beginning to feel like he was in the middle of a movie; everything was slightly off-center, slightly out of control.

"There's about five hundred large there," Blanks announced. "Too many small bills, though. That's how come it seems like so much more."

Najowski looked at Blanks for the first time. He was sitting at a desk in a corner, smiling broadly. A tall black man sat next to him on the edge of the desk. He was smiling, too.

"Ain't this place a bitch, Marek?" Blanks said. "The way you came in is the *only* way in. Every other entrance is bricked up by the city. But there's three ways out. Three tunnels. The pigs'd have to send a fucking army to get up them stairs. By the time they got here, I'd be long gone." He stopped for a moment, still smiling. Waiting for a reply, but not surprised when Marek remained silent. "By the way, I want you to meet my partner, Muhammad Latif. He's a black Moslem, but not a Black Muslim, if you take my meaning. We met up in Attica. Watched each other's backs for a couple of years, then decided to pool our connections. You know how it is, right? I mean after ya go through somethin' like that, ya just make natural partners." Blanks' grin broadened. "Am I right, or what?"

"How's it movin'?" Latif asked by way of a greeting.

"Fine," Najowski replied. The single word hung painfully in the air. Marek, who could think of nothing except the insult being paid to him, noted Blanks' continued smile. He tried to smile himself, struggling with it at first, but eventually grinning his broadest grin. No sense in showing his anger here. Much better to let the asshole have his triumph. Let the asshole think he was on top of it.

"Give us some privacy, Muhammad," Blanks said. "Me and Marek are gonna talk business."

"No problem, bro. I'll see you tomorrow. So long, Marek. It was a pleasure to meet you."

Marek said nothing, waiting patiently for the black man to leave the apartment. "You shouldn't have brought me here," he said as soon as they were alone.

"It was an emergency," Blanks explained. "We got a runaway posse in the North Harlem Houses. Think they're too tough to pay for their crack. If they get by with that bullshit, we gotta fight a war with every fuckin' crew in Harlem. What we're tryin' to decide is if we wanna dump the crack business altogether.

Just walk away and forget about it. Most of our business is in Hell's Kitchen, anyway. Maybe we oughta chill a few of the kids who fucked us and get out." He stopped suddenly, breaking into laughter. "It seems like now that I'm a man of property, I don't have the heart for a battle no more."

"Well, before you retire," Najowski said, "you better take another look at your property. We got a lot of problems. The cops are making noises about HPD taking the building away from us. And there's a councilman named Connely sniffing around for potential publicity. The fire hurt us bad. It was supposed to be a warning, but it made the old Jew into a martyr. I thought only Christians were martyrs, but now we got the first Jew martyr. The first *two* Jew martyrs. The old man is a martyr, too."

"I don't see what's the big deal," Blanks replied calmly. "The pigs can't move against the building until they make some arrests and, so far, they ain't busted nobody. Besides which, all the dealers are squatters. We didn't actually rent them any apartments, so I don't see how we can be held responsible."

"You don't understand New York real estate any more than I understand the economics of cocaine. If Councilman Connely gets HPD to attempt a seizure, we'll be tied up for years. Between the three properties, we've already got fifty units empty. That's a potential five million dollars, even if we never sold another apartment. We'd have our money back and we'd still own the rest of the apartments, a situation which I define as a sure winner. I don't see any reason to risk everything. All we gotta do is cooperate for a month or so. Maybe do some repairs. Try to force the squatters out, but fail, because of the Legal Aid bitch. The trick is to make it look good. To make us appear to be innocent until the papers and the cameras forget all about us. Until we're yesterday's news."

"Ya know somethin', Marek, I think ya lost ya nerve. The way I see it, we only got one *real* problem and that problem's got a name: Stanley Moodrow. That's the ex-cop who's runnin' around with the Legal Aid lawyer. He used to be a detective on the Lower East Side, which is the only reason I didn't set up there. I know this pig real good, Marek. He's fuckin' crazy. He never gives up. Never. I guarantee right this fuckin' minute he's lookin' for the one who made that fire. If we don't do somethin' about him, he's gonna come knockin' on *my* door."

"How can he find you?" Marek asked incredulously. He was afraid of real things, of city agencies and courtrooms. Not a retired flatfoot.

"He's gonna take some of the assholes we got livin' in them apartments and smack their heads until they say who put them in there. Then he's gonna go to the people they name and do the same thing until he finally gets to me." Blanks shook his head decisively. "I'm not gonna wait around until he blows me away, man. I'm gonna have his ass by the end of the week. Once he goes, the whole Jackson Heights deal is gonna fall into our laps."

Marek walked over to the pile of money and began to heft the stacks of bills. He felt perfectly calm now. A thought floating just beyond his consciousness suddenly crystallized: he had the buildings and the tenants were on the run. What did he need Blanks for? "Let me see if I have this right, Martin," he said finally.

"You have a million dollars invested in real estate. In the long run, you stand to make ten million. You could, without doing anything else, make two or three million right now. But you're willing to risk that in order to eliminate a retired cop from the Lower East Side because he might come looking for you ten years from now. You want to murder a retired cop."

Blanks shrugged. "You wanna make it sound crazy, go ahead. But you don't know shit about cops, Marek. In your life, cops are people to ask directions from. I'm tellin' ya there's pigs who take their shit personally. I met guys in the joint who got busted two years after they fucked up because some pig wouldn't quit."

"And if I vote against it, partner?" Marek was surprised to find his voice so calm.

"He's goin', Marek." Blanks didn't even bother to look up. "See, there's somethin' else you didn't tell me about. You didn't tell me about the empty apartments. You didn't say that we can't have more than ten percent vacancies if we wanna sell the apartments. Sometimes I don't think you wanna tell me what the fuck is goin' on."

"That's nothing," Marek fumed. "Those apartments have to be empty for a year before they count as being warehoused. Plus I know a dozen brokers who specialize in putting buyers into empty apartments. Plus if we do major renovations, we can get a waiver." He stopped to draw a deep breath. "Try to hear what I'm saying, Marty. If we don't ease up for a month or so, this whole deal's gonna blow wide open. We'll have the cops all over us. I can almost always deal with HPD bureaucrats. I give them money and they look the other way. But not if I'm a celebrity. Then everybody wants to get a piece of your ass. Every judge, every cop, every inspector, every reporter. You want to see a headline: *Who Is Bolt Realty?*"

Blanks finally raised his eyes to meet his partner's gaze. He looked surprised, perhaps annoyed. "Forget about it, Marek. Two . . . three days the most. Moodrow's gone. And it's all because you were right. When you told me this was my big chance and I should take it? You were a hundred percent right, Marek. Maybe you think I don't know what happens the next time I take a fall, but I do. This is my *only* chance, mother-fucker, and I ain't gonna play it like a pussy."

TWENTY-FOUR

April 20

A CARESSINGLY warm Friday morning, the kind of a spring day that destroys the will to work. A morning when the bright yellow forsythia growing freely along the Grand Central Parkway beckons to the commuters crawling past LaGuardia Airport, reminding them of other times. Reminding them of young love and long-forgotten resolutions to find a different way. Of dreamers crushed by the relentless grind of the city as surely as Sylvia Kaufman was crushed by the greedy dreams of Marek Najowski and Martin Blanks.

Betty Haluka, driving out to the 115th Precinct with Stanley Moodrow, thought of her aunt even while she noted the annual miracle. The yellow flowers grew so thickly it seemed as if an artist, in a sardonic moment, had decided to paste a swatch of bright yellow over a field of soot and litter. The forsythia, she knew, grew completely wild, like the laurel thickets in southern mountains, though on a much smaller scale. Of course, one expected beauty in the wild mountains of West Virginia. The sudden, brief appearance of the forsythia (to be completely forgotten with the onset of the broiling summer) always came as a surprise, even to veteran New Yorkers who'd been plying the same commuter routes for decades. A surprise, an intrusion, a silent, uneasy memory.

"What are they called again?" Betty asked. "The yellow flowers? All I can remember is that it's a word that begins with 'f' and I could never pronounce it."

Moodrow stirred alongside her. "I been thinking the same thing. Funny, I never saw this before. Whatever it is, there's an awful lot of it. You think someone planted it?"

"I don't know." She paused as a giant Pan Am jet crossed the parkway a hundred feet above them. So loud it seemed to shake the world. "Forthithitha," she said after the plane had safely dropped onto the La Guardia runway a quarter mile to the east. "Damn! I can't say it. I could never say that word. Fasythitha."

Rabbit Cohan didn't want to get up when the alarm rang. He didn't want to get into the shower or get dressed, either. In fact, he hadn't been awake at eight o'clock in the morning since he'd come out of the service in '86, not since he'd been initiated into the economic mysteries of cocaine by his twin older brothers, Ben and Mick.

But it was their own progress into those economics that had him out of bed after three hours' sleep. The Cohan brothers were about to move up (assuming the job went off all right) and moving up was what it was all about—moving up to Jaguars and Porsches and North Shore mansions on Long Island Sound.

The best part was that he'd never done cocaine. Never done it and never been tempted. His relationship to the white lady was that of protector. He and his brothers protected shipments and money exchanges for bigger, stronger people who would, sooner or later, realize the value of the brothers Cohan. Who would properly evaluate their industrious sobriety and give them a piece of the mother-fucking action. In the meantime, they lived from contract to contract, augmenting their incomes with the odd hijacking.

"Big day comin', boyo," Mick Cohan said as Rabbit went by. "You ready to work?"

"Fuck you, too," Rabbit answered smartly. Mick had a thick scar under his right eye. Without it, Rabbit could only tell the twins apart by their behavior. Mick was the aggressive one. He gave orders and the brothers obeyed. Ben was quiet, almost sullen. For some reason, Pop had liked his little Mickey. He'd never, so far as anyone could tell, liked anything except Budweiser before Mickey'd come along and he clearly disliked Ben, beating the boy as often and as casually as he beat his wife.

Still, the old man hadn't been able to come between the twins, who stood by each other (and by their mother and, later, their little brother, Rabbit) despite their father's tyranny. Predictably, Pop had died in his early fifties when his heart had followed his liver into the alcoholic toilet, and "making it up to Ma" became the second most important goal in the brothers' lives.

"Whatsa matta with ya filthy sinners? Can't yer stop that mastrubatin' long enough to have a breakfast before ya go off ta work?"

"We'll be there in a minute, Ma," Rabbit called. He threw himself out of bed, pulling a Kelly green T-shirt over his head. Green was the family trademark and the brothers never left the house without proudly displaying a bit of the Irish. This despite the fact that only Rabbit had ever seen the "old sod" and he'd done it via a four-day pass while stationed in Paris.

As usual, breakfast was a massive affair—eggs, pancakes, ham, bacon, toast, fruit, coffee, juice. Lunch, if Ma got to serve it, would be just as heavy, and dinner was a challenge the boys loved to accept. Rabbit sat before his plate and reached mischievously for his coffee.

"Say yer grace," Ma warned, swiping at his hand with the flat of a knife.

"Blessusohlordandthesethygifts . . ."

"Not like that, ya heathen bastard." Her voice rose into a familiar screech. "Y'll say yer prayers like a proper Catholic or ya won't eat in this house."

She raised her knife again, but Rabbit hastily apologized, running through the prayer calmly and clearly.

"Are ya givin' yer saintly mother a hard time?" Mick asked, reaching for his own coffee. It was a ritual they observed whenever they assembled, although Ma never seemed to get the joke. But then, Ma was, indisputably, the brains of the gang.

"We'll go through it one more time," Ma announced. "If ya can stop stuffin' yer mouths. It's a wonder yer not fat as pigs. Ben, let's hear you say it."

Ben, sullen as ever, continued to chew his food and Ma went into a frenzy, her lined face trembling as if she had Parkinson's disease. "If that's the way it's gonna be," she declared, "yer can all stay home and we'll go on the welfare. Yer incompetent bastards, I'd sooner have three Brits than a gang of fools like yourselves."

"C'mon, Ben," Mick said quietly, "let's just do it."

Ben finally looked up, muttering, "We already did it fifty times."

"Then once more wouldn't hurt, boyo," Mick observed, tossing brother Ben his friendliest smile. "Wouldn't wanna make a mistake and do the wrong pig, would we? Don't think we'd get no second chance."

"I'm the driver," Ben said, his gaze returning to his plate. "Mick and Rabbit are the shooters. We wait on 37th Avenue between 72nd and 73rd Street until we get a call on the cellular phone that Moodrow's leaving."

"Do yiz have the photos?" Ma interrupted. "So ya know what in the name of God yer shootin' at?"

Ben held up Moodrow's photo (taken three days before with a telephoto and supplied by Blanks' man, Mikey Powell) for his mother's inspection. "Then I drive to the front of the building and double-park until he comes out. As soon as I see him, I nod to Mick and Rabbit. They open the van door and start firin'. If Moodrow runs, I follow. If he runs toward the front of the van, I try to keep the side door lined up with him. If he goes toward the back, Rabbit kicks open the rear doors and they fire through the back. The boys have two twenty-five-round clips taped back to back. When the clips are empty, I go, even if the pig is still alive."

"Well," Ma observed. "So ya can talk. I didn't think ya had it in ya. But how is it possible ya forgot about the masks? Is it because yer as stupid as ya look?"

"Yeah," Ben muttered. "Before we move in, we put on ski masks, so's the witnesses think we're a bunch of niggers."

She paused to let the information sink in, then went on. "And you, little Rabbit, what do yer do if there's other people around when the pig comes out? What do yer do if there's darlin' little children returnin' home from school?"

"We blow 'em into the next fuckin' universe."

Ma actually smiled for a moment. "They should all be as quick as you, me lovely boy," she said. "But I'll be pleased if ya'll watch yer filthy mouth as long as yer livin' in my home."

Moodrow and Betty found Paul Dunlap in his office, playing with a computer terminal. They called out quick greetings, then helped themselves to coffee before sitting down next to his desk.

"Since when did they start letting cops use computers?" Moodrow asked. "I always thought we were too stupid to use computers. If I wanted access when I was working, I had to beg some civilian."

"Well, it's the old good news and bad news routine," Dunlap explained. "The bad news is the captain won't give me any other men. He's not convinced the fire was deliberate."

"Is he a fool?" Betty asked. "What about the wiped vials? And the syringes?"

"He says it could have been by accident. Maybe the marshal mishandled them. Maybe the druggies wiped 'em for some reason. Also, even if it is arson, most likely the print belongs to some junkie and the perp missed it when he was wiping down the vial. It's enough to keep the case open, but not enough to spare any homicide dicks. Meanwhile, I should work on it in my spare time. He *did* manage to get a print man over to do the basement, though. Dusted the doorknobs and like that. We found out the doors and the glass weren't wiped, but that's as far as the captain's willing to go without more evidence."

"And that's where the computer comes in, right?" Moodrow observed wryly. "So you can do the work by yourself. I take it you're hooked into the FINDER system."

The FINDER system, only a few years old, had been created by the FBI to allow the computer to cull probables from among the millions of prints in FBI files. The probables were then given over to humans for closer comparison.

Dunlap shrugged. It was warm in the precinct and he was beginning to sweat, but he knew the captain wouldn't trigger the air conditioning for another month at the earliest. By then, Moodrow would probably have him on the street. "I only wish I could, but it's not gonna be that easy. All we have is a piece of a central pocket loop. Eight ridges of one fingertip. There's not enough potential points of comparison for the computer. I tried to feed it to the FINDER system anyway, but the computer spit it out. I'm using the state system now. First I'm gonna pull a list of all known arsonists working out of the city. Go back about ten years. Then I'll cull out the ones in jail or dead. That'll leave me with about four hundred names. I'll punch the names into the computer, one by one, and get a screen on the right little finger. From there I can make the comparison by myself."

"You know that's gonna take you about . . ."

"I know," Dunlap interrupted. "I have it figured. Five-minute delay between keying the name and getting a screen on the print. One minute for comparison. One minute to punch in the new name. Seven minutes times four hundred names equals twenty-eight hundred minutes. Forty-five hours of work. Now, if you've got something better for me . . ."

"Sounds like you spent some time in the John Jay College of Criminal Justice," Moodrow teased.

Dunlap smiled ruefully at the name of the school. "Yeah, I went to John Jay. About five years ago I had this flash that I could get off Community Affairs by studying forensics and I took eighteen credits before I gave up. I'm not saying I'm an expert, but if we get an exact match, I'll know it." He turned to Betty. "The print we took off the vial has a triple bridge to the left of the loop. That's rare enough to use for a key. I'll check for the bridges first and if there's no match, I'll move to the next name. That triple bridge is how come I can do a comparison in sixty seconds. If the print we're looking for was more common, it'd take forever."

"I'd say forty-five hours is pretty close to forever," Betty said. "Do you have enough points to go into court?"

Dunlap shook his head. "I can't be sure, but I don't figure to get more than ten points. We need twelve to get it admitted. Maybe I could stretch it, maybe not. Of course, there's enough so *we'll* know who set the fire, assuming the print belongs to the perp *and* he was printed in the city some time in the past ten years."

"Did the captain at least canvass the neighborhood?" Moodrow asked.

"No way. I canvassed the building myself, but nobody saw anything out of the ordinary. As for the rest of the neighborhood . . . I think my time's better spent working on the print."

"Well, I gotta take a few hours of that time," Moodrow said. "Me and Betty are on the way to brace the political, Anton Kricic. I checked him out and he's serious about the squatters. He's some kind of housing freak. A leftover from the 60s or maybe a new breed altogether. I can't tell anymore, but I'm hoping he's bright enough to feel something for Sylvia Kaufman. If I can get him to explain how he heard about this building, I can start digging down to the bottom of the bullshit."

"So what do you need me for?"

"I'm not a cop," Moodrow explained simply. "Kricic doesn't have to give me the time of day. If you flash your shield, at least he'll talk to us."

Paul Dunlap came within an inch of asking Moodrow why he, an NYPD sergeant, should take orders from a civilian, but he held himself in check. "Yeah, but let's do it fast, so I can get back to work."

According to the Cohan brothers, their biggest challenge was keeping themselves occupied until the hit went down. Once they had the van parked near the Jackson Arms, all three would move to the rear of the van and wait for a phone call from an anonymous spotter inside the building. If Moodrow decided to spend the day talking to the tenants, the wait would seem like forever. They'd voiced their objections to Ma when she announced the plan, but she'd screeched their objections away. Calling them "sissyboys" and "homos."

"It's our chance in life, boyos," she'd explained. "Marty Blanks told me personal that he'd be more than grateful if this man was relieved of his life. Since when does the likes of Marty Blanks personally call the likes of us? And here's another question for yer bunch of lazy bastards. If ya will risk such a chance for lack of a morning's entertainment, what sort of men are ya? Are ya even men at all? I tell ya, the curse of an Irish muther has always been the Irish son."

It wasn't a long drive from the Cohans' home in Woodside to the Jackson Arms (the neighborhoods lay against each other), but the brothers, mischievous as ever, took a detour into Astoria. They went to an attached home on 28th Street near the Con Ed plant, cruising slowly past the house before pulling to the curb near the corner. Five minutes later, Katerina Nikolis trotted down the block and climbed into the back of the van without a word. Though she still lived with her parents and still spoke Greek at the dinner table, Katerina was one soldier in a growing army of middle-class New York children addicted to crack cocaine. At fifteen, without money and not yet ready to commit herself to the street, she would do almost anything for the man (or men) who supplied her with the drug. Curiously, she *never* thought of this as prostitution. When she looked in the mirror, she saw a siren with black hair and black, black eyes, milky skin, and full lips. As far as she was concerned, her flat abdomen and the patch of dark pubic hair so startling against her white flesh merited the slavery of the men who gladly spent hundreds of dollars to feed her habit (a habit which, coincidentally, inflamed her own sexual desire, making the whole business that much easier).

Katerina lay back on the waterbed in the rear of the fully-customized van Rabbit had liberated from a north Jersey parking lot the night before. Smiling happily, she reached for the crack pipe and the tiny vials in Mick Cohan's palm. As she fired up the first hit, she raised her knees to allow her short skirt to slide up toward her waist. "Top o' the mornin', boys," she called in her heartiest false-Irish voice. "Top o' the mornin'."

Moodrow began to suspect that it was going to be a bad day when he pushed open the front door to the Jackson Arms (without benefit of a key) and found Ino Kavecchi waiting in the lobby. At first, the paralegal turned to Betty, reeling off a list of court dates, and Moodrow was momentarily relieved, but then, after passing Betty several manila envelopes enumerating legal precedents in the various actions they were pursuing, Kavecchi turned back to the ex-cop.

"Hey, Moodrow," he screeched. "What's the matter with these people? I never seen anything like it. They won't even let me in the door. 'Don't wanna get involved. Don't wanna get involved.' Whatta they think, they're invincible? The Chinese don't wanna talk to the Indians. The Indians don't wanna talk to the Irish. The Koreans must think they're goddamn Japanese, because *they* won't talk to nobody. *They* think they're too good for Jackson Heights, anyway, so they don't mind moving out, which is what they're doing. The rich ones are buyin' two families out in Flushing and the poor ones're gonna be the tenants. I mean it just amazes the hell out of me. I could go up to Harlem and the first thing anyone asks is when we're gonna throw a rent strike. Nobody talks about running. These fools . . ."

"All right, Ino." Moodrow put his hand on the paralegal's chest, shutting him off abruptly. "Why don't you tell me what you want. We've got a lot of work to do."

Kavecchi, offended, stepped away from Moodrow. "Hey, look, I couldn't care less. I'm just trying to let you know what's happening out here. I mean it's your party and all, but I think you oughta realize that the building's gonna be empty of bona fide tenants if things don't turn around. I been doing this a long time and it's my experience that if the people don't wanna stand up for themselves, the courts and the politicians don't wanna stand up for 'em, either."

"What about the city councilman, Connely?" Betty interrupted, trying to smooth Kavecchi's ruffled feathers. "And HPD. I thought they were all involved."

"They're involved for right now because of Birnbaum's publicity, but the cops're gonna drop the gun charge and the public is gonna forget. If you wanna keep the bigshots in the ballgame, you better hope something dramatic happens. The new super, Henry something, fixed the main lock yesterday, but somebody busted it out again last night. By three o'clock this afternoon, when the kids get home from school, there'll be dealers out by the ramp leading to the basement and . . ."

Once again, Moodrow interrupted. This time, though, his voice held little annoyance. He spoke in a matter-of-fact monotone. "I'm sad to say it, but I think you're right. Most of the people here don't have any fight in them. Maybe they think paying taxes entitles them to a safe world. What I see is that the first ones to move out were the last ones to move in. They don't have any sense of home and they pay the highest rents. I thought about it all last night and I came to the conclusion that none of this makes a problem for me. I'm looking for an arsonist and whoever told him to make a fire. That's what I'm good at. I can't make miracles, but I can bust scumbags and that's what I'm gonna do. So if you got something specific you want from me, I'll be glad to help out. Other than that, I don't have any advice."

Rabbit Cohan, temporarily satiated, sat on the rolling waterbed with his back against the front seat of the van. He watched in amazement as Katerina Nikolis alternately pulled at the smoking glass pipe and at his brother Mick's cock. Mick was lying flat on the bed and Katerina, kneeling with her bare ass high in the air, worked him over as earnestly as she worked the pipe. She seemed blissfully unaware of Rabbit's scrutiny and, as far as Rabbit was concerned, her twin preoccupations were just two more indications of the power of the white lady. Especially when reduced to her purest state in the form of rock cocaine.

Rabbit, at twenty-seven, had never done crack or any other drug (excepting, of course, Irish whiskey, which is or isn't a drug, depending on which end of the American schizophrenia happens to be wagging the dog), but he'd seen the power of drugs many times. First it was boyhood companions, kids he'd been playing with since he was old enough to go out on the streets. Half of them tried heroin and a quarter became desperate junkies. A number were dead—of an overdose or of AIDS. Cocaine had offered another enticement altogether, a controlled pleasure that smacked of affluence as surely as gold chains and German automobiles. Rabbit had been in Europe, a soldier, when the coke epidemic had exploded on the American public, and he was glad the lessons had been learned before he was faced with the temptation.

On the other hand, Ben and Mick, Rabbit's brothers, had been right in the thick of it, but had never been tempted to try the white powder. They were unionized construction workers who supplemented their incomes during the slow winter months with armed robberies, ripping off poker and craps games, and drinking themselves into a brawl every Saturday night. Their big break had come when they'd run into an old friend, a lawyer named O'Brien. O'Brien knew a number of cocaine entrepreneurs who needed occasional, reliable muscle. Mick and Ben, with their big Irish grins, were nothing if not muscle.

So the power of the lady had then seduced Ben and Mick as surely as it owned the sweet, white ass of Katerina Nikolis. Rabbit, focusing on the van again, noted that her dedication hadn't flagged. She was lying on her side, her head buried in Mick's lap. Ben had curled up behind her and she was pushing back against him as he attempted to enter her. Somehow, all through the various switches, she kept her head up with nearly constant pulls on the crack pipe. Rabbit felt himself beginning to stir again. He smiled brightly, listening to his brothers moan and grunt, considering *exactly* what he'd make the whore do next.

Stanley Moodrow was the only one of the three interrogators confronting Anton Kricic in his first floor Jackson Arms apartment who wasn't surprised to find Kricic intelligent and purposeful.

"I'll talk to you," Kricic explained, once they were inside, "because I hate arsonists even more than you do. There's no place for poor people to live in this city and the torches keep destroying what little there is. But there's gotta be some ground rules and the main one is you accept that I mean what I say. Don't worry about *why* I give a shit, just respect that I do."

Moodrow understood the demand to mean that Kricic not only wouldn't succumb to pressure, he'd walk away at the first hint of it. "Whatever you say, Kricic," he announced. "I tell ya the truth, I don't have any use for landlords, either. In fact, I'd go so far as to say that *everybody* in New York hates landlords. The goddamn real estate people run this city and they always have. The landlords and the banks and the fucking politicians."

Betty glanced at Moodrow, probing for a sign of insincerity, but Moodrow's face was completely blank, as was that of Paul Dunlap. Suddenly, she realized what ordinary people dislike about cops—they're *never* sincere. They'll say anything to make a clean collar. "My name's Betty Haluka," she announced, extending her hand. "I'm a Legal Aid lawyer. In most cases, we'd be working together, but I expect we're going to be on opposite ends of this deal before it's over."

Kricic almost smiled, taking her hand. "You're against warehousing apartments," he announced, "but you're also against homeless squatters in middle-class neighborhoods. No surprise, right?"

Betty held firm, despite the sarcasm. "If we start that argument now, we'll never get to our real business. You say you hate arsonists and I presume that you're not supporting drug dealers. Those are just two of the calamities that have come down on the people living here. Six months ago, the Jackson Arms was fully occupied by middle-class families and elderly people on social security. We know the building changed hands in November, but we don't know who bought it."

"I hope you don't think *I* know," Kricic responded angrily. "If you think I'm working for the landlord . . . Man, that's the worst insult I ever heard."

Moodrow, convinced that Kricic (innocently, no doubt) was part and parcel of *somebody's* plan for the Jackson Arms, nodded his head approvingly. "You know what, Kricic? I'd have to be even crazier than I am to believe you'd work for *anybody* you didn't approve of, and one thing I'm not is crazier than I am. But what *I* was wondering is how you found out about this building. You're not even from this neighborhood. In fact, last time I heard of you, you were living in an HPD tenement on 7th Street. Likewise for the dopers and the juicers: they don't have empty apartment radar and neither do you. Somebody had to tell you about us, and we think . . . wait a second, lemme get it right." Moodrow paused, his eyes down, as if he didn't know what he wanted to say. "We think if we can find out how all these people heard the Jackson Arms was giving out free apartments, we can find the scumbag who set the fire that killed Sylvia Kaufman."

Kricic turned away, shrugging his shoulders. "I couldn't really tell you who the dude was that told me about this building. You were right about where I was living—on 7th Street in a condemned twenty-family tenement that HPD took over when the landlord walked away. I went in there in '84, just knocked down the cinderblocks in the doorway and moved inside. First, I got the water turned on, then I pirated enough electric to keep the apartment lit. Little by little, people began to join up with me. In '88 we applied to the city to become a co-op. We offered to do all the work necessary to get a certificate of occupancy if the city would give us the building, but the bastards kept putting us off. They were too chickenshit to throw us out, but they weren't going to surrender a valuable property to a gang of homesteaders who have to beg Legal Aid for a part-time lawyer. Now the mayor and his HPD flunky are getting ready to auction off *all* the abandoned buildings and empty lots on the Lower East Side. That whole neighborhood's coming up and the sharks are making fortunes. Anyway, the city was too scared of publicity to evict us, so it was pretty much a standoff until someone made a fire. That was a month ago and the back wall of the building was burned out so bad it looked like it would fall down any minute. But we hung on, anyway. We got an architect from Pratt Institute to come in and show us how we could put the walls back together."

Moodrow waved his hand impatiently, but Betty moved closer to him, urging Kricic to continue. "Go ahead, Anton, I'd like to hear this."

"We were scared shitless most of the time," Kricic admitted. "There were times we'd be sitting around drinking beers and hear chunks of the back wall break off and crash onto the floor. But we didn't have any place to go. Maybe I could have found a place, but the others were really poor. They were uneducated and unskilled, some had been in jail and most had passed through drugs or alcohol addiction. So we hung in until the city came by with a demolition order and enough cops to throw us out. They claimed the building was going to fall down on top of us unless it was knocked down. Naturally, we decided to make a fight out of it—take the publicity if that was all we could get, and somehow enough neighbors showed up to make the city give us three days to move our possessions. Man, we threw some party that weekend. We knew we weren't gonna be in there come Monday night, but if we drank enough beer and wine, we didn't have to admit it."

"Is that when you heard about the Jackson Arms?" Betty asked gently.

"Yeah. I was in the kitchen with a guy named Bill, who I knew from college, and a black dude named Dayton, who I didn't know. We were talking about landlords who hold apartments off the market. Some newspaper guy had written an article claiming that 70,000 units were being warehoused. These are the cheapest apartments in the city. That's why the landlords don't wanna rent 'em out. Think about it—you got families living in shelters because there's no apartments and landlords are deliberately keeping the same apartments these homeless families *can* afford off the market. Anyway, I was pretty drunk and Dayton was going on about this place in Jackson Heights where homeless were already moving in. I started thinking about what kind of craziness I could make by establishing a homeless community in a privately owned middle-class building. It's gonna take a year, even if the landlord is serious about throwing us out— which I *don't* believe for a second—to get the court to issue an eviction notice. By that time I'll have the building organized, and every camera in New York'll be on hand to record the battle."

Thank God we have our pants on, Rabbit thought, as the call came through on the portable phone. Somehow, the brothers had fixed on the belief that Moodrow would be spending the entire day in the Jackson Arms and the eleven A.M. call announcing his imminent departure from a first floor apartment would have led to panic had the trio not been temporarily through with Katerina Nikolis. Katerina, of course, was still naked, lying dazed on the waterbed with the pipe clutched between her small breasts. *That*, Rabbit knew, was truly unfortunate. It meant their plan to dump her before doing the deed on Stanley Moodrow was out the window and they would have to think of something in a hurry. For a long moment, the brothers were paralyzed by indecision, but then Rabbit, who *knew* he was the smartest, grabbed Katerina by her hair, and pulled her erect before slamming her against the paneled wall of the van between the rear and side doors.

"Stay there, bitch. Don't move a fuckin' muscle," he said.

Rabbit's sudden action set the twins in motion. Ben climbed into the driver's seat and started the engine. Mick opened a long, narrow cabinet built into the paneling on the side of the van and removed two 9mm Uzis, passing one to Rabbit. The magazines had already been inserted and the gray metal weapons, their stocks folded, looked as lethal as they actually were. Lethal enough to make Katerina's eyes widen, to pull her back into the present. In an instant, in the time it took for Rabbit to jack a round into the chamber of the Uzi, the cocaine burning in her nerve endings turned from warmest pleasure into darkest terror. She leaned forward to grab at her skirt and blouse, but Rabbit kicked out at her, driving her back against the side of the van.

"I said to stay put," he yelled, putting the barrel of the gun against her throat. "By fucking Jesus, I swear I'll blow your eyes outta ya goddamn head if ya make another move."

"Please, please lemme go," Katerina begged, the words spilling out, one on top of the other. She'd given them *everything* and now they were going to reward her by killing her.

When Paul Dunlap pushed open the front door of the Jackson Arms, Betty Haluka and Stanley Moodrow in tow, the first thing he noticed were three black youths, obviously children and obviously dealers, standing off to one side of the entrance. The sight grabbed at his attention, enraging him. The little bastards didn't even have the good sense to run. He knew their defiance meant they had neither drugs nor money in their possession. They were advance men, bracing potential customers and steering them to the proper apartments.

"Do you wanna take them out?" Dunlap asked seriously. "Slap their faces, show 'em they're not in charge."

Betty pulled Dunlap to a stop fifteen feet from the doorway. "I'm a Legal Aid lawyer," she said evenly. "Except for the color of their skin, you have no reason to harass those children. Remember 'probable cause'? If I witnessed an unprovoked attack on civilians, I'd have to do something about it."

"That's easy for you to say, Betty," Dunlap argued. "But all three of us know those bastards are dirty. If I have to wait until they actually shoot someone, I'll never get their respect."

"Respect?" Moodrow gestured toward the trio, who still held their ground. One, the tallest, wore a Yankee cap with the brim turned to one side and pulled down over his ear; he openly watched the two cops and the woman, seeming more curious than concerned. "Forget about it, Paulie," Moodrow continued. "What you gotta do to these kids if you want respect, you're not gonna do surrounded by civilian witnesses." He gestured toward Inez Almeyda and her three children coming up the walk. Inez, her mouth already moving, was marshaling her complaints and Moodrow exchanged a private look with Betty, his arm encircling her waist as he prepared himself to absorb Inez's energetic onslaught.

"How come you no do your job?" she shouted (much to Stanley Moodrow's relief) at Paul Dunlap. "How come these pigs stay here and deal their drugs without no police come to arrest them?" She gestured at the dealers who, uneasy now, began to move slowly away, their shoulders dipping and rising contemptuously, their manner screaming, "We'll be back."

When Rabbit pushed the side door open, slamming it toward the rear of the van until it locked, Katerina's mind shut down altogether. Like Sylvia Kaufman's first reaction to the smoke pouring into her bedroom, Katerina could only form a single thought: escape. She had no idea where she was, no idea of the landscape that awaited her if she managed to get out of the van. She didn't realize that she was naked or that her pulse, already pushed to a flutter by the cocaine driving through her nervous system, had been accelerated by terror and now pounded behind her eyes at better than 200 beats per minute. The same fear that had frozen her against the side of the van suddenly twisted her body through the open door and she ran screaming into the street.

Curiously, both Mick and Rabbit had exactly the same reaction to Katerina's sudden and unexpected flight. "Fuckin' bitch," they said in unison, raising their rifle barrels until the black holes were in line with her retreating back. The first salvo of six shots, fired off as fast as the brothers could pull the triggers, pushed Katerina forward in a series of jerks, like she was being shoved repeatedly by an invisible giant. A seventh shot, fired by Rabbit after an instant's pause, took her in the back of the head and pitched her forward on her face.

"Get the pig," Ben ordered curtly from the front seat. "Wake the fuck up and chill that pig. Ma's gonna kill us if we blow this deal."

Rabbit was the first to jerk his eyes away from the naked, twitching body on the sidewalk. He raised the Uzi and tried to point it at Moodrow, but couldn't seem to keep it aimed; he was seated on the waterbed, his legs folded under him, and the recoil from the first volley of shots had set the water in motion. It was like trying to shoot geese from a speedboat.

"We didn't put the masks on," Mick observed, startling Rabbit, who began pulling the trigger as fast as he could.

If asked beforehand, Moodrow would have insisted, with full sincerity, that *he* was the real cop and Paul Dunlap a Community Affairs facsimile, but it was Paul Dunlap who reacted in proper cop fashion to the naked woman and the volley of shots from inside the van. Moodrow froze initially, but then, as if protecting a child from the blows of an angry parent, turned and took Betty Haluka in his arms, crushing her against his chest. Though his back was completely exposed to the gunshots exploding so close to each other they made a single crashing roar, he had no awareness of personal danger. He was on a street corner in midtown Manhattan, trying to warn the woman who waved to him from across the street.

"Watch out, watch out, watch out" he yelled over and over again. Trying to warn her before it was too late. Seeing two scenes at once, seeing another woman and a younger helpless cop unable to protect her. The sounds of the present jumbled into a series of separate impressions. Like a cubist painting in which the parts cross, but never touch. The roar of gunshots; the chink of bullets slamming into brick; the chunk of 9mm slugs entering the flesh of Inez Almeyda; the high-pitched wail of a terrified infant; the voice of a frightened cop holding his woman. It was all happening in pieces—random sounds garnered from a dozen old movies. It would have taken sight to put those sounds together and Stanley Moodrow's eyes were tightly closed and pressed into the hair of Betty Haluka.

Paul Dunlap, on the other hand, took no notice of the bullets ripping past his body. He saw Katerina Nikolis go down, her body erupting blood from a half-dozen holes, and all the anger in his being exploded at once. He'd been passing empty days for more than a decade, filling the time with a few well-practiced hobbies. Working out with his .38 at the police practice range (in preparation for a competition he never found the nerve to enter) was his oldest hobby. Without a second thought, he drew his revolver with practiced skill and blew Ben Cohan's brains out.

The Irishman fell against the steering wheel, turning the van sharply into the curb, throwing the already bouncing shooters away from the door and into each other. For a second, as the barrel of Mick's Uzi swung up toward him, Rabbit Cohan thought his own execution was somehow part of his mother's arrangement with Marty Blanks. He was surprised when Mick's chest fell apart under the onslaught of a dozen rounds from his own weapon. He was even more surprised when Porky Dunlap appeared in the open door of the van, his .38 thrust forward, and fired two rounds directly into Rabbit's chest, killing him instantly.

TWENTY-FIVE

IN some ways, the transformation of the entranceway to the Jackson Arms from slaughterhouse to official NYPD crime scene was more chaotic than the original attack. The first rule in the protection of crime scene evidence is to limit access to the primary detectives, the medical examiner, and the Crime Scene Unit (formerly "Forensics"). On the other hand, when the crime scene is outdoors and bodies are lying one atop the other and the wounded are screaming for help, such considerations go out the window. The first uniform on the scene (in this case, a portable assigned to the front of the subway station two blocks away) had a dual function: to secure the scene and to act as a recorder, noting name and rank as well as the time when various cops entered or left the crime scene. The second and third cops to arrive (two uniforms on sector patrol) were expected to control the crowd, keeping civilians (with a special emphasis on reporters) as far away as possible. Unfortunately, all three patrolmen responded to the carnage by turning over the bodies of Inez Almeyda, Katerina Nikolis, the Cohan brothers, and a young black male who no longer looked like a hardened drug dealer. They were searching for signs of life.

The homicide dicks who caught the squeal, two veterans named Jackson and Goldberg, were horrified at the chaos on 37th Avenue. They were late getting there, having been in the middle of an interview when the call had come through. The actual crime, they knew, had been committed at least thirty minutes before they arrived, but there were no ribbons of yellow plastic surrounding the Jackson Arms. Worse yet, they could see civilians touching the van and reporters taking photographs as the EMS paramedics ran back and forth with their folding gurneys and portable oxygen tanks.

Lesser men would have panicked, but Jackson and Goldberg were wily veterans, who immediately recorded the time of *their* arrival in their notebooks, following that piece of information with the names of the first three cops on the scene. Later on, when the lieutenant—or worse, the Queens Chief of Detectives, a monumental prick with the sensitivity of a drill instructor—cornered them, they would offer these three uniforms as sacrificial lambs. They felt no guilt at this betrayal; sacrifice, in their opinion, was better than the stupid bastards deserved anyway. Now the area was too compromised to establish the sequence of events by using crime scene evidence. They (and they knew it) would have to rely on witness interviews to get a picture of the drive-by, drug-related shooting both believed to be at the bottom of the incident.

But the surprises weren't over for Jackson and Goldberg. Having separated and catalogued the witnesses, they expected to proceed in a routine manner. What with the presence of Sergeant Paul Dunlap and the ex-cop, Stanley Moodrow, the statements were sure to be concise and accurate. What they didn't expect was an ex-cop with a big reputation, a thirty-five-year veteran, who could tell them nothing of what happened.

"Explain something to me," Jackson said in the course of the interview.

"Explain what?" Moodrow's voice was sharp and impatient. He had to get out of there, but he was trapped. As a civilian, he had no right to leave until the detectives decided to release him.

"That thing beneath your jacket . . . That bulge over there. Is that a gun?"

"Yeah, it's a gun."

Jackson took his time with the next question. His partner and five other detectives were in different parts of the Jackson Arms lobby, conducting interviews with the various witnesses. The crime scene was at last secured and the victims, wounded or dead, had been carted away to Elmhurst Hospital or the morgue.

"You got a license to carry that gun, right?" he finally said.

"You already seen it." Moodrow's voice began to rise, both in tone and in volume. He'd conducted thousands of civilian interviews, but had never sat on the other side, never had to deal with the deliberately slow pace of the questioning. He knew that Jackson would slow down still further as they went along, would cut from one subject to another without transition. The game was designed to increase the anxiety of the guilty, to make a suspect indiscreet. Of course, Moodrow was not the perp, a fact which only aggravated his sense of being needled.

"And how long have you had this permit?" Jackson, a tall black man, was also aware of the game, but he was more than unhappy to discover that his second-best witness, a man trained to observe accurately, had had his eyes shut throughout the incident.

The answer Moodrow wanted to shout began, *Ever since your mother . . .* But he knew that defiance wouldn't get him out of there. In the course of his own career, he'd almost always reacted to defiance with a further application of whatever abuse he happened to be dishing out. And he *had* to get out of there. It was that simple. There were too many things to put right and he might never get to the end of them if he didn't start immediately.

"Since I came on the job. 1952."

"Have you ever *used* your gun?"

Moodrow put his hand inside his jacket and pulled the .38, holding it gently on his lap. "You mean *this* gun?" he asked.

"That one."

"Yeah, I used it a lot. One time I had the record for active cops. That was before the Rambos came into the job."

Jackson turned away angrily. "Put the weapon back in the holster," he ordered.

"I'd like to put it in your mouth and pull the trigger until your brains go into orbit."

Moodrow giggled. The words had come unexpectedly; they were so *wrong* in terms of his real needs that he found it funny. Now Jackson, if he had any balls, would drag Moodrow's ancient ass into the precinct and hold him there for eight or nine hours as a lesson in good manners.

"What'd you say?" Jackson sounded like he was in shock.

"What I said is that I'm not a fucking suspect. I'm a witness and I don't wanna be cross-examined as if I pulled the goddamned trigger." He smiled up at Jackson. Challenging him. The action made him feel much better, but did little to prepare him for Jackson's response.

"Tell me how come," Jackson said evenly, "you didn't pull the gun when the shit went down? Tell me how come you turned around and hid your head? I just wanna know for my own curiosity. Like, did you crap your panties? Or maybe you settled for pissing down your leg." He stared directly into Moodrow's eyes, his hands on his hips. "The whole thing amazes me. The perps fire more than forty rounds before Dunlap takes them out. You're listening to screaming civilians and you have a legal gun inside your jacket. But you don't pull your gun. Oh, no. You don't protect them. You turn away and close your eyes. Now, all of a sudden, you're a hot shit again. You threaten me and I'm supposed to be afraid, but I gotta tell you I don't see anything to be afraid of. What I see is an old man with his balls shriveled up into his asshole."

Jackson stopped for a moment, giving Moodrow a chance to reply, but Moodrow, having no desire to explain his actions to Detective Jackson, held his peace until the detective went on. "I'll be at the precinct from nine to eleven tomorrow morning. You get your ass in there and make a statement. I want your chickenshit response in writing, so I can send a copy to the boys in the 7th Precinct. Now get the fuck out of here."

On his way out, Moodrow noted Betty Haluka and Paul Dunlap; they were huddled in a far corner of the lobby with the Chief of Patrol, a silk from One Police Plaza who stood just behind the Commissioner in the hierarchy of the NYPD. The presence of the chief, a man named Sean Murphy, meant the media was playing up the shooting as a major incident. Moodrow recalled the spring day a couple of years before when a black and Hispanic wolfpack had beaten a woman jogger over the head with a pipe before raping her. The jogger had been white and what might have passed unnoticed (by the TV stations and the papers, anyway), had it taken place in the South Bronx, became a source of page-one headlines for weeks. The presence of the Chief of Patrol in an obscure Queens precinct meant the Jackson Arms was getting that kind of attention. Good news for the tenants; bad news for the dealers. Moodrow knew from long experience that the department, faced with the kind of situation that *could* be resolved, would undoubtedly respond with a show of force designed to end the problem in a hurry.

"Moodrow." The voice was deep, full of humor. It belonged to Franklyn Goobe, the Chief of Detectives for New York City.

"What's up, Franklyn?" Moodrow wondered if he was about to get another lecture. He'd never gotten along with Goobe, never liked the pompous bastard.

Goobe straightened up, giving his carefully blow-dried mane of white hair a quick shake. "What's the situation here, Moodrow?"

"Speak to those people over there," Moodrow said, waving at Betty, Paul, and the Chief of Patrol. "I really have things to do."

"Don't be such a hard-on," Goobe said. "I thought when you retired, you'd ease up a little."

"Maybe I'm dedicated," Moodrow said. "Maybe I try harder."

Goobe nodded solemnly. "What I can't really see is how this incident affects the detectives. Sure, there's the shooters and the question of who, if anyone, sent them, but that investigation should go over to narcotics. The Commissioner's calling for one of his 'special efforts,' but I don't see what the detectives can do."

"You know something, Goobe? For once I gotta say you're a hundred percent correct." Moodrow had already come to the conclusion that he'd been the target of the brothers Cohan. In his opinion, the presence of the three dealers in front of the building had been nothing more than a lucky (from the killers' point of view) accident. "What you got here is a drug-related shooting in which the perps are dead. Of course, the detectives are supposed to find out who sent the shooters, but we both know that's a long-term project. *At best.* Your move is to give it over to narcotics and forget about it. Let Patrol move anticrime into the building—make it a dozen men. And don't pull 'em out as soon as the reporters disappear. Let 'em stay here for a couple of months. I guarantee the problem's gonna disappear."

It was almost five o'clock when Moodrow, released by Franklyn Goobe, pulled Betty's Honda to the curb outside the offices of Precision Management (he knew Dunlap would arrange to get Betty home) and settled down to wait. Even with the seat all the way back, the Honda's interior was too small for him, but he felt no discomfort. He was working.

The employees of Precision Management began to leave the building at five o'clock. They continued to leave for the next twenty-five minutes, and by a quarter to six everything was quiet. Moodrow was waiting for Al Rosenkrantz; he planned to follow Rosenkrantz home, to find some private place for a conversation. The kind of criminal who'd send two assassins into a quiet neighborhood, with orders to keep firing no matter how many people got in the way, was very new to Moodrow. Even during the worst of the heroin wars in the 60s, some attempt had been made to confine the carnage to fellow combatants. The man (or men) responsible for the violence that had taken place in front of the Jackson Arms was certain to come back to do the job right, which not only put Moodrow at risk, but threatened any poor innocent who happened to be standing within a hundred feet of him. Moodrow was looking for the short road.

He waited until six o'clock before going inside, expecting Rosenkrantz to be long gone, and found the security guard, an elderly black man, sitting in a folding chair at the top of the stairwell leading to Precision Management's offices.

"Whatta ya say?" Moodrow grunted.

"All right," the man answered. His nametag, a black bar with silver letters, read *T. Sawyer.*

"Glad to hear it." Moodrow, wondering if the "T" stood for Tom, flashed his ID at the guard. "I'm looking for Al Rosenkrantz. I didn't see him come out."

"The fat boy's workin' late tonight. He's up in his office."

"You mind if I go up?"

"Don't mean shit to me."

The main floor was deserted when Moodrow crossed it. With no humans scurrying about, the offices appeared even dirtier than on his first visit. The wastebaskets, each surrounded by a halo of crumpled paper, focused Moodrow on the contrast between the patches of white paper and the dirty brown tile floor. The condition of the offices hinted of corruption, not violence, and Moodrow came to the firm conclusion that Rosenkrantz could be no more than an office boy in this operation—a mouthpiece for the violent center. The only question was whether Rosenkrantz was a collaborator or a dupe. And the only important information to be gained was the source of his instructions.

Moodrow wasn't surprised to find Rosenkrantz still in his office, despite having been convinced, only a few moments before, that Rosenkrantz had gone home. The tension growing inside Moodrow's body was familiar and pleasant; it was like the memory of something especially helpful, something he should have known all along. He pushed open the door and stepped inside the small office, noting the sudden leap, from surprise to fear, that flashed across the fat man's features. Rosenkrantz knew what had happened and he knew Moodrow was the target.

"You're gonna fall," Moodrow said. "You *gotta* fall. How's about doing me a favor and not taking all day about it?"

Though he liked taking orders—carrying through was what he was *good* at, he'd never been creative—Al Rosenkrantz hated to be pushed around. Like many civilians who hadn't had a fight since junior high school, he thought of himself as a tough guy, willing to look any tenant right in the eye before launching into a line of bullshit. He liked saying "Trust me" to people he intended to destroy and felt himself stronger than any man who played by the rules. Of course, the simple fact that Moodrow had no intention of playing by the rules was manifestly obvious, but without any other real option, Rosenkrantz decided to test Moodrow anyway. He was a large man, six foot tall and well over 250 pounds; when his bullshit hadn't worked, he'd often used his size to intimidate building inspectors as well as tenants.

"Do me a favor," he said, before realizing just how far he had to look up to meet Moodrow's eyes, "and get the hell out of my office."

Moodrow responded by slapping him across the face, an openhanded blow that, nevertheless, had most of the ex-cop's shoulder behind it. It sent Rosenkrantz sprawling over the wastebasket beside his desk and he hit the floor with a very audible splat.

"You'll pay for this," was the best response Rosenkrantz could manage to formulate as he rose to his feet. His voice nevertheless conveyed defiance; he clearly meant to stand up to Moodrow's harassment. Unfortunately, when he raised his left hand to the side of his face (which seemed to be on fire), he exposed his ribs and, despite the heavy layer of protecting fat and muscle, Moodrow's fist exploded against the bones just beneath his heart like a two-pound hammer against a bag of peanuts. This time he had the good sense to stay on the floor, and when he spoke, his voice was much more conciliatory. "What do you want?" he asked.

By way of an answer, Moodrow took Rosenkrantz by the lapel of his jacket and, despite the fat man's 250 pounds, hauled him to his feet. "You tried to kill me," Moodrow said flatly, pushing him up against the filing cabinets. "And I'm gonna hurt you for it."

"I didn't," the fat man started to protest. "Please . . ."

Rosenkrantz saw Moodrow draw back his left fist, but, with his back up against the filing cabinets, he was unable to move away. The best Precision Management's Project Supervisor could do was cringe, and cringing had no effect on the intensity of the blow that crashed into the right side of his rib cage, driving him, once again, to the floor.

This time he made up his mind not to get up under any circumstance, not to get up even if Moodrow kicked him to death. He curled himself into a ball and grabbed at the handles of a locked filing cabinet. When he wasn't immediately attacked, he relaxed slightly, hoping against hope that the nightmare was over. Like a child pretending to evade a raging parent, he squeezed his eyes shut, opening them only when he felt Moodrow's weight drop onto his chest. What he saw—the barrel of a .38 caliber Smith & Wesson less than twelve inches from the end of his nose—was so frightening, his bladder released and he began to urinate. Curiously, he was unaware of the sensation of warm fluid on his thigh; it was the odor, sharp and acrid, that made him realize what he'd done.

"Please don't kill me," he moaned softly. "Please, please, please, please . . ."

Though he had no intention of really hurting Rosenkrantz, Moodrow knew he was using more force than necessary. He also knew that, of all the guilty ones, Rosenkrantz and the lawyer were the most likely to walk away unscathed. As a cop, he would have accepted this reality; he understood law enforcement as a series of compromises. As the target of fifty rounds of 9mm ammunition, however, he had a vested interest in seeing Al Rosenkrantz squirm, and he cocked the hammer of his pistol without cracking a smile. "You tried to kill me," he repeated.

"I didn't. I didn't. Oh, God, believe me. I didn't know anything about it."

Moodrow eased the hammer down, but kept the gun barrel in the fat man's face. "When did you find out?"

Rosenkrantz, though still terrified, had a dim realization of the reality that any convict would have understood the minute Stanley Moodrow came through the door. Moodrow wanted information; the violence was only a way of demonstrating his side of the deal. And Rosenkrantz's answer, should he decide to give it, would be the same as signing the contract.

"I got a phone call from Holtz about twenty minutes ago." To his surprise, the dominant emotion sweeping through him was shame, not relief. Nevertheless, he continued. "That's why I stayed late. He calls me this time every week."

Moodrow, recognizing the fat man's total capitulation (and anxious to put some distance between himself and Rosenkrantz's wet legs), stood up, holstered his weapon, and took the visitor's chair next to the desk. "C'mon, asshole," he said, pointing to Rosenkrantz's chair, "get off the fuckin' ground. It's time to spill your guts." He waited until Rosenkrantz was seated, then took a small cassette recorder from his jacket pocket and laid it on the desk. "On the way over here, I picked up this recorder and five tapes. After I load the tape and get it going, I'm gonna ask you some questions. If your answers give a hint of the fact that I'm forcing you to submit, I'm gonna shut down the recorder and load another tape. Nowadays the experts can tell if you erase the tape and that limits me. I can only go through it five times, so you should remind yourself that it definitely pays for you to make sure I don't run out of tape."

"Are you going to try to use this in a courtroom?" Rosenkrantz was careful to keep his voice soft.

"Could be."

"But I don't have a lawyer."

"Oh yeah, that's very interesting." Moodrow, the tape inserted and ready to go, put the tape deck in his lap. "It used to be, when I was still a cop, that I'd have to do all kinds of shit before I could ask you any questions. But now that I'm retired, all the rules have changed. It don't matter if I gotta break the law to obtain evidence against you. I mean you could always go to the precinct and make a complaint against me. Maybe you could even get me arrested. But none of that would make the evidence inadmissible. *Miranda* doesn't have anything to do with civilians. You understand what I'm sayin'?"

Moodrow turned the recorder on, labeling it with the day, the date and the place, then laid it on the desk between himself and Rosenkrantz. "So when did you find out that someone tried to kill me today?"

"I got a call from the lawyer . . ."

"Say his name."

"Holtz. Bill Holtz. From Bolt Realty."

"He told you I was the target of the hit?"

"No, no. He told me there was a shooting in front of the apartments and he gave me some instructions."

In the end, Moodrow was disappointed. Rosenkrantz freely admitted his part in the assault on the tenants of the Jackson Arms—he went so far as to admit participation in a dozen similar schemes—but he completely denied having any part in the violence. He'd helped to select the targets for eviction and deliberately fired the old superintendent, but his main function was to keep the tenants from organizing. To convince them that Precision Management would handle the problems. At no time was he part of the general planning. Nor did he personally meet any of the squatters, though he'd furnished the lawyer with a list of empty apartments. And, most of all, he had absolutely no idea who, if anyone, stood behind William Holtz.

TWENTY-SIX

MOODROW drove directly from Precision Management to Betty Haluka's apartment in Park Slope, Brooklyn. He was hoping for a quick trip, but as Precision Management was in eastern Queens and Park Slope was in west-central Brooklyn and it was only seven o'clock, the trip was long enough and slow enough for him to face his disappointment. He'd hoped (even though he knew better) that Rosenkrantz would lead him directly to the owners of Bolt Realty. A futile hope that was doomed from the beginning. Bolt Realty had gone to great lengths to keep its owners away from public scrutiny and there was no reason to suppose the principals would trust their security to a flunky like Al Rosenkrantz.

As he drove, Moodrow tried to occupy himself with the question of who, exactly, had been the target of the brothers Cohan. His initial conviction, that he had been the one slated for execution, had come instinctively, but now, like any good investigator, he had to subject it to an application of cop logic. Working backward, he quickly eliminated the obvious. The attackers were white males, nearly thirty years of age, and clearly atypical in terms of the crack wars of the 80s and 90s. Those wars were being fought on the streets of black and Hispanic ghettos, not in middle-class Jackson Heights. They were also being fought, in the main, by ultraviolent savages masquerading as children. A prime example—the dealers hanging out in front of the Jackson Arms were no more than fifteen years old, ten years younger than the youngest of the assassins. There was a reason, of course, why these children were allowed to function unimpeded by their elders in the drug business. Any dealer with half a brain divorced himself from the street as soon as he had enough capital to participate in the wholesale end of the industry. Those too stupid to make the jump inevitably capped their careers with long, hard periods of incarceration. If they survived at all.

But even if the three dealers had not been the target of the Cohan brothers (they'd actually had their identification in their pockets, another example of their ultimate stupidity), that didn't mean their target was Stanley Moodrow. One by one, as he drove up onto the Brooklyn–Queens Expressway, Moodrow went over the others present at the scene: Dunlap, Betty, the Almeydas. They were all replaceable: Paul Dunlap, from the killer's point of view, was only one of 30,000 cops in New York (his cop status also made him an extremely unlikely target for assassination); Betty Haluka was a Legal Aid lawyer, one of thousands, and her efforts to halt the decay of the Jackson Arms amounted to nothing more than harassment; Inez Almeyda, a housewife with little more than anger to contribute to the struggle to save her home was, of course, the most innocent of innocent bystanders.

He, on the other hand, private investigator Stanley Moodrow, was the man pursuing the source; he had already made up his mind not to stop until he found Sylvia Kaufman's killer. (And the killer of Inez Almeyda and Katerina Nikolis and a fourteen-year-old crack dealer named Roy "Pinwheel" Johnson.) He was also the man who had decked Al Rosenkrantz, a fact certainly reported to the fat man's employers. His willingness to step away from the narrow line of the law was certain to set off an alarm in the mind of a criminal, criminals being only too aware of the short-term advantages to be derived from a highly developed contempt for the law.

Of course, there was always the chance that the Cohan brothers hadn't been after anyone in particular. Maybe the attack had been no more than a faked drive-by with assault rifles, a message to send the tenants packing while the cops searched their files, looking for Queens crack czars. Nevertheless, prudence dictated that he consider himself a target. For the same practical reasons, he should have considered Betty a target, as well, but he wasn't ready to face what he'd done at the scene. Sooner or later, he would have to probe his actions with the same cop logic driving his present speculations, but not then and there. Better to deal with the victims, to psych himself up for the chase.

Betty's apartment was empty when Moodrow finally arrived, and there was no sign that she'd come home and gone out again. A phone call to the 115th Precinct produced a detective named Downey who told Moodrow that all the witnesses had given statements and gone home. Likewise for Porky Dunlap and, yes, the Legal Aid lawyer had been given a ride back to somewhere, maybe Brooklyn. How long ago? At least two hours.

A sudden feeling of apprehension washed over Moodrow as he laid the phone down and went back to the car. The fear had no basis in "cop logic"; not even in the "cop instincts" sitting at the source of his pride. Maybe she was angry with him. Maybe she thought him a coward or . . . But he didn't want to think about alternatives. He wanted to drive home and find her waiting for him and he did it quickly, cutting in and out of the heavy traffic on Flatbush Avenue. When he climbed the stairs to his fourth floor apartment and found her sitting with her back against his door, he was so relieved, he stopped in his tracks.

"Stanley," she said, "you son of a bitch. I thought you were dead. Where did you go?" She came off the floor in a hurry, running toward him, throwing her arms around him. "You bastard. You dirty bastard. How could you disappear like that?" Crying, as much from the remembered fear as relief to find him in one piece. "I want to go inside. I want us to get undressed and into bed. Please, Stanley. I've been thinking about it for hours. I want to get into bed and I want you to tell me what happened."

Ten minutes later, the front door bolted behind them, they huddled under the covers, sipping at glasses of bourbon, speaking softly, darting around the central issue. Inez Almeyda was dead, as was Katerina Nikolis and the dealer. The Almeyda children were unhurt, though devastated by the violence, while their father, Andre Almeyda, was in shock, alternately vowing revenge and weeping uncontrollably.

The Chief of Patrol, Sean Murphy, had made his will known to Inspector Mario Gerardi, his hatchetman, who'd passed it on to Captain George Serrano, Commander of the 115th Precinct. All illegal tenants (regardless of political conviction) would be arrested for criminal trespass and charged with breaking and entering. Despite there being virtually no chance for any convictions, the apartments would be classified as crime scenes and padlocked as they were cleared. They would not be rerented without NYPD approval. The landlord (or his agent) would be sought out and informed that only cooperation stood between Bolt Realty and a full-scale, multiagency investigation. Once things had settled down, anticrime would keep the building under surveillance until Serrano was sure nobody was coming back.

"So that's it for the Jackson Arms," Moodrow said. "The bad guys lost. Along with everybody living there."

"The price was too high," Betty said. The bourbon, which under other conditions would have made her choke, was sending a warm glow directly to the place where the fear had been. She could feel the muscles in her back relaxing, one by one. Casually, she turned toward Moodrow, throwing one leg across his thighs.

"The price is the price," Moodrow said. "How do you figure it's too high?"

"A lot of innocent people died, Stanley. And the mother-fuckers tried to kill you. Don't pretend it's not true. I've been thinking about it for hours and it's the only thing that makes sense. If they wanted to frighten the tenants, they'd do it at three o'clock when the kids come home. Or at five when people come home from work."

"You're right." Moodrow cut her off. He was amazed (and very happy) to discover that she'd seen through the charade. "I think they were after me. It could have been you or Paul Dunlap, but I think it was me."

"And it's because they're afraid of you?"

"Most likely that's it."

"And they'll probably try again."

Moodrow grunted. "They came after me and it completely destroyed their project. Maybe they'll learn a lesson. Maybe not. But either way I figure they don't have more than a couple of weeks until I catch up with them. I'm not really too crazy about getting shot at."

They were quiet for a few moments, lying close to one another. Moodrow, his arm around Betty's shoulders, could feel the ebb and flow of her breathing. He expected her to fall asleep and her question caught him off guard.

"What happened this afternoon?" she asked. "My head was buried in your chest and I couldn't see any of it. Tell me what happened."

"Paul Dunlap . . ."

"I mean with you and me, Stanley. I mean about what *you* did."

Moodrow sat up in the bed, turning his back to Betty Haluka. He was very uncomfortable; it wasn't in his nature to say things to another person that he couldn't say to himself. On the other hand, if he remained silent or tried to evade the truth, Betty would know it immediately and her knowledge would have consequences that also frightened him.

"I wanted to protect you," he said. "But it was bullshit protection. I should have thrown you to the ground, but all I could do was hold you. Military weapons like those Uzis can shoot through car doors. My back wasn't any protection. By holding you upright, I only put you in greater danger."

Betty laid one hand gently on his shoulder. She was going to pull him around until she could see his eyes, but thought better of it. "Still, in your own mind, you believed you were protecting me."

"I didn't think at all. I wasn't even there." He drew a deep breath; he didn't want to talk about this and he could feel resentment beginning to grow. He knew it was better not to let that build up. "Do you know about Rita?" he finally asked.

Betty, as she felt the blush rising in her throat, was glad she hadn't turned her lover around. She'd spent an afternoon with Rose Carillo talking about Moodrow's former girlfriend, Rita Melengic. Gossiping behind Moodrow's back had been delicious. "She used to be your girlfriend."

Moodrow didn't stop to consider how Betty had come by the information, though he'd think about it later on. "I was crazy about her," he announced, his voice dropping to a whisper. "It was very unexpected, because I had chances when I was younger and I hadn't felt that way before. We had only been living together about a month when it happened. She and I were tryin' it out, thinking about getting married, but what happened was that I saw her get killed. I don't wanna get too dramatic, but in some ways it was like this afternoon. They weren't after Rita. She was standing on a corner waiting for me and I was coming up Sixth Avenue. I had no idea what was about to happen, just like today. It'd be very strange if I hadn't been in some tight spots after thirty-five years in the job, but I could see those situations coming. When you're walking down a dark corridor toward an apartment where you expect to find large amounts of contraband, you get yourself ready for gunfire. But when it's someone you care about, when you're not expecting it at all, it comes on you very different. I remember that the afternoon was real hot and I don't do so well in the heat. We were going shopping at A&S in Herald Square and, naturally, all the big stores were air conditioned, so that's what I was thinking about. I saw Rita standing in front of the store from about half a block away. She was waving to me and then she was gone. I was about to step into the street. My foot was in the air and then she was gone. Today, when . . ."

Moodrow's voice trailed off. Like a talking doll when the string winds back into its body. Betty wanted to take him in her arms. A dozen questions jumped to her lips, but she held back somehow. As if her hand, still resting gently on his shoulder, had already passed her thoughts between them.

"You always believe those things eventually go away," Moodrow began abruptly, his voice stronger. "You have to believe that, because if you don't, you'll lose control. You expect to feel bad for a while. Maybe you even get torn up, but sooner or later it goes away. That's what I always believed, but this afternoon I didn't know where I was. I had my eyes closed and I was seeing Sixth Avenue, but I could hear what was happening in Queens. Every sound was sharp and clear. They just didn't match the movie playing in my head. All I could really think about was losing you." He shrugged her hand away, then turned to face her. "I think I've had enough of that in my life."

By the time Leonora Higgins called, at ten o'clock, Betty and Moodrow had done what lovers do to restore basic equilibrium. Their lovemaking, complemented by the bourbon, had driven their fear into hiding; now the job was to keep it penned up. Betty had dozens of questions about how Moodrow expected to proceed and what he intended to do if he got to the source of the violence, but she held them back. She recognized, dimly, that her own role was probably over. Inspector Gerardi, in her presence, had made a phone call to William Holtz, attorney for Bolt Realty, explaining the delicacy of the situation and casually mentioning the possibility of a joint task force composed of Fire Department, HPD, and NYPD personnel. Gerardi had explained exactly what he intended to do to the squatters and Holtz had assured him of Bolt Realty's full cooperation—the padlocked apartments would not be rerented without approval. Holtz had even offered to furnish Gerardi with an accurate list of unleased units.

None of this, of course, brought Moodrow any closer to his quarry. Leonora's phone call, on the other hand, brought a piece of information that gave Moodrow considerable optimism for the immediate future. Leonora's voice was chipper. She had no sense of the scene she was interrupting.

"How's Betty doing?" she asked, ignoring him altogether.

"She's doing okay," Moodrow returned. "I'm gonna put her on the extension, if you don't mind."

Betty and Leonora exchanged greetings, then Leonora, perhaps in deference to the hour, got into the meat of her information. "I finally gained access to the Department of State computer by pretending I was from the Department of Finance investigating a failure to file a corporate tax return. They change the password for those files every few weeks and it's hard to get it. Anyway, Bolt Realty is owned by a Delaware Corporation called, if you can believe this, the Flatbush Realty Corporation."

"Are you serious?" Moodrow interrupted. "Another corporation? This is bullshit."

"Wait a second, Stanley. It gets better. When you file an application for a corporate charter in New York State, someone has to swear to the truth of the information and that someone has to be an officer, though not necessarily a stockholder. The charter for Bolt Realty was filed by the president of the company, Simon Chambers. I have an address for him, but no phone number. Why don't you take it down?"

Moodrow fumbled for a pen, then took the address, a street in Sheepshead Bay on the southern end of Brooklyn. He was looking for a way to get off the phone without insulting Leonora (maybe a quick thank-you for the information, followed by a good-bye and the instantaneous acknowledgment of his sudden need for rest) when Leonora floored him with a piece of information she, herself, considered old news.

"Congratulations on getting the arsonist," she said matter-of-factly.

"What're you talking about?" The sentence, much to his dismay, was nearly a scream.

"I thought you knew about it. Dunlap matched a print last night. He was all over the Queens District Attorney's office, trying to find out if it's enough for an arrest warrant. The cops are looking for the torch right now."

"How come you heard about it?" Moodrow demanded. The anger was rising between his ears like the steam in a sixty-year-old tenement. "You're in Manhattan."

"The Jackson Arms is a big story. Can't you see the headline: Crack Comes to the White Folks. It's like Man Bites Dog."

Moodrow laughed bitterly. "Is that what they think? That it's drugs?"

"That's what I hear." Leonora stopped, abruptly. "I suppose you think it's something else?"

"I don't have any proof," Moodrow offered lamely.

"Do me a favor, Stanley. When you get proof, give me a call. Now that you're a civilian, I'll need a head start if I'm gonna save your ass."

"Good night, Leonora."

"Nighty-night, Stanley. Night, Betty."

TWENTY-SEVEN

April 21

ON the following morning, Moodrow got himself out of the bed just before the sun came up, rising to the smell of the percolator and Betty, in her red terry-cloth bathrobe, moving purposefully about the kitchen.

"You want coffee, Stanley," she called cheerfully.

"Bless thee, woman." It was a little after six and the Lower East Side was beginning to stir. Moodrow liked being up at this time, drawing his own work energy from the men and women trudging toward the subway. His working days inevitably began within his own mind, with problems that needed resolution (usually, the same problems he'd gone to sleep with) and Betty's presence made no difference. He used her, as he'd once used a woman named Rita Melengic, for a sounding board.

"I think the best thing about this President of Bolt Realty . . . What's his name? Simon Chambers? The best thing about him is that I don't have to find a way to confront the lawyer, Holtz." Moodrow had high hopes that, between the lead given to him by Leonora Higgins and the identification of the arsonist, the end of the road was well within reach. On the other hand, Holtz was undoubtedly the hub of the operation; he would know virtually everything about the criminals who ran Bolt Realty, but Moodrow could not simply walk up to an attorney and lean on him the way he'd leaned on poor Al Rosenkrantz. The concept of fang and claw didn't apply to lawyers: you could beat them down with paper, but not with your fists.

"I've given Mr. Holtz a lot of thought," Betty said. "I think of him the way you'd think of a corrupt cop. I know lawyers aren't supposed to have any honor, but I've always been too much of a *shmuck* to be completely cynical. I don't think Holtz committed a crime and I don't think you can make him pay for being a merciless scumbag, either. Merciless scumbaggery is not, to my knowledge, a violation of the penal code."

"Why do I get the feeling you don't like this guy?" Moodrow grinned, but Betty's anger was too strong.

"Yesterday," she said, "some bastard tried to kill me. I still can't believe it. Whenever I close my eyes, I hear the sound of gunshots. I want revenge and I think Holtz was as responsible as the rest of them. Him and that bastard, Rosenkrantz."

"Rosenkrantz," Moodrow groaned, "The whole reason I took off yesterday was to go see Big Al." Quickly, he outlined his futile interview with Rosenkrantz, including his means of persuasion. "A dead end," he concluded. "But I got a tape out of it. The prick admits he took his orders from William Holtz; he was told to fire the super and to prepare eviction notices for people who always paid the rent. Rosenkrantz figures the plan was to clear the building out, but he never actually discussed it with Holtz. It wasn't any of his business."

Betty shrugged. "That's about the way I figured it. Rosenkrantz's job was to keep the people confused until it was too late to do anything. He might have succeeded, too, if he tried it ten years ago, but the druggies are more violent these days. That's the difference between crack and heroin. Anyway, I have to go into my office for a while. We're going into court Monday and I plan to ask the judge to force disclosure of Bolt Realty's stockholders. With everything that's happened, he might even agree. If Holtz is stupid enough to make a personal appearance, I'll put him on the stand as a hostile witness and ask him, under oath, who he gets his orders from."

Moodrow was on the phone, trying to reach his old friend, Jim Tilley, before Betty closed the front door. It was typical of Moodrow to have contingency plans in case individuals failed him and Porky Dunlap's apparent defection was no exception.

Rose Carillo answered the phone and then woke her husband.

"What? What? Who is it?" Jim Tilley didn't sound especially ready to face another day.

"It's me. Moodrow. Wake up a second. I need your help."

"Stanley? I heard the mutts chilled your ass yesterday."

"Very funny," Moodrow said. "But, as a matter of fact, I escaped serious injury. Which you're not gonna, if you don't stop being a wiseass."

"Hang on a second, Rose's bringing coffee. Gee, that's good. Not as good as sex maybe, but right up there with hitting the john after five hours staked out in a closet. Rose says to tell you she's happy you didn't get killed."

"Will you stop with that shit, already," Moodrow said. "I gotta ask you a favor and I'm getting distracted."

"First, I have to ask *you* a question." Tilley drained the mug before continuing. "I wanna know if you think you're more likely or less likely to get me to do you a favor by referring to my humor as 'that shit'?"

Moodrow responded by ignoring the remark altogether. "It looks like Dunlap's gonna cop out on me," he announced.

"You mean the Community Affairs Officer?" Tilley was still amused. "What'd you expect?"

"I expected," Moodrow said honestly, "that if he didn't come across, I could count on you. That's because I remember you *already* offered to help."

Tilley sighed. "Whatta ya need, Stanley?"

"Time."

"Lemme hear the whole thing."

"Dunlap matched one of the arsonist's prints. Last night. Only he didn't call me with the arsonist's name. I mean the guy's been calling me every time his little brain turns a half-click, but now he can't find the phone." Moodrow paused long enough to ease his frustration, then continued. "I'm going out to see him as soon as I finish with you and I got the feeling he's gonna tell me it's a police matter. When I think about it, I have to admit he's got a point. I'm retired and this particular arsonist is wanted for a homicide. Also, Dunlap is an asshole. Now that all the boys are patting him on the back for putting down the Cohan brothers, he'll probably wrap himself in the department. Last night, Leonora gave me the name of the president of Bolt Realty Corporation. I wanna pay him a visit this afternoon and I could use a badge to back me up."

"No problem. I spent the last two weeks sitting on a rooftop on East Broadway. A total waste, as it turned out. The mutt was picked up at his brother's house in Boston. Anyway, the Whip says the job can't afford overtime this month, so I have to take six days compensatory time. Yesterday was the first day and I slept it through. Now I'm awake and I'm bored. Besides, I'm not forgetting that even if you escaped serious injury, somebody tried to kill you. I wouldn't have any objection to meeting up with that person. That's because me and Rose love you, Stanley."

Paul Dunlap wasn't in his office when Stanley Moodrow arrived at the 115th Precinct; he was standing in the middle of a circle of admiring detectives, repeating the story of the Jackson Heights massacre with full gusto. Moodrow, coming into the squadroom on his way to Dunlap's office, couldn't help but notice the rotund Porky Dunlap as he demonstrated the various shooter's positions he'd taken during the course of the attack.

"You come back to give a statement?"

The voice belonged to Detective Jerome Jackson, and Moodrow, though he'd forgotten all about his promise to give a written statement, could see no way to get out of it. He spent the next half hour sparring with Jackson while Dunlap studiously ignored the both of them. In the end, after Jackson's final snotty remark, Moodrow had to approach Dunlap and ask for a moment's time.

"Sure, Moodrow," Dunlap said, "let's go into my office."

As they walked away, Dunlap threw the detectives a look, (eyebrows raised, half-smile tugging at one corner of his mouth) that left no doubt that he considered Moodrow to be, at best, a ludicrous figure and, at worst, a coward. Curiously, Moodrow took no offense whatsoever. He had no intention of working with the NYPD and if it appeared that Dunlap was rejecting him, so much the better.

"I know what you're going to ask me," Dunlap said as soon as the door closed behind them. "And I can't do it."

"What's that?" Moodrow asked innocently.

"You want to know the name of the arsonist."

"Actually, I'd settle for knowing why you didn't phone me last night."

Dunlap leaned back confidently. "Captain Serrano called me in for a talk after you left yesterday. This was *before* I matched the print. He told me in no uncertain terms that the investigation was official and civilians should be left out. He mentioned you in particular and told me that *any* leaks would come back on me: I was responsible for keeping the investigation within the job. Right after that, I matched the print."

"I see what you're getting at," Moodrow answered, "and I realize you gotta do what you gotta do. Remember, I was in the job, too. I just wanna know how the department's gonna handle it. Are you putting the arson with the shooting?"

"*I'm* not doing anything." Dunlap paused dramatically. "I've been appointed to the detectives; I'm going to work with the Task Force on Organized Crime. That's why I didn't call you. One more day and I'm out of here."

The information came as no surprise to Moodrow. If Dunlap had had any heart, Moodrow knew, he wouldn't have been able to spend all those years in Community Affairs. And, of course, now that Dunlap considered himself a "real cop," he certainly wouldn't want to tarnish his status by taking orders from Stanley Moodrow.

"So you can't even tell me how you're treating the case?" Moodrow asked sadly, his hands pressed between his knees.

Dunlap smiled paternally. The past sixteen hours had been the best of his life and the reversal of his relationship with Stanley Moodrow was, in some ways, the best part of it. "Look, Moodrow," he finally said, "I don't know that much about it. It's not my squeal. Never was, really. But from what I understand, the arson is gonna stay in the house and the shooting's going over to Citywide Narcotics."

Moodrow smiled. "Thanks, Paul," he said. "That's the way I figure it, too. A drive-by over a drug location. Christ, we *saw* the damn dealers ourselves, right?"

"Right." Dunlap nodded his agreement.

"And, also, I understand that Serrano's gonna bust up the squats. Haul 'em out and seal the apartments." Moodrow paused, but, as Dunlap's head continued to go up and down, he started again before the sergeant had a chance to reply. "That should be the end of the problems for the Jackson Arms. My only complaint is that they should have done it a month ago. A lot of lives could have been saved."

"A hundred percent correct," Dunlap encouraged. "But you know how it is. It takes a ton of dynamite to get the department off its collective ass. Always has."

They both chortled at Dunlap's newly found cynicism. "So there's nothing for me," Moodrow said. "My job is basically done."

"And you did a great job, too," Dunlap quickly agreed. "You were the one who provided the energy to get the giant in motion, but now that it's moving . . ."

Moodrow stood abruptly, extending his hand. "Paulie," he said, "it's been a pleasure working with you. I won't insult you by asking you for the name of the arsonist, even though I gotta admit I bear the fucker a major grudge."

"I'm glad you feel that way." Dunlap rose to his feet as Moodrow made his way to the door. "Take care of yourself, Moodrow," he said. "I owe you one."

Moodrow went directly from Paul Dunlap's office to the precinct detention cells in the basement of the One One Five. He was looking for the Precinct Attendant, an ordinary patrolman, usually a veteran, who took responsibility for prisoners, supervising detainment until a Corrections bus hauled them off to the courts for arraignment. Moodrow, a detective for more than twenty-five years before his retirement, had had the foresight to build up sources of information within the department as well as within the criminal world outside. His goal, at one time, had been to establish an informant within each precinct. He'd never fully succeeded (Staten Island, considered a foreign country by many New Yorkers, had eluded his best efforts), but the One One Five had yielded several well-placed individuals and Moodrow was looking for the best of them.

Robert McTeague was a professional Irishman who'd spent the better part of his life avoiding the twin pitfalls that seemed to plague his countrymen—booze and violence. A third generation cop, he'd come into the job for obvious reasons. Once in it, however, he'd taken great pains to keep himself away from the mainstream of policing. Using his father's clout, he'd wormed himself into the position of Precinct Attendant (a job usually reserved for alkies or the disabled) and now rarely left the precinct during his tour. An eighteen-year veteran, he'd been at the One One Five for fifteen of those years and knew everything there was to know about his precinct.

It was still early in the day when Moodrow came up to the cell block. The unit, having been cleared an hour before by a Corrections Department bus, was completely deserted. McTeague was asleep in an ancient wooden desk chair.

"Wake up a second," Moodrow said, shaking the patrolman gently.

McTeague opened one eye, fixing it on Moodrow. The eye was red with sleep, as bloodshot as that of any Irish alcoholic though McTeague hadn't had a drink in fifteen years. "Moodrow," he said after a moment's thought. "I heard you almost bought it yesterday." A cautious man, he didn't add the rest of the rumor—that Moodrow had performed in a cowardly manner.

"I need some information," Moodrow said, knowing McTeague was not a man who could be coaxed with words; the patrolman responded only to the flash of money. "I want the name of the arsonist Dunlap identified last night."

"Fifty," McTeague announced without a moment's hesitation.

"C'mon, McTeague, have a little fucking mercy. Didn't you hear that I'm retired?"

"Maybe you been retired too long, Moodrow," the attendant returned equably. "Maybe you never heard about inflation. Them days when you could flash a twenty and get the color of the commissioner's underpants are long gone. Pay up or lemme go back to sleep."

"You oughta be sleeping in the goddamn cell instead of out here," Moodrow responded, counting out the money.

"The perp's name," McTeague began, folding the bills and stuffing them into his pocket. "Is Maurice Babbit. Served time in the Clinton Correctional Facility for an arson committed somewhere upstate. Last known address is a halfway house on West 102nd Street, but he left there about a year ago when he finished his parole. Babbit's a white male about thirty years of age. Five foot ten inches tall, average build, blue eyes, sandy hair."

"How the fuck you know this?" Moodrow asked, shaking his head in wonder. "The detectives are upstairs and you're down here. You seem to know this shit before they do."

"I fill out the reports," McTeague announced. "I fill out the booking reports and the arraignment forms while the boys go out for coffee. Do all the finger-printing by myself when it's not too busy. The suits show their appreciation by keeping me informed. I think it's a fair trade."

Moodrow shrugged. "Maybe it is. Anything else I should know about Babbit?"

"His parole officer claims he's a nut case. Shoulda been in the crazy house instead of the pen. The guy goes around scared shitless all day long which means you gotta be careful when you take him. Guys like that are liable to do anything."

"And what about a picture?" Moodrow, already moving down the corridor, fired a hopeful parting shot.

"I thought you'd never ask," McTeague responded. "It'll cost you another twenty-five. Just fill out an envelope with your name and address. I'll run Babbit's sheet through the copier and mail it out tonight."

Despite Jim Tilley's rambling complaints about his current partner, a twenty-year man named Peter Bonomare, Moodrow was more than happy to be riding across Brooklyn with his old partner. Tilley had had the foresight to bring his own car, a '79 Buick with approximately sixteen times the leg room of Betty Haluka's Honda, and Moodrow was luxuriating in the unaccustomed space while his partner drove from light to light on Ocean Parkway. They were headed for the foot of Nostrand Avenue, just off Shore Parkway, in Sheepshead Bay. Moodrow knew the area well: it was white and middle class, a quiet residential neighborhood populated by working couples, small-business owners, and young professionals trying to get started.

They drove all the way to Emmons Avenue, to the waters of Sheepshead Bay, before Moodrow's antennae began to tingle. Something was wrong, but he couldn't put his finger on it until Tilley pointed out 6548 Nostrand Avenue. It was right where it was supposed to be, taking up the entire east side of Nostrand, between Voorhies and Shore Parkway. The reason Moodrow hadn't seen it was because the Longview Nursing Home didn't seem like a place where the president of Bolt Realty could possibly reside.

"I don't like this," Tilley said. "We're gonna get screwed here."

They were treated with courtesy by the staff of the Longview Nursing Home, a small favor which made the reality of Simon Chambers a little more palatable. Louise Eller, administrator for the home, received them promptly, offering them chairs by her desk. "Yes," she said, "we have a patient named Simon Chambers. But I don't think you'll be able to talk to him. Mr. Chambers had a series of strokes after he came to us and no longer communicates."

"How long ago, Ms. Eller?" Tilley asked. "Was the stroke recent?"

"Fairly recent." She looked down, consulting Chambers' medical records. "He was in an automobile accident a little more than two years ago. Came to us from the hospital. The strokes occurred about fifteen months ago."

"What about family?"

"No family. He's an elderly widower. Childless. All his affairs are handled by an attorney named William Holtz."

Moodrow tried to contain a rising excitement. Maybe the trip wouldn't be wasted after all. "Do you think we could take a look at Mr. Chambers?" he asked. "The reason I'm asking is because I gotta make sure it's the same guy we wanna talk to. I really don't think it can be him, because the Chambers we wanna talk to has been active within the last year, but if I could take a look, I'd be sure."

Louise Eller activated the intercom, asking her receptionist to send in "Nurse Rawlins." A few minutes later, a middle-aged black woman opened the door without knocking and stepped inside.

"You want me, Louise?" she asked.

"I want you to take these officers to Simon Chambers' room. Let them have a look at him. It shouldn't take them more than a few minutes to make an identification."

The message was clear enough. They could have their look, as long as it didn't take too long and they left when they were finished; Nurse Rawlins was along to see that things went smoothly. Not that Moodrow had any objections to being rushed. His main interest was in separating the Longview Nursing Home from Bolt Realty, to determine if Chambers' presence was entirely innocent.

The tall nurse, her manner utterly unconcerned, led the way through a series of corridors to a single room at the southern edge of the building.

"One second, Ms. Rawlins," Moodrow said, before they'd gotten inside. "Could I ask you a couple of questions?"

"About Adolph?" The nurse giggled.

"Who's Adolph?"

"That's the name we had for Chambers. He was a son of a bitch before he had his stroke."

"So, you called him 'Adolph' because he was nasty?"

Rawlins laughed again. "We called him 'Adolph' because he was a damn Nazi. He's even got a tattoo on his arm. In fact, he's got two tattoos on him. He got a swastika on his right shoulder and two lightning bolts on his left. The lightning bolts have something to do with a political party. His legs were all broken up from the accident. He couldn't do anything for himself, but he used to tell the people who were helping him exactly what would happen to them once his party took power. The guy was crazy and when the blood vessels started popping off in his brain, the whole staff had a party."

Tilley laughed on cue, his nerves tingling just as Moodrow's were. "This guy have any visitors?" he asked.

"Just the lawyer. I don't know his name."

"Can Chambers write? Could he sign a document?"

"No way," Rawlins said firmly. "He's paralyzed. Damaged on both sides of his brain and twisted up like a pretzel."

"Doesn't sound like you're too sympathetic," Moodrow observed.

"Chambers used to call us subhuman. He'd say, 'Ah, here comes a subhuman. Does it think it can find a minute to do its job?' You hear that for a few months and you start saving your sympathy for the people who appreciate it."

TWENTY-EIGHT

April 25

BETTY HALUKA knew it was raining hard the minute she got out of bed. She knew it was raining, despite the closed windows and drawn shades in Stanley Moodrow's apartment, because the giant sitting at the kitchen table, sucking on a hot cup of coffee, was soaking wet. So wet that his fingertips were wrinkled, like those of a child left too long in the bathtub.

"What happened to you?" Even through bleary, pre-coffee eyes, Betty could sense Moodrow's distress.

"You remember how beautiful it was yesterday? The sun was out all day, right? Could you believe it was gonna get down to forty-four degrees in less than six hours? It was like summer when me and Jim decided to put out the word that we were looking for Babbit. We did the bars until they closed, then hit the social clubs. Around four o'clock, Jim took the car and went home to Rose, but me, I decided to look up an ex-con named Montrose who hangs at a club on Avenue D. The mutt wasn't there, and when I came out, it was pouring. I can't run no more, Betty. I had to walk the whole way home."

"Any luck?"

"With finding Babbit?"

"What else?"

"Nothin'." Moodrow was unperturbed. "Probably don't come from around here. We'll take him, though. The Lower East Side's been torch heaven since the city announced they were gonna auction off the empty buildings. The bars are like gossip columns, only instead of talking about movie stars, they talk about who's pulling off which scam. I'm not saying we'll find Babbit today, but sooner or later, if the guy's a professional, which he obviously is, he's gonna pop to the surface."

"And you spent all night doing this?"

"It's a slow process," Moodrow explained. "And last night was just the beginning. Last night was the easy part, talking to bartenders and regular neighborhood people. Tonight, I'm gonna look for some of the informants I had when I was still in the job. I turned Jim onto my snitches before I retired and we're gonna dig 'em up and lean on them a little."

"Well, you better get into the shower." Betty slowly crossed to the stove. "You're gonna catch cold if you don't get out of those clothes."

"Yeah. You're right." Moodrow pulled himself out of the chair. "I better change before Leonora gets here." Oblivious, he trudged down the carpeted hallway, leaving a series of wet pools behind him.

"What's with Leonora?" Betty called.

"I think we maybe got Holtz."

Betty filled her cup quickly, dumping in a minute amount of milk and a packet of Sweet 'n Low, before following the trail of Moodrow's wet clothing into the bathroom. Moodrow was sitting in the tub, the shower beating down on him, surrounded by a cloud of steam.

"Jesus," he said, "I didn't realize how cold I was. I didn't realize how tired, either. Ten years ago, I could put in forty-eight hours without thinking twice about it. Now after one night, I feel like a side of beef in the freezer."

"Why don't you just tell me what happened?" Betty demanded unsympathetically.

Moodrow leaned back in the tub. The water was rising, the heat putting him to sleep. "Supposedly, the Department of State has Simon Chambers' signature on file in Albany. Supposedly, Simon Chambers swears, in writing, to the accuracy of the information in Bolt Realty's corporate charter. Supposedly, Simon Chambers is the president of Bolt Realty. Only problem is that Simon Chambers is lying in a nursing home in Brooklyn. He stroked out fifteen months ago. Not only can't he sign his name, the doctor says there's nothing happening between his ears at all. I personally eyeballed Chambers' predicament and the doctor's not kidding. Not even a little bit."

Betty, careful to put the cover down, sat on the edge of the toilet and thought for a moment before speaking. "You think Holtz is involved in some kind of securities fraud?" she finally asked.

"I stopped off at Leonora's last night. I gave her the tape I made with Rosenkrantz and told her about Simon Chambers being too sick to sign his name. She seemed to think there's a case to be made. Anyway, she's taking it up with the Attorney General's office."

Despite Moodrow's exhaustion, Betty insisted on cooking breakfast. She was going to Inez Almeyda's funeral later that morning, a chore she was dreading, and she wanted to spend a few minutes alone with her lover before he dropped off to sleep. She started butter melting in a frying pan, cracking eggs into a bowl despite his weak objections. "Stanley," she asked over the hiss of scrambled eggs dropping onto hot fat, "do you really think you're going to find the people responsible for what happened?"

Moodrow, surprised, looked up from his coffee. "Of course I'm gonna find 'em. What'd you think? Look, Betty, this kind of work is full of disappointment. You have to be prepared for frustration, which is exactly why you *can't* be pessimistic about the outcome. You can't check out a lead with the feeling that you're doing bullshit work and you're never gonna get anywhere. You'd go crazy."

"Don't evade the question," Betty responded, her voice harder than Moodrow had ever known it. "I need to know if you're going to catch them."

"Why?"

Moodrow's question was sincere and Betty, recognizing that sincerity, also recognized the necessity to respond. "Ever since it happened," she began, "I've been thinking about the bastards who set it up. I wish I could have done what Paul Dunlap did. That I could have a gun and kill the three brothers. Hell, I almost wish the brothers were alive, because at least I'd have a focus for the hatred I'm feeling. And that's what it is, Stanley—it's plain, naked hate. Every time I close my eyes, the scene pops into my mind. Intense, like a movie. It plays exactly as it happened, except that Dunlap fades away and it's me standing next to the van. It's me pulling the trigger. I kill them and I feel good about it."

Even while Betty Haluka was driving off to Inez Almeyda's funeral (and Stanley Moodrow was pulling the covers over his head), two of Inez Almeyda's murderers, Marek Najowski and William Holtz, were meeting to discuss the future of the Jackson Arms. Martin Blanks was attending to his own business in Hell's Kitchen; he hadn't been invited, despite the fact that his character was at the center of their discussion.

"Ya know something, Marek," Holtz observed. "I have to admit that I never liked Marty Blanks. Too much of a wiseguy. He thought he knew more about this business than you did. I've done a lot of criminal law and that know-it-all crap seems to come with the territory. I never met a hotshot criminal who didn't want to tell me how to try his case."

"It's not being a criminal that screwed up Marty Blanks," Najowski said. "It's being Irish. I mean the Irish are whiter than white, but they're cursed with that Papist bullshit. And with the British. Between the Roman Church and the British, the Irish can't see their own best interests."

Holtz smiled at this observation. "The Irish," he asserted, "are stubborn and stupid. They've always been that way. That's because they spend their lives grubbing in the earth for potatoes. They substitute poetry for analysis, which, as far as I'm concerned, is the ultimate proof of their corruption."

Najowski laughed dutifully while Holtz retreated to a small refrigerator and took out a magnum of Moët et Chandon Brut, a moderately priced (by William Holtz's standards) French champagne he thought in keeping with the dual nature of their meeting.

"Here we go, Marek," Holtz said, pouring, "I propose a toast to your success." He noted Marek's grimace, but held the glass out until his client accepted it. "Indulge me, all right? Drink."

Najowski sipped at the champagne, then put the glass on Holtz's desk. "It's okay wine," he observed, "but I don't see how it's a celebration. We're gettin' our asses kicked."

"I didn't want to tell you before," the lawyer said smoothly, "because I didn't want to stir up false hopes, but just before you arrived this morning, I got a call from Moe Grebnitz. I think you know him. He specializes in outer-borough properties and our Jackson Heights parcels have caught his attention. He's made a firm offer of nineteen million. Even considering the enormous fee I intend to charge for my services, you should show a profit of about three million. *Without* going through any of the disclosures involved in co-op conversion."

Marek sipped at his champagne, then shook his head. "I was looking for a profit of twenty million dollars. Should I celebrate settling for three and a half?"

"In some ways," Holtz observed, "you should celebrate just getting out with your ass in one piece. And three and a half million isn't bullshit, no matter what you were expecting."

Marek grinned crookedly. "You talk like I didn't have a partner."

"Isn't that what we're here to discuss?"

Marek got up and began to pace the room. "Of course, I have no intention of splitting any profit with the bastard who cost me ten million dollars," Najowski said firmly. "If Blanks hadn't been such an asshole, we'd have brought off our original plan. Now, he's gotta pay. I assume there won't be any problem on the corporate end."

Holtz shook his head. "None at all. Blanks owns fifty percent of a corporation registered in the Bahamas. His sale of that stock to Marek Najowski will be on file the moment Blanks is no longer in a position to protest the transfer. Nobody on Grand Bahama Island will ever question the deal. The way I see it, the only question is how we find someone to do the job."

"Forget about it," Najowski said firmly. "No question about who's gonna do it. I've already checked it out. See, the one advantage I have over an asshole like Marty Blanks is that he thinks he's so goddamned tough, I wouldn't dare take him on. He has no idea of my resources, of what I've done in the past or what I might do. I treated Blanks as an equal and he rewarded me by destroying my investment. All because he thought some ex-cop was coming to get him. When I reminded him that we were partners and should make decisions together, he laughed at me. Him and his nigger partner. They shit all over me and I'm gonna pay them back."

"I presume the ex-cop is Stanley Moodrow? The private investigator who came to my office."

"Exactly."

"He's an asshole." Holtz refilled their glasses. "An old man trying to be tough. Maybe your partner's been sniffing his own cocaine. Maybe the drugs have made him paranoid."

Najowski waved the lawyer away. "I don't care what made him do it. What I give a shit about is making him pay for it. Maybe I'm not Olympic caliber, but I've been target shooting competitively for ten years. You get me within two hundred yards and I won't miss."

It was seven o'clock by the time Moodrow, in Betty's Honda Civic, arrived at the Jackson Arms to interview Pat Sheehan. The few days since the shooting had brought a number of changes to the building. The first, the new locks on the lobby door, caught Moodrow off guard and he had to use the intercom to get inside. He rang Mike Birnbaum instead of Pat Sheehan, because he couldn't be sure how Sheehan would react to his visit. Moodrow preferred to make his first appearance at the ex-con's door. Just in case Sheehan was feeling antisocial.

But Pat Sheehan let him in without a murmur of protest and the reason became evident as soon as Moodrow passed through the door. Louis Persio was not lying on the couch—even the small pieces of his life were absent: the brown medicine vials, the oxygen mask and the green tank of oxygen, the newspapers and magazines piled on the coffee table, the gauze pads, the surgical tape, the clamps and scissors. Moodrow spent a moment taking it in.

"Louis go to the hospital?" he finally asked.

"Louis is dead, Moodrow. I buried him on Sunday."

"I didn't know." It was all he could think to say.

"Nobody knew," Sheehan responded. "Nobody wanted to know. Even in the hospital. I took him there myself, because 911 couldn't tell me when the ambulance would get here. No big deal, really. Louis was having trouble breathing. It happened every time his fever went up. I took him over to Elmhurst General."

"And they didn't wanna take him?" Moodrow felt a familiar tug. By playing the sympathetic acquaintance, he could maneuver Sheehan into talking about Maurice Babbit. That was why he'd come. At the same time, Sheehan, slumped in a worn easy chair, was so deep in his grief, a nonprofessional would have backed away immediately. Moodrow, on the other hand, was a thorough professional; he'd interviewed the families of victims on dozens of occasions. Instinctively, and without any lessening of sympathy, he kept Pat Sheehan talking.

"You go in the city hospitals and the first thing you see ain't a nurse," Sheehan said. "Forget the nurse. First you gotta get past the security. By the time the taxi dropped us off, Louis was very weak. I carried him into the hospital and it was like nothin'. It was like carryin' a pile of sticks. Only the sticks were hot. They were burnin' up."

"What'd the security say? He try to stop you?"

"No. He took one look at Louis and he went back to find the nurse. See, I found out later from the same guard that you're better off comin' in by an EMS ambulance, because then it's registered and if they let you lay around without treatment, you could come back at them. If you just walk in, it's your word against theirs as to when you arrived. The nurse came in about five minutes later—the guard was practically dragging her—but I could see she wasn't too interested in Louis. 'AIDS,' she said. Real short, as if he got sick on purpose. The only thing I could say good for the bitch is that she didn't make us wait in the waiting room. There musta been twenty people in that room with AIDS. You could see 'em tryin' ta sit up in them plastic chairs. Most of 'em were alone and they didn't look as bad as Louis. At least they could walk in by themselves."

Moodrow settled down on the couch. Patience and a willingness to listen are the most important ingredients of nonviolent police interviews. "The city hospitals have been disaster areas for about five years."

"Yeah," Sheehan agreed. He looked up at Moodrow through swollen eyes. "That was the one thing I couldn't afford for Louis. I couldn't afford private hospitals. I woulda got insurance if I could, but I didn't think of it until after he got sick and by then it was too late. Nobody wants to sell insurance to someone with AIDS. They'd have to be crazy."

"So you got stuck with Medicaid."

"Yeah, that's the story. Not that it woulda made no difference. The nurse put Louis on a bed in the corridor because the rooms were full. Shit, even the corridor was full. People were everywhere: cryin', moanin', pukin'. One drunk was bleedin' so bad the sheet on the bed was soaked. His head was cut open and he was holdin' his bandage in his hands from where he pulled it. Pulled the stitches open, too, but nobody was doin' shit about it. The nurse listened to Louis' heart for about five seconds, then told me to wait for the doctor. I told her that Louis needed to see someone right away, but she said if I made any trouble, the security guard would put me out of the building. She said she only had seven nurses and six doctors instead of twelve nurses and eight doctors and it was Friday night and they already had five gunshot wounds. So we should just wait."

Sheehan paused for breath, watching Moodrow closely. Like all mourners, he needed to talk, but his relationship with Louis Persio had isolated him from his old prison buddies, as well as the straight world. "What could I do? I didn't think he was that bad. Plus I expected the doctor would come any minute. Louis was still talking to me. He was talking about how I came back to him after I got outta the joint and he never expected it. He told me—I already knew this part—how his parents dumped him after the first time he got busted and when they found out he was gay, they made it permanent. Even sent him a letter sayin' please don't come home for the holidays. Louis said I should mail the letter back to them on the day of his funeral. His voice was very soft and I was havin' a hard time hearin' it, because of how crazy it was in there. One man started screamin' in Spanish. He was already handcuffed to the bed, but the security came anyway. They held him down while a nurse gave him a shot. I don't know what was in it, but about twenty seconds later, he lights up with a big toothless grin and starts goin', '*Gracias, gracias, gracias.*' Me and Louis both laughed and you can't blame me if I thought he was gettin' better. Then he just stopped breathin' and I screamed so loud the doctor musta figured Louis got murdered. He was a Chinese guy and he checked Louis out for a few seconds and shook his head. 'No, no. So sorry.'"

"You got anything to drink?" Moodrow asked after a moment's silence.

"I don't want nothin'."

"Well, I do," Moodrow said firmly. "Do me a favor, if you got it, tell me where."

"Look in the freezer. There's a bottle of vodka in the freezer."

Moodrow retrieved the bottle and two glasses, then returned to the living room. The irony of the situation wasn't lost on him. A grieving ex-convict, a middle-aged ex-cop—not the most likely combination. Moodrow was faced with an ancient cop dilemma: how to intrude on grief and suffering without being crushed by it.

"I said I didn't want none." Sheehan pointed to the second glass.

"Just in case," Moodrow said. "So I won't have to make two trips." He poured three inches of vodka into his glass, then sipped speculatively. "This shit doesn't have any taste to it. I like bourbon. Then I know I'm drinking something. It's awful, but it's there."

"Why'd you come, Moodrow?"

"Look, I didn't mean to bother you." Now that the moment was at hand, Moodrow found himself reluctant to get started. Better, he decided, to let Sheehan push a little. "If I woulda known about Louis, I wouldn't have come. At least not this soon."

Sheehan sighed without looking up. "I owe you, Moodrow. No question about it. I owe you for makin' Louis feel a little bit easier. Most of the people in the world took one look at Louis and ran for the holy water. You treated him like any other human being. He laughed about it. No shit. Who could of believed that the last person, besides me and the nurse, who could stand being next to Louis would turn out to be a cop? That meant more than the favors."

"It wasn't any big deal," Moodrow said. He was actually blushing. "Don't make a big fucking thing out of it."

"Tell me what you want, Moodrow."

"I'm still trying to locate the people behind what happened here. I was wondering if you spoke to any of the dealers. You know . . . What we talked about last time I was in the apartment."

"I talked to a few people, but I don't have no answers for you. My sense is that most of 'em came from Hell's Kitchen, but I couldn't find out *why* they came. I didn't get close enough to ask that kinda question. Maybe if I had more time . . . But they're runnin' for cover, now. Word's out that the cops are gonna close the place down."

"That's definite," Moodrow said. "The dealers are gonna get busted for criminal trespass and the building's gonna be patrolled by street cops for the next couple of months."

"I guess that's it for me, too," Sheehan said. "My name ain't on the lease."

"Don't give up too soon." Moodrow refilled his glass, then filled Sheehan's. When he offered the drink, the younger man accepted it without comment. "Talk to the paralegal. What's his name, again?"

"Kavecchi." Sheehan twisted his face into a grimace. "That guy makes me crazy. He complains about everything."

"Well, he also knows everything about housing. Between him and the fact that the landlord's scared shitless, you might find a way to keep your apartment." Moodrow hesitated momentarily, looking down at his hands. "There was one other thing I wanted to ask you about. We got the name of the scumbag who set the fire. The arsonist. We got it through a print he left behind, but we can't find him. When I pulled his package, I noticed that he was up in Clinton the same time you were."

"Yeah?" Sheehan, interested, sat up straight. "A white guy?"

"Right. Name of Maurice Babbit."

"Babbit? No shit."

"You knew him?" Moodrow couldn't keep the excitement out of his voice.

" 'Knew him' is a little too strong for it. Babbit was a crazy and I kept as far away from the nuts as possible. You gotta remember there ain't that many white people in the joint, so when you get one who's crazy enough to set people on fire in their cells, you learn who he is before he torches *your* cell. Babbit got out two years before me."

"That's right. He's off parole and we can't find him."

"You think I know where Babbit lives?"

"Actually, I don't. I thought you might know people who were close to him. Maybe one of his buddies is on parole. It'd give me a way to go."

Sheehan, sitting back in the chair, took his time considering the request. "I don't think I could give you no names," he finally said. "It's too late in life to start rattin' people out. If I knew where Babbit was, I'd tell ya, but if I give ya the names of guys who used ta be friends of mine and you go leanin' on 'em . . . People been leanin' on me and Louis for too long. Neighbors, parole officers, Medicaid doctors, emergency room nurses, landlords. I don't want it on my conscience that I put you on someone who used to be my friend."

"I'm not gonna lean on anyone."

"Bullshit."

Moodrow giggled, putting his hand to his mouth. "Yeah," he admitted. "It's bullshit. If I had to press someone to get to Babbit, I would. Still, if you're sayin' you know people who were close to Babbit, there's gotta be a way we could do this."

"There's a way. There's always a way. That's why you came here." Sheehan raised his head. "I'm not goin' back to work for a week, because I ain't got the heart for the packages and the traffic. Which means I got enough time to check it out. Ya know, Sylvia Kaufman's face was the only face I could count on for a smile in this building. That would be reason enough to finger a crazy motherfucker like Maurice Babbit, even if I didn't owe you, which I admit I do. Plus I gotta be doin' somethin' and right now it can't be work."

TWENTY-NINE

April 27

MAREK NAJOWSKI decided not to use his competition rifle, a heavily customized Anschutz Super Match, because, despite its accuracy ("accuracy" wasn't really strong enough for the half inch groupings he customarily shot), Marek couldn't be certain the Anschutz's .22 caliber ammo would kill Marty Blanks. Not from a hundred and twenty yards out; not when the target was moving. Better to use ammo guaranteed to cause massive damage. Even if you were off by an inch or two, the shock alone was enough to kill. There wasn't *that* great a loss of accuracy, anyway. In fact, Marek had long felt that the Weatherby Mark V, fitted with a 2x-7x scope and a 26" barrel, should have its own competition. Even geared up to handle .458 Win. Mag. ammunition (enough to put down a charging elephant, though there wasn't much of *that* anymore, either), the rifle, at two hundred yards, would shoot true in a hurricane. Of course, the competition would have to be very exclusive. How many people could afford a rifle of that quality? The Weatherby had cost him $4000. The inlay on the stock alone, parallel ivory triangles set deep in the French walnut, went for more than a thousand dollars.

Naturally, some people, especially assholes like Marty Blanks, would sneer at the bolt action Weatherby ("One shot at a time? You gotta be kiddin' me"). But the sort of people who favored drive-by shootings with semiautomatic (or, God forbid, *fully* automatic) weapons had never interested Marek Najowski. Marek was too concerned with style; he was convinced that, without style, life would be completely unbearable. He'd seen a lot of pain in his time; he still touched it whenever he visited his mother. (He'd never get used to that, *never.*) The best response, as far as *he* was concerned, was an equal measure of stiff upper lip and all-out revenge.

Besides, drive-by shootings, perfect vehicles for the deliverance of terror, were part and parcel of Marty Blanks' experience and, thus, protecting against a massive attack would form the base of Blanks' security. A true assassination, on the other hand, was beyond Blanks' imagination (and, thus, beyond the scope of his defenses), but perfectly compatible with the goals and methods of Marek Najowski.

Even as Marek Najowski made himself comfortable amid the dirt and rubble of an abandoned tenement, Marty Blanks seated himself in the kitchen of his 49th Street condominium, along with Muhammad Latif and Muhammad's sister, Lily Brown. Blanks was discussing Stanley Moodrow and his inexplicable escape. Without any knowledge of Katerina Nikolis and the undulating waterbed, the ex-cop's survival seemed, to Blanks, like one of those miracles the nuns used to talk about. Curiously, Blanks' obsession with Stanley Moodrow and the danger Moodrow presented, didn't surprise Latif at all. Latif had grown up in the 7th Precinct on the Lower East Side and knew all about the giant detective with the tombstone face. The last thing Latif felt he needed was Stanley Moodrow sniffing around his door. Even *if* Moodrow was after Blanks for a crime that didn't really involve Latif.

"I been gettin' stories back," Lily Brown said. One of her functions, as a trusted lieutenant in the Latif–Blanks organization, was to service many of the dealers at the Jackson Arms. "From some of the Queens crew. Them white boys you picked out, Marty? They fucked it up bad." She sniffed loudly, her contempt for whites (with the sole exception of Marty Blanks, who'd backed her brother when they jailed together) more than obvious.

"How?" Blanks was still amazed. "The assholes had Uzis and the cop was twenty feet away. How the fuck could they miss? I mean it. *How the fuck could they miss?*"

"Word, my man," Lily counseled. "You know the riff about all black men got their brains in their johnsons? Seem like your white boys made us look like Catholic priests." Lily Brown shook with laughter. "Up and down, Marty. Up and down and all around. Your shooters were lovers, not fighters. They took a little white bitch with them to help pass the time. When the shootin' started, she come out the van like the devil was goin' up her ass. Damn, but your boys was mad. Fact, Marty, they was so mad they chilled the bitch instead of the cop."

Latif, who loved Blanks like a brother, couldn't resist the chance to kid his friend. "Jus' be grateful, bro. Be grateful the assholes got themselves killed. If one of them Irish boys *survived*, Moodrow'd be here right now."

Blanks stared at his partner for a moment, then smiled. "I got an interestin' piece of news for ya, Muhammad. The cops emptied the building today. We knew it was comin' and got our people out. Only the asshole, the political dude, got busted and he can't bring nobody back to us. I ain't expectin' to send no more people in there, man. Fuckin' street cops're all over the block."

"What about the investment?" Lily asked.

"That shit don't worry me. Najowski pisses his pants whenever I'm in the room."

Marek Najowski pulled a torn and broken easy chair up to the window, laid newspaper on the arm, and sat down to wait. In some ways, he thought, still-hunting is as great a test of hunting skill as facing the charge of an angry buffalo. It not only tests patience, it tests the hunter's understanding of the quarry's territory. Marek was in the fourth floor bedroom of an abandoned tenement on Ninth Avenue, a position which offered a clear view of the short stoop leading to the 49th Street home of his partner, Marty Blanks. Sandwiched between two decrepit tenements, Blanks' newly renovated building stood out like a Porsche between Volkswagens. There could be no mistake.

And the streetlight, with its halogen bulb, set conveniently at the foot of the stoop, only added to Marek's confidence. As did the floodlights installed by a condo board terrified of crime. At one point, before he had reconnoitered the scene, Marek had planned to use a Litton nightscope. The nightscope could amplify available light several thousand times, but the image it delivered was often unclear and there was the danger that he, like the Cohan brothers, would shoot the wrong man. Now, of course, with the building lit up like the endless parade of whores working Eleventh Avenue, identification would be sure and certain.

What wasn't certain, though, and what Marek hadn't prepared himself for, was the number of tenants and visitors going in and out of the building. Marek was certain that Blanks was inside the building, but he was taking no chances; he scoped every head that passed through the doorway, snapping the Weatherby against his shoulder and sighting down in less than three seconds.

He would take Blanks out with a chest shot. Blanks was broad chested. (How many times had he watched Blanks inflate like the ape he was?) Marek's shot could miss by four or five inches and kill Blanks, anyway. It would certainly knock him down and keep him down long enough for Marek to get off a second shot. Not that he'd need a second shot. Not that he needed *anything*, but the death of Marty Blanks.

Marty Blanks was drinking his third Miller High Life. Miller was, in *his* opinion at least, the perfect choice for a celebration. Didn't the brewers call

Miller "The Champagne of Bottled Beers"? And he hated *all* wine, especially the bubbly shit. Champagne had a place; he'd admit that. The only thing was that its place was grandma and grandpa's 50th wedding anniversary.

"Say again?" Muhammad asked. "What we celebratin'?" Muhammad was pulling on a joint of super grade Thai weed. It had come to him, sticky as tar, from a low echelon dealer looking for a better connection.

"We're celebratin' me at last gettin' ta do what I been wantin' ta do since the first day I laid eyes on Marek Najowski. First, I'm gonna make him refund my investment, plus interest. Then I'm gonna bust him up."

Lily Brown, sipping a glass of Chivas, giggled. "You sure do hate that partner of yours, Marty. Truth, man, I would *never* have a partner I didn't like. I feel like if I don't like someone, I can't trust 'em."

"I don't *gotta* trust the asshole," Marty grunted. "Marek came to *me* for muscle. If he could've supplied it himself, I never woulda heard his fuckin' name. Which woulda made me ten times better off."

Muhammad held out the joint to Marty, who waved it away, then opened another beer. Blanks was beginning to feel good, to shake off his disappointment at falling back into dependence on dealing. "See," Marty continued, "I'm thinkin' that Marek was makin' me a *guarantee*. I didn't go to him. He came to me and he said, 'Do this and do that and you'll make ten million dollars. You'll be rich and you can retire forever.' Didn't I do exactly what he told me? Shit, I done it better than good, but here I am with my tail between my legs. Who am I gonna blame? Myself? Word, Muhammad, if I thought Marek had the bank, I'd beat the whole ten million out of his ass."

After midnight, the traffic in and out of Marty Blanks building virtually stopped and Marek Najowski was denied even the small diversion of sighting down on potential targets. He was beginning to feel some fatigue, but his contingency plan, in case Blanks didn't show by one o'clock, was sitting securely in his jacket pocket. Eight plans, actually—real beauties. Real *black* beauties. Taken every six hours, they'd keep him awake and alert until Blanks made his last appearance. They'd sharpen him, hone his desire, tighten his finger.

Still, even though his eyes were riveted to Marty Blanks' front door, Marek's mind began to drift. He thought about his early life, remembered the period before Flatbush had been overrun by the expanding black ghetto as being idyllic. It had all changed after his mother had been attacked. His father had spent his off-hours in the hospital with his mother, leaving the children to fend for themselves. His two sisters had married early. Irene, the oldest, took a garbage-man to her bed when she was seventeen. She'd been dropping babies ever since. Mary-Jo had done a little better. She'd married a bookkeeper who drank himself to death before he was thirty-five.

" 'And the sins of the fathers are visited upon the sons,' " Marek said aloud. The failures of his family only emphasized his own fitness. He had survived. They had drowned. He was rising. They continued to sink.

One by one, the lights began to go out in the occupied tenements on 49th Street, a small, homely drama that had Marek sighing for his own home. He wouldn't be seeing Brooklyn Heights for a while. He was heading upstate—just in case Muhammad Latif decided to avenge his partner. There was always the chance, though he couldn't *know* who pulled the trigger, that Latif would strike out at everybody. But Muhammad's memory would only last as long as his next big deal. In the drug world, short term profits are measured in days, not fiscal years.

In fact, by the time Marie showed for her regular visit, on Saturday, the whole business would probably be over. Of course, he wouldn't be there, but that wouldn't matter. George Wang would yell at him in high-pitched chinky-English: "Why you make me bankrupt? I no can afford send girl for nothing." And Marek would pay up, too. He'd pay for the chance to break her down, to erase, once and for all, the disrespect at the bottom of her discipline.

He thought about slavery, about the possibility of owning her. God, those were great days. Slavery had once been universal, the common fate of the common man. He felt himself beginning to sink into the fantasy and held himself back. After all, business *did* come first.

But he'd love to buy her once and for all, to buy and own her instead of merely renting. If he owned her, he'd break her down in a minute. She could maintain her illusion of control only so long as she was paid. But if there was force, if she performed for him because he forced her to perform, all dignity would be lost. Perhaps he could find a way to use force without angering George Wang. Maybe . . .

When the thought came to him, he pulled away from the window and shook with pleasure. Wang was even greedier than the whore: whereas sweet Marie would *do* anything for money, George Wang would *sell* anything for money. What Marek would do, as soon as he settled down upstate, was arrange to buy a full day of Marie's time, with the single proviso that Marie shouldn't be told. Let her come to him expecting an ordinary session, then be forced to stay. Let her perform without knowing when (or *if*) she was going to be released. He'd make it up to her later. Hell, he knew she'd do anything for money. And, if she wouldn't . . . How much, he wondered, would the Chinaman charge if she *never* came back?

Marty Blanks was pretty drunk when the call came through. He didn't usually allow himself to get drunk, but he'd been under a lot of strain and he wasn't expecting to go out. Still Marty Blanks had put a protective routine into place when he first moved into the building and he wasn't about to deviate just because he'd downed a few too many *cervezas*. He called his bodyguards into the kitchen where Lily and Muhammad were already present.

"We gotta go up to the Bronx," he announced. "Little Benny's holding and I wanna get to him before he offs the load. Hustle it up, but keep your eyes open. It's late and we'd make easy targets."

"You and Lily goin', too, Muhammad?" Mikey Powell asked. "If you guys're gonna go, we better take the van."

"Lily's goin', but not me," Muhammad responded. Blanks and Latif rarely traveled together. "Y'all take good care of mah sister, now, and don't be playin' with ya johnsons."

Mikey's puzzled look only set Muhammad and his sister laughing. "Hey, forget about it, Mikey." Blanks slapped his bodyguard on the back. "They're makin' fun of *me*, not you. Just go out and get the car. And keep your eyes open."

"Does that mean we should take the Buick?" Stevey Powell asked.

Blanks thought for a moment, then shook his head. "No, we been takin' the Buick too much. It's like wearin' a sign that says, 'Here Comes Marty and Muhammad.' Let's take Mikey's Ford for a change. Maybe I'll buy it. Or trade it for the Buick. I got an itchy feelin'.'"

The first thing the Powell brothers (who lived in studio apartments on either side of their boss) did was check the roof door to make sure it was locked. Then Stevey Powell checked the stairwell, while his brother secured the lobby. If their boss made a buy, they wouldn't be coming back; they'd be going to a much more secure location. Blanks never kept drugs or cash in his apartment. He kept his merchandise all over the city, carefully dividing it so as to make a disastrous hit impossible.

"Everything all right?" Mikey asked when his brother stepped out of the elevator.

"No problems," Stevey responded.

"You think somethin's wrong with the boss?"

Stevey Powell grunted. "He's drunk. Don't mean nothin'."

Leaving his brother to guard the lobby, Mikey Powell proceeded west on 49th Street to a Tenth Avenue parking garage. His '84 LTD, a full size car designed for the taxi trade, was parked on the first floor, as were all the vehicles belonging to the entourage. The Ford, again like all the other vehicles, was fitted with a two-way radio. The radio, with a range of twenty miles, operated on an extremely narrow, unused frequency. Its very presence was a clear violation of FCC regulations, but as there were dozens of illegal car services in New York doing exactly the same thing, the gang's small theft of the airways was unlikely to draw undue attention. As a security device, however, the two-way radio was extremely important to the safe operation of their business, and Mikey Powell was on the radio with Marty Blanks before he put the Ford into gear.

"Startin' out," he announced, neither receiving nor expecting a response. He drove up Tenth Avenue, peering into parked cars and watching vans for any sign of movement. He was looking for cops or killers (or, maybe, cops *and* killers) and he announced every turn. "Tenth Avenue, clear. 50th Street, clear. Ninth Avenue, clear. 49th Street, clear." When he got to the front of the condominium, he double-parked, announcing, "In front" to the radio while signaling to his brother in the doorway.

"Mikey?" Marty Blanks' voice crackled in the radio's speaker.

"Yeah, boss?"

"Check out the blue van across the street. It's new on the block."

Mikey Powell, without a word of protest, left the Ford, walked to the van and punched it with his fist. Punched it hard enough to shake up anyone inside, then calmly walked back to the Ford.

"Nothin', boss," he said into the mike.

"I'm comin' down."

Marek's heart began to pound as soon as Mike Powell's face appeared in the doorway of Blanks' home. It was one thirty and the first black beauty was rushing over him like the quick rush of anticipation at seeing Powell's face.

"Game time," Marek whispered, turning the scope back to Blanks' doorway. He had never killed a man before, but he had no doubt that he would pull the trigger when his target appeared on the stoop. It was as if his association with Blanks and the violence that followed had removed the last piece of bullshit tying him to ordinary human values. If he wanted to be honest with himself (and he did), he had to admit that he was responsible for *all* the violence at the Jackson Arms. It had been his plan from the beginning and he had no regrets.

He watched the Ford pull in front of Blanks' building, watched Powell stroll across the street and pound the innocent van. It was coming now, coming soon. He wasn't angry anymore, just excited. Like a grateful son the first time his daddy takes him hunting.

The scope was already against his eye when Blanks appeared in the doorway. Already focused. Marek put the cross hairs on his ex-partner's chest and muttered five words before pulling the trigger.

"Am I right, or what?" he said.

THIRTY

April 28

DESPITE it being a Saturday and her day off, Betty Haluka was nursing a cup of tea in the kitchen when Moodrow arrived home in the early morning. Her night had been full of unsettling dreams, dreams of terrifying danger, of hate and revenge. Dreams alternating with periods of wakefulness in which she tried to put all the events of the last few months together: Stanley Moodrow's appearance in her life; the dark fire that had sought out Sylvia Kaufman; the overwhelming crash of exploding weapons; the cries of fear and pain stabbing at the empty silence—waking or sleeping, events chased through her mind like tumbleweed blowing through a Western movie. The inability to escape terrified her.

She'd spent most of her life working in what she liked to call "the justice industry," but her work had been with the criminals and not the victims and now she was a victim herself. By her own characterization, her career had involved nothing more than doing the dirty work necessary to keep the country going, to keep the Constitution strong. There are very few places in the world where "rights" have any meaning larger than the power flowing naturally from the barrel of a gun; or where individuals have more "rights" than a single ant in an ant heap. Yet, in Betty's mind, individual rights were the abstractions that defined Western civilization, and the reality of a lawyer for every criminal (even a lawyer overburdened with work) was just as important to the existence of her country as the cops and District Attorneys who protected the victims.

But now she was an undeniable victim. Her sympathy for defendants had disappeared like footprints in a blizzard, and she was left with an enormous void. No matter how hard she tried, the void kept filling with anger; it seemed that anger was the only emotion that *could* fill that particular emptiness. The anger made her afraid, as did the loss of the assumptions which made up the foundation of her intellectual life.

If he'd been home, Moodrow could have told her how natural, how common, these emotions were. The drama of revenge, no matter how unlikely, *always* played itself out after a violent crime. In the days and weeks following an attack, the victim reworked the scene until the terror that accompanied helplessness and violence was finally smoothed by time. Of course, Betty would eventually return to something approximating her usual equilibrium; she was a strong woman with a well-established system of values. But for the present, she was compelled to imagine the most basic of human motivations: revenge.

When Moodrow finally did arrive, at six thirty, Betty was seated at the kitchen table imagining a confrontation with Al Rosenkrantz, in which Rosenkrantz, already half-dead (having had his arms and legs shot off with a pistol the size of a cannon) was begging for mercy. As Moodrow came through the door, she reluctantly abandoned her daydream and looked up expectantly.

"Any luck?" she asked.

"Nothin'." Moodrow poured himself a cup of coffee and sat down at the table. "But me and Jim'll get him. And we'll get the prick who sent him."

"How long is that supposed to take?" Betty asked, her voice tentative.

"I can't say," Moodrow admitted. "Could easy be the cops'll get to him before we do."

Betty shifted in her seat; she was wearing a blue terry robe over a short cotton nightgown and her eyes were red with insomnia. "What are you going to do when you catch him?"

"Babbit? I'm gonna ask him a few questions and then I'm gonna hand him over to the cops. It turns out the print they took off the vial had enough points to go into evidence. Juries love fingerprints."

"What if he pleads?" she persisted.

"You're a plea bargainer—what do *you* think? How's the DA gonna handle a killer arsonist?"

"Probably take second degree murder. Drop the arson counts."

"And what's the penalty for second degree murder?"

"Twenty-five to life."

"That means he's gotta do twenty years minimum and he'll probably do thirty. Babbit is thirty-two years old, so by the time he comes out, he'll be sixty-two. With that kind of time hanging over his head, I don't feel a strong need to get personally involved in his punishment. Not that I wouldn't prefer seein' the skell fry in the electric chair until his skin crackled, but whatta ya gonna do, right?"

Betty stared up at him. "I want to do it myself," she announced. "I keep dreaming about finding him and the man who sent him and every time I have the dream, it's me who administers the punishment."

"Judge, jury, and executioner?" Moodrow smiled. "I was there myself, once. When it was a question of personal revenge. That's what came back to me a few days ago. *Kill the fuckers. Kill 'em!* All I could think of was how bad I fucked it up. How I put my head in the sand and saw what I wanted to see when the worst rookie asshole would of known what was going on. I was saying to myself, "What if I would of done this? What if I would of done that? Then they might all be alive. Inez and Sylvia and the kid they had in the van." He stopped for a second and sipped at his coffee. "But I must be gettin' old or somethin', because I'm lost in it now—lost in the hunt—or maybe talking to you made it better. Now my revenge is catching the mutts. Catching them and turning them over to the lawyers and the courtrooms. That's all the revenge I'm allowed and that's what I'm gonna settle for." He giggled softly. "Unless, of course, there's some kinda reason why the perp can't be prosecuted. Like, for instance, if there's no direct evidence of an undeniably guilty fucking perp's undeniable fucking guilt. That would present another problem altogether."

As they went off to bed together, to make love and, then, to sleep, Betty had a sudden flash of illumination. "The worst part," she thought, "is that the anger will go away. The anger will retreat and harden into something permanent and ugly. Something far removed from the original terror."

It was early afternoon before Moodrow stirred in response to someone pounding at his door. For a moment, he was tempted to push his head into the pillow and wait for the noise to go away. But as he was expecting "the big break" to make its appearance at any time, he felt morally obliged not to hide until it went away.

"The big break" cracking its fist into his front door turned out to be a thoroughly annoyed Pat Sheehan. Dressed in black jeans, a gray T-shirt, and an olive fatigue jacket, he looked every inch the street junkie.

"What the fuck is the matter with you?" Sheehan stared at the enormous man standing in his underwear.

"I was sleeping," Moodrow explained.

"It's one o'clock in the afternoon."

Moodrow yawned himself awake, then took a closer look at Pat Sheehan. He was looking for any sign that Sheehan, who'd been on the streets for several days, was back to using drugs. Sheehan, without being asked, shrugged off his jacket, revealing bare arms free of fresh needle marks.

"I take it you didn't come here to pass the time of day," Moodrow said casually.

"I found Babbit," Sheehan announced. His eyes were swollen and tired.

"Where?"

"He lives up in the northern end of Manhattan. Inwood."

"Let's go make some coffee. I gotta get myself awake."

Moodrow, trailing Pat Sheehan in his wake, trudged through the living room to find Betty already waiting in the kitchen.

"What happened?" she asked, nodding to Pat Sheehan.

"I found Babbit," Sheehan announced.

"How'd you do it?"

"Easy. I always kept in touch with a few of the cons I did my bit with, so I just went and paid a visit. After a few drinks, me and the boys started talkin' about the good old days. Nat'rally, that turns to somethin' like, 'Hey, you remember that crazy fuckin' torch who burned up Rufus Johnson?' Then some dude goes, 'Yeah. Yeah. I see him around once in a while. He's a pro, now. Hangs out at a topless joint called the Sizzle Club. On Broadway around 104th Street.' So I run up there and wait a couple of nights till he shows, then follow him back to his apartment. I tell ya the truth, the whole thing didn't amount to no big deal. It just took a long time."

"Did he recognize you?" Moodrow asked.

"He saw me, but I don't think he knows who I am. He got out less than a year after I arrived and I wasn't one of the famous cons. In fact, I made it my goal to keep away from maniacs like Babbit as much as possible, so it ain't too surprisin' that he don't know me."

Betty poured out three cups of coffee and they waited in silence until Moodrow, fully dressed, came back inside, drained his cup, then turned to Pat Sheehan.

"I think I need a favor, Pat," he said.

"Ain't we even yet?"

"We're even," Moodrow admitted, "but I still got a problem. My ex-partner, Jim Tilley, can't make it. He's up in Albany trying to execute a fugitive warrant."

"I thought he was on vacation for the next few days," Betty said.

"In the department, you're only on vacation until they say you're not. The captain didn't have anyone else, so he called up Jim and that was that. Rose says he won't be back until tomorrow. And that's if the skell's lawyer doesn't contest the warrant."

"So whatta ya want from me?" Sheehan asked.

"I want ya to pretend to be a cop while I interrogate Babbit. He'll sit for it better if he thinks you're a cop."

"Why don't you be the cop?"

"Well, see, after he rats out the guy who ordered the fire, I wanna hand him over to the real cops, but I don't want him sayin' I impersonated an officer."

Sheehan sat straight up in his chair. "What about me? I'd do ten years if they caught me with a badge."

"You're gonna be long gone before the cops get there. Let's face it, Pat, I could most likely do it by myself, but havin' you there helps in a lot of ways. Babbit's no punk. He's done hard time and I don't know what kinda problems I'm gonna run into. With another pair of hands, at least I win the psychological battle."

Moodrow, taking Sheehan's silence for agreement, turned to Betty. "I guess I gotta offer you the chance to come along," he said, "but I'm warning you that I may have to do things you don't wanna see. And I'm also telling you it'll get better if you wait it out. Then you can go back to Legal Aid and your regular life. On the other hand, if you go with us, you're gonna have to pretend not to see things you've spent your whole life fighting."

Betty touched Moodrow's lips with her finger. For a moment, they were the only two people in the room. "I can't go," she said. "I love you too much to take a chance. It's better if I keep on seeing the best side of you. But I still want you to get them. Get Babbit and get the one who sent the brothers. I don't think I'll ever feel right until they're . . ." She fumbled for a word to describe how she felt, then realized that all serious possibilities were extremely violent. "Until they're gone," she finally said.

THIRTY-ONE

MAURICE BABBIT was dreaming of fire when Stanley Moodrow pounded on his door. He was dreaming that he was a child again, setting trail fires in the backyard grass. Trail fires were great fun, but they required some kind of fuel. Gasoline, kerosene, alcohol, lighter fluid, cleaning fluid, turpentine—little Maurice was a master of deception, stealing flammable liquids and setting out complex trails like other kids stacked rows of dominoes on a kitchen table.

He wasn't so little in this dream, though. He was older, at an age when he'd already abandoned trail fires. But he didn't notice this oddity, because he was focusing his concentration on making the trail. It was a very ambitious trail. Somehow, he'd gotten hold of five gallons of gasoline and he was creating an enormous spiral that began at the very center of the yard and extended almost to the back porch. The arm of the spiral was narrow, the blades of grass only wet enough to keep the line of fire moving toward the drenched circle of grass where four mice, maddened by the sharp smell of gasoline, swarmed over the bars of their cage.

The mice had been a Christmas present from his parents; they had been given at the urging of Maurice's therapist, who'd felt that Maurice needed to bond to something. If he couldn't come close to another human being (not even his eternally perplexed mother who loved her only child more than she loved herself), perhaps he'd be able to love a creature as absolutely nonthreatening as the tiny mice his grinning father brought home to him.

But Maurice hadn't loved the mice any more than he loved the grass or the gasoline. They were only the tools he needed to complete his given task. Of course, Maurice had no clear idea why his given task had been given to him, but, not being especially reflective, he contented himself with knowing what the task was. Method was Babbit's strong point, anyway; he was always calm and careful when he made a fire, no matter how small and insignificant the blaze. Even in his dream, he was carefully pouring the gas—laying out a trail while imagining the quick rush of the flame as it tore along an ever-narrowing circle, as it finally exploded outward, as the cloud of oily black smoke (along with the souls of four white mice) rushed toward the heavens.

The emotions stirred up by his expectations were especially intense, which explained Babbit's reaction to the pounding at his door. He was confused for a moment, trying to bring himself back to adulthood, to New York City, then he was angry.

"Fuck you, Boris," Babbit screamed. "Come back later. The garbagemen ain't never gonna show up on a fuckin' Saturday."

But the pounding actually increased, as if the super knew that he could beat the door forever without disturbing the other tenants, and Maurice finally surrendered to the inevitable. Stepping into his pants and shoes, he quickly substituted Boris Krakov, the superintendent, for the mice in his dream.

"What're you, nuts?" Babbit screamed as he opened the door. He was fully prepared to add a long description of Krakov's Russian ancestors, but Moodrow's enormous body drew all his attention. Even while his mind screamed, *COP! COP! COP!*, his mouth grunted, "Wha? Wha? Wha?"

Then Pat Sheehan popped up alongside Moodrow's left arm with a badge in his hand, shouting the word, "Police." He pushed Maurice back into the room, he *followed* Maurice into the apartment. It was going to be very bad—the big cop was smiling and Maurice figured the smile was meant to frighten him, but then the big cop said, "See, it ain't as hard as it looks," and *that* made no sense at *all*.

"What's your name?" the little cop shouted.

"How long you been living here?" the big cop roared.

"Do ya like ta set fires, ya little fuck?"

"Why'd you go to Queens?"

"Ya know how much time you can do for an arson–murder in New York State?"

Maurice continued to back away and the two cops continued to advance, not grabbing for him, but not giving him enough room to turn and run either. He backed through the rubble crowding his apartment, through stacks of yellow newspapers, twisted toy trucks and rusted cars, headless watersoaked dolls. He noted the drums of gasoline against the wall, the propane torch and the flamethrower he should have been given in Vietnam, but had had to make himself from a ten-pound can of pickles, a plumbing valve, and a cylinder of oxygen. Everything was out of reach; the men facing him were too big, too strong.

It was like prison had come out from behind the walls to get him. Like the niggers were facing him down, calling him "soft" and "sweet." But he *showed* the niggers; they gave him a little time and he burned one until his body was a lump of boiling fat on the cell floor. That was great. That was a *great* day. He was so overcome that he hadn't remembered to run away and he actually got to watch the prick dance the "fire dance." Like he'd watched the mice dance *their* "fire dance."

But the cops would never give him the time to get to his tools. They were going to beat him, because they were shouting at him and the prison guards always shouted at him before they beat him. They shouted questions and when he couldn't answer (because he was terrified and the words they screamed were no closer to language than the pounding of a pneumatic drill) they always beat him.

Babbit began to whimper softly. There was *no* place to go; his legs were smack up against the bed. This was the way the guards had done it. They'd forced him back into his cell, forced him back until he could no longer retreat. The big cop was reaching out to him; his hands were enormous, like plates, like thick slabs of cold white meat.

"What the fuck is goin' on here?" Moodrow asked. He was staring down at a shivering Maurice Babbit, knowing his original tactic, to alternate promises of a deal with physical bullying, was out the window. Like all cops, Moodrow had worked with crazies before, and he was afraid that if he pushed Babbit too far, the information he wanted would slip away altogether. "What the fuck is goin' on here?" he repeated.

"Maurice's looney-tunes," Sheehan pronounced calmly. "I told ya he was crazy before we even came here. What were you expectin' from a man who makes fires for fun?"

"I know he's crazy. You think I can't see he's crazy?" Moodrow was becoming thoroughly annoyed with his string of lost opportunities. "What I'm trying to ask is how we're gonna talk to him? How we're gonna communicate if the asshole don't even hear what we're saying?"

The questions had been purely rhetorical and Moodrow was surprised when Sheehan responded with a command. "Handcuff Babbit to the steam pipe and let's go in the other room," he said. "I got an idea you're gonna love."

Five minutes later, as they were walking away from a thoroughly secured Maurice Babbit, Pat Sheehan explained his idea. "What I think is that you're gonna have to use shock therapy if you wanna reach Maurice. He's livin' somewhere in the past and you gotta bring him back to the present. You gotta zap him hard enough so he pays attention."

"Look, Pat, I seen a lotta nut cases before. Mostly, when you put pressure on them, they get crazier. They get so you can't talk to 'em at all. I could always throw Babbit to the cops, but I want more and I don't have no other leads. Understand what I'm saying? If I lose Babbit, I gotta close up shop."

"All the more reason you gotta act now," Sheehan said. "How long could you keep Babbit tied up here? How do you know someone won't come lookin' for him? Remember how he was yellin' about the garbage? That means he was expectin' someone. Maybe you could flip a badge and keep people away for a few hours, but not forever. Sooner or later, someone's gonna call the *real* cops and then you gotta give him up. Face it, Moodrow, right now is the only chance you're gonna get."

Maurice wanted to collapse in a heap—collapsing was what he *always* did when the guards came after him—but the cuffs wouldn't slide past the steel rod anchoring the pipe into the wall. On top of that, the rod was high up on the wall, so he couldn't even cover his head, which is what he always did. He tried to think of something to do, but his mind was clouded with the waiting, which he hated as much as the beating. They did that every once in a while—threw him in his cell and left him until he thought he was safe. Then they came back, like the two cops were coming back, and beat him all the harder.

"Take it easy, Maurice, I'm not gonna hurt ya." The little cop was standing right next to him. He was smiling and speaking very softly. "It's my partner that you should worry about. And ya know why that is?"

He didn't answer, because he knew from his own experience, that *any* answer was the wrong answer when they came to beat you. Besides, he was too busy watching the big cop tearing up his newspapers. He didn't like people going through his things; people always put his things down. That was another trick the guards had—ripping your cell to pieces, destroying your things. Once they had found turpentine in his cell and the beating, on *that* awful day, had put him in the prison hospital.

"See, Maurice, my partner's got a bug up his ass about a fire you made in Queens. On 37th Avenue."

The big cop was bunching sheets of newspapers, crushing them into balls and throwing them at him, but even when they hit him in the face, they didn't hurt him. What was the point of it? That's what he *wanted* to ask, but he knew better than to open his mouth.

"The fire in Queens, Maurice. You made a fire there about a month ago. We have your fingerprint on one of the little crack vials you left. Remember?"

Even though there was no way he could retreat, he kept trying to swivel behind the pipe, trying to stuff his entire body into a two-inch space. The big cop was going to do something terrible to him. He *knew* the big cop was really going to hurt him.

"Jeez, Maurice." The little cop was putting an arm around him, whispering in his ear. "My partner's a mother-fucker. Even I don't like some of the shit he pulls. But what can I do? He's too strong for me. And he outranks me, too. In fact—and I wanna be honest, Maurice—I can only think of one thing to make the cocksucker go away. Tell him who paid you to make the fire in Queens. Or if you're too scared of him, tell me, and I'll tell him. Then he'll go away."

What was he doing? What was the big cop doing? He had a lighter in his hand, a little brown BIC that looked as tiny as a thumb and he was flicking it on and off. How many times had *he* passed the time with a lighter, watching the little sparks coming off the flint and the small explosion of flame that followed. Or lighting pieces of paper and watching them burn down in his hand. The big cop was doing the *same* thing. He was lighting a ball of newspaper and throwing it onto the pile.

"Holy shit." The small cop stomped on the paper, putting the fire out before it could spread. He put his face real close, until his lips were brushing Maurice's ear. "Can ya hear me?" He put his arm around Maurice's waist and pulled him in tight. Maurice could feel the small cop's groin pressing against his hip. "I hope you can hear me," the little cop said. "I need your help and I hope I'm gonna get it soon, because I got a problem and that's that I gotta go to the toilet. What's gonna happen when I'm gone? Just thinkin' about it scares the shit outta me."

The big cop grinned—this time, Maurice *knew* the grin was meant for him alone—and flicked the lighter on and off. Maurice desperately tried to concentrate on what the little cop was saying, but his hip was hot where it pressed into the cop's crotch and he loved the fire so much . . . He felt himself getting an erection, despite the fear. Or maybe the fear made it *better.*

"Don't be ashamed, Maurice. I understand. I know how much you love the fire. Maybe you'd even *like* to get burned up. Is that it? Would you like to get burned up?"

The big cop began to light ball after ball, casually throwing them into the pile at Maurice's feet. The little cop kicked a few out of the way, but then stepped back, forcing Maurice to kick at the newspapers until he could feel the heat burning into his calves. What would happen if his pants caught on fire? Would they let him burn? The big cop was so angry, but the little cop said there was a way to get out of it. That was what the words about the fire in Queens meant. That was the way to get out of it.

He tried to remember. Remember quick before it was too late. He was getting very tired, but if he stopped, he'd burn up. Where was the fire? It must have been a very small one, or else he'd remember it. Maybe a shitty one? Maybe a small shitty fire with hardly no flame at all? There had been one like that, but he didn't know that anyone died. He didn't think anyone died, because the fire wasn't *supposed* to kill anyone. It was just a message fire if that was the one they were talking about.

Maurice's thoughts were interrupted by the unmistakable sizzle of liquid on fire and the sharp stink of ammonia. He twisted against the cuffs, trying to make sense of it, and found the little cop, penis in hand, groaning with relief.

"How 'bout that?" the little cop said, grinning madly. "Talk about killin' two birds with one stone, right? I'm really happy I figured out a way to take care of my physical need without havin' ta leave you alone with my crazy partner."

While he spoke, the little cop tucked his penis into his pants, then stepped in close again. His partner was balling up sheets of paper and throwing them, unlit, into a pile around Maurice's feet.

"Can you hear what I'm sayin?" the little cop asked gently.

"Yes," Maurice whispered. If he could only *remember*.

"Don't be afraid. I'll help you." He put his arms around Maurice and drew him in close, pressing a thigh into Maurice's crotch. "It's not gonna be so hard. It's not gonna be hard at all. Do you remember a fire in Queens? You set it a few weeks ago."

"I don't remember it." He felt himself becoming erect again; this time the swelling was stronger, more insistent. He liked the little cop's words now, because he was sure the little cop would help him.

"I'm gonna try to save ya," the little cop whispered, "but I gotta warn ya that we don't have a lotta time. Believe me, Maurice, I know my partner and I can see that he's gettin' ready to act crazy, so try ta stay with me. Okay?"

"Okay."

"You made the fire in a mattress in a basement. Do you remember the mattress? All the way in the back? The mattress had papers stuffed into the middle and you made the fire in the papers."

"And I put dope stuff all around it," Maurice cried triumphantly.

"That's right. So nobody would know you made the fire on purpose."

"So they would think the junkies did it by accident."

"The fire was very smoky, wasn't it?"

"I don't know." Maurice began to feel sad. He didn't like to think about this part of it. "I couldn't stay and watch. I made it way in the back and I hada get out right away."

The little cop pressed Maurice even closer. "You didn't go from here ta Queens just ta make a practice fire, did ya? Ya musta got paid for it, right?"

"That's right. I got paid."

"And who paid ya, Maurice. Who gave you the money?"

"Marty Blanks. Marty Blanks asked me to set that fire. It wasn't much of a fire. It wasn't supposed . . ."

Maurice stopped abruptly. The big cop had stopped balling up newspapers. He was grinning happily now—grinning a wolf grin that could eat Maurice in a second. The little cop seemed stunned, though. He was stepping away, letting his hands drop to his side.

"Bad luck fa you, Moodrow," the little cop muttered. "Marty Blanks is dead."

"All I could tell you is what I said before," Sheehan explained for the fifth time. They were inching toward a toll booth on the Triboro Bridge, heading back to Jackson Heights. "Blanks came out of his apartment on 49th Street a couple of nights ago and someone shot him. I heard about it in a social club near 42nd Street, but I didn't think much of it."

"Did you know Blanks? Do you know about him?"

"We were all up in Clinton together. Me, Blanks, Babbit, and Blanks' partner, Latif. Of the three, I knew Blanks the best. He controlled all the dope in North Block, which was not an easy thing to do, because the blacks made it a question of racial pride. That's why Blanks took Muhammad Latif as a partner. Latif is black."

Moodrow snorted. "Muhammad Latif, eh? I knew the fucker when he was living in the projects on Pitt Street. Tell me something, Pat, do Muhammad Latif and Marty Blanks sound like two guys who'd go into real estate together?"

Pat Sheehan thought for a moment before answering. "Not by himself. He came up through the streets, not through the system. He wouldn't know shit about real estate."

Moodrow continued to push the Honda through the heavy traffic while they both thought it over. The implications were more than obvious.

"Blanks had to've had a partner," Sheehan said evenly. "Had to."

"That's just what I figure, Pat. Now if you could just tell me where I could find Mr. Latif, I'd be most grateful."

"No problem, Moodrow. Blanks and Latif lived together. Latif was in the apartment with his sister when Blanks went down."

THIRTY-TWO

IN some ways, Muhammad Latif had more in common with Marek Najowski than with his partner, Marty Blanks. Like Marek, Latif enjoyed style for its own sake, while Marty Blanks had been committed to drab colors and a lower-than-low profile. Their differences had begun at the very roots of their experience. Blanks had grown up in an Irish Catholic neighborhood, had been taught (at least before he was sent off to the baby jails society euphemistically calls reform schools) by celibate nuns in long black robes. The men in his father's world favored navy pea coats and black watchcaps. The women wore dark cotton dresses and rarely went outside without covering their heads with faded silk scarves.

Latif, on the other hand, had passed his formative years in the Baruch Houses on the Lower East Side. He'd seen poverty at its worst—seen economically devastated human beings who owned little more than the clothes they put on their backs. No surprise that clothing then became a major form of self-expression for those who couldn't penetrate the system.

"In New York, they built cages for their niggers," Latif had explained to Marty Blanks. They were in Clinton at the time, caught in a lockdown after a small disturbance. "They called these cages 'the projects' and they said, 'You niggers can live here cheap. You can't leave, but you can live here cheap.' It was always the man's property that he was *lettin'* you live on. Like the plantation was for the slaves. Word, Marty, from the time I got my hands on my first money, me and all the brothers I ran with, I put it on my back. 'Get fresh' don't refer to no sister buyin' a new couch. We leave that for the integrationists. 'Get fresh' means a new suit, a ruby ring, a mink coat."

"That's a nice story," Blanks had returned evenly, "but you ain't in the projects no more."

"Say what? Marty, them projects are in my damn soul. I'm gonna die with them projects."

"Look here, Muhammad," Blanks had smiled, "bein' Irish, I nat'rally have some cops in my family, so I can tell you for a fact that cops hate it when people like us throw it in their faces. Cops ain't machines, Muhammad. Cops are mostly kids from the neighborhoods. If they think you're shittin' on 'em, they stop puttin' out their hands and start bustin' heads. You know it just as well as I do: if the pigs make you a target, you're goin' down."

In the end, once they were out and establishing their business, Latif had given in to his partner's paranoia. Low profile was central to Blanks; he went about his business as quietly as a Mafia don. Nobody moved unless movement was absolutely necessary and travel *always* involved bodyguards and elaborate pre-cautions.

No surprise that, despite Muhammad's sincere grief (he felt a chunk of himself, solid and fleshy, go into Blanks' grave), he felt like a man who'd just escaped from prison. The gold jewelry came out of the drawer and the 500 Benz sedan with the heavily tinted windows and the three-hundred-watt stereo came out of the garage. Instead of surreptitious visits to his cousins and his mother, he had every intention of mingling with the other big players at the most exclusive uptown social clubs.

"Baby," Latif explained to his sister, Lily Brown, "Marty was the best friend I ever had. Shit, he was the *only* friend. The only man I ever let that close to me. But he had one big fault that I could never show him. The boy thought he was gonna live forever without gettin' himself busted or killed. Man was a pure fool about that. Way I see it, my life is gonna be damn sure short, so I wanna make it damn sure sweet."

Lily Brown, who had her own priorities and her own business, nodded patiently. "Without Marty, it's gonna be shorter still." She was referring to Blanks' near legendary savagery. It had always kept the ogres at bay.

"You remember the time he broke on Paco Santiago?" Latif asked, shaking his head. He'd cried at the grave and, again, on the ride back into the city. Now he felt the tears building.

"Marty was *always* buggin' out on people who fucked with him," Lily said, taking her brother's hand.

"When Paco tried to jump the price on us, Marty was ready to beat him down in a minute. Didn't matter that Paco had most of the guns in the room. Marty squeezes his face together, like he does when he's pissed, and screams in Paco's face: 'Man, you *fuckin'* wit' me.' Like he can't believe what's goin' down.

"Paco says, 'I can' no hep it, man. The Customs got half my keeeeelos. I got to pay the man in South America, don' I?'

"Marty says, 'I don't care if your mother took the coke and stuffed it up her greaseball ass. You ain't jumpin' no fuckin' price on me. You think I done twenty years in jail to get ripped off by a punk?' "

Lily Brown shook her head in wonder. "You must've thought you was one dead nigger."

"Check it out, Lily. You coulda cut the vibes in the room with a knife. There was three of us and six of them and all the mother-fuckers was *armed* to the max. Right then, I knew Marty Blanks was up in the zone somewhere, but I was pickin' out my targets, too. Gettin' ready for my dyin' day. Only Paco opens his mouth and smiles like hate is chippin' his teeth. Prob'ly, he's thinkin' if the shit goes down, Marty's gonna take him out first, but whatever way it is, he does the deal at the original price and me and Marty's reps are *made.*"

Lily smiled and shook her head again. Without thinking much about it, she bent her head to the mirror lying on the kitchen table and drew up a line of cocaine. Muhammad grinned at her. "That's somethin' else Marty didn't approve of."

"The boy was hard," Lily declared. The coke was nearly pure; she could already feel it taking her up. "If you gonna be hard like that, what you need with money? Might as well get a straight job and live in the projects."

Two hours later, a very stoned Muhammad Latif and his equally stoned sister, Lily Brown, emerged onto 49th Street. It was almost two in the morning, but a knot of junkies crowded around the steps leading to a basement apartment and a number of homeless alkies slept in doorways. Muhammad, who felt like a kid sneaking out of school, looked the street over and saw nothing frightening. The big players rarely fucked with each other, as long as payments were made on time. It's the small dealers fighting over street corners who make the tabloids hum.

Lily's 500 Benz, the one with the vanity plates that read HOMEGIRL, was parked at the curb, untouched by vandals. Muhammad ran his fingers over the pearl gray surface. He could see himself reflected in the paint. Not on the surface, but deep within the metal.

"Don't you love this car?" Lily asked, a huge smile spread across her face. "Don't you just love this mother-fuckin' car?"

"I do, Lily," Muhammad grinned, "I do love this *mother*-fuckin' car."

They got inside with every intention of heading for the bright lights, but the mother-fuckin' car only made it half a block before Muhammad Latif received a strong reminder of Marty Blanks' warnings. It was almost as if Blanks had reached up out of the grave to deliver a final lecture. Lily Brown, having carefully pulled out of the parking space, was still accelerating when an ancient Buick slid from between two vans and planted its nose directly in front of her right fender.

Fender benders are very common in the heavy Manhattan traffic. For the most part, they are never reported, either to the cops or to insurance companies. The three-year rise in insurance premiums comes to more than the cost of the repairs. For the same basic reasons, Manhattanites, unless they're very, very rich, don't like to drive new cars and have contempt for people who do.

Lily Brown, on the other hand, wanted her new car *because* most New Yorkers have to make do with dented clunkers. She was pissed when she got out of the car, and the contemptuous smile on the face of the white boy who got out of the Buick to meet her only fueled the anger rolling within her skull like cocaine boiling up in a pot of baking soda. Sensing Lily's mood, Muhammad opened the passenger door and climbed out to calm her down. Lily was his older sister and he'd felt her temper more than once when they were growing up. The one thing they didn't need, considering they had an ounce of cocaine in the glovebox, was a street fight.

"Lily," Muhammad said in his gentlest, most reassuring voice, "Lily, I think . . ." He was so involved in defusing the potentially dangerous situation that he didn't see the obviously drunk derelict wander out of the doorway behind him. He didn't hear the alkie, either, but he felt the press of metal against his ribs, and when he looked down to see a sawed-off 12 gauge, an ancient double-barreled Ithaca with its two triggers hidden by the finger that caressed them, his voice (along with his basic psychological state) jumped into terror.

"Please. Don't. Please. Don't. Please."

Lily, alerted to the drama behind, started to turn around, but was restrained by the driver of the Buick. Astounded by his touch, she spun back to face a gold shield and .38 S&W.

"Stay out of this, miss. It ain't your problem."

Muhammad Latif expected to be killed on the spot, just like in the movies. It wasn't until after the alkie ordered him into the Mercedes, that he found the courage to raise his eyes from the shotgun to his assailant's face. "I know you," he said. "I *know* you."

"If you say my name, I'll kill you where you stand," Moodrow replied evenly. "Get in the fuckin' car right now."

Muhammad found himself complying without ever making a clear decision to obey. Lily, further from the shotgun, was much less frightened, especially after she saw the badge. Dealers are used to being hassled on the street by ambitious narcs and she was sure the badge was genuine.

"If y'all want money," she said contemptuously, "why don't you just name your price. 'Stead of all this *bull*shit."

The cop didn't answer; he put his shield back in his pocket, but kept his hand on the butt of his .38. Lily, helpless, watched Muhammad get into the car, then push across the seat. The other cop, the big one, got in next to him.

"I'll be back," Muhammad called to Lily, as he slid the Mercedes by the Buick. "Soon as I find out what the man wants."

He was rewarded by the twin barrels of the shotgun jamming into his ribs. The orders that followed were crisp and businesslike. "Work your way over to the West Side Highway. Head downtown. We're goin' over the Brooklyn Bridge."

"Look, Moodrow, if . . ."

"Don't say a fuckin' word, Muhammad. Not a word."

Moodrow's voice radiated danger. Latif felt it, but couldn't eliminate the possibility that it was designed to get something from him. He decided to keep his mouth shut, to wait until Moodrow was ready to say what it was he wanted. At the same time, he made a second decision: he vowed that if God spared him, he would forever adhere to the lifestyle espoused by his dead partner. The only certainty in this mess, as far as he was concerned, was the inescapable fact that Marty Blanks would never have fallen into this trap.

Twenty minutes later, having made their way around the edge of the deserted island, they crossed the Brooklyn Bridge, then cut east, down Tillary, to Flushing Avenue. Moodrow barked instructions (reinforcing them with the barrels of the Ithaca) as they drove beside the old Brooklyn Navy Yard and onto Kent Avenue in industrial Williamsburg. It was after three and the streets were temporarily deserted. Later, around six, when the small manufacturing lofts opened their doors, the hookers who serviced the truckdrivers would come out onto Kent Avenue, but at three, even the burglars seemed to have gone home.

"Slow down. Slow down and make a left."

"Hey, man, this here's the damn river."

"Take the fucking left and turn your lights off."

The tires crackled over a gravel drive and onto a wooden pier, one of dozens that had formerly served the shipping industry. The industry had gone to New Jersey twenty years before, leaving the piers behind to rot.

"Stop the car. Gimme your left hand."

"You're crazy, Moodrow. You're *goddamn* crazy."

"Shut the fuck up. Gimme your left hand."

Moodrow closed one end of his handcuffs around Latif's left wrist and yanked him across the car, sliding the cuffs through the bars on the headrest before locking him in.

"You got to talk to me, mother-fucker," Latif yelled. "You *got* to talk to me before you pull this shit."

Moodrow responded by getting out of the car and walking slowly around to Latif's window. "You tried to kill me," he said, reaching inside to yank the gearshift into neutral. "You and your scumbag partner, Marty Blanks." Without any seeming effort, he began to push the car along the pier.

The minute the Mercedes' tires began to turn, Muhammad Latif lost all control of his bladder and his mouth. The East River, so black it was nearly invisible, lay dead ahead. "I never had nothin' to do with it," he screamed. "That was Marty's shit altogether."

"It wasn't enough to half burn the fucking place down. Raping old ladies, beating old men . . . that was just baby shit for Muhammad and Marty. That was just warm-ups for the main event. Well, I'll tell ya a little story, asshole. You shoulda hired some better shooters, 'cause there's only one thing worse than trying to kill me and that's trying and missing. Now you gotta pay, mutt. Play, then pay. That's the rule, ain't it?"

"It wasn't me. I swear on my mother, man. I didn't know nothin' about it. Please. I can't deal with the water. I hate the fucking water."

"You were Blanks' partner when you were in the joint. For all I know, you mighta even been asshole buddies. In fact, from the way you're shitting your pants right now, I'd have to guess you were doin' the bend-and-spread the whole time you were inside."

The crunch of the tires moving slowly across the wooden planks of the pier echoed in Latif's ears like the sound of three Uzis firing into a crowd in Jackson Heights. He yanked the cuffs hard enough to rip into the skin around his wrists and blood began to flow along his forearms.

"Ain't no nigger doin' no real estate," Latif shouted in desperation. "I never was involved in no shit like that."

Moodrow pulled the car to a halt, then leaned through the window. "Say it again?"

"I come out the projects. I know about dope. I seen dope all my life through. But I don' know shit about no real estate. Marty wanted to get out of the life, that's why he went along with Najowski. Me, I ain't got nothin', *but* the life."

"What was that name?"

"Najowski. Najowski. Marek Najowski. Lives in Brooklyn Heights and real estate is *all* he does. He's the one who talked Marty into buyin' them buildings. Sayin' how Marty was gonna get so rich he could stop dealin'."

"Well, he can stop dealing forever, now that he's dead. Tell me how Marty found Najowski?"

"Shit, man, I don't know. I didn't have nothin' to do with it. Anyways, Marty didn't find Najowski. It came the other way around. I think it was a lawyer. Right, man. That's it. It was Najowski's lawyer who came with the deal. I can't recollect his name, but he had connections through his clients. Najowski knew about buyin' buildings. He wanted Marty to supply muscle so the people livin' there would run."

"Take a deep breath and hold it, Muhammad." Moodrow leaned into the car, shifting it forward on the springs, then let off when Latif began to cry.

"Please. I can't take no water, man. I don't swim. I don't even go near no beaches. Please, Moodrow. The fucking river is *black* out there. I can't go in no black water."

"Give me the bullshit name again."

"Marek Najowski. I'm tellin' you straight, man."

"Where does he live?"

"He's got a co-op in Brooklyn Heights. I don't know the exact address, but Marty told me it looks over the water at Manhattan."

"You don't know where Najowski lives?"

"I *never* been there. That's what I'm sayin', man. But there can't be no more than one Marek Najowski livin' in Brooklyn Heights. Like the *operator* could give you the address."

Moodrow reached inside the car and jerked the gearshift into park. "How much time you done, Muhammad?"

"Say what?"

"I asked you how much time you've done. I know you were upstate with Marty Blanks."

"I did six years in Clinton."

"And before that?"

"Small bits on Rikers. What you wanna know this shit for?" If Muhammad's spirits had begun to rise when Moodrow first stopped pushing the car toward the river, his very essence was flooded with relief when Moodrow locked the transmission. Now, in the face of Moodrow's new line of questioning, he was uneasy, sensing bad news coming on like the rush of cocaine in reverse.

"You got coke in this car, Muhammad?"

"Yeah. I got an ounce in the glove compartment. Take it, man. Take it and let me go."

Moodrow patiently walked around the car. Covering his hand with a white handkerchief, he opened the small door, took out the coke in its Ziploc bag and laid it on the seat next to Latif.

"What you doin', Moodrow? What the *fuck* you doin'?"

" 'In plain view' is what the lawyers call it." Moodrow walked back to the driver's side of the car. He reached inside, flicked the light switch, and an old Buick with a badly dented fender pulled slowly onto the pier. "It don't matter that Blanks had another partner. You knew what they were doing and you didn't warn me. You knew it and you were perfectly willing to let me die. In fact, I'd go so far as to say you didn't consider my safety or the safety of any of the poor bastards your partner killed even one little time. You think I'm such an asshole, I'm gonna let you get by with that, just because you told me a name? A coke-dealing, murdering fuck like you? You done a lot of time, Latif. What with the dope laws bein' as tight as they are and the judges handin' out years like fuckin' Christmas candy, you'll do fifteen if the cops find you first. See, what I'm gonna do is turn on the headlights before I go. That's bound to attract some attention, because people around here get nosy about fifty-thousand-dollar cars parked on deserted piers. Now, if I was you, I'd start prayin' real hard. I'd pray, Dear God, please let the pigs find me *before* the wolves."

THIRTY-THREE

April 29

MOODROW was up and waiting for Jim Tilley before dawn, though Tilley wasn't due to arrive until nine o'clock. He wanted a chance to think about the last stages of the chase, to savor his victory. He'd been called an old man, an ancient, a dozen times in the last few weeks. *"If you were still a cop . . ."* He'd even said it to himself, blaming his failure to foresee the events in Queens on some incipient senility. Now he knew that his inept analysis was part of the process of learning his new job. As a cop, he'd worked with strangers; here the strangers became his friends. He'd liked Sylvia Kaufman from the beginning and her death had flooded him with self-reproach, opening old, supposedly healed wounds. Sitting at his own kitchen table with the inevitable cup of coffee, he accepted his mistake for what it was: an error in judgment based on limited information. Blaming himself would do nobody, especially him, any good. It might, on the other hand, sweeten the endgame.

Clients were not the same as complainants: if he was going to function in retirement, he would have to get used to it. Cops were like doctors, carefully maintaining enough distance to ensure proper perspective. That wasn't possible here; he was going to have to serve individuals and not the state. He allowed his mind to re-create the shooting in front of the Jackson Arms. While it no longer frightened him, Inez Almeyda, blood pouring from her eyes and ears, still cried out for revenge. As did Sylvia Kaufman, Mike Birnbaum, Yong Park's mother, Katerina Nikolis . . .

Stubbornly, he pushed the victims away. There was no profit in anger. Maybe he *did* have the last conspirator in his sights, but he didn't have a shred of evidence to connect him with either Marty Blanks or the Jackson Arms. A single fingerprint had led to Maurice Babbit, who had led to Marty Blanks, who *should have* led to Marek Najowski. Now the chain of evidence was irrevocably severed. Perhaps the lawyer, William Holtz, could be persuaded to turn on his master, but the lawyer wasn't his problem: pressure on the lawyer would have to come from Leonora Higgins. His own options were far more limited. He would confront Najowski; let him know that he'd been identified, that he couldn't hide behind his partner's death. Perhaps Najowski would panic. If not . . .

Moodrow glanced at the clock over the sink: five thirty. He rose and drifted across the room to the stove, pouring out a second cup of coffee. At this rate, he'd be floating in caffeine before the day was over. There was a time when he . . .

It was nearly six o'clock before he finally acknowledged the only important question left to consider. What would he do if there was no legal way to reach Najowski? What if Najowski was safe? What if he was safe and he *knew* it? Once again the faces rose up; he could see Sylvia Kaufman clearly, serving tea and cake while organizing her rebellion. The acrid smell of the blackened basement assaulted his nostrils. Sylvia's body had been found halfway between the bed and the door. She had tried to get out, had known what was coming.

Suddenly, he had a vision of Yong Parks' daughter, the little girl with the red ribbon in her jet-black hair. She'd witnessed the brutal attack on her grandmother, seen the rape. In spite of himself, Moodrow began to re-create the actual scene: the helpless woman, the attacker lowering his trousers, ripping at the woman's clothing, penetrating.

"The mother-fucker pays," he said aloud. "One way or another."

"Who pays, Stanley?" Betty Haluka wandered, half-asleep, into the kitchen.

Moodrow ignored the question. "I got something I wanna ask you, Betty. About confessions. See, I can't think of any way to pin Najowski for what he did."

"That's what you said last night."

"Well, the situation hasn't changed."

"Maybe the lawyer will turn on his client," Betty suggested hopefully.

"Maybe he will," Moodrow admitted, "but I can't sit and wait for that to happen. For all we know, the lawyer's just accepting rent money and paying the mortgage."

Setting down her coffee, Betty came up behind Moodrow and began to massage his neck and shoulders. As always, she was impressed with his bulk. He seemed to be made of hard rubber, to be without bones, even at the point of his shoulder or the back of his neck.

"I feel much better today, Stanley," she said finally. "I didn't dream about it last night. For the first time. I didn't see it again."

"I knew that would happen," Moodrow said, covering one of her hands with his own.

"But that doesn't mean I want to see anyone get off. It doesn't mean that at all."

Moodrow smiled, then changed the subject abruptly. "What interests me this minute is confessions. Now that I'm not a cop anymore, do I still have to give the same warnings? What if I grab Najowski and shake him until he opens up? Put it all on videotape. Would it be admissible?"

"What makes you think you wouldn't be arrested for assault? If there was any sign of duress on the tape, you could be the one making the confession. But don't worry, Stanley, I'll defend you for . . . let's say half your pension."

"What if I took a confession without appearing on the tape?" Moodrow ignored the humor. "What if I passed the tape, along with any documents connecting Najowski with Blanks or the Jackson Arms, to Leonora Higgins? Suppose *she* got the lawyer, Holtz, to turn on Najowski. What would happen if you put it all together?"

"No judge will admit a confession that was obtained under duress. Even suspected duress. Judges think the state should be able to build a case without confessions. Also, how will a judge know that evidence you seize illegally really came from Najowski's home? A document with Najowski's name on it is evidence, but a pound of cocaine might have come from anywhere. A private citizen doesn't have the same kind of believability as a cop."

"Suppose," Moodrow said, "I find a way to trick Najowski into confessing? Suppose I do it in a way that he can't claim he was forced?"

"Stanley, criminals testify against each other all the time. A man goes into jail, talks too much to his cellmate and the next thing he knows, the cellmate is testifying against him in court. There was no *Miranda* warning given, because the cellmate wasn't an agent of law enforcement. But if the police put an undercover cop in the cell and the accused made the same confession, it would be completely inadmissible."

Moodrow seemed to relax for the first time. "With that much room," he announced, "I don't think it's gonna be a problem. I'm bound to figure something out."

When Leonora Higgins called from her office, Moodrow and Betty were in the shower, disproving the cliche that equates a clean mind with a clean body. Moodrow, who was waiting to hear from Jim Tilley, stumbled out of the steamy bathroom, grabbed the phone and muttered something like, "I'll call ya back in a fuckin' minute, all right?" Then hung up.

The phone rang again before he closed the bathroom door, and this time Leonora began speaking before he could say a word.

"Don't you dare hang up the phone, old man," she said. "*I'm* the one who only has a 'fuckin' minute.' *You're* the one who's unemployed, remember?"

"Leonora," Moodrow groaned, reorienting himself as he went along. "I thought it was Tilley. What's up?"

"Good news, Stanley. Holtz is going down. We're arresting him this afternoon."

Moodrow felt his spirits rising—in direct contrast to his penis—as she spoke the word "arresting." "What have you got him for?"

"Forgery in the first degree. Falsifying business records. Offering a false instrument for filing. Tampering with public records. Insurance fraud. Conspiracy in the second degree. Two E felonies. One D felony. Two C felonies. One B felony."

"If you run that consecutively, he'll come out of jail on a respirator," Moodrow observed happily. "What's the conspiracy?"

Leonora laughed. "Rosenkrantz fell apart. Cried like a big, fat baby. He says Holtz ordered him to cut off services to the building, to violate leases, to hire thugs to break the locks and mailboxes. He says Holtz supplied him with a list of criminals to fill the vacant apartments. Stanley, the head of the securities division says we can use Holtz to get to the owner of the Jackson Arms. Trade some years for some names."

"I already have the names, Leonora. I'm not as retired as everybody wants to believe." Quickly, he ran down the last few days' events, including Babbit (who was already in police custody), Babbit's connection with Blanks and the legally useless means by which he'd gotten the name of Marek Najowski. "I guarantee," he finished, "that Blanks hired the Cohan brothers and Maurice Babbit. That lets Najowski off the hook for any of the big stuff."

Leonora's voice was resigned, the voice of someone accustomed to the vagaries of justice. "We can still get him for conspiracy. That's a B felony and it calls for a minimum six years. Six to twenty-five. That's not chopped liver, Stanley."

"It ain't justice, either. I'll see ya later."

Jim Tilley began to bang on the front door before the phone was back on the hook. Like a silent movie comedian, Moodrow gazed wistfully at Betty, who peered around the shower curtain, her naked body a shadow against the running water. Accepting the inevitable, she plucked a towel from the rack and threw it out to Moodrow, then climbed into her bathrobe and headed for the bedroom. Moodrow stopped her briefly as she went past him.

"See how it is?" he asked. "You flop around like a walrus out of water, working your ass off and getting nowhere. Then you hit the right track and you get pushed along with no effort at all. Ever watch the sea gulls over by the Jersey palisades? They come off the river struggling so hard you think they're gonna sink back into the water, then they catch a rising air current and jump a hundred feet in a few seconds."

An hour later, Jim Tilley and Stanley Moodrow were sitting outside a five-story brownstone at 1010 Grace Court, in Brooklyn Heights. Tilley had gotten Najowski's unlisted phone number and address by giving a shield number (not his own) to a NYNEX supervisor. A test call had been rewarded with Najowski proclaiming that he was on vacation, that his machine was doing announcements only, that no messages would be recorded.

"I think we've gotta stake the place out," Tilley contended. "The message says he'll be gone for a few days. He'll turn up if we wait."

"By then, half the NYPD is gonna be waiting with us. I don't give the lawyer's honor twenty-four hours. Guys like Holtz crap out before they get into a cell. Jail's what they're really scared of, anyway. They can do the time, but they don't care for the company. Holtz'll give up Najowski and the detectives will show up to make an arrest. I was kinda hoping we could get to Najowski first."

"I can't say as I blame you," Tilley responded, "but I still don't see how we're gonna find your boy in twenty-four hours."

"You're right. That's impossible. The fucking guy could be anywhere and if we start questioning his neighbors, it'll get back to him. What I was thinking is that I got this ex-con who works with me a little. Name's Pat Sheehan. Specializes in locks and safes. Claims he can use picks, drills, explosives. What about if we send him inside? There might be documents in the apartment. Some link with Blanks."

"A fuckin' convict? Why would you wanna work with an asshole like that? You could never count on a criminal. He'd sell you out in a second."

Moodrow pushed back against the seat, reveling in the comfort of Tilley's Buick. "I'm not asking the guy to fucking marry me. He wants to work and I got work for him. Besides, I think he's all right."

Tilley stared at Najowski's building for a moment, before changing the subject. "Did I tell you what my partner did to me last week?" he asked.

"I don't think so." Moodrow was settled in for the time being, watching and waiting. Hoping someone would come along to lead them to Najowski—a friend, a deliveryman, a business acquaintance.

"We worked a full week on a precinct homicide. Staked out like we are now. We knew who did the killing, asshole named Oray Donaldson, but we didn't know where he was and we were watching a soup kitchen on Rector Street where he liked to go to eat. One day, my partner calls me and says his wife's sick and he's not coming in, which is okay by me because I can't stand the bastard. Meanwhile, there's nothing wrong with his old lady. He found out through one of his snitches where Donaldson was hiding out and made the arrest by himself. Now the lieutenant wants to know where I was. Was I fucking off? How come I'm not ambitious? Maybe I was appointed to the detectives too soon. And I gotta stand there and take it."

Moodrow held up his hand. "Cool down a second, Jim. Partnerships in the job are temporary. Why don't you ask for a new assignment?"

"Oh, I'm looking for a new assignment, all right. I'm thinking about leaving the department altogether. When you retired, I was real gung-ho about working for the community, but I don't see how I'm gonna do it. I know for a fact that Captain Ruiz is trying to get me out of the 7th. He's got a hatchetman, named Ocasio, who 'deals with potential problems before they happen.' Ruiz thinks I'm a potential problem and I think he's right."

"What does Rose say about this?" Moodrow, stunned, managed to ask.

"Rose's making $45,000 working for the city. It's enough to keep us going while I start something else."

"And what would that be?"

Tilley's voice suddenly dropped two octaves as he gestured toward the black woman standing in front of 1010 Grace Court. "What do you make of that?"

Moodrow didn't know whether Tilley was referring to the woman's strange wardrobe, a lustrous peach jacket over a torn gray housecoat, or the fact that her finger was pressing on the second of three buzzers, the one belonging to Marek Najowski. He understood the question, though. Nothing pleases a cop so much as a situation that demands an explanation.

THIRTY-FOUR

MARIE PORTER didn't know whether to be angry or relieved. On the one hand, she'd come all the way out to Brooklyn for nothing. Marie was one of those Manhattanites who equated a trip to the outer boroughs of New York City with a journey to the Twilight Zone; whenever she left "the city" on business, she expected to be well-rewarded. On the other hand, when repeated pushes on Marek Najowski's buzzer brought absolutely no response, she realized that she wasn't going to have to service the Freak and that made her happy. She wouldn't have to cook his dinner. Or respond with downcast eyes when he called her. Or scrub an already spotless floor.

Marie took a deep breath, pulling the mild spring air into her lungs. Small clusters of sturdy tulips bloomed in tiny front yards, echoing the first rush of lacy young leaves to trees that seemed to grow out of the sidewalks. She had almost six hours before her next date. Where would she go? The Brooklyn Heights Promenade, with its spectacular view of lower Manhattan, was only a few steps away. It was a place she often sought after a session with the Freak, a place to get clean again. But this time she wanted to feel earth instead of concrete beneath her feet. The cold towers of Manhattan, even against the blue spring sky, would not feed the day's desires.

Suddenly she had a delicious idea—a taxi to her home, a change of clothes, a drive up to Central Park. There were huge beds of tulips throughout the southern reaches of the Park, as well as trees and shrubbery from all over the world. A long walk in the park instead of sex with the Freak? A light lunch at Tavern on the Green instead of a pail of hot soapy water? The best part was that she was going to charge George Wang for every bit of it. She'd wanted to dump the Freak a month ago, but George Wang had merely raised the price and sent her back. Maybe this would convince him to cut the Freak loose, once and for all.

As she came back along the short walkway, Marie looked up at the glowing leaves on a young sugar maple and took another deep breath. She felt as if she could fly away, as if the breeze would pick her up and float her across the river to Manhattan. She might have stood there for a long time, willing herself into weightlessness, if Moodrow hadn't come up behind her. His homely words provided the anchor that brought her back down.

"What're you supposed to be," he asked, "the fuckin' earth mother?"

"Pardon me?" Her first impression was one of size. The man confronting her was enormous. It wasn't until she raised her eyes far enough to see his face, that she put the word "cop" and the word "big" together.

"Police officer," Jim Tilley said, stepping around Moodrow to display his gold shield.

As a black woman from the vast ghettos of northern Manhattan, Marie Porter's initial reaction to Moodrow and Tilley was automatic. She felt a blind street impulse to run. Then she reminded herself that she wasn't committing a crime by walking through a white Brooklyn community (how could she, with her co-conspirator nowhere to be found?). Even if Brooklyn Heights *was* a certified landmark neighborhood. Her second panic (once she'd cleared herself of prostitution) centered around drugs and drug paraphernalia. After years of low-level addiction, the fear of arrest and involuntary drug withdrawal was very real, even if there was no probable cause for a search and she'd eventually be released. Except that Marie Porter was no longer using illegal drugs and hadn't used them for more than a year.

Suddenly, she was very angry. And not with the two cops who stood in front of her. The cops weren't after her; they were after the Freak and somehow she was involved. A wave of hatred, as physical as nausea, swept through her body, twisting her mouth into a tight frown.

"My name's Tilley and this is Moodrow," the smaller man said. "We'd like to ask you a few questions."

She hesitated for a moment, then nodded. There was nothing she could do about it, anyway, and she followed them back to the old Buick without a protest.

"You're here to see Marek Najowski, right?" Tilley said.

Marie, unable to fabricate a plausible lie, nodded once.

"And what was your business with Mr. Najowski?"

The question, from the same cop, was expected, and Marie answered without pausing. "I'm the maid."

"The maid?" Moodrow's voice was filled with contempt. "That's fucking pitiful." He pointed to her shoes, a pair of two-hundred-dollar Karl Lagerfeld boots from Saks. She'd drooled over them for months before buying them, waiting so long to see them on sale, she'd become afraid they'd be discontinued before she got her hands on them. "I suppose those're some kinda scrub boots?"

"Just because I'm a maid, it doesn't mean I don't like nice things." Her shoes, of course, along with the peach jacket, would have been removed the minute she entered Najowski's apartment.

"You're a hooker," the big cop said flatly. "Not that we give a shit. We're after Najowski and we want your cooperation. Excuse me, one way or another, we're gonna *get* your cooperation. What's Marek to you, anyway? Why would you wanna protect a trick?"

"I haven't done anything wrong," Marie protested.

Moodrow pointed to the healed punctures on the backs of her hands. "You're also a junkie," he announced. "You got tracks."

"I *was* a junkie," she admitted. "I'm clean now." The big cop, she realized, was being deliberately antagonistic. His voice was filled with suspicion, as if she was Marek's business partner instead of his sexual partner. Not that she cared if he made her for a whore. She *was* a whore. "Why do you want Marek?" she asked with genuine curiosity.

"I thought *we* were asking the fucking questions," Moodrow said to his partner. "I thought we were the cops. Jim, you better help me out here. I'm gettin' confused."

"Be cool, Stanley," Tilley said, stepping in front of his partner. "I think the lady wants to help us. That right?"

"Sure," Marie said agreeably.

"What's your name?"

"Marie Porter." She might as well admit it. All her identification, including her credit cards, were in her real name. It'd been *that* long since she'd been on the street.

"Well, Marie, your pal Marek's been a very bad boy," Moodrow said. "He made a fire and this little old lady got killed by the smoke. He had another little old lady raped. And an old man got beat up and a sixteen-year-old kid got killed. Things like that. I mean he might be good in the sack. Or maybe he's very generous. But he's also a killer. In fact, he even tried to kill me. That's why you're gonna help us out."

Marie felt the anger rush back into her body as she recalled the Freak's hands on her flesh. The humiliations he demanded flashed through her consciousness like a series of rapid-fire slides from a projector. "I knew he was sick," she admitted. "I tried to get out of seeing him, but my pimp . . ." Marie could feel the cops' interest, not unlike the sexual organs of her male customers, rising.

"What do you want to know about Marek?" she asked. "I mean I wasn't exactly *close* to him."

"We're interested in some property he owned. He had a partner from Hell's Kitchen."

Marie tried to recall the exact details of a conversation she'd listened to while confined to Najowski's spare bedroom. Najowski's partner had been a dinner guest and they'd spoken of their plans for some building in Queens. "I don't remember exactly," she said carefully. "Some tricks like to talk. You know what I mean, right? After you take care of them, they go on and on. I don't usually pay much attention, but I do recall a building in Queens that he was trying to get people out of. He was checking leases and moving dealers, cocaine dealers, I think, into the vacant apartments. He was real proud of himself, but I got the impression that the violence was coming from his partner."

"Do you have any idea where Marek is now?" This time, the young cop's voice was actually friendly, encouraging her to go on.

"Maybe," Marie said. "Back in my apartment. I might have another address for him in my trick book."

"Where's your apartment?"

"In Manhattan. On East 95th Street, near York."

She could feel the cops' hesitation and she was afraid they'd either turn her down or send her home with instructions to call them with the information. But then, without words, they seemed to come to an understanding.

"You drive her home," the young cop said. "If there's anything to it, come back and pick me up. I'll maintain the stakeout."

As they drove back across the Brooklyn Bridge and up the Drive, the big cop recited the various crimes committed in the name of money at the Jackson Arms. He went through them chronologically, detailing the exact nature of each assault. "I was hoping to find some kind of a witness, so I brought some proof with me. I brought some pictures to show."

The photos, taken routinely by the Crime Scene Unit, were so gruesome as to appear staged: Sylvia Kaufman, her face twisted in agony as she fought for oxygen; Inez Almeyda with the left side of her face blown out by three separate exit wounds. There were others, and Marie, to Moodrow's surprise, studied them intently, her breath sharp and shallow as she absorbed what she was seeing.

"He did this for money, right?"

"That's right. There was nothing personal to it. He never met any of them." Moodrow grinned. "And the truth is that he's probably gonna get away with it. The partner you met is dead and the only one who can tie Najowski in is his lawyer, who may not know a fucking thing about what went on."

Marie, though quite aware of Moodrow's intentions, allowed herself to share in the cop's righteousness. She walked him past the doorman, who made the cop for a trick and threw her a broad wink, even though it'd been more than a year since she'd brought a client back to her apartment.

"What the fuck is that?" Moodrow said as they rode up in the elevator. "This guy must come from fucking Romania that he shouldn't know I'm not a john. The guy is a complete asshole."

"Actually, he's from Bulgaria, and the only thing he's aware of is the little envelope I pass him every month."

They were walking down the hall toward a one-bedroom apartment that cost Marie $1800 a month. Despite the adjective "luxury," which seems to describe every apartment on the Upper East Side, the rooms were not luxurious. Small cubicles devoid of architectural flair, they did nothing more than hold Marie's furniture. Even the view from the picture window in the living room, though they were more than two hundred feet in the air, revealed only the anonymous windows of another building less than thirty feet away.

Marie picked up her address book, the one she used for her business, thumbed through it, then slammed it down. "I don't have the address," she announced. "I remember, I went upstate somewhere about a year ago. To some small town. I'd never find it again in a million years."

"I hope you're not jerking me off," the big cop said. "I'm not in the mood for it today."

"I want to get him as much as you do," she announced. The words had come to her automatically, but her sincerity was apparent, to her and to the cop.

"You sure you don't have it somewhere else?" he asked.

She hesitated momentarily. "I could call my pimp," she said softly. "He saves everything and he probably still has the address. The only thing is, you have to promise not to hassle him." She looked up into Moodrow's eyes, trying to read him. "Because if I lost George Wang, I'd be out on the street."

The big cop, to her amazement, began to giggle. "*George Wang?*" he said. "Are you bullshitting me or what?"

Marie put a hand on his arm. "Wang's been my pimp for so long that I forgot how weird it sounds to someone who doesn't know him."

She walked into her bedroom, a riot of brightly colored fabric spiced with the faint scent of jasmine, then laughed at Moodrow, who hesitated in the doorway. It was clearly a place of seduction.

"You got messages," Moodrow said as she tugged his arm. "On your machine. Maybe one of them's from Najowski."

She frowned and turned away to pick up a pad and pencil. "It can't be Najowski. I never gave him my phone number. He had to go through Wang."

Moodrow folded his arms across his chest. "Don't worry," he said, "I won't be embarrassed at what I hear."

Realizing that he had no intention of moving until she retrieved her messages, Marie rewound the tape and pushed the play button. The first message was from the pimp.

"Guess what, Marie? Marek loves you so much, he wants you to do a special trick. Plus he's going to pay for not being home this afternoon. Call me as soon as you get in."

"Bingo," Moodrow said, his face lighting up with a grin that seemed even more dangerous (though not to her, thank God) than the Freak's hatred. "Call the pimp, Marie. He sounds like he's in a hurry to hear from you."

Resigned, she picked up the receiver, only to have the big cop order her to use the speaker phone. "I wanna hear both ends," he announced. "There shouldn't be any mistakes here. No mistakes at all."

"George," Marie said, when the pimp answered on the third ring, "it's Marie."

"You're on for tomorrow," Wang crowed happily. His voice was sharp despite a severe echo. "Marek says he's ready to pay for everything."

"All day?" Marie groaned, looking over at Moodrow.

"Yes." Wang, reveling in the potential profit, ignored her tone. "The only thing is, you have to pretend you don't know what's happening. Marek says when you try to leave, he's going to pretend to hold you prisoner. You're not supposed to know this, by the way. I'm supposed to say it's a regular two-hour trick, but I never lie to my girls. You pretend you're a prisoner. Make the customer happy."

"And if I don't want to?" Marie asked, noting the startled look on the big cop's face.

"You have to go." Wang's voice jumped a full octave. "Marek won't pay for today unless you come. We're talking about fifteen hundred bucks here, understand? He's willing to pay a grand for his upstate adventure. Must be real horny, right? He told me that only Marie can supply what he needs. I swear I think the man's in love with you."

Marie sighed loudly, playing George Wang as smoothly as she played her tricks. "Give me the address, George. I'll take care of it."

The pimp's directions involved a train ride upstate, then a taxi to the "Schroeder House" located in the hills north of Kingston. Najowski would deal with her as usual, right up until it was time to leave. Then he would refuse to let her go, holding her against her will, threatening to keep her indefinitely. While it was up to Marie to prepare a suitable response to her imprisonment, George Wang felt defiance, followed by groveling fear, was more than appropriate.

"Do you really do that shit?" the big cop asked in wonder after she'd hung up.

"I'm a specialist," Marie explained. "I give folks the fantasy as well as the fuck."

"You mean the whole fucking fantasy?" Moodrow giggled again. "You gotta be an actress."

"It's more acting than sex," she responded. "That's for sure. That's what all the money's about."

"That's right. That's why I say you gotta be good and why I feel safe in asking that you help us out some more."

"Yeah." Even though she was hoping for just this, she feigned wariness. "I gave you the address. I don't owe you anything else."

"You didn't owe me anything to begin with," Moodrow responded, his tone dropping suspiciously.

"Tell me what you want," Marie said quickly.

"I want you to go in and get him talking about what made him run away from New York. Talk about the building in Queens. Think you can do it?"

Marie sat on the bed without answering the question. "And he plans to hold me prisoner," she said, more to herself than to Moodrow. "The mother-fucker wants to hold me against my will. He offers money to Wang like I was a machine he was renting for the day." She sat silently for a moment, remembering the feel of his hands, the grunt of satisfaction as he penetrated her, the gesture of dismissal as he paid her. "Why not?" she said, looking up at Moodrow. "I can get the bastard to say anything. You want me to wear a tape recorder?"

"A transmitter," Moodrow said. "We'll tape it in the car. If you get in trouble, we'll come in. Do you have to strip for him? Can you conceal it on your body?"

"He never touches my breasts. I don't know why, but he never does. How big is the transmitter?"

"A matchbox."

She nodded. "I can do it. No problem."

"I want you to stay with me tonight. Don't take it the wrong way, but I have to make sure you don't get in touch with Najowski. And we should talk about what you're gonna do."

"I have another appointment tonight, but I'll cancel it." She smiled brightly. "I'll claim the whore's only legitimate excuse—menstruation."

"Call it 'the curse,'" Moodrow advised. "It'll go over better."

Marie laughed brightly. "See? All I have to do is *think* about that and I need to use the little girl's room. Excuse me for a minute." She forced herself to stroll into the bathroom, to shut the door slowly before locking herself inside. She even took a quick glance at her reflection in the mirror over the sink. Then, her heart racing with desire, she reached behind the toilet and removed the Smith & Wesson revolver taped to the tank. A Model .38 Bodyguard with a two-inch barrel, it fit easily into her oversized purse, its fourteen ounces barely noticeable. The man who'd given it to her was a retired cop with a strong need to be raped. So strong that he'd insisted the gun be loaded, and she knew, theoretically, how to use it. The cop had finally disappeared, as customers tend to do, but she'd kept the gun. Now, as she sat on the edge of the tub remembering the Freak, she knew why.

Moodrow and Marie were on their way back to Brooklyn and Jim Tilley, when the news about William Holtz came on over the radio. According to the announcer, Holtz was being transported from his office to an ordinary patrol car when he bolted, running between the patrol car and a double-parked van into the path of an M101 bus. The incident, gory enough to attract attention all by itself, was made even more newsworthy by Holtz's association with the drive-by shooting in Jackson Heights. According to the newscaster, Holtz was to have been charged with several violations of New York State securities law when the incident occurred. A spokesman for the NYPD was quoted as saying that proper procedure had been followed and Holtz, who had been handcuffed, had given no warning before running away from the stunned officers.

"Is that about Marek?" Marie asked, when the report was finished.

"Yeah," Moodrow admitted. "That was Marek's lawyer."

"Does it mean I'm the only game in town?"

"That's what it means."

"It also means that Marek will know it was me who set him up."

"Don't worry about Marek. Once we take him, he won't come back out to bother you."

"But he'll *know* it was me, right?"

"Yeah, he'll know."

"Good. I like that very much."

THIRTY-FIVE

April 30

MAREK NAJOWSKI sat in the kitchen of the small summerhome belonging to his former adviser, William Holtz, and stared between pale yellow curtains at the raw spring day. The small yard, extending less than forty feet before surrendering to the winter forest, revealed no hint of the caressing warmth that had inspired Marie Porter on the previous day. This far north and west of the Atlantic coast, the cold days usually stretched out until mid-May. True, a few hyacinths, short and spare, hugged the earth, waiting for intrepid honeybees despite the weather, but their colors were muted, their fragrance smothered by a ground fog that refused to lift.

Not that Marek Najowski was aware of the scenery or the weather. In his own way, he was celebrating. Celebrating the death of William Holtz. He'd spoken to Holtz's personal secretary less than an hour before and, though details were scarce, it was clear that Holtz, the last person able to link Najowski to the violence at the Jackson Arms, was dead. At one time, Najowski had wanted to eliminate Holtz the way he'd eliminated Blanks (he'd enjoyed that tremendously) and now fate had stepped in to do the job for him. Holtz's accident (or his suicide), had miraculous overtones; Marek felt like a child waking up to find a hated rival moved to another state.

In a few days, he'd return to his home in Brooklyn Heights. When the authorities put the name of Marek Najowski to the Jackson Arms and its twins (it wouldn't take long; with Holtz dead, he'd have to reveal himself to Precision Management immediately), he, as an absentee landlord, would shrug his shoulders and point to William Holtz.

"I trusted the man . . ."

Marek began to imagine the scene, fleshing it out with detectives (*real* detectives, not like the private cop who had Marty Blanks peeing his pants). The interview would take place in the offices of his lawyer (his *new* lawyer) and the detectives would be suspicious: "Do you mean to tell me that you weren't involved in the day-to-day management of your own property?"

"That's why I used a management company, officer. Because I didn't *want* to get involved. I've never been the sort of landlord to go from door to door collecting rents. Finding good, efficient management is the key to success in real estate."

The cops, of course, would know that he was lying, they could tell that much from his sneering smile, but they'd write their reports and go back to more profitable investigations, leaving Marek to congratulate himself on the first decision he'd made after deciding to pursue the adventure. Except for the literal ownership of stock, he'd never put anything in writing, never spoken to anyone, but William Holtz or Marty Blanks. Now that he was free and clear, with sole possession of Bolt Realty—Holtz's last act on behalf of his client had been the transfer of Blanks' stock to Marek Najowski—he would move to put space between himself and Jackson Heights as quickly as possible. He would sell the property, count his profit (and his blessings) and move on.

The idea of profit warmed him as surely as the coffee percolating on the kitchen table, and he began to drift into his favorite daydream. It was ten years into the future, a year or two after the moral majority woke up to assert its might. America's southern border was sealed now, except for official checkpoints. Sealed by an army committed to fire at anything moving through the deserts of northern Mexico. Legal immigration was limited to white Europeans who would eventually become white Americans. The founding of America had *always* been the historical and spiritual mission of Europe.

There were camps, of course, but not the death camps predicted by the doomsayers. These were work camps, created for the tens of thousands of junkies when America decided it couldn't afford to support a permanently unemployed, (permanently stoned) underclass. There was plenty of work to be done in America. The cities were filthy with human garbage while the countryside was dotted with toxic dumps. Inner city bridges were falling apart; the interstates were dotted with crater-deep potholes; the nation's rivers were polluted with the detritus of industrial profits.

It was nearly noon and ferociously hot in the desert. The convicts, mostly black, though there were nearly as many women as men, were stumbling out of the buses. Wasn't it amazing how quickly most of them had lost that ferocious look? How their innate aggression had been transformed into fear and confusion? They'd been packed in for days and, unlike the Jews of Germany, the stronger ones had refused to share a daily ration of water sufficient for the needs of all. In fact, the dominant males had doled out food and water like jailhouse kings dealing passes to the evening movie.

The young women, girls, really, had suffered especially. He watched them, dazed and frightened, as they looked to something or someone for support.

When the order to strip followed immediately (the de-lousing process began, as it should, *before* the animals were brought into the zoo), they looked up in despair. Most of the bitches, as Marek expected, were heavy. Their breasts sagged to where the smooth skin of their abdomens should have been, while their abdomens, in a parody of modest concern, hung down over bloated thighs. Fortunately, there were a few teenage girls with lithe muscular bodies that begged for humiliation: miraculous bodies, bursting with sexual vitality.

The sergeant walking alongside Marek noted the numbers as he pointed to this or that girl. They would be brought to the special barracks (*his* barracks, his due as Camp Warden) where he would confront them with the hope of escaping the worst aspects of the camp. Yes, they could live comfortably, sleep in a real bed, eat enough to maintain body weight, but the requirements were strict. Obedience, immediate and absolute, of course, but beyond obedience, a (hopefully feigned) sexual enthusiasm vigorous enough to convince a nasty old cynic like Marek Najowski.

Leaning back into his chair, Marek looked at his watch and calculated the time until Marie would appear. His crotch was on fire.

Stanley Moodrow, sitting in the front seat of Jim Tilley's Buick, with the engine running and the heater on, was parked behind a thick stand of young hemlocks a hundred yards from the cottage where Marek waited for Marie Porter. Despite the short distance, the car, enclosed by the heavy forest, was invisible from the house. Moodrow, in the driver's seat, was close to the road, but he couldn't see the rented car Marie Porter drove toward the front door. He could hear her, though; the transmitter concealed between her breasts was broadcasting an amazingly clear signal. It had been designed to work in the unpredictable canyons of New York, where signals echo crazily and contact with street cops is routinely broken.

Marie had the car radio tuned to a light rock station and Moodrow listened quietly while John Lennon advised the world to "Imagine." He was at the end of the chase, as he'd been so often in his career, and he could almost taste the exhilaration. And the triumph. He'd given up the badge—they'd made him give it up, that was the truth of it—but he could still hunt. It might not be the *only* thing that mattered to him, but without the hunt, he wouldn't be able to enjoy the rest. Food, sex, love, friendship—all depended on the administration of justice. His administration. His justice. It was stupid, but he'd long ago stopped denying it, especially to himself.

Not that Marek Najowski was gift-wrapped and ready for the Grand Jury. Moodrow would have to be even more senile than he suspected to believe Marie's story about Marek confessing to her. They were into some kind of master-slave bullshit, all right, but Marie wasn't exactly dressed like the master. That's why Moodrow had left Jim Tilley in Manhattan. He wasn't sure what Marie was planning to do to Marek Najowski and he didn't particularly care. As long as it was bad.

* * *

"I thought I told you to take a cab?" It was Marek's voice, hard and commanding. *"Don't you like to obey me?"*

"Yes sir, I do like to obey you."

"I won't continue to ask why you brought the car, because I know that you don't know why you do anything. Get started in the kitchen and stay there until I get off the phone."

Moodrow managed to pay attention for almost three minutes. He listened to Marie fill a bucket and begin to scrub the floor, before he shook his head in disgust. So much for voluntary confession. He inserted a pair of Sony earphones into the side of the transmitter and turned off the tape recorder. There was one possibility left and that, of course, was violence. Not that he minded. As long as the right person was on the receiving end, violence was a perfectly acceptable way to end a hunt. In fact, when you thought about it, it was almost traditional. Unconsciously touching the butt of his .38, he opened the door and stepped out into the cold, wet, mountain air.

When the Freak pulled a straight-backed, dining room chair into the kitchen and settled himself directly behind her, Marie Porter felt the excitement buzzing through her body. It sang like the relentless hum of energy rushing through high tension wires. Slowly, deliberately, she dredged up memories of all the times she'd put her body on the line, of the various fingers, mouths, and cocks that had been thrust inside her in the name of pleasure. She'd never known Moodrow's glib justice; she'd never known luck or fairness, either. Her fortune had been earned by surrendering pieces of herself and the fact that George Wang made it easy couldn't restore what she'd given up.

"How come you colored folk got such big asses?" the Freak asked, as he always did at some point in their visits together.

"I don't know, sir," she replied for the hundredth time. "It must be God's will, sir."

The Freak smiled, then knelt beside her, running his fingers over her flanks. "How would you like to stay with me permanently, Marie? There's a lot of work around here and I need a good slave to get it done."

"No, sir. I can't do that. I've got appointments, sir."

"Oh, Marie." He shook his head like a parent humoring an imaginative child. "You've got to stop fibbing. I *know* you don't like me. I know that's why you won't stay here."

"I like you fine, sir. But I'm so busy, I . . ."

"Guess what, Marie? I'm not really *asking* you to stay." The Freak's voice was perfectly calm, as if he was talking to a machine that just happened to understand language.

"What do you mean, sir?"

"What you've got to remember, Marie, is that you're a junkie whore and not really entitled to make your own decisions."

"I thought this was a free country, sir."

"You're ignorant, Marie. That's your problem. *America* is a free country, but you're not in America. You're in Najowskiland. How do you like it?"

"What about George Wang?"

She allowed herself to drop the "sir" for the first time, but the Freak didn't seem to notice. He began to laugh loudly, his sharp features narrowing even further.

"You mean 'Chung King'? All that slanty-eyed pimp thinks about is money. If you disappeared off the face of the Earth, he'd calculate your value and settle out of court."

Marie smiled to herself, remembering her conversation with George. The Freak really was insane; he was (she recalled the term from the only psych course she'd taken) deluded. He thought he was in control, that he could manipulate her as he chose.

"Are you going to hurt me?" she asked, drawing up a voice that hinted of barely repressed terror, that promised the authenticity of nightmare.

"That depends on you, Marie. It depends on whether you're a good girl or a bad girl."

Marie saw a glow of desire rise into the Freak's eyes, just as she'd seen it in the eyes of so many of her tricks. She used this desire as a measure of her own success, because it inevitably made its appearance when the tricks bought her act.

"I'll be good, sir," she said, her eyes slowly rising to Najowski's waist, then holding steady. "How long do I have to stay here, sir?"

"Until I let you go. Don't you want to stay with me?"

"Yessir, I do. But *when* will you let me go?" She persisted as a dog might, scratching at a closed door to get to a bone. She persisted dumbly, without letting any hint of defiance touch her voice. Only her eyes, even with the Freak's chest, might have warned him.

But the Freak didn't read the warning. The Freak turned his back and laughed, shaking his head in wonder.

"You don't understand. It doesn't surprise me, of course, but you *don't* understand. Your stay will be somewhere between the next minute and eternity. It really depends on you." His smile dropped away as he put on his most dangerous face. Narrowing his eyes and tightening his lips in imitation of every Camp Commandant in every WWII movie, he turned back to face Marie Porter and the .38 she held in her hand.

When Marie Porter pulled the .38 from her purse, Stanley Moodrow grunted in satisfaction. Now the cards were on the table. Marie Porter had no way to persuade Marek Najowski to confess. She could force him into it, of course, but the confession would never hold up. Which was just as well. Moodrow didn't much believe in confessions, anyway.

"Do it now," he whispered to himself. He was kneeling in the wet mud of the garden, peering through the window curtains. His knees already hurt and the longer he stayed the worse it would be. Marek's back was to the window and his attention was riveted to the gun Marie held, but Moodrow kept his head down anyway. "Don't wait. Don't talk," he advised. "Just do it. Get even for all the humiliations."

He tried to will her into pulling the trigger, pushing the message out to her through the closed window, but she began to talk and he groaned in frustration. She probably thought she was working herself up, but the words would dissipate her energy, like opening the window on a fart. Moodrow could hear her clearly, even through two panes of glass, and what she did was entirely expected. She began to question Najowski.

"Do you *really* think you own me? Did you *really* think I came up here without knowing what you wanted to do with me?"

Marek took his time answering. As if the question was meant to draw a response. "If you knew all about it, then what are you doing with that gun?" He was still playing the tough guy. Trying to be the master despite the intensity of his slave's rebellion. Moodrow thought there was a chance that he would do something really ugly. Ugly enough to make Marie pull the trigger without thinking about it. The notion cheered him, but, of course, he couldn't allow himself to rely on it. Without taking his eyes off Najowski, he pulled a small Browning automatic, a double-action 9mm, from an ankle holster and drew back the hammer. Najowski was less than ten feet away from the window and his back was turned.

"Maybe it's for the old lady you burned up in her bed."

Marek shook his head paternally. "Ignorance, Marie. Remember? It's your biggest problem. The old bitch didn't burn. She was smoked out. Get it? Like that fish her people smear on bagels? Smoked out?"

Marie sat back in her chair and Moodrow read her reaction in the slump of her shoulders. She looked stunned and angry at the same time. Like Marek's glib admission was the only thing she *wasn't* expecting.

"What about the others?" she asked, the gun still aimed straight for his chest.

"What others?"

"I was in the bedroom. I heard you talking to your partner. The things you were going to do. The things you did."

Marek smiled, and Moodrow read the future with the precision of a Gypsy psychic. Marek was going to make a try for the gun. He was just waiting for his best shot. Moodrow reminded himself that Najowski had almost certainly killed Marty Blanks, a man who knew something about self-protection. Marek might be too insane to be afraid, but he wasn't too insane to kill Marie Porter.

Moodrow was also sure that Marie wouldn't be able to pull the trigger. No matter what she thought. Killing looks so easy in the movies. Bang! Bang! Bang! Blood spurting everywhere. She'd probably spent the night imagining Marek's death, playing out the scene again and again. What she hadn't imagined was the difference between her dreaming and reality. She knew nothing of the special quality that allows some people to kill in cold blood and she therefore couldn't know that she lacked it altogether. Unless, of course . . .

"I was only a cook," Najowski said. "Using a tried and true recipe, I mixed various insects together and the heap took care of itself. The heap provided the explosion. Which is no surprise. Am I right, or what?"

"What you are is crazy."

Marek took a step forward. A quiet, unhurried step, designed to cause no anxiety whatsoever. "You think *I'm* nuts? Well, I think that any slave who rejects the path to freedom—the *only* fucking path there is—was born to be a slave."

Moodrow struggled to his feet. There was a time, he noted, when he could have jerked his 250 pounds upright without a second thought. Now it seemed that each piece required a separate effort. He assumed a shooter's stance, square to his target, both hands supporting the automatic, and sighted down on the left side of Marek's back. A bullet off to one side would spin Najowski away from the prostitute. A second and third shot would finish him. "If I had half a fucking brain," he said aloud, "I'd do it now." But he couldn't shoot an unarmed man. Like Marie, he had to wait for justification.

"Ya know, Marie," Marek continued, "the truth is that I didn't actually control who went into that building." He took another half-step forward. His belt buckle was almost touching the gun. "That was my partner's end of the deal."

"Why are you telling me this? Don't you know that I came here to kill you?"

"What I was telling you about was how my partner was too good for our mutual good." Marek knelt in front of Marie's chair, bringing his shoulders level with the gun; he gestured with his hands as he spoke, ignoring her comment altogether.

"Get back away from me. Get back." Her hand shook, the barrel of the revolver bouncing slightly, but her finger remained frozen on the trigger.

"I came at him in a totally unexpected way. He thought I was gonna use lawyers and I used a Weatherby. It was a nothing shot. Just like Blanks was a nothing. Am I right, or what?"

Marie leaned back in the chair, trying to put some distance between Najowski and the barrel of the .38, but the few inches she gained didn't put her out of reach. Marek slowly raised his left hand above his head and Marie followed the movement with her eyes. Then Marek's right hand swept across his body. He grabbed the gun and yanked her forward onto her face.

The .38 exploded once, discharging a harmless round into the ceiling. The sound was still echoing when Stanley Moodrow fired into Najowski's left shoulder, spinning him around. Marek dropped the revolver as he spun, though Moodrow couldn't tell whether he meant to surrender or was in too much pain to hold on to it. It didn't matter, anyway, because Marie, all barriers down, picked the .38 off the floor and began to fire it from point blank range. Tiny fountains of blood pushed back through the wounds as the slugs broke up in

Marek's body, tearing the veins and arteries in his neck and back, splattering Marie's face, soaking into her hair and her dress.

"Not a bad shot," Moodrow said to himself as he eased down the hammer. It was too bad, of course, about Marie's ammo. Through-and-throughs usually bled out the exit wound. Now she was gonna have to take a shower and find some new clothes before they got out of there.

THIRTY-SIX

May 10

As if in perverse celebration of the winter's events, the purple lilacs in front of the Jackson Arms exploded into blossom during the first two weeks of May, filling the air with the favored perfume of grandmothers everywhere. The early spring had been warm and damp and the bushes Morris Katz had planted in 1970 were two weeks early. They were the only flowers in the small austere yards fronting his buildings and when their blossoms (the ones that hadn't been snatched by tenants or neighbors) fell to earth, it would mark the end of spring and the beginning of summer for the residents, just as it had for twenty years. Untended for the most part, the lilacs had thrived on the wet Eastern weather and become a fixture in the lives of tenants like Mike Birnbaum and Paul Reilly, who sat on lawn chairs, enjoying the bright sunlight and seventy-five-degree weather.

But the beautiful spring morning was not the topic of the old friends' conversation. They were far more concerned with the fate of the Jackson Arms, which had begun to slide downward again. True, the drug dealers had been eliminated, but the promised repairs had stopped almost as soon as they'd begun. A Precision Management spokesman (*not* Al Rosenkrantz) was claiming the company no longer represented the landlord, because the landlord's attorney no longer existed and they had yet to be contacted by anyone with the authority to make decisions regarding the property. Not only did Precision Management call off the carpenters and painters working in the Jackson Arms, they refused to accept rent checks; the buildings and the tenants, their spokesman insisted, were not Precision Management's problem.

Both Stanley Moodrow and Betty Haluka, who stood on the grass beside Reilly and Birnbaum, knew what the problem was. Moodrow had told Betty the truth about Marek Najowski. He'd told it without embellishment, admitting that he'd gone there with the intention of making sure justice was done.

"If Marie could've gotten the confession without pulling a gun, I would've been glad to take it to the cops. I would've been satisfied to see Marek doing a long bit in Attica. But the truth is I never thought it was gonna be that easy. I knew she was full of shit, because I went through her purse while she was sleeping, and I found the gun."

"You didn't take it away?" Betty had asked quietly. "An illegal weapon?"

"I never thought about taking the gun away. Not for one second. I thought about what she wanted to do with the gun and whether she had the stomach for it and what I was gonna do if she didn't." He'd waited for Betty to respond, to become angry, to scream, but she'd kept her eyes on the kitchen table. "Najowski was gonna walk away, Betty. How could I let that go? You remember Inez Almeyda lying on the concrete. You remember the holes in her face?"

"I can't forget."

"Now remember her the way she was *before* Marek Najowski came into her life. Imagine her with her children. With her husband. Imagine her cooking dinner while the kids watch television, while her husband has a beer." He'd stopped again, waiting for her to make the accusations, and, again, she'd held her peace. "I once looked up the word 'murder' in a dictionary. It was a long time ago and I forget exactly why I did it, but I remember what it said. According to the pocket dictionary I was using, murder was 'unlawful killing.' That simple, Betty. Nothing about good and evil. Or about justice. According to the dictionary, what the Nazis did in Germany wasn't murder, because the same Nazis who did the killing wrote a law saying the killing was legal. I'm not gonna live with that bullshit. Why should I? The truth is, if you wanna look in the dictionary, killing Najowski was murder. Me, I've got my own definitions."

"The problem is," Betty had finally said, "that I don't *know* how I feel about it. I've been nursing this revenge fantasy ever since it happened. In fact, there's someone inside me who keeps wishing you'd done it slower. But I've been fighting all my life against cops who think they're judges and juries."

"I'm not a cop anymore. I'm a private citizen who witnessed a homicide without reporting it. I'm a private citizen who cleaned up the scene and walked away."

"That makes you a vigilante."

"Like the Equalizer, except younger, right?"

Neither of them laughed. Instead, they took Najowski's death with them when they drove to Jackson Heights, Moodrow once again folded into the hated Honda. Birnbaum had called Betty after receiving a certified letter from Precision Management announcing that Precision Management would no longer accept rent and would not be responsible for day-to-day maintenance. Betty intended to petition the court to appoint a receiver to care for the property until the landlord (or his heirs) could be located and she wanted to prepare several affidavits as well as view the problems for herself.

"Let me see if I've got this right," Betty said to Paul Reilly. "You suffer from emphysema and you're currently being treated by a physician?"

"Yeah," Reilly answered. "By Dr. Musari at the Veterans' Hospital. That's why it's very hard for me to walk the stairs. The elevator went out two days ago and the super can't fix it. I called up to complain, but the lady at the management won't talk to me, either. Now I hear the porters didn't get paid yesterday, so they won't carry down the garbage. I have to do it myself or live with the stink."

"Every time something gets better, it gets worse. How can this be?" Mike Birnbaum's bruises were healed and the reporters had stopped coming around, but his basic attitude was unchanged. "It used to be a paradise . . ."

Mike stopped suddenly, his mouth dropping open. For a long moment, Betty thought he was about to collapse, but then he sat upright in the chair, pointing one long shaking finger at an old man coming up the walk. The man, leaning heavily on a cane, wore a Hawaiian shirt over light cotton trousers and sandals on his feet instead of shoes. When he saw Mike Birnbaum begin to stand, he accelerated into a stumbling shuffle, raising the cane as he went.

"It's Morris Katz," Reilly explained to Moodrow and Betty.

"It's Beelzebub!" Birnbaum screamed. "It's Satan!" The old man spluttered on for a minute, unable to form a coherent word, then finally gasped the appropriate insults. "Did you bring matches with you?" he screamed. "Did you come to finish the job your hoodlums started? Maybe you came to hit me on the head? The one thing you *didn't* come to do is commit a rape, because you only get a hard-on when you rub your *putz* with five dollar bills."

As Morris Katz's face began to redden, the spray of freckles across his nose and cheeks lit up. He waved his cane threateningly, but when Birnbaum proved to be fearless, let it fall back to the ground. "Why," he implored, raising his face to the heavens. "Why did You bring me back here? For what reason? To get one last piece of torture out of my life? Wonderful people You take every day. Saints You take. Infants in their cribs You take. Why do You let this man live who made every minute of my life in New York a misery? This bastard of a *schnorrer* who never once in thirty-five years paid the whole rent. He's an old man, Lord. Take him tonight."

"Pay the rent?" Birnbaum shook with anger. "For this pigsty? Did you even one time send up enough heat? Plaster falls off my wall and I gotta beg for a painter. The hallways are greasy and I practically gotta crawl so I don't break my back. The . . ."

"You should fall and break your *head*!"

"Then I could sue until you're so poor you gotta live in your own buildings."

The combatants paused for breath, leaving Betty enough room to interject a question. "My name is Haluka," she said. "I'm an attorney and I represent the tenants here."

Morris Katz, his breath coming in gasps, turned to Betty and bowed deeply. "My name is Morris Katz and I'm holding the mortgage on these buildings. For two months I haven't seen a check, so I call the company and they tell me the new owner is missing. Also his lawyer is dead, so nobody's in charge. I'm in the court tomorrow."

"What are you planning to do?" Betty asked.

Morris smiled as if at a child. "You are Jewish?" he asked gently.

"Yes," Betty answered, grinning in spite of herself.

"In my life I've made many mistakes. In fact, I got to admit that certain people think I'm a *shlemiel*. Me, I don't argue. What for? I'm a *shlemiel* who doesn't give up no matter how many time's he falls in the soup. I'm a *shlemiel* who persists."

"A *shlemiel?*" Mike Birnbaum yelled. "More like a *shmuck.*"

"You see how he talks?" Morris replied to Betty. "You see the language that pours out of his mouth? That's what comes of eating *trayf*. You talk like a *goy.*"

This time Betty responded before Mike Birnbaum could frame a reply. "Mr. Katz, would you mind giving me the name of your attorney? Maybe we could work out some details and go into court together. It'd make everything happen much faster."

"What attorney?" Morris sniffed the air suspiciously. "You think I worked all my life to make some shyster rich? A lawyer I don't need. I'm gonna fix this place up like a dream. New windows, new roof, new elevator. I'm tired of the Bahamas. The water, the sun . . . it's disgusting, already. I can't even breathe the air. When I go in the casino, I don't care if I should win or lose. I got a forty-foot yacht—it should sink in the bay."

"It should sink with you in it, you bastard," Birnbaum raged.

Betty looked up at Moodrow, finding him expressionless, as usual—only his eyes held any hint of the pleasure he took from the scene. He met her glance and they began to edge away from the combatants.

"They're just getting going," Moodrow complained.

"That's what I'm afraid of." She took his arm and marched resolutely toward the car. "It's funny, but I was under the impression that Mike loved Morris Katz. Now he acts like he wants to eat Katz's liver."

"From Mike's point of view, all landlords are greedy thieves who get sexually aroused by shutting off the heat on New Year's Eve. Morris was a saint only as long as he was the *ex*-landlord." He eyed the Honda with distaste, then unlocked the passenger door and passed the keys over to Betty. "Your turn," he said.

Betty accepted the keys, but remained standing while Moodrow folded himself into the front seat. Finally, she walked around the car and got in next to him. "Stanley," she said, "I've been thinking."

"How did I know?" Despite the weak humor, Moodrow understood that some decision had been reached.

"Remember I told you about how much I wanted to do it myself. To . . ." She hesitated, then finished it. "To kill Najowski."

"Yeah, I remember."

"And I told you how my job, which I've been doing all my life, complicates it." She paused and he felt compelled to mutter the compulsory, "Yeah."

"Well, there's another complication and that's that I'm in love with you. I thought love was supposed to conquer all, but this love makes it harder."

Moodrow tried to straighten up, but only succeeded in jamming his head into the roofliner. "Does that mean you're not taking off on me? The way you say it, I'm not sure."

"I've decided to leave my job. I've got more than twenty years in the pension, so I should be okay for money. As for the rest of it . . . I'll just have to wait and see."

Betty maneuvered the overloaded Honda through the traffic at Queens Plaza and onto the 59th Street Bridge, dodging a bus that moved between the cars like it owned the street. "If I leave Legal Aid, I don't know what I'll do with myself," Betty said, once they'd settled onto the outer roadway. "I can't just clean my apartment all day. Not after twenty years in a courtroom. I have to have a little action. I'll have to find something."

The Honda's windows, in deference to the warm weather, were rolled all the way down and the noise of the traffic was almost as loud as the Honda's engine as it struggled to push the little car up the steep grade. A quarter mile ahead, the towers of midtown Manhattan, softened by the spring light, rose up on either side of the silent couple.

Once again, Moodrow tried to shift position. His knees still hurt from when he'd knelt in the mud outside Najowski's window. Most likely, he reflected, he shouldn't have told her what happened. Most likely, he should have kept it to himself. Or at least softened the truth by admitting that he loved and needed her. But there were times when manipulation didn't work. When the prize was so enormous, it justified any risk. When the truth really did set you free. One way or the other.

He looked across at Betty as she drove her little Honda along the raised expansion cracks in the roadway. The tires were shifting back and forth rapidly, though the car continued to move in a straight line, and Betty's mouth was slightly open, the point of her tongue a lighter pink against her lower lip.

In My end is My beginning.

The words stole into Moodrow's consciousness as he watched the evening light play across Betty's features. It came from someplace in the Bible, though he didn't know where, a memory, most likely, from a reading of the Gospels at a long-forgotten Sunday Mass. He did feel as if he was ending and beginning at the same time, that there was no difference between the two. Only a gap, a pause for breath in which it was possible to see the end without fearing it.

"Do you believe this?" Betty asked, tossing the point of her chin at the sunlight reflecting from a million panes of glass. "I love the city when it gets like this."

Moodrow agreed silently. He'd defined his life by facing down the ugliest aspects of urban life, by staring at the Medusa without being turned to stone. Now, drenched in spring light, he could admit that he loved the city. He could admit that he loved it as he loved his life and his work. That, if truth be told, he'd never loved it more.